PRAISE FOR GRA

"Readers looking for a good historical mystery/romance or a historical with a little more kink will enjoy *The Duke Who Knew Too Much*."—*Smart Bitches, Trashy Books*

"*Her Husband's Harlot* is a pleasing, out of the ordinary read."—*Dear Author*

"Grace Callaway's book is the first in her 'Heart of Enquiry' series, and this excellent brew of romance and intrigue and emotion is also *Stevereads* best Romance novel of 2015."—*The Duke Who Knew Too Much* named the #1 Best Romance of 2015 by *Stevereads*

"I discovered a new auto-buy author with [*M is for Marquess*]… I've now read each of Grace Callaway's books and loved them—which is exceptional. Gabriel and Thea from this book were two of the best characters I read this year. Both had their difficulties and it was charming to see how they overcame them together, even though it wasn't always easy for them. This is my favorite book of 2015."—*Romantic Historical Reviews*

"Erotic historical romance isn't as plentiful as many would think, but here you have a very well-written example of this genre. It's entertaining and fun and a darn good read."—*The Book Binge*

"I devoured this book in a couple of hours!.... If you love a story with a heroine who is a wallflower with a backbone of steel or a damaged hero then you will love this one too."—5 star review from *Love Romance Passion* on *Her Wanton Wager*

"I found this to be an exceptional novel. I recommend it to anyone who wants to get lost in a good book, because I certainly was."—A Top Pick from *Night Owl Reviews*

"I thoroughly enjoyed this story. Grace Callaway is a remarkable writer."—*Love Romance Passion* on *Her Prodigal Passion*

"The depth of the characters was wonderful and I was immediately cheering for both of them."—*Buried Under Romance* on *The Widow Vanishes*

"Callaway is a talented writer and as skilled at creating a vivid sense of the Regency period as she is at writing some of the best, most sensual love scenes I've read in a long while. For readers who crave sexy, exciting Regency romance with a fresh plot and intriguing characters, I would highly recommend *Her Protector's Pleasure*."—*Night Owl Reviews*

"You know when a book is so good that you are still reading it at 2 am....This book had it all: drama, laughter and a few tears as well. The chemistry between Harry and Tessa just sizzled off the pages....If I could I would give this book ten stars, but I'm only allowed to give 5/5 stars."
—*Boonies123 Book Review* on *The Duke Identity*

ALSO BY GRACE CALLAWAY

GAME OF DUKES
The Duke Identity
Enter the Duke
Regarding the Duke (May 2019)

HEART OF ENQUIRY
The Widow Vanishes (Prequel Novella)
The Duke Who Knew Too Much
M is for Marquess
The Lady Who Came in from the Cold
The Viscount Always Knocks Twice
Never Say Never to an Earl
The Gentleman Who Loved Me

MAYHEM IN MAYFAIR
Her Husband's Harlot
Her Wanton Wager
Her Protector's Pleasure
Her Prodigal Passion

CHRONICLES OF ABIGAIL JONES
Abigail Jones

The Duke Identity © Grace Callaway, 2018.

All rights reserved. Without limiting the rights under copyright reserved above, no part of this publication may be reproduced, stored in or introduced into a retrieval system, or transmitted, in any form, or by any means (electronic, mechanical, photocopying, recording, or otherwise) without the prior written permission of the copyright owner.

This is a work of fiction. Names, characters, places, brands, media, and incidents are either the product of the author's imagination or are used fictitiously.

∽

Cover Design: © Erin Dameron-Hill Graphics

Cover Image: © Period Images

The Duke Identity

Game of Dukes

Book One

Grace Callaway

PROLOGUE

WEST MIDLANDS, ENGLAND, 1838

"Bennett, we 'ave to talk," feminine tones said from the bed.

Harry Kent—or Sam Bennett as he was known in the railway camp—stilled in the act of dressing. In the three months since Roxanne Taggart had first approached him, she'd never made this request. In fact, conversation had not featured highly in their interactions...unless one counted her rather profuse utterances in bed. He, himself, preferred quiet during the act.

He finished pulling on his shirt, shoved his spectacles on his nose, and went over to the bed. They were in his rented room at the boarding house not far from where he worked as a navvy or laborer of the railway. Roxy reclined against the pillows, her dark blonde hair tumbling over her shoulders, her large breasts on full display.

"What about?" he asked politely.

"You and me, lover."

Her serious manner was new and unexpected. With an unpleasant jolt, he wondered if she was the merry widow he'd believed her to be. History had taught him that his judgement when it came to females wasn't exactly sterling.

His gut knotted as he thought of Miss Celeste De Witt, the woman he'd once loved. The woman whose betrayal had destroyed his good name and career, his lifelong ambition to be a scientist. Because of her, he'd been ejected from The Royal Society, leaving Cambridge under a cloud of scandal and disgrace. For the last two years, he'd built a new life for himself as Sam Bennett, rock blaster with the Grand Midlands Railway.

At least he'd been able to put his experience in the laboratory to good use. Blasting rock had been a practical application of his academic study of explosives, not to mention damned cathartic. It wasn't intellectually stimulating work, but the grinding physical labor had brought him, if not a measure of peace, then at least a degree of numbness.

He'd always been a private man, not the sort who enjoyed strong sentiment. It had taken months to calm the turbulence caused by his foolish entanglement with Celeste, and he'd vowed to never again let his emotions override his rationality. His brain was far more trustworthy than his heart, and now it was warning him to beware of the glint in Roxy's eyes.

"I wasn't aware there was a problem between us," he said.

"It ain't a problem, lover." Naked, she crawled over to the edge of the bed where he stood. Kneeling on the mattress, she placed a hand on the exposed part of his chest, her fingers trailing coyly over the tensed slabs of muscle. "We've been 'aving our fun for some time, and I got to thinking that we should make the arrangement more...permanent."

He froze. Devil take it, did she mean...marriage? The idea had never occurred to him.

"I believe we discussed this at the outset," he said carefully. "I made it clear what I was looking for, and you agreed that you wanted the same thing. We had an understanding."

"Maybe we did," she said with a pout. "But things change,

don't they? Our understanding *then* ain't the same as our understanding *now*."

This was precisely the sort of feminine reasoning that he found confusing. He liked women, had sisters whom he adored, but that didn't mean he understood them.

Still, he didn't want to hurt Roxanne.

"My understanding hasn't changed," he said quietly. "Nor will it."

Something in his tone must have told her it was futile to continue the discussion. She dropped her hand from his chest and got out of bed. Marching over to her pile of discarded clothing, she began yanking on garments.

"If you don't want me, Tom Wilkins does," she snapped. "'E asked me to marry 'im last week."

Harry hadn't known she was seeing anyone else. Another surprise...not that it mattered. He didn't know how she expected him to respond, so he remained silent as she finished dressing and stormed up to him.

"Don't you got nothing to say?" she demanded. "I just told you I'm marrying another man!"

I don't like being manipulated. He didn't think that was what she wanted to hear.

He said, "I wish you the best."

∽

"Find yeself on the losing end o' an argument, did ye, guv?" Emerging from the tunnel with several others, Johnson, a fellow navvy, set down his pick-axe, his dirt-streaked face split into a grin.

"Something like that," Harry muttered as he packed up his satchel.

His jaw still throbbed from Roxanne's right hook.

"Should've asked me for pointers. I could've made a living as a prizefighter, if I wanted," Johnson boasted. "Ne'er been in a brawl I didn't win."

In the past, boxing had been Harry's favorite form of exercise. He'd practiced at Gentleman Jackson's and knew damned well how to fight. But he would never hit a woman.

Which was more than he'd say for some of the present company. To be fair, the womenfolk were no more peaceable than their men, Roxy being a prime example. As the men downed ale in the sweltering afternoon sun, belching and telling bawdy tales, a dark mood set upon Harry like a London fog.

He couldn't shake off the recognition: he wasn't where he wanted to be.

He got on with his fellow workers well enough. At first, some had been suspicious of his "gentlemanly ways," but since he did the job that made theirs easier, one that no one else was keen to take on, they'd come around. The vein of his discontent ran deeper, his awareness of it triggered by the scene with Roxanne.

The last navvy emerged from the tunnel, calling, "She's all yours, Bennett."

Hefting the sack of blasting devices he'd made, Harry took a lamp and entered the dark mouth of the tunnel. The dank air was suffocating. As the path split, he took the smaller tunnel he and the others had cut away, broodingly aware of the cause of his restlessness.

He was bored. With the mindless grind of his days, the casual depravity of his nights. He wasn't steering his life in the proper direction—in *any* direction. He'd once had a vision of happiness that included being a scientist, a respected member of the Royal Society...and a husband and father.

At two-and-thirty, however, he was none of those things.

He was...adrift.

He arrived at the section of rock he was to clear away. Relieved to have a distraction from his rumination, he embedded the shells of gunpowder into the craggy wall and attached the fuse.

Lighting it, he sprinted out. Sunlight struck him at the same time a panicked voice did.

"Larkin ne'er came out. 'E's still in the tunnel!"

Devil take it. Heart hammering, Harry turned around, running back into the darkness. Not enough time to get back to the fuse, to disable it. He had to find the missing navvy.

"Larkin," he shouted as he charged deeper into the main section of the tunnel. "Get out!"

Larkin staggered into sight, obviously drunk.

Harry grabbed the man's arm. "Run, goddamn you—the rock is going to blow!"

He shoved Larkin toward the exit, and the other finally stumbled into motion, Harry right behind him. As the light neared, Harry heard the terrifying whoosh of air being consumed, felt the ground rumbling beneath his feet, rocks pelting from all directions.

An instant later, the earth roared, and darkness buried him.

1

THREE MONTHS LATER, ST. GILES, LONDON

Despite the smoky dimness of the Hare and Hounds, Miss Tessa Black-Todd spotted Dewey O'Toole straightaway. The ginger-haired bastard occupied the best table at the center of the rowdy public house. He was swilling ale with two comrades, a tankard in one hand, a joint of mutton in the other. As Tessa watched, he dropped the meat to grab at a passing barmaid, marking her skirts with his greasy paw-print.

Tessa curled her hands at her sides, fighting the impulse to go over.

Better to let the blighter come to me.

And O'Toole would come to her, she knew, because she'd transformed herself into irresistible bait. At present, her long, dark tresses were tucked beneath a short brown wig and cap. A moustache and side whiskers further obscured her feminine features. She'd bound her chest—for once, she was grateful that there wasn't much to hide there—and donned the bulky garb of a country lad. A roughly knotted neckerchief completed her outfit.

She hadn't much time to snag her prey; the latest bodyguard

her grandfather had hired to watch over her was bound to discover her missing sooner or later. She headed over to the bar that lined one side of the room, hoisting herself onto a stool.

"O'er 'ere, my good barkeep!" she said in the deepest tones she could muster. "Name's Tom Brown, and I'm new to Town."

The pub's proprietor was a heavyset man known throughout St. Giles as Stunning Joe Banks on account of his flamboyant cravats. The puce and magenta checkered cloth surrounding his thick neck did indeed assault the eyeballs. He didn't spare her a look.

She tried again. "I 'ave a mighty thirst. What do you recommend, my good sir?"

Stunning Joe continued filling tankards from a cask. "Ale."

"What kind o' ale?"

"The kind I put in front o' ye."

"Some o' your finest ale, then—"

A tankard was slammed in front of her, foam splattering onto the bar's scarred surface.

She picked up the sticky vessel and sipped, her nose wrinkling at the watered-down libation. Surreptitiously, she surveyed the clientele using the cracked looking glass behind the bar. At the center of the room, Dewey O'Toole and his cronies were still drinking, laughing without a care in the world.

Fury smoldered beneath Tessa's breastbone at she thought of her friend Belinda's battered face. The tears that had trickled over bruises, mingling with blood as Belinda had wept over her stolen savings.

You're not getting away with it, O'Toole, Tessa fumed. *Not while I'm breathing.*

She felt a wriggle of agreement from the inner pocket of her jacket.

"Patience, Swift Nick," she said under her breath, and the wriggling obediently ceased. "The rotter will pay the piper soon enough."

Louder, she said, "Barkeep."

"Wot now?" Stunning Joe grunted.

"Seeing as I'm celebrating, I'd like to buy a round for all the fine patrons 'ere."

Fine patrons, her arse...or *derrière*, as her French tutor would say. (Apparently, the lessons at Mrs. Southbridge's Finishing School For Young Ladies, or *The Old Dragon's Dungeon of Doom*, as Tessa dubbed it, had not gone entirely wasted.) The Hare and Hounds catered to cutthroats, thieves, and fences; while Tessa held no prejudice against those occupations, for she knew how her bread was buttered, she did judge a man by his moral character.

A man's only as good as 'is word, her grandpapa oft said. *'Ow 'e treats 'is kin and those under 'is command—that's the true measure o' a man, Tessie.*

By any of those standards, Dewey O'Toole was a blackguard through and through.

Stunning Joe swiped a rag against the counter. "Ale don't come for free."

Deliberately, Tessa dropped a coin purse onto the bar. The heavy, unmistakable clink of gold drew gazes the way the bells of St. Mary-Le-Bow did worshippers. Stillness as reverent as a prayer spread through the room as she withdrew a guinea, letting the gold catch the light.

"Will this suffice?" she said innocently.

"Nan! Alice!" Stunning Joe barked at the serving wenches. "Drinks for the 'ouse courtesy o' our young friend 'ere."

The ensuing cheer shook the rafters. Within seconds, Tessa was surrounded by new "friends," most of whom would sell their own grandmothers for a sovereign. Which still made them less dangerous than the milk-fed twits who'd been her classmates. Society ladies, she thought grimly, were the most cutthroat of all. They would stab you between the shoulder blades whilst smiling and sipping tea with their pinkies lifted.

Pushing back the painful memories, she answered a sly-faced coster's question about the source of her windfall.

"The fortune was left to me by my Uncle Jim, God rest 'is soul," she said, emulating a clodhopper's earnestness. "Ma always said 'er brother was a good-for-naught—"

"If this uncle o' yours was such a lazy prat," a grime-streaked sweep cut in, "'ow'd 'e get 'is 'ands on a fortune?"

"Uncle Jim 'ad a lucky 'and at dice and won a 'undred quid. Gor, that's fortune enough, ain't it, but then 'e used 'is winnings to buy some pieces o' paper..." She scratched her ear as her audience watched her with rapt expressions. "*Certificates o' share,* that's what the solicitor called 'em. Something to do with iron 'orses. Now, me, I don't trust any 'orse that don't eat and shit, pardon my language, but my uncle 'ad a gambler's 'eart, 'e did. Paid off, too: those papers are now worth *five times* what 'e paid for 'em."

She could almost hear rusty gears turning as the cretins worked out the arithmetic of her supposed inheritance. Just then, a movement at the end of the bar caught her eye.

Her heart stuttered. A curious tingle danced over her skin.

The stranger was standing a few feet away. He hadn't been there moments ago, and she didn't know how she could have missed his arrival. He was tall and broad-shouldered, lean of hip, built like a medieval knight from the tales she'd heard at her grandpapa's knee.

He had one arm braced on the counter, a large hand wrapped around a tankard. His clean but worn clothes fit his sinewy physique like well-used armor. His boots clung lovingly to his muscular calves. The tavern's dim light glinted off the thick, dark waves of his hair, flickering across his profile and glinting off...spectacles?

She felt an odd flutter in her belly.

His head turned, and her breath hitched at her first full glimpse of his face. He did indeed resemble a knight: one who had returned from some perilous quest and bore the travails of his journey. The clean structure of his broad cheekbones and square jaw was offset by the scar slanting through his left eyebrow. The scholarly spectacles were an intriguing contrast to that scar, as was his brooding intensity. There, on his face, she saw his true armor: his expression was as impenetrable as tempered steel.

Mind your own business, dunderhead, she chided herself.

It wasn't like her to be distracted by a man. Her father owned a bawdy house, and she'd grown up surrounded by wenches who'd warned her of the dangers of animal attraction. At four-and-twenty, she'd never experienced that supposedly brain-obliterating force; she wondered if she ever would.

"You there," Dewey O'Toole's nasally voice called out.

She pushed aside thoughts of the stranger, her purpose taking center stage.

Concentrate and play your part. For Belinda's sake.

"Me, sir?" she said with as much diffidence as she could muster.

O'Toole crooked a stubby finger, kicking out the chair next to him. "Come 'ere."

The crowd parted like the Red Sea, clearing the path to O'Toole's table: no amount of gold, apparently, was worth the trouble of crossing the O'Toole family. For Dewey was the heir to Francis O'Toole, a famous cutthroat.

Indeed, Francis O'Toole was one of the seven men who ruled the London underworld—men so powerful that they were known as "dukes." O'Toole was the Duke of the Docklands, and his territory encompassed the wharf-side areas from Bluegate Fields to the Isle of Dogs. However, as powerful as O'Toole and the other dukes were, every one of them paid homage to the mightiest of them all: Bartholomew Black.

King of the Underworld. And Tessa's grandpapa.

At the thought of her beloved grandfather, pride burgeoned in her. Grandpapa was a legend for he'd put an end to the bloody territorial wars that had once torn the stews asunder. While some might call him a cutthroat, he did whatever was necessary to keep the peace. He cared for the welfare of those under his rule. While the government enacted laws that benefited the upper class but left many in the underworld starving and destitute, Bartholomew Black found ways to feed and employ his people—the legalities of society be damned.

Of late, however, Grandpapa had had too much to contend with: an assassination attempt, the death of one of his most loyal dukes, and a deadly explosion at a brothel. For the first time, Tessa could see his many burdens wearing upon him, and it filled her with worry. She wanted desperately to help, yet he refused her. Refused to see that she had the ability to serve him, to help him make the underworld a better place.

Instead, he wanted to marry her off to some overbred blueblood. She scowled. As much as she loved her grandfather, she wasn't going to let him barter her off like chattel at Smithfield Market. She might be a female, but she was of the House of Black. Protecting the underworld and its denizens was in her blood.

If Grandpapa didn't let her stand by his side, then she would have to serve him on her own.

And she would begin by delivering justice to Dewey O'Toole.

Going to his table, she doffed her cap. "Tom Brown, at your service, sir."

"O'Toole." He waved carelessly at the brutes across the table. "Barton and Smithers."

"Pleased to make your acquaintances," she said as she took a seat.

She knew O'Toole's cronies by reputation. Barton was a swarthy hulk capable of beating a man to a fare-thee-well, but it was Smithers who made her wary. Narrow-faced and twitchy, Smithers was known to be a weasel—an insult, Tessa thought indignantly, to weasels everywhere. Nonetheless, he was the brains of the trio, and her breath caught as his beady gaze roved over her. Luckily, he didn't seem to notice anything amiss, his attention returning to his leader.

"O'erheard 'bout your windfall." Greed glinted in O'Toole's eyes, which resembled currants pushed into puffy dough. "Four 'undred quid, is it?"

"Five," Smithers said, then cowered at O'Toole's glare.

"Five—that's wot I said." O'Toole's fist slammed against the table, setting plates and cups a-clatter. "Wot are ye, deaf?"

"Beg pardon," Smithers sniveled. "My fault for mishearing you."

"Ye got bacon for brains," O'Toole snarled.

"Bacon for brains." Barton slapped his tree-trunk-sized thigh. "Good one, O'Toole."

O'Toole scowled. "Now where was I afore I was interrupted?"

Seeing as how she didn't have all night, Tessa slung her leather coin bag onto the table, where it lay like a fatted calf. "You wanted to know about my inheritance. It's in this purse."

"You can't fool me," Barton scoffed. "Five 'undred guineas wouldn't *fit* in that purse."

Lord above, what kind of morons am I dealing with?

She resisted the upward pull of her eyeballs. "The clerk at the bank said this paper,"—untying the purse strings, she took out a fifty-pound note—"is as good as gold."

O'Toole snatched the banknote, squinting at it. With a grunt, he shoved it across the table.

Smithers held up the banknote and perused it expertly. "It's the genuine article."

Crafty looks were exchanged amongst the three bounders.

"What are you planning to do with all that blunt?" O'Toole said.

Finally.

"The truth is," she said in a confidential timbre, "I've a fancy for cards. 'Eard there are places in Town where the sky's the limit when it comes to the stakes. Say, you fellows wouldn't know of any such fine establishments, would you?"

"You don't need no gaming 'ell," O'Toole declared. "We'll 'ave us a game right 'ere."

Tessa made an apologetic face. "Kind o' you to offer. I was looking for, er, a larger game."

"Think I don't got the stakes, that it?"

"Oh no, sir, I'd ne'er—"

"'Ere's a 'undred quid." O'Toole flung his coin bag onto the table. It skidded into hers, the pair of purses nestling like twin piglets. "And plenty more where that came from."

A hundred pounds is twice what you stole from Belinda, you blackguard. Thus, you'll be paying her back—with interest.

Hemming and hawing, Tessa scratched her ear. "I ain't certain this is a good idea."

"We're playing." O'Toole snapped his fingers at Smithers. "Fetch some cards, you stupid git."

"I've a deck," she said quickly.

Tread carefully. Don't rouse suspicion.

Reaching into the outer pocket of her jacket, she pulled the deck out halfway then shoved it back, mumbling, "Ne'er mind. It ain't decent."

"Not decent? What the bloody 'ell does that mean?" O'Toole demanded.

As if embarrassed, she averted her gaze. "Fellow who sold 'em to me pulled a fast one. 'E claimed they were all the rage in the fine gent's clubs. Now 'ad I known they were indecent—"

"Give 'em to me."

With sham reluctance, she placed the deck in O'Toole's outstretched hand. He spread the cards out on the table, forming a rainbow of debauchery. Each card depicted a naked couple in some variation of sexual congress. Their expressions were lascivious, body parts improbably magnified.

"God's bollocks, they're all doing the buttock jig," O'Toole chortled.

Peering over, Barton sniggered. "That one's giving 'er a green gown, 'e is!"

"Oh ho, look at *this* one." Chin jiggling with delight, O'Toole pointed at the three of spades. The illustration featured a woman sitting astride a man, her back to his chest, her eyes heavy-lidded as she impaled herself on his engorged sex. "St. George is riding the dragon, eh!"

Smithers scurried over from the other side of the table. "I want to see, too!"

Men were so *predictable*. A bit of obscenity reduced cutthroats to giggling schoolboys. Borrowing this deck from her chum Alfred had been a stroke of inspiration. Distraction was the key to successful sharping, after all. The trio was so diverted by the fornicating figures that they failed to notice a critical fact: the cards were marked.

"Let's play," O'Toole said between snorts of laughter.

She nudged them into a game of *vingt-et-un*, with O'Toole starting as the dealer. To build his confidence, she let him win a few rounds and take fifty pounds from her. Then it came her turn to deal, and, being cautious, she gave him another round, totaling her losses to a hundred pounds. By this time, onlookers had gathered around the table, eager to watch the high-stakes play and placing their own side bets on the outcome of each round.

As the game paused for O'Toole to toast himself, a scent cut through the *eau de tavern* of greasy meat, stale ale, and unwashed bodies. The clean smell—soap, leather, and male—tickled her nostrils, released a rush of awareness. Without looking, she knew that the stranger was standing behind her. Unable to resist, she turned slightly in her chair and looked up.

And had to tilt her head to look farther up.

The eyes that met hers were a deep elemental brown, the color of rich earth and polished wood. The intelligence gleaming behind the wire-rimmed spectacles made her shiver. His gaze shifted to the game, and she saw where it landed: on the Knight of Spades, a rather hirsute fellow who was inserting his lance into a lady on all fours.

The stranger's eyebrow, the one with the scar, winged upward.

She spun back around in her chair, her cheeks pulsing with heat. The cards had never discomfited her before. In truth, she'd found their absurd depravity amusing. Why, then, did they cause her insides to feel as quivery as an aspic when she saw them through the stranger's eyes?

Shaking off her reaction, she resumed the game, dealing a face-down card for all the players.

Checking his card, O'Toole gleefully said, "I'm in for a 'undred quid."

Barton and Smithers placed smaller bets.

Tessa passed out the second cards, face up. O'Toole's was an eight, hers a five—a deliberate move on her part to feed his overconfidence. He went for the bait.

"Let's make this more interesting and double the stakes, eh? Everything I got in 'ere,"—O'Toole jabbed a finger into his bulging purse—"plus all my winnings."

"You're certain, O'Toole?" Wetting his lips, Smithers said, "You're already ahead—"

"Shut your bloody gob!" O'Toole glared at his crony, who fell silent, cheek twitching. "When Lady Luck spreads 'er legs, a real man don't walk away. 'E swives 'er, and swives 'er *good*."

"You tell 'im, O'Toole," Barton crowed.

Still aware of the stranger behind her, Tessa decided it was best to hurry things to their conclusion. "Double it is."

O'Toole shoved his pile of money forward; she matched with two hundred pounds of her own.

She dealt the third cards. The groans of Barton and Smithers came as no surprise seeing as she'd busted them, giving them both above the value of twenty-one. O'Toole received an ace of clubs; when he saw her third card, another five, his grin widened.

Chortling, O'Toole, flipped over his first card. "Ace o' diamonds brings it to twenty for me. Pot's mine, unless you got—"

She flipped over her hidden card.

"Mary's tits, it's an *ace o' hearts*," an onlooker breathed. "Wiv two fives that makes *twenty-one*. Tom Brown wins!"

Cheers went up. O'Toole's face turned a violent shade of red.

Sensing the direction the wind was blowing, Tessa swept her cards and winnings into her satchel and rose. "Much obliged for the game, sirs. Now I fear I must be off—"

"Not so fast, you buggering cheat." O'Toole surged to his feet, his glare menacing.

Uh oh. She took refuge in righteous anger. "Got no right to besmirch my good name, sir. Won fair and square, I did, and you've no proof elsewise."

Murmurs of assent rose. Even among thieves, beggars, and fences, no one liked a sore loser.

"Don't need no proof, you wily bastard. I *know* you fleeced me." O'Toole jabbed a finger at her. "Barton, Smithers, get 'im!"

She made a run for it. She dodged past Barton, who was big but slow, and almost made it past Smithers. Unfortunately, the latter was quicker than he looked. He caught her arm and wrenched it, causing her to cry out.

"Got you—what the bleeding 'ell is that?" Smithers shrieked.

In a flash of champagne-colored fur, her ferret, Swift Nick, burst free of her inner pocket and dashed up to her shoulder, still imprisoned in Smithers' grip. The animal rose on its hind legs, hissed, and sank its fangs into her attacker's hand.

Smithers screeched.

She tore free from his slackened grip. Tucking her furry rescuer safely into her pocket, she dashed toward the back exit. By this time, the entire tavern had erupted into a joyful free-for-all, and she had to dodge brawling bodies left and right. Barton's heavy footsteps pounded behind her. Just as she felt his hot breath upon her nape, he let out a howl of rage. Pivoting, she saw that the stranger—*her* stranger—had charged to her rescue.

Mesmerized, she watched him take on her pursuer. Barton threw a punch. The stranger evaded and executed an uppercut, and her blood quickened at the man's power and precision. The blow connected solidly with Barton's jaw, the latter's head snapping back.

Barton groaned, toppling like a felled tree.

"Now *that's* a facer," she breathed.

"Don't countenance troublemakers 'ere," Stunning Joe's voice growled from behind her.

Before she could turn, his meaty hand closed around her collar, lifting her clear off the ground. She kicked and cursed, straining to reach one of the daggers hidden in her boots when her neck cloth loosened, fluttering to the ground.

"*Christ Almighty.*" Stunning Joe released her, stumbling back. His gaze was riveted on her throat: on the gold medallion now exposed. "Didn't know who you were, I swear—"

"Now you do." Bending, she snatched up the linen. "And you'll keep your lips buttoned about it. If anyone discovers I was here tonight, I'll know who to come find."

"A-aye, anything you—"

The stranger sprinted toward them, his fists readied for another fight.

Tessa subtly lifted her chin at Stunning Joe, and the barkeep backed away, hands raised. She knotted her cravat in place just as the stranger arrived.

"Tom Brown, at your service," she said breathlessly. "And you are?"

A roar sounded, a recovered Barton knocking aside bodies like pins as he charged toward them. More of O'Toole's brutes had arrived, the pack following at Barton's heels.

"Introductions can wait." The stranger grabbed her arm. "For now—*run.*"

2

"Through here," Harry's companion said. "We'll lose 'em in the tenement."

Ducking to avoid a low-hanging beam, Harry Kent followed his guide into the decrepit building. He knew "Tom Brown" was no lad, but his plan was to play along for now. The other had navigated the rookery's maze with spritely agility, dashing through dark alleyways and twisting streets, pushing through the Saturday night crowds spilling out of taverns and gaming hells. Even now, in this dilapidated warren, Tom seemed to know exactly where he was going.

Harry trailed his companion past rooms overflowing with raggedy folk of all ages. None of the occupants paid any mind to two passing interlopers. Poverty decimated privacy, exposing everything: the shouting, fornicating, and drinking. The squalor and lawlessness reminded Harry of the railway encampment. Of the accident that had nearly ended his life.

Trapped in elemental darkness, he'd felt not just panic but suffocating regret. That he hadn't made more of himself. That he'd lived and died without making a difference to the world.

His schoolmaster papa's teachings had come to him. *Character is determined by choice not opinion. What is the essence of life? To serve others and do good.*

In that moment, Harry had known that he didn't want his legacy to be defined by scandal and failures. Summoning his strength, he'd fought his way through the darkness, through the wall of rock to the shouting voices and promise of light. In the end, he'd been lucky to escape with only a small scar, and he'd taken it as a sign.

It was time to stop licking his wounds. To stop running from the past. To find his future.

Thus, he'd bid Sam Bennett adieu and returned to London. His older brother Ambrose owned a successful private enquiry business and had offered him a position, but Harry didn't want to ride on his brother's coattails. He wanted to strike out on his own, find a job in which he could take pride. One that would make a difference in the world and help him regain his sense of purpose.

Thus, a fortnight ago, he'd signed on as a constable with the Metropolitan Police Force. How better to serve his fellow citizens than by upholding justice? His first case involved murder. A fiery explosive had razed The Gilded Pearl, a popular Covent Garden brothel, killing over a dozen occupants. Acid burned the back of his throat as he recalled the charred bodies he'd viewed his first day at Scotland Yard, the police headquarters.

Death had been delivered by a brutal hand.

Hence, Harry's present mission. Although he couldn't save those victims, he could find the culprit, perhaps prevent future carnage. And his gut told him that the figure scampering ahead of him was the key.

A whistle made him look ahead. A blonde exited from a curtained room along the narrow corridor, one that Tom had just passed. As Harry neared, she blocked his path.

"Lookin' for some sport, luv?" Her coy tone, combined with

her scantily clad form and painted face, left no doubt as to her profession.

"No, thank you," he said shortly. "Let me pass."

"I like a gent wiv manners," the prostitute cooed. "Certain you won't join the fun?" She yanked aside the curtain, revealing a tableau of debauchery.

Harry had seen a lot at the navvy encampment; he'd never witnessed anything quite like this.

Men and women occupied mattresses strewn on the floor. Naked bodies tangled in eyebrow-raising permutations. Couples, trios, and more. Bodies formed an undulating chain, slapping flesh and moans and groans spilling into the hallway.

Heat crept up Harry's neck as Tom came back to his side. He wondered how the "lad" would react to the depraved scene. Glancing at the carnality, Tom evinced no sign of discomfort and turned to face the whore.

"Cast your ha'penny lures elsewhere." Scowling, Tom hitched a thumb at Harry. "The cove's with me."

"Like *that*, is it?" She smirked.

Before Harry could respond, Tom turned to him, saying imperiously, "Stop gawking at the cut-rate goods. O'Toole's minions ain't far behind."

"I wasn't gawking—" Harry found himself talking to his companion's retreating back.

Exasperated, he strode after the other, who was no country bumpkin. He was certain that the minx ahead of him was none other than Miss Thérèse-Marie Todd, the only daughter of brothel owner Malcolm Todd *and* the only grandchild of the most infamous cutthroat of the age:

Bartholomew Black, King of London's criminal underclass.

And cold-blooded murderer.

According to Inspector Davies, Harry's supervisor, Black was responsible for numerous deaths. For years, the police had tried to hold him accountable for those and other crimes. All to no avail.

Mouths shut. Evidence disappeared.

The underworld protected its own.

We'll get the bastard this time. Determination had hardened Inspector Davies' time-worn features. *Even Black cannot incinerate more than a dozen people and get away with it.*

Davies had briefed the new constables, including Harry, on Black's family members and known associates. He'd assigned a round-the-clock watch on the cutthroat's fortress in St. Giles, his officers in civilian wear for the sake of discretion and their own safety. Harry had been on duty tonight when he'd spotted a diminutive figure making a furtive exit from the walled estate. Recalling that Black had a granddaughter who was known for mischief, he'd made the decision to abandon his post and follow. At the Hare and Hounds, he'd seen through Miss Todd's disguise, observed her shenanigans, and gone to her aid.

The last part had been instinct. She might be a member of London's most dangerous family, but she was still a female and a dainty one (at least in size). Neither his code nor his conscience would allow him to stand by and watch while she was beset by a gang of ruffians.

Even if her behavior was reckless, bold, and that of a lunatic.

One thing had led to another, and now he was caught up in a mad chase through the stews with the suspect's granddaughter. A female who dressed like a lad, fleeced cutthroats at cards, and didn't blink at the sight of an orgy.

The apple doesn't fall far from the tree, he thought darkly.

Yet there was no going back, only forward. He would worry about what to do once he got Miss Todd and himself out of the present predicament. They came to the end of the passage, a heavy door blocking their way.

She tried the knob. "Blast it, it's locked. And I don't have any hairp—"

At the slip, her first thus far, Harry felt his brows rise.

"—picks." She caught herself. "Forgot my lock picks, I meant to say."

"Allow me." Removing a set of picks from his pocket, he set to work. The lock clicked in seconds.

"Zounds, that weren't your first time, were it?" Beneath her short wig, her eyes were a light, mysterious color that the dimness refused to yield. But there was no hiding that they were wide and fringed with the thickest, curliest lashes he'd ever seen. Intelligence sparkled in that gaze, along with an exuberance that seemed oddly...innocent.

Yet appearances could be deceiving—especially when it came to women.

Harry's jaw clenched. He was no longer the greenhorn he'd been back at Cambridge. He wouldn't fall for feminine wiles, and especially not those of *this* chit who was, according to Inspector Davies' report and Harry's own observations this eve, about as harmless as a loaded pistol.

Footfalls thudded, and voices grew louder.

In the next heartbeat, Miss Todd was through the door. He went after her and found himself in a luxurious courtyard. It was as if he'd stepped into a different world.

Perplexed, he took in the majestic wall of trees that shut out the shabbiness of the bordering buildings. Here there were blooming flower beds and marble statuary, a white marble fountain that tinkled a merry tune. Mews occupied the far end of the courtyard. Miss Todd headed over, and he trailed her, his boots crunching on the graveled path, the sky a dark canopy of diamond-studded velvet.

Reaching the mews, Harry saw wooden steps leading to the groom's quarters above the stalls. He scrutinized the upper floor for any sign of occupants: the panes remained dark, moonlight reflecting off their fathomless depths. Miss Todd opened the door to the stables with obvious care, the well-oiled hinges making no sound. She craned her head this way and that before entering, gesturing him to follow.

Inside, the space was softly lit by lanterns. The stalls were occupied by sleek horses which would fetch a pretty penny at Tattersall's. Miss Todd continued down the window-lined row to the stall at the end. She opened the Dutch door and ushered him into an empty cubicle piled with sweet-smelling hay.

"We can wait 'em out in 'ere," she said.

He didn't see a back door. "If our pursuers come in, there's no escape route."

"They won't dare come in."

"How do you know that?"

A hint of pink crept above her fake mustache. "Just, um, a hunch."

Before he could question her further, there was a sudden movement beneath her coat.

"What the devil?" He blinked as a line of fur darted from her jacket pocket. It wound its way up her body, looping itself around her neck like a collar. The animal was cream-colored, with dark brown accents on its tail and paws. The strip of brown around its eyes resembled a mask, and, along with its pointed ears and twitching pink nose, gave it the look of an inquisitive bandit.

"You brought...a ferret?" he asked stupidly.

"This is Swift Nick Nevison. Where I go, he goes."

The fact that she had a ferret named after an infamous highwayman was bizarrely fitting.

"Swift Nick," she chided, "we don't hiss at friends."

The ferret stopped hissing at Harry and bared his fangs instead.

"Pleased to make your acquaintance as well," Harry muttered.

Apparently determined to carry on her masquerade, Miss Todd swept him a jaunty bow. "My thanks for your assistance tonight. Your name, sir?"

Voices sounded, silhouettes growing larger in the window.

Harry acted on instinct, tackling her into the pile of hay. He twisted to bear the brunt of the fall, and Miss Todd let out a little "*oof*" as she landed atop him. Swift Nick, who'd been detached from his mistress during the process, hopped up and down on the ground beside them, hairs raised and spitting mad.

"Hush, Swift Nick," she said breathlessly. "Go hide. Don't come out until I tell you."

After a lingering glare at Harry, the ferret scrambled off.

Harry remained stock-still, his arms around Miss Todd, their heartbeats thudding in unison.

"They're in there." The voice belonged to Barton, the lout Harry had given an uppercut. "I can smell 'em."

"Let's go in," another brutish voice said.

"*Stop*. We have to leave at once." Smithers' sniveling tones emerged. "This courtyard is Black's territory."

Harry's head jerked, his gaze meeting Miss Todd's. Hers was unflinching, and she didn't seem to realize that her moustache had been lost in the scuffle. Without that strip of hair, her mouth was revealed as pink and plump, the sensual dent in the bottom lip distractingly feminine.

She wriggled, making him aware of her other attributes as well. With her draped over him, he could feel her shape through that bulky disguise. She was slender yet delicately curved in all the right places.

"Bugger Black. I ain't afraid o' 'im." Barton's bravado filtered through the stable walls. "Codger's old now, weak. Mark my words, a new King is coming—"

"Shut your yap," Smithers hissed.

A shot blasted, followed by a sharp cry. Harry instinctively rolled over to cover Miss Todd's body with his own. Shouts sounded outside.

"Bloody 'ell, Barton's dead! Bullet between the eyes!"

"There's a shooter above the stables!"

Another shot rang out.

"Run, the bastard's still shooting!"

Footsteps pounded as the brutes made their escape. Then...silence.

Harry mouthed, "Stay here," to Miss Todd, who remained perfectly still, eyes wide and luminous. He got up, hearing the almost imperceptible creak of steps outside...someone stealthily descending from the groom's quarters. Removing his flintlock, he exited the stalls, horses nickering as he passed. Through a window, he glimpsed Barton laying on the ground, eyes open, blood trickling from a neat hole in his forehead.

Harry neared the door. Soles scraped just beyond. His grip on his weapon tightened.

The door flung open, and Harry found himself face to face with a Chinese. The man's hair was bound in a long ebony braid, his wiry figure clad in a high-collared tunic. His eyes were steady... as were his hands, which held a shotgun.

Both men kept their weapons raised, aimed at each other.

"Ming, don't shoot!" Miss Todd came dashing toward them.

"Miss Tessie?" The Celestial—"Ming," apparently—blinked. "Why you here? And dressed like boy?"

"I, um, got in a bit of a bind."

Sliding Harry an abashed look, she peeled off her side whiskers, removing her cap and wig. She shook out the pins, and his breath hitched as luxuriant sable curls tumbled to her waist.

"Please put the gun down, Ming. This gentleman came to my aid." She smiled at Harry, her eyes shining, and his chest tightened oddly. "He's a *hero*."

Slowly, Ming lowered his weapon, shaking his head. "Mr. Black not like this. Not like *at all*."

3

THEY ARRIVED AT THE BLACK RESIDENCE AT MIDNIGHT.

Ming had insisted that Harry come along, and his shotgun had brooked no refusal. Thus, Harry found himself entering the veritable fortress which occupied an entire block in the heart of the rookery. His past reconnaissance hadn't allowed him to see beyond the guarded spiked gate and dense wall of brush. Now, with a word from Ming on the driver's perch, the pair of guards let them through, iron bars clanking shut behind them as their carriage rolled down the pebbled drive.

With wary anticipation, Harry watched as Black's lair came into view. Moonlight dappled the gothic mansion, an eerie silver-plating of the turrets and arches. When the carriage stopped, he exited first, turning to help Miss Todd down. Her hand felt soft and dainty engulfed in his. She ended the fleeting touch, ascending the front steps with nimble grace.

As he followed her up to the recessed entry, he had a feeling of being watched. He glanced up, saw dark silhouettes huddled along the roofline. The cloud cover passed, and the exposed moon shed light upon stone gargoyles. They stared down at him, some grinning evilly, others keeping a brooding vigil.

Bartholomew Black knew how to set a stage.

Once inside, Ming told Miss Todd to go upstairs and change.

She bit her lip. "Do you think I ought to leave Mr. Bennett alone?"

During the short ride over, she'd again asked Harry his name, and he'd hesitated. If he let his true identity be known, Bartholomew Black might trace him to the police force. Knowing the underworld's animosity toward law enforcement, Harry didn't think the cutthroat would take kindly to a constable embroiled in his granddaughter's affairs. Moreover, he couldn't risk compromising Davies' surveillance.

Thus, Harry had introduced himself as Sam Bennett, the identity that combined his father's first and his mother's maiden names. He'd lived as Bennett for so long that, in some ways, it didn't feel like a lie.

"Upstairs. Change," Ming said to Miss Todd.

"But you *know* how Grandpapa can be." Miss Todd worried her lower lip with her teeth. Her eyes, it turned out, were an uncommon shade of green with a touch of grey...like verdigris, the compound produced from soaking copper plates in acid.

"I don't want Mr. Bennett to be alone with him," Miss Todd was insisting. "You know how easily Grandfather's temper can spark."

"Master see you dressed like boy, you see more than spark. You see Chinese fire flower."

At the calm words, Miss Todd flashed an impish grin. "All right, Ming. You win." She dashed to the stairwell, pausing there to add, "Keep an eye on our guest, will you?"

"I can take care of myself," Harry called out—as usual, too late.

Miss Todd had disappeared up the steps.

The imperturbable Ming took Harry to the drawing room to await Black's arrival.

Left alone, Harry took stock of the surroundings. The

polished mahogany furnishings and thick Aubusson rugs radiated luxury. He might have been in a grand Mayfair drawing room, or, indeed, any one of his siblings' homes. Although he came from country-bred, middling class stock, his brother and four sisters had, much to the *ton*'s and their own surprise, married into the Upper Echelons.

The Kents had come a long way from their humble beginnings in Chudleigh Crest. As fate would have it, several members of Harry's family had even crossed paths with Bartholomew Black. Although Harry wasn't privy to all the details, he knew that, many years ago, his brother Ambrose's wife, Marianne, had paid off some debt to Black. And Andrew Corbett, the man who'd wed Ambrose and Marianne's daughter Rosie, had also had encounters with Black.

Corbett was a product of the underworld, and, as he told it, he'd barely survived Black's incendiary wrath as a young man. This supported Inspector Davies' belief that fire was Black's modus operandi and that the cutthroat was behind the fiery explosion at The Gilded Pearl.

I must make the most of the opportunity. Harry firmed his resolve. Things might not have gone as planned this evening, but now he had rare access to the suspect's domain. He would not waste it.

His boots moved soundlessly over the plush rugs as he traveled the perimeter of the high-ceilinged room. He didn't know what to search for. Keeping an eye on the door, he rifled through the drawers of an escritoire: nothing but candle stubs, an inkwell, and some broken quills. He continued on past several seating areas, one of them around a carved stone fireplace. His shadow glided over a silk-covered wall lined with columns. Between the columns hung gilt-framed portraits in the style of famed painter Benjamin West.

Intrigued, Harry peered at the signature...make that *by* West.

Upon closer perusal, he saw that gold placards beneath the portraits identified the subjects as members of Black's family.

There was one entitled "Althea Bourdelain Black," showing a regal matron, her dark hair bound in a pearl-studded coronet. Framed by crimson curtains, she sat by a table, her beringed hand resting delicately on a bible. The paint brought out the richness of her forest green eyes, the blood-red of her heart-shaped ruby pendant and ring.

The next several portraits were of Black's only child Mavis, spanning her development from girl to womanhood. In all of them, the painter had emphasized her doe-eyed fragility. The last picture depicted her as a young lady, sitting on a swing beneath the bowers of a leafy oak.

Harry came to the portrait at the end. It was one of Black himself, dressed in the style of the previous century with white silk breeches and an embroidered jacket. Beneath a powdered wig, Black's piercing dark eyes seemed to stare directly at the viewer.

"They don't make painters like they used to," a voice boomed.

Harry turned to see Bartholomew Black framed in the open doorway.

Black looked as if he'd stepped out of his own portrait. He had on the same type of old-fashioned wig and breeches, his waistcoat blooming with exotic stitchery. Instead of a jacket, he wore a maroon silk banyan.

On any other man, the outmoded get-up might appear foolish. Nothing, however, could diminish the palpable aura of power and ruthlessness that swirled around the King of the Underworld. It reminded Harry that the civilized ambiance was just for show. Lives had been brutally cut short by this man's command.

Muscles tensed, he reviewed his plan. *Keep your identity hidden. Learn as much about the suspect as you can. Stay alive.*

As Black neared, Harry noted that there were a few differences between the man in the portrait and the one in the flesh. Even London's most powerful cutthroat couldn't escape the ravages of time. Deep lines were etched into Black's broad face.

He had a walking stick, not just for decorative purposes. Harry observed the weight Black put on the cane, the white-knuckled grip on its brass knob.

Black stopped next to Harry. He was shorter by several inches, but his husky, barrel-chested figure gave him the presence of a larger man.

"Know who did these portraits?" he demanded.

At the non-sequitur, Harry said warily, "Benjamin West, I believe."

"Bloody right, it was. West was 'ead o' the Royal Academy, only the best for my family. But the damned codger 'ad to go and cock up 'is toes before 'e could paint my Tessie."

Black grunted as if he took West's death some twenty years ago as a personal affront.

"Inconsiderate, I'm sure," Harry said wryly.

Gaze thinning, Black pointed his walking stick at a chair by the hearth. "Sit."

Harry thought it best to comply.

Black took the adjacent studded wingchair, a throne-like affair several inches higher off the ground than Harry's seat. Nonetheless, Harry's height brought him eye to eye with his host.

"Explain yourself," Black commanded.

Here goes. "My name is Sam Bennett—"

"Know your name. Know you were found with my Tessie in my stables," Black growled. "What I want to know is whether I need to gut you like a pig."

Bloody hell, there's an introduction. "I don't believe that's, er, necessary."

"Then spit it out. What were you up to with my granddaughter, eh?"

He decided to stick to the truth as much as possible. "I was at the Hare and Hounds when Miss Todd appeared to be in a predicament. At the time, I thought she was a lad, since she was disguised as such," he added as Black's mien darkened. "I saw she was outnumbered and lent a hand. The brutes gave chase, and she led the way to the stables, where we were hiding. Your man Ming chased off the villains,"—*and blew one's brains out*—"and brought us here."

Moments ticked by. Black said nothing, the flames of the hearth casting demonic shadows over his face. Just as Harry was beginning to wonder if his body would be found floating in the Thames, his host said gruffly, "Nothing else 'appened? 'Twixt you and my Tessie?"

"No, sir. 'Pon my honor."

"Honor, eh? We'll see." Black's fingers drummed on the arm of his chair. His gold signet ring, a crested affair, gleamed in the firelight. "'Ow much?"

"I'm afraid I don't follow."

"'Ow much do you want for 'elping my granddaughter out of 'er *predicament*, as you call it?"

"I don't want anything." Harry frowned. "I did as any gentleman would."

"For your silence, then."

"That cannot be purchased either," he said evenly. "You have my word, however, that I would not harm a young lady's reputation."

"My Tessie is a lady," Black declared.

Deciding it wise not to disabuse the other of the notion, Harry said nothing.

"Sent 'er to the same finishing school wot trained the *ton*'s broods. My Tessie's as accomplished as any nob's daughter. Speaks French like a Frog, plays violin like a maestro, and paints like that fellow wot did that chapel's ceiling."

Harry wondered what the point of this was.

"Thing is, she's clever. Got brains as well as looks. Takes after me in that respect—ain't from 'er father's side, that's for certain." Black snorted.

It was a well-known fact that Bartholomew Black did not

hold his son-in-law, Malcolm Todd, in high regard. Inspector Davies had described Mavis' second husband and owner of a chain of brothels as a cold-blooded and ambitious man. Miss Thérèse-Marie Todd was, in actuality, Todd's daughter from his first marriage, which meant she had no blood tie to Black. Nonetheless, she was Black's only grandchild and the apple of his eye.

"Now some men, they don't know 'ow to 'andle a classy female like my Tessie." Black leaned forward, his gaze keen. "What's your opinion o' spirited, intelligent females, eh?"

As Harry had four spirited and intelligent sisters, he said honestly, "I think highly of them, sir."

"Good. You're 'ired."

"Hired?" He stared at his host. "To do what?"

"To protect my Tessie, o' course. To be her bodyguard," Black said impatiently.

What the devil? "Why, er, does she need a guard?"

"I'm the most powerful man in the stews. Got more enemies than a dog 'as fleas. I'm constantly exterminating vermin, and I can't be worrying about 'er welfare while I'm doing it."

As the cutthroat's expression darkened, speculation ran through Harry's head. Who were Black's enemies? Was the fire at The Gilded Pearl Black's way of "exterminating" them? Was there a hidden motive that, once uncovered, could pin Black to the crime?

Keep him talking. "Vermin, sir?"

"Ev'rywhere I look. And the worst pestilence o' all? Peel's Bloody Gang. More plentiful than lice, those bastards."

Harry's gut clenched at Black's derogatory reference to the police. *Does he know I'm one of them? Is this some cat-and-mouse game he's playing?*

"You have trouble with the police, sir?" he said cautiously.

"Peelers ain't nothing *but* trouble. They're the real threat to an Englishman's liberty." Black's beringed hand clenched the arm of his chair. "If I 'ad my way, I'd squeeze every one o' those nits 'til they bloody popped."

At least the animosity didn't seem aimed at Harry.

"Point is, I got my 'ands full," the cutthroat went on. "I need to know that my Tessie's out o' 'arm's way. I've plans to get 'er out o' my world, to launch 'er into the *ton* where she belongs."

Thinking of the naughty card-wielding, trouser-clad mischief maker, Harry doubted that a catapult could accomplish the feat.

"Indeed," he said in neutral tones.

"Got a nob lined up. Cove's got a title so mossy it'll open any door for her. Problem is, Tessie don't agree with my plan." Black scratched irritably at his wig. "She's gotten accustomed to doing as she pleases. Ain't 'er fault, mind you. 'Er father's ne'er given a piss 'bout anything but 'is own 'ide, and my daughter Mavis ain't got the constitution to manage the minx. Result being, Tessie's always danced to 'er own tune. Now she chafes at the idea o' marriage—says she wants to stay by my side. As if I'd let 'er rot away on the shelf. That's why I need you to keep an eye on 'er."

Harry was no nanny. "Seems to me what she needs is a female companion."

"One o' 'em tight-lipped bombazines?" Black's eyes rolled toward his bushy grey brows. "Tessie 'as 'em calling for smelling salts afore they get in the door. No, my granddaughter needs a firmer hand. That's why I moved 'er in with me. But I'm a busy man so I got to find a guard who can keep up with 'er. In the past month alone, she's gone through three."

Harry lifted his brows. "Gone through?"

"Don't condone failure." In a blink, Black went from doting grandfather to menacing criminal king. "I trust you to guard my treasure, you don't betray my trust. If you do,"—Black stabbed a finger at him—"prepare for consequences."

Hairs stirred on Harry's nape. At the same time, the possibility flitted through his head: as Miss Todd's personal guard, he'd have access to Black's inner sanctum. He could search for evidence of Black's guilt in a way the police hadn't been able to do.

The risks would be many. He decided to play along for now. As long as he survived the night, he could consult with his superior on the best plan of action.

"How do you know I'm the man for the job, sir?" he asked. "You don't know me—"

"Know your name's Sam Bennett. Know you've the manners o' a gent, but you ain't no fribble." Black jerked his chin at Harry's hands. "Didn't get those calluses idling about Brooks's."

Harry answered Black's unspoken question. "I was a navvy."

"Real work. The kind that makes a man." Black nodded with what might have passed for approval. "Despite the fact that you're a four-eyes, you gave a fine accounting o' yourself at the 'Are and 'Ounds. Took down three bastards—could've been a prizefighter with that uppercut o' yours."

Devil and damn, how does Black know all that?

"Got eyes and ears everywhere, and don't you forget it." Black's warning was unmistakable. "You'll start on Monday."

"Yes, sir." It seemed the safest thing to say.

"One more thing. You guard Tessie with your life. You touch 'er for any other purpose, I'll string you up and yank your guts out from your throat. That clear?"

Egad. Only a fool would play with that sort of fire. "Very."

"Good." Black gave a satisfied nod. "Now take your lumps if you 'ave to, but keep Tessie out o' trouble. The swell I got lined up for 'er is a bona fide stickler. Got 'im by the balls and purse strings, don't I, but 'e still won't marry 'er unless 'er reputation is as white as the driven snow."

Before Harry could contemplate what Black meant by taking his "lumps," the door flew open. He rose, an odd stutter in his chest at Miss Todd's transformation.

Devil take it, she's...beautiful?

The puckish lad had been replaced by a vibrantly attractive

young lady. Miss Todd's dark, lustrous locks were piled on her head, exposing the graceful curve of her neck. With her disguise removed, her heart-shaped face came into focus. She had a charming retroussé nose, creamy cheeks, a piquant little chin. Her eyes sparkled like a sunlit pond, and that mouth of hers...

Uncomfortably aware of the hot pounding in his veins, he jerked his gaze away. A mistake. For it landed on the rest of her, where her camouflage had apparently been the most effective at hiding her charms. The pink frock she now wore displayed her delicate bosom and nipped-in waist, the femininity of her form. The form that had felt delectably soft draped over him.

Swallowing, he reminded himself of how he'd been duped by Celeste. The one time he'd allowed sentiment and desire to rule over rationality had resulted in catastrophe. And the stakes this time were even higher: not just scandal but...death.

No, he wouldn't make the mistake of placing his future in a woman's hands again. In matters pertaining to the opposite sex, he would be guided by his intellect. And he would need his wits about him in order to deal with the troublesome Miss Todd.

4

"Good evening, Grandpapa," Tessa said.

"Don't you *Grandpapa* me," her grandfather grumbled as he held his cheek out for her kiss. "Ought to turn you o'er my knee, missy, make sure you don't sit pretty for a week."

Tessa kept her smile bright. She wasn't at all afraid of her grandfather, who was all bark and no bite, at least when it came to her. When it came to Mr. Bennett, however, she hadn't been quite as confident. Not wanting to leave him alone with her overprotective grandparent, she'd changed as quickly as possible.

Studying Mr. Bennett, who stood next to her grandpapa, Tessa was relieved that he appeared his strapping self. Not that she'd been truly worried: after the way he'd charged to her aid, taking brutes down left and right, Bennett was clearly a man who could take care of himself.

A hero who'd come to her rescue.

She'd so rarely had anyone in her corner. A foreign, heady feeling came over her, as if she'd imbibed champagne. When he bowed, an unruly lock of dark hair slid onto his brow; she had the strangest desire to sweep it off with her fingertips.

To hide her reaction, she curtsied and smiled at him. "All in one piece, I see."

"Why wouldn't I be, Miss Todd?"

At his emotionless tone, her smile faltered. His expression was polite yet not exactly warm. Behind the lenses, his intelligent brown eyes were scrutinizing her. In a flash, she recalled how he'd initially watched her at the Hare and Hounds, as if she were an insect under a magnifying glass, and he wasn't entirely approving of the species.

Truth be told, she was no stranger to rejection. Although she loved her father, he'd always treated her like a minor nuisance: a fly he ignored until it became too annoying and he had to do something about it. Worse yet, there was her experience at Old Southbridge's Vault of Horrors.

She'd attended under the alias of Miss Theresa Smith, the "distant niece" of one Baroness von Friesing, an impoverished noblewoman whom Grandpapa had employed to be her sponsor. Her tomboyish ways and lack of social polish had made her an outcast from the start.

Lady Hyacinth Tipping's honey-soaked tones rang in her head. *What a* delicate *bosom you have, Miss Smith.*

I don't have my lorgnette. Miss Sarah St. John (Hyacinth's lackey) had a brittle laugh that plunged into one like a shard of glass. *I'm afraid one can't see her bosom without them.*

Perhaps, my dear, if you water them, Lady Jane Perrin (lackey number two) said archly, *they might grow?*

Tessa fought the urge to cross her arms over the part of herself—one of many—that her peers had mercilessly ridiculed. While Ming had taught her how to defend herself against physical attacks (she was an expert in the use of flying daggers), she'd had no shield against social weapons: the barbs, gossip, and circles that closed whenever she neared. Her attempts at retaliation had only led to further ostracism, and, as tempted as she'd been, she couldn't very well throw one of her trusty blades at the problem.

Although she'd left Southbridge's years ago, her time there had left its mark.

She was quick to sense rejection and didn't trust easily.

Bennett came to your aid, she chided herself. *There's no reason to doubt his regard or motives.*

"It ain't Bennett's neck I ought to wring, is it?" Grandpapa said sternly, waving her toward the striped settee. "Got some explaining to do, missy, and you best do it quick."

She sat, feeling like a wayward schoolgirl. Bennett took the seat beside her. His demeanor remained distant and cool, ratcheting up her unease.

"Well?" Seated in his customary wingchair, Grandpapa pinned her with a stare. "What 'ave you to say for yourself?"

"Does it matter?" she said. "The verdict's obviously been decided."

"You watch your tone, Thérèse-Marie. Ain't got patience for your lip."

The fact that Grandpapa was using her full name did not bode well. Since he'd first come into her life when she was four, he'd insisted that any granddaughter of his ought to have a proper English name. He'd christened her "Tessa," and she'd adored his pet name almost as much as the other name he'd given her: Black.

"I wasn't giving you lip," she protested. "I was merely pointing out the fact that it doesn't matter what I say. You've obviously decided that I'm in the wrong."

"O' course I 'ave! Got witnesses, don't I, that you were making mischief in the 'Are and 'Ounds, dressed like a bloody lad!"

Some might have found Grandpapa's bellowing intimidating.

Tessa was used to it.

Eyes narrowing, she said, "Was it Stunning Joe Banks who ratted me out?"

A Black never forgot a wrong. The ability to mete out justice was a measure of success, the way one gained respect. To that end, Tessa kept a List of Retribution. When it came to vengeance, there was more than one way to skin a cat, and she preferred clever tricks over brutality. Mentally, she added Stunning Joe to her list.

"Ain't the point and you know it," Grandpapa thundered. "What reason could you possibly 'ave to antagonize the son o' Francis O'Toole?"

Dash it. Her grandfather's network of informants was even more formidable than she'd given them credit for. The problem was that she couldn't tell Grandpapa the truth. She was already worried that he was overburdened. Moreover, in these contentious times, he might place more value on keeping the peace with the O'Tooles than on the welfare of a single wench.

A ruler's got to make 'ard choices, he'd say. *The needs o' the many outweigh those o' the few.*

To Tessa's mind, the "few" also deserved justice. Yet when Belinda had sobbingly confessed that Dewey O'Toole, after taking his pleasure, had beaten and robbed her, she'd made Tessa vow not to tell anyone.

"At least let me talk to Father," Tessa had insisted.

"*No.* Mr. Todd already knows what 'appened, and 'e told me to keep my mouth shut. Your pa said if I offended an O'Toole, 'e'd beat me 'imself and toss me out on my ear. I *need* this job, Tessa, so you mustn't breathe a word to your father or grandfather or *anyone.*" Belinda's swollen lip had quivered, her eyes pleading in the mask of bruising. "*Promise me.*"

Reluctantly, Tessa had given her word. Just because her family wasn't willing to offend an O'Toole, however, didn't mean that *she* couldn't avenge Belinda. Thus, she'd devised her plan to get her friend's savings back.

She was close to accomplishing her goal. She'd regained Belinda's money and then some. Now all she had to do was deliver it back to her friend and honor her word. For Belinda's sake, she had to keep the matter under wraps…even from her grandfather.

"I wasn't out to antagonize anyone. I was out on a lark," she lied glibly. "Dewey O'Toole happened to be the fat pigeon that waddled my way. I didn't force him to do anything; he was the one who insisted on playing cards with me."

"That true, Bennett?" Grandpapa barked.

Tessa blinked. It wasn't like him to invite the opinion of strangers. He'd apparently taken a liking to Mr. Bennett, and she couldn't blame him. There was something distinctly solid and trustworthy about the cove, with his warrior's hands and gentleman's manners.

And anyone who would step in to assist an outnumbered stranger was, she thought wistfully, that rarity of rarities: a man of honor. As chivalrous as the knights of old.

She felt that strange giddy sensation again.

Mr. Bennett adjusted his spectacles. "It is true that Mr. O'Toole approached Miss Todd."

Tessa sent him a grateful smile. Wasn't he the *best* chap? A real stand-up fellow.

Grunting, Grandpapa said, "So my granddaughter wasn't at fault then?"

"I wouldn't say that exactly."

Tessa's smile wavered.

"While Miss Todd didn't do the approaching, she did set the trap," Mr. Bennett went on. "And O'Toole took the bait, just as she'd planned."

"Now wait just one moment," Tessa said indignantly. "I didn't—"

"Silence," Grandpapa demanded. "I want to 'ear what Bennett 'as to say."

Pressing her lips together, she crossed her arms.

"Now, Bennett," her grandpapa said, "why do you think Tessie would want to bait O'Toole?"

"As to Miss Todd's motivations, that is a matter of conjecture." Bennett's voice had taken on an annoyingly pedantic tone. "I do have a hypothesis, however."

Hypothesis? Who does he think he is, a bloody professor? I can't believe I trusted the pompous ass!

"Let's 'ear it," Grandpapa said.

Go on, then, she fumed. *Talk about me as if I'm not even here.*

"Based on Miss Todd's actions this evening and those that you described earlier, I would say she was looking for diversion. Entertainment. In short," he pontificated, "my guess is that she was bored and trying to amuse herself."

Mr. Bennett's words struck her like a slap across the face. Her cheeks burned. *Entertainment?* To have her intricately plotted and brilliantly executed plan for revenge reduced to naught but the frivolous amusement of a bored twit...

With anger came an odd deflating sensation in her chest, as if her heart were a hot air balloon on a rapid descent. She ought to have known better than to hope that once, just dashed *once*, someone might see her for who she was. Might recognize her true abilities. Might...like her.

She shoved aside the ninnyish longing. The true frustration, she told herself, was that she couldn't defend herself. Couldn't reveal her true motivations without threatening Belinda's wellbeing.

What do I care what Bennett thinks of me anyway? she thought resentfully. *After tonight, I'll never have to lay eyes on the interfering prig again.*

"'Ow many times 'ave I told you, Tessie?" Grandpapa's censorious tone riled her further. "You can't be running about pell-mell through the streets. Ain't safe, for one, and you're a lady now, so best start acting like one."

The unfairness of it all made her want to scream.

Instead, she went to her grandfather's chair, crouching at his side and taking his hand. The way she'd done so many times as a girl. Back then, he'd listened to her. Indulged her. A tin of her favorite lemon drops, a miniature pony, a trip to Astley's Amphitheatre: the world had been her oyster.

But the best times had been when he'd taken her with him to Nightingale's, his favorite coffee house and the place where he conducted business. In between his meetings, he'd tell her tales of King Arthur and his knights. Of quests fulfilled or forsaken. Of honor and duty and unbreakable loyalty. People from the stews had come to seek his help and pay him homage, and she'd watched on with fierce pride.

Because Bartholomew Black was a *king*. And all she'd ever wanted was to be his trusted vassal. To sit by his side at the long table at Nightingale's, helping him bring peace and order to his unruly kingdom. She might not possess the physical strength or sheer ruthlessness of his dukes, but she would offer up what she had: a clever mind and determined heart.

Since she'd entered womanhood, however, everything had changed.

Her grandfather no longer paid heed to her desires. He'd gone from being indulgent to critical. He'd forced her to attend the ghastly Mrs. Southbridge's, to trade trousers for tight-laced corsets, to abandon her identity as a daughter of the stews in an effort to win over the snobs of the *ton*. Despite Tessa's hurt and confusion, she'd done her best to please him...but enough was enough.

She would *not* be parted from the streets. From her world. From her *home*.

"I don't want to be a lady," she said with fierce urgency. "I want a place by your side, Grandpapa, to help you—*especially* now, when there are threats facing our family." She darted a glance at Bennett, not wanting to say more about the assassination attempt on her grandfather in front of a stranger. "Why can't you understand that?"

Why can't you see that you need me? Why can't you see...me?

"Time you faced facts, Tessie. If you were a man, things would be different. But you ain't," her grandfather said bluntly. "You're a female, and you ain't got no place in my world. If you want to help me, you get married to the nob I got picked out for you. Give me great-grandchildren. That's your duty."

Pain bled through her. A dagger in the chest would have hurt less.

"My biggest regret was that I was too soft on you, Tessie," her grandfather went on heartlessly. "Let you run wild for far too long. No longer. From 'ere on in, you do as I say. You're going to act like a lady. Like the future bride o' the Duke of Ranelagh and Somerville."

When her grandfather had first announced his plan to marry her off to the Duke of Ranelagh and Somerville, she'd thought he was making a poor jest. But he'd become increasingly adamant on the subject, and none of her arguments could sway him.

"The duke is a known *rake*," she said desperately. "He'll make a terrible husband!"

"All that matters is that 'e'll keep you safe."

"I don't need him to keep me safe. I have you—"

"Won't be around forever, Tessie, and won't spend what time I got left arguing with you neither. Baroness von Friesing will be 'osting a supper for us, and 'Is Grace will be there. You'd best be prepared to make a good first impression."

His casual reference to his own mortality churned her insides with dread. At the same time, his high-handedness made her furious.

"I will *not* marry some stupid duke and breed a high-nosed litter!" She raised her chin. "I belong here with you, with the people whose lives I make a difference in. You can't force me to do anything I don't want to do!"

"Won't 'ave to. That's Bennett's job now." Grandpapa's smile was smug. "Meet your new bodyguard."

"*What?*" She turned to Bennett, who'd risen when she had. "I don't need another bodyguard!"

"'E's your only one. 'Ad to let the other one go," Grandpapa muttered. "Worthless git."

"Your grandfather has your best interests in mind," Bennett said. "You'd do well to abide by his wishes."

As if her grandfather's rejection wasn't enough, now she was being *lectured* by this blighter? She'd credited Bennett with being an intelligent man, and he'd seen her in action this eve: her clever disguise, her duping of O'Toole, her agility in the stews' streets. Yet he still believed her to be a *bored* miss in search of diversion? Some useless ninny who needed a keeper?

Her rage and despair found a fresh target.

"How much is my grandfather paying you?" she said acidly.

"None o' your business, Tessie," Grandpapa cut in.

She ignored him. "How much?"

"We haven't discussed terms as yet," Bennett said.

"Well, I can assure you that no amount of gold will be worth the trouble I'll cause. If you take this job, you're adding yourself to my List of Retribution," she vowed.

He stared at her. Unbelievably, his lips quirked. "Your, er, List of Retribution?"

"An eye for an eye," she said succinctly. "A Black never forgets a wrong."

Instead of looking afraid, or even wary, amusement glinted in his eyes. "I'll take my chances."

"You *will* regret this." Enraged, she poked him in the chest and was further irked when it felt as if she'd jammed her finger into a slab of granite. *Ouch.* Resisting the urge to rub her smarting digit, she stormed past him.

"Good evening, Miss Todd," he called after her, and her face burned at the humor in his deep voice. "'Twas a pleasure to make your acquaintance."

You don't know me, Bennett, she thought darkly. *But if you insist on crossing me…you'll find out* exactly *what I'm capable of.*

5

AFTER LEAVING BLACK'S RESIDENCE, HARRY TOOK A ROOM AT an inn rather than return to his lodgings. He couldn't risk Black tailing him and discovering his true identity from the landlord. He caught a few hours of sleep then left in the darkness, taking detours and making sure he wasn't followed. He arrived at the Lambeth Stairs and took a river boat helmed by a man named Salty Finn.

As Salty Finn rowed him out onto the dark river, towards Inspector Davies' waiting barge, Harry mulled over the recent events in preparation for the report he would have to make.

He'd begin by sharing what he'd learned about Tessa Todd. The facts were clear: she was a miss who donned deceptive disguises, cheated at cards, and didn't blink twice at orgies or a man being shot between the eyes. Moreover, she'd admitted that her night's adventures had been a *lark*. She was the wickedest miss he'd ever met—with the possible exception of Celeste De Witt, who'd used her seductive wiles to help her father steal Harry's work. Who'd played a part in branding Harry a thief and liar.

As Sir Aloysius De Witt's distinguished features resurrected in his memory, Harry felt a bitter anger. Celeste's father was celebrated in scientific circles, but Harry knew what the man really was: a cunning, ruthless fraud. His only comfort was that, as far as he'd heard, Aloyisus' scheming hadn't done the other any good; as he'd told the bastard, some fires were too dangerous to be tamed.

Shoving aside the past, Harry objectively reviewed Miss Todd's brash, bizarre, and, some might say, *bordering on criminal* behavior. He was aware that his intellectual assessment didn't quite line up with his personal reaction to her. He couldn't deny that Tessa Todd stirred up a certain degree of...fascination. She was like an experiment with wholly unpredictable results: the kind that had once kept him in his laboratory night after night, trying to understand the phenomena.

He told himself it was only Miss Todd's uniqueness that roused his curiosity. Recalling her threat to put him on her "List of Retribution," he felt his lips quirk. What made up the complex alchemy of this woman who was unlike any he'd met before? Miss Todd's willfulness eclipsed even that of his sisters, whose delicate appearances belied strong-willed natures.

He knew one thing for certain: she was trouble. Thus, he would do the rational thing. He would acknowledge his reaction to her, let it go, and do his duty.

Arriving at his destination, he boarded the covered barge in the middle of the river. Ducking, he entered the cramped cabin, where his supervisor stood waiting.

"You weren't followed?" Inspector Davies said without preamble.

"No, sir." Water lapped against the boat's sides as he and his superior took adjacent seats. "I took extra precautions."

The flickering glow of the single lantern deepened the circles under the police inspector's eyes. Though his wiry grey hair and deeply creased face placed Davies in his fifties, he had the energy of a younger man. In a way, Davies' vigilance reminded Harry of

Ambrose; indeed, his brother and Davies knew each other for, years ago, both had worked for the Thames River Police.

Ambrose had described Davies as an ambitious fellow with the single-mindedness of a bloodhound on a hunt. Harry would agree: his supervisor was devoting full resources to establishing Black's guilt. Not only had Davies set up a rotating watch on the cutthroat's home, he had every constable report in to him personally after the shift. He held the meetings here, in the dark oasis of the Thames, beyond the reach of eyes and ears.

"Give me your report," Davies said.

Inhaling, Harry recounted the night's adventures.

Davies' straight eyebrows levitated toward his hairline. "You mean to say Black hired you to be his granddaughter's guard? And you *agreed*?"

Having broken protocol, Harry knew he deserved censure.

"Yes, sir," he admitted. "I didn't want to tip him off that he was being investigated by the police. Given the circumstances, I also didn't wish to contradict him. So I humored him."

"Do you know what you've done, Kent?" Davies said slowly.

Something in the other's manner made the ever-present knot tighten in Harry's chest. He'd expected a reprimand...but was he about to lose his job? Damnit, why hadn't he seen this coming? For two years, he'd lived in the shadow of disgrace, with the foreboding sense that disaster could erupt at any moment. Now, when he ought to have been prepared, he wasn't ready.

He steeled himself, readying for the talons of failure to strike.

"You've given us a way in. At long last." The barge rocked as Davies slammed his fist into his palm. "After *years* of pursuing Black, we've finally got him in our grasp. With you on the inside, we can collect evidence of his guilt."

Relief pulsed through Harry. Along with surprise. "You mean... you want me to take the job?"

"*Yes*, by God." Davies's expression was as fervent as an

acolyte's. "This is a *once in a lifetime* opportunity, Kent. For years, I've been pursuing Black, but each time he's got away with everything from theft to pillaging to murder. There's never been sufficient proof to find him guilty: even this time, when we have this."

From his pocket, Davies withdrew a gold medallion. Harry recognized it from the initial briefing of the constables. Davies had found the medallion around the neck of The Gilded Pearl's bawd. The disk of gold spun upon its chain now. A pair of crossed swords was stamped on one side, a tiny blood-red gem dripping from the tip of the right blade. The other side held a single, engraved word: *Adsum.*

Latin for *I am here.*

"This is Black's insignia. He left his bloody *calling card*,"— Davies' hand fisted around the chain—"and still I was able to do nothing."

Davies had gone to question Black the day after the fire; Black had denied any wrongdoing. The cutthroat had acknowledged that the medallion was that of the House of Black but had refused to elaborate further. Moreover, there were no witnesses—none willing to risk their necks anyway—and Black had an alibi for the time of the fire: he'd been at a dinner party given by his daughter, Mavis Todd, his presence vouched for by at least a dozen others.

"I walked away empty-handed, but I won't do so again. You're going to see to that."

As Davies tucked the medallion away, Harry saw frustration flash in the other's gaze. He wondered what it must be like to witness all the suffering that Davies had over the years. To wage a tireless war against evil.

"What do you want me to do?" Harry said quietly.

Davies rested his arms on his knees, his expression pensive. "Earn Black's trust. The bastard has a small inner circle: if you're allowed entry, you'll have access to valuable information. Keep your eyes and ears open for any details—about his business, his family—that might help us connect him to The Pearl. But *observe only*: we don't want another Popay situation on our hands."

Harry nodded. A former member of the force, William Popay had worked in civilian clothes to infiltrate the National Union. His overzealousness had earned him the label of "spy," fueling negative public opinion about the police.

"Be on the lookout for any motive, any piece of evidence that can tie Black to the destruction of The Pearl...or any other crime. I don't care what we get him for as long as we get him," Davies went on starkly. "Through this, you must keep your true identity hidden. You must eat, breathe, and sleep as Sam Bennett. One false move and you'll be paying with your life, understand?"

"Yes, sir." Hesitating, he said, "What should I do if I'm recognized?"

Although he and Black lived in different worlds, overlap was possible. London might be a metropolis, but in certain neighborhoods it felt like Chudleigh Crest, the village of his youth, where one was bound to encounter a familiar face. To Harry's advantage, he'd lived outside of London for two years, and, before that, in Cambridge. Moreover, working as a navvy had changed his demeanor and appearance, offering him further anonymity.

"Hide, or run," Davies said succinctly.

An honest, if not reassuring, reply.

Another problem occurred to Harry: his family. The Kents were a close-knit bunch. Since his return to London, his sisters, in particular, had been badgering him to socialize. His eldest sister, Emma, the Duchess of Strathaven, had put it in her usual forthright way: *You must hold your head up high, dear brother. No matter what anyone says, you know the truth, and that is what matters. And you must know you have our full support.*

He did know, but he had no intention of letting his family fight his battles for him. And while he knew Em and his other sisters were well-intentioned, he'd also declined their offers to introduce him to "nice young ladies." Being a private man, he didn't want them meddling in his affairs.

Now he would need his family to stay away so as not to compromise his first mission.

"I'll have to talk to my brother—" he began.

"I can fill him in on your assignment. Of all men, Ambrose Kent understands discretion, and I'd wager he can keep the rest of your family, ahem, at bay."

The inspector's wry expression suggested that he knew something of Harry's sisters. The Kent ladies were rather famous (or infamous, depending on who one asked) for their unconventionality and for marrying well in spite of it. Emma had met her duke while trying to solve a murder. Likewise, Harry's other sisters—Thea, Violet, and Polly—had proved their mettle during adventures that had brought them together with their respective lords.

"Ambrose will know what to do," Harry said.

Davies nodded. "The mission will bring great risk, but the reward will be commensurate. If you help me bring Black down, I can promise you a raise and a promotion in rank."

The inspector said no more. Harry knew the other was leaving the door open. It was up to him whether or not he would cross the threshold. The decision wasn't difficult. Here was his chance to do what was right, and, hopefully, in the process, redeem his good name.

"How will I communicate with you, sir?" he said. "When I have news to report?"

Davies' eyes lit with triumph. "Good man. We'll use the mudlarks."

The "mudlarks" were children of the stews who scavenged to survive. They'd earned their moniker because they were oft found along the banks of the Thames, knee-deep in muck, sifting out anything of value. Due to their ubiquitous presence, the mudlarks were uniquely positioned to be messengers. Their speediness and famed discretion were worth their weight in gold.

"Is there anything else, Kent?" Davies asked. "Do you anticipate any problems carrying out the assignment?"

An image flashed of green-grey eyes and riotous sable curls, a mouth shaped like temptation.

He dismissed it and said firmly, "Nothing I cannot handle, sir."

6

Bloody hell, I can't take another day of this.

Or, more precisely, I can—but I might end up throttling Tessa Todd.

These were Harry's first thoughts upon awakening.

It had been a week since he'd started guarding the recalcitrant miss. A week of pure hell. When she'd claimed he would regret taking on the job as her bodyguard, she hadn't been jesting.

Groaning, he slung an arm over his eyes. He'd experimented with explosive chemicals. Used incendiary devices to blast tunnels through mountains. How could he have guessed that guarding a mere slip of a female would be the most dangerous job he'd ever had?

She'd run him through the bloody gauntlet. It turned out that Miss Todd was not only clever and devious, both of which he'd gleaned from their first meeting, but she also had the sense of humor of an adolescent boy. He had two young nephews who would undoubtedly snicker at her pranks. Being on her List of Retribution, however, was no laughing matter.

It all began on his first day as her guard. He'd refused to allow her to visit some "chum" of hers named Alfred. Not only would it be improper for her to visit the blasted fellow unchaperoned, but this Alfred lived in one of the worst parts of Whitechapel. When Miss Todd insisted that she'd been visiting Alfred on her own for years, Harry had been appalled.

What had her family been *thinking* to allow her behavior to go unchecked for so long?

He'd put his foot down; she'd gone to sulk in her chamber.

Afterward, whether for her own amusement or to punish him, she'd started practicing violin. He'd heard cats copulating with more grace. Just as he suspected that his ears might be bleeding, one of the maids brought him a tea tray. Grateful for the respite, Harry had added generous spoonfuls from the sugar bowl before taking a gulp. He'd instantly spat the *salty* liquid out.

Miss Todd's laughter had echoed from the other room.

The next day, he'd accompanied her to Potter's, a Covent Garden tea shop that appeared to be the equivalent of Gunter's for the wealthy denizens of the underworld. In the light-filled dining room, well-dressed patrons ate ices and cakes that arrived on tiered plates. He'd planned to wait outside, but Miss Todd had insisted that he stay. When he'd eyed the tea she'd poured for him, she'd flashed him a *challenging* grin.

"I solemnly vow that I've added nothing to your beverage... this time," she'd said impishly.

Reluctantly, he'd taken a seat in the chair beside her, and the moment his arse hit the chintz seat cushion, an ignominious sound had trumpeted through the room. His face flamed as he recalled the shocked stares, gasps, and titters of the other patrons. All the while, Miss Todd had tried—unsuccessfully—to stifle her chuckles behind a napkin.

From beneath the cushion, he'd removed a device made from a pig's bladder. One that made farting noises, for God's sake. Then came her *pièce de resistance*.

Harry got up from the cot and lit a lamp, his living quarters flaring into view. He'd been assigned the room in the mews behind the house, and the space was comfortable and utilitarian.

He splashed his face at the washstand, his reflection in the looking glass showing his dark mood. After Potter's, he'd taken the high road and offered her a truce: he would take her on an outing of her choice, as long as it was suitable for a lady.

She'd decided to go shopping.

Arriving at the Pantheon Shopping Bazaar, she'd asked him quite prettily (that in itself ought to have tipped him off) to hold her reticule while she and her maid went inside a shop. After ascertaining that there was no secondary exit to said shop, he'd agreed and had been waiting for her to emerge when two guards suddenly descended upon him, truncheons in hand.

Apparently, a young miss had reported a man of his description stealing her purse. It had taken no little explaining to extricate himself out of that predicament. Passing patrons had looked at him as if he were horse shit clinging to their shoes.

Why are you surprised? His chest burned. *Being humiliated by a woman is nothing new.*

The memory of his desperate desire to please Celeste De Witt, how stupidly he'd fallen for her ethereal looks and seeming fragility, tore at his gut. For four years, he'd worshipped the ground she'd walked on. As a man uncomfortable with flirtation, he'd nonetheless conjured up awkward compliments and flowery sentiments in order to gratify her. If Celeste had requested that he fetch the moon, he'd have asked if she wanted the stars as well.

Well, he'd learned. He no longer believed in angels or putting women on pedestals.

He saw Tessa Todd precisely for what she was: a devilish brat who ought to be turned over his knee. At the thought of spanking the minx, an inexplicable surge of heat flooded his groin.

He cursed, raking a hand through his hair. He didn't understand his physical reaction to the chit, and he didn't trust things he didn't understand. Logically, he couldn't deny that Tessa Todd was attractive. Her eyes shifted between green and grey depending on her mood and flashed verdigris fire when she was angry (he ought to know). Her features were delicate and fresh, her figure enticingly petite, and, if she wasn't such a hellion, she might bring to mind a porcelain figurine.

Nonetheless, he *knew* who she was. Celeste had hidden her true nature behind a façade of demure virtue, but Tessa Todd had no qualms about being a wicked, spoiled miss through and through. In fact, she seemed to take *pride* in it. Knowing her capacity for deception and manipulation ought to have neutralized his attraction to her, yet his baser instincts warred against his rationality—and the latter, he realized with self-disgust, was far from claiming a decisive victory.

Perhaps he'd just been celibate too long. He hadn't been with a woman since Roxanne, hadn't wanted distractions while he was finding his footing. But now he recognized the pent-up need building in him, putting him on edge.

Do not let Tessa Todd get under your skin, he told himself. *You have a mission to complete. Rein in the troublesome chit—and your own bloody self.*

With brisk efficiency, he finished dressing and reached for his boots. This was his spare pair: his favorite Hessians had been ruined by Miss Todd, who'd somehow managed to furtively fill them with honey. Scowling, he took the precaution of sticking his hand into the battered leather footwear—unadulterated, Praise Jesus...though a bit shoddy.

The state of the boots was due to the fact that he found shopping as enjoyable as a visit to the tooth drawer. His wont was to get fitted once, have multiple duplicates made, and wear the items until they could no longer be decently worn. Or until his glamorous sister-in-law, Marianne, declared his wardrobe a state of emergency and corralled him into a shopping expedition. Luckily, Marianne wasn't here, so he donned his boots, which were old but comfortable, and vacated the room, heading across the dark courtyard to the kitchen.

The cavernous room was warm and bustling with activity. A

black stove lined one wall, pots and pans hanging neatly from hooks. The servants were milling about the large central worktable, preparing for breakfast. The smells of frying meat and fresh bread permeated the room.

Harry returned the friendly greetings and received more than one sympathetic look.

"Ready for another round, are you, Bennett?" Jim, the second footman asked, grinning.

"Hush, Jim." Mrs. Gates, the bespectacled housekeeper, looked up from the list she was consulting on the worktable. "If the master hears you speaking with disrespect, you'll find yourself out on the street, and you'd deserve it."

Jim snorted as he hefted up a tray. "Master would have to be 'ome to' ear me, wouldn't 'e?"

The footman had a point. Since Harry had started work, he'd seen little of Black. He hadn't been able to do much in the way of reconnaissance due to Miss Todd keeping his hands full. She was an early riser, but it was not yet dawn, so he had some time before she started to wreak havoc anew. Now was a good time to gather information.

"Has something been keeping Mr. Black busy?" he said casually.

"Just the usual murder and mayhem," Jim called before he disappeared up the steps.

Murder and mayhem? Is he referring to The Gilded Pearl?

"Pay Jim no mind," Mrs. Gates said, a reproving line between her brows. "If he spent half as much time on improving his skills as he did on idle chatter, he'd be a first footman by now."

She turned to chastise a pair of chatting housemaids, who scurried off to do her bidding.

Seeing the cook's arms tremble as she lifted a large saucepan from the stove, Harry strode over to assist. "Allow me, Mrs. Crabtree."

She relinquished the heavy pan with a grateful smile. "Much obliged, Bennett."

"My pleasure." With her plump, pigeon-like figure and frizzled hair, the good lady reminded him a little of his own mama. He set the pan down on the worktable, next to a dish of baked eggs. "The cream sauce smells delicious."

"It's the tarragon." Her eyes twinkled. "And the splash o' sherry."

"My mama made shirred eggs in the same fashion."

"Do your kin live in London?"

He hesitated. "My parents passed some time ago."

"I'm sorry to 'ear it."

"Thank you." Although his mama had died when he was twelve and his papa a decade after that, Harry still felt a pang when he thought of them. Marjorie and Samuel Kent had been a loving couple and devoted parents; sometimes, he wondered if he would ever experience the security and happiness of his early years again.

"It ain't easy losing kin. I lost mine when I was a girl." Mrs. Crabtree spooned the sauce carefully over the eggs. "If it weren't for the master, I'd have ended up in the orphanage or worse."

"Mr. Black took you in?" Harry couldn't keep the surprise from his voice.

"Owe 'im everything, I do. 'E provided for my care, saw that I got trained in a trade. And I ain't the only one 'e's 'elped. With the Corn Laws leaving folk starving in the streets, 'e funds the free kitchens o' the parish churches and finds work for the men where 'e can. The government may not care 'bout the common people, but Bartholomew Black does."

Her assertions astonished Harry.

"And contrary to Jim's palavering, the master was busy this week looking after poor Miss Mavis—Mrs. Todd, I mean," Mrs. Gates put in. "A more loving father I've never met."

"Poor Mrs. Todd." Mrs. Crabtree clucked her tongue. "She

relies upon 'er papa during 'er spells. Lord knows she 'as no one else."

The cook and housekeeper shared a knowing look.

Recalling his instructions to collect any information about Black and his family, Harry asked, "What about her husband?"

"That one." Mrs. Crabtree snorted. "All 'e cares 'bout is filling 'is coffers. If Mr. Black weren't there to keep 'im in line, 'e'd ne'er show 'is face around 'is own 'ouse."

He filed the fact away. "And Miss Todd? Is she close to her parents?"

"Poor girl always looked up to her father, not that she saw much of him," Mrs. Gates said. "She and her stepmama are fond of each other, but Mrs. Todd needs her peace and quiet."

"Both of which are in scarce supply around Miss Todd," he muttered.

Mrs. Crabtree chuckled, and Mrs. Gates looked as if she was fighting a smile.

"You're faring better than most, Bennett." Approval glinted in the housekeeper's bespectacled gaze. "Most of your predecessors didn't last a sennight. Ran off with their tails between their legs. Takes brawn and brains to keep up with our Miss Tessa."

"Now she may like to play 'er tricks," Mrs. Crabtree said in a consoling tone, "but beneath that pluck, the girl's got a 'eart o' gold. Treats all o' us below stairs wiv kindness, ne'er forgets a birthday, is always the first to 'elp when there's trouble. Remember when Mr. Black's old valet broke 'is arm, Mrs. Gates?"

The housekeeper nodded. "Miss Tessa went personally to visit him and bring supplies to the family. She visits the orphanages, too, you know. I don't know what the children like more: the food she brings or the tricks she's taught Swift Nick to perform."

"Like 'er grandfather, that one," Mrs. Crabtree declared.

It was a compliment, Harry knew. Still, he was having a difficult time reconciling this new perspective on Black and his granddaughter with what he knew of them.

Heavy steps shuffled into the kitchen, and Mrs. Gates greeted the newcomer. "Good morning, Lizzie. Is Miss Tessa ready for her tray?"

Lizzie, a robust woman with a perpetually downturned mouth, shook her head. "Told me last night that she weren't to be disturbed this morning. Wanted to stay abed, she said."

The words roused Harry's suspicion. "From what I've observed, Miss Todd is an early riser."

"A week and you got her pegged, have you?" Lizzie's arms crossed beneath her ample bosom, her expression reminding him of a bulldog's. "Well, I've been with Miss Tessa *ten years*, and I daresay I know her better than you."

Of the staff, the lady's maid had been the only one to take an antagonistic attitude toward Harry.

Aping her mistress, no doubt.

"It is my job to understand Miss Todd's patterns," he said.

"It's *my* job to see her wishes obeyed," Lizzie shot back. "And she don't *want* to be disturbed."

Rather than argue, he headed for his charge's bedchamber.

The house had servants' passages constructed throughout, and he took the stairs to the first floor, Lizzie huffing and puffing behind him. He paid her no mind, opening the panel and exiting onto the hallway. Passing gilt-framed landscapes, he strode towards Miss Todd's suite and knocked briskly on her door.

"Miss Todd, this is Bennett," he said.

When there was no reply, premonition knotted his gut.

"She's still sleeping." Lizzie's indignant voice came from behind him. "Stop that racket before you wake her up."

He knocked louder. "Answer me, or I'm coming in."

"Don't you dare open that door!" Lizzie screeched.

He tested the door handle. Locked. *Of bloody course.*

Rearing back, he charged shoulder-first at the door. The barrier flew open, and he had an instant to register the empty room before an icy torrent rushed over him. Dumbfounded, he swung his head up, swiping at his spectacles to clear his vision.

Through the clinging droplets, he saw an empty bucket over the door. It was suspended by a system of ropes and pulleys, the mechanism triggered by a string tied to the door handle. He might have been impressed by the complexity of the apparatus if he wasn't so furious.

Steam fogged his lenses.

"Told you not to open the door," Lizzie said.

At his smoldering glare, she shrugged and left.

A drop of water slid down his brow. He ripped off his spectacles, searching his coat pockets for a handkerchief. A snarl left him when that came out sopping wet as well.

This is the last bloody straw. He stalked down the hallway. He'd played by a gentleman's rules, taken the higher road—no more. He was going to hunt the chit down and when he did...there would be hell to pay.

7

"You *didn't*," Pretty Francie gasped.

"Oh, yes, I did," Tessa said. "As I speak, Sam Bennett is likely getting the soaking of his life."

Her three friends—Pretty Francie, Belinda, and Daisy—looked at her. At each other.

Laughter rang through the room.

A half-hour earlier, Tessa had slipped into The Underworld, the pleasure house owned by her father. She'd been coming to the club for as long as she could remember. When her mama had died giving birth to her, her father had been left with the care of an infant. A busy man who couldn't be bothered with domestic details, he'd simply brought her along to work.

Tessa couldn't recall if he'd ever hired a nanny for her; she'd never needed one for the wenches had taken her under their collective wing. The Underworld was her second home, and, at the early hour, she'd caught her friends just as they were getting to bed after a night's work. Now they were enjoying a chat in Pretty Francie's chamber.

The women wore bright, clingy peignoirs while Tessa was once again in a lad's get-up. This time, she'd chosen slim-fitting trousers and forgone the scratchy wig, tucking her plaited hair beneath a cap. Even during daytime, a woman alone in the stews invited danger. Without the hindrance of petticoats and skirts, Tessa moved with confidence through the streets, her daggers tucked snugly in her boots.

As she chatted with her friends, Tessa surreptitiously monitored Belinda. Since being beaten and robbed by O'Toole, Belinda had lost some of her natural vivaciousness. The bastard had taken more than money from her: he'd punched a hole in her self-confidence.

If Grandpapa would give me a seat at the table, I'd stand for Belinda and all the women like her, Tessa thought fiercely. *I'd make bastards like O'Toole think twice about taking advantage of the defenseless.*

Thankfully, Belinda appeared more like her old self this morning, her honey-colored curls bouncing as she giggled, the bruises around her right eye faded to a mottled green. Swift Nick Nevison had his front paws on her generous lap, munching on pieces of cold mutton that she fed him from a plate.

"I almost feel sorry for this Bennett fellow." Pretty Francie lounged on her bed, her trademark auburn hair tied in rags. Her handsome face was heavily painted. At thirty-four, she was now the club's madam and rarely serviced customers, but she liked to keep up appearances. "'E didn't know what 'e was taking on."

Years ago, when Pretty Francie had been a house wench, she'd been especially kind to Tessa. Daisy and Belinda had joined The Underworld some time later, and Tessa considered them, along with Francie, to be her bosom friends.

Sitting at the foot of Francie's bed, Tessa shucked her cap, tossing it onto one of the bedposts. "He knew perfectly well what he was in for because *I warned him*. Said flat-out that I wouldn't tolerate having my freedom curtailed. Why would I need a bodyguard when I'm perfectly capable of handling myself?"

"Our Tessa ain't no milk-fed miss," Daisy, a saucy brunette, said with a wink. She and Belinda occupied the adjacent settee. "Can take care o' 'erself, she can."

Tessa beamed at what she considered to be the ultimate compliment.

"But after wot 'appened to your grandfather at Nightingale's," Belinda put in hesitantly, "don't you fink you might be be'er off wiv some protection?"

At the reminder of the murderous attempt, a cold droplet slid down Tessa's spine.

The shooting had taken place a month ago, right outside Nightingale's. Luckily, the would-be assassin had missed, and Ming had returned fire with deadly accuracy. To maintain order, Grandpapa had suppressed gossip; Belinda and the others only knew about it because Tessa had confided in them. Since then, there'd been no other threats, but the event had left Tessa shaken. Her grandfather was not invulnerable...and he was down a man.

John Randolph, the former Duke of Covent Garden, had died in a carriage accident two months ago. In the never-ending struggle for power in the underworld, Randolph had been a staunch ally to her grandfather, and his loss, Tessa knew, was a big blow.

It made her more determined than ever to stand by her grandfather's side.

Where he needs me. Whenever she was out in the underworld, she acted as his eyes and ears. Aware of the importance of appearances, she was also a proud ambassador of the House of Black.

"We Blacks will not be intimidated," she declared. "Am I right, Swift Nick?"

The ferret's eyes were alert in his furry brown mask. When Tessa gave a subtle nod of her head, he mimicked the motion vigorously, giving the impression that he was agreeing with her.

Belinda laughed. "Howe'er did you train 'im to do that?"

"It was easy. Swift Nick is the cleverest fellow who ever lived and all the protection I need, aren't you, dear?"

In answer, the ferret loped over to Tessa. He clambered onto her lap, rolling over, and she obliged his request for a tummy rub. He made *took-took* sounds, the ferret equivalent of purring.

"That ferret may be clever, but it ain't no guard." Brow pleating, Francie said, "Belinda 'as a point, luvie. Maybe you shouldn't be comin' 'ere alone."

Frost spread over Tessa's insides. Her grandfather had tried to curtail her visits, and her father went along (not because he cared, but because he wanted to curry his father-in-law's favor). She ignored their orders, continuing to come in secret: no one was taking away her friends, her home.

"The lunatic who shot at my grandfather is dead," she said firmly. "There's no threat."

"Are you certain o' that?"

At the seriousness in the other's gaze, Tessa sat up straighter. "What have you heard, Francie?"

Francie hesitated, confirming Tessa's suspicion that her friend *did* know something. Too often, people underestimated prostitutes, believing that because they made their livings on their backs, they didn't have anything between their ears. Tessa, however, knew the truth.

Her friends had minds as keen as her daggers. Not only were the women observant and shrewd, they were also privy to all manner of secrets. Men in their cups, and in the throes, were less likely to be discreet. Most of them didn't think they had to be with an "empty-headed" wench.

Which meant Francie and the others had access to prime information. Others might believe that money was the currency of the stews; Tessa knew better.

Nothing, but nothing, made a man (or woman) more powerful than information.

"It might be nuffin'," Francie said.

"Tell me," Tessa insisted. "You know I'd never tell anyone where I heard it."

Francie licked her lips. "There's been talk. Rumors that your grandfather..." Her voice lowered. "That 'e ain't as powerful as 'e once was. Some are takin' The Gilded Pearl as proof o' that."

The Gilded Pearl had been a bawdy house in Covent Garden. A fortnight ago, an explosive fire had killed all those trapped inside. Tessa had witnessed her grandfather's fury over the disaster for, like any good king, he held himself responsible for those under his protection.

Her blood chilling, she said, "That was an accident. Grandpapa said so."

"What with John Randolph's death, there's been a few too many accidents in Covent Garden," Francie said darkly. "Rumors are flyin' that Black's rule is nearing an end."

Codger's old now, weak. Barton's last words echoed in Tessa's head. *Mark my words, a new King is coming...*

She balled her hands in her lap. "Who said that?"

"Ain't loose lips you need to worry about." Francie slid a look at Belinda. "To make matters worse, after what Dewey O'Toole did 'ere, in your father's establishment, and your father not retaliating... It makes your entire family look weak. And bastards like O'Toole more powerful."

Frustration bound Tessa like a tight-laced corset. Although she didn't agree with her father's stance, loyalty made her stand up for him. "My father is *not* afraid of a blackguard like O'Toole. I'm sure if I were to ask him why he didn't—"

"No!" This came from Belinda, her bruises pronounced against her paling face. "You *promised* you wouldn't say anything to Mr. Todd. I can't lose this job. I got nowhere to go!"

Seeing the fear in her friend's eyes, Tessa bottled her frustration. No matter how much she wanted to confront her father, she would never betray her promise to her friend.

She crossed over to the other, put a hand on the blonde's trembling shoulder. "I'm a woman of my word, Belinda. I said I wouldn't tell, and I won't."

"Thank you," Belinda said tremulously.

Tessa had planned to return Belinda's money in private, but she realized she couldn't wait. It was imperative to demonstrate, even to friends, that her family was a force to be reckoned with. That Blacks and Todds had the power to uphold the stew's most sanctified tenet of reciprocity.

She whistled at Swift Nick, nodding at her jacket which she'd earlier slung onto a chair. The ferret hopped over to the garment, disappearing into the folds. He emerged with the coin bag between his teeth.

"Give it to Belinda," Tessa said.

The ferret dragged the heavy bag over, depositing it at Belinda's feet.

"Wot's this, then?" Belinda picked up the bag, untied it, and let out a squeak. "Gor, there's a bleedin' *fortune* in 'ere!"

"It's what O'Toole owes you," Tessa said.

"But this is more than a 'undred quid—"

"He owes you every cent and *more*," she stated. "Consider it payment with interest."

Belinda clutched the purse. "'Ow—'ow did you get the blunt from O'Toole?"

"Never mind that. Just know that a Black will *always* see justice done."

"We'll go see a goldsmith straightaway," Francie put in. "'E'll turn that blunt into silver and keep it safe for you, too."

Belinda's throat worked. "Oh, Tessa, I don't know how I'll repay—"

"Your friendship is payment enough." She went over, squeezed the other's shoulder. "You've seen me through thick and thin, and I'm merely returning the favor."

Tessa would never forget the kindness of her friends. They'd been her safe harbor during the lonely years of childhood and the stormy ones of womanhood. After yet another day of being bullied and ridiculed at Mrs. Southbridge's, she'd arrive at the club, dejected and feeling alone.

Belinda had always had a kind word and gentle hug, Daisy an amusing rejoinder.

And Francie had been the fount of wisdom.

"As your friends, Tessa," Francie said, right on cue, "we don't want you getting 'urt. What 'arm would it do to 'ave a guard?"

"He wouldn't let me come here, for starters." Tessa plopped back onto Francie's bed. "Bennett is like a Professor of Propriety. He's always lecturing me, telling me what I can and cannot do. I think he enjoys enforcing Grandpapa's orders to keep me in line."

"Enforcing?" Belinda's voice quivered. "Is this Bennett a brute?"

Bennett...wasn't. That was the problem: he wasn't like any man Tessa had dealt with before.

"He's not," she said grudgingly. "I mean, he *is* rather large, in a tall, muscular sort of way, but he's not a lummox like the previous guards. He's intelligent, and he's got a gentleman's polish...though he's no fribble, either. In a brawl, he can hold his own as well as any prizefighter."

"So let's see if I got this right. This Bennett is a virile, brainy, well-mannered toff who's good wiv 'is 'ands." Daisy made a droll face. "I can see why no woman in 'er right mind would want 'im about. 'E don't 'appen to be a looker, too?"

Tessa's cheeks warmed. She'd eat her cap before admitting that Bennett was attractive.

"I haven't noticed his looks," she lied. "The point is I don't like his manner."

"What's wrong with his manner?" Daisy wanted to know.

He's too observant. Overbearing. And he never loses his temper.

She found Bennett's equanimity particularly irksome. Yet she appeared to be the only one for Mrs. Gates was constantly praising his amiability and Mrs. Crabtree his steady, considerate nature. Tessa, however, didn't trust a man with good manners.

Perhaps it was because she was used to men who expressed their displeasure in no uncertain terms. Both her father and grandfather had volatile tempers. In contrast, Bennett's calm rationality was dashed *unnatural*. When she played a prank on him, he didn't shout or threaten or show much emotion at all. In fact, he regarded her with calm brown eyes, gave her a lecture in cool, rational tones, and moved on...as if nothing had happened!

This, perversely, egged on her bad behavior. Made her want to get some reaction from him. To pierce his blasted armor of control.

"He's high-handed and controlling." She crossed her arms. "Can you believe he had the gall to prevent me from seeing Alfred? To tell me what to do?"

"He's a man, luvie," Francie said. "Telling a woman what to do is what they do best."

"Well, I don't need some dictatorial keeper. Especially one whose sole purpose is to ensure that the Duke of Ranelagh and Somerville gets a pristine bride," she said bitterly.

Bennett's complicity with her grandfather's plans angered her most of all. For a brief instant, when she and Bennett had been on the run together and he'd let her guide the way, she'd believed that he saw her as an equal. That the respect she'd felt was mutual. Instead, he thought she was some bored twit who ought to do whatever she was told.

Francie quirked a brow. "Your grandfather is still set on marrying you off to Ransom?"

Society had given the Duke of Ranelagh and Somerville the moniker of "Ransom." It was not only a clever contraction of his two titles but also a reference to his popularity with the ladies: according to the *on dit*, he held female hearts hostage wherever he went. If the situation weren't so dire for her personally, Tessa would have snickered at the *ton*'s absurdity.

"I have to meet the blasted nob tomorrow night," she said mulishly.

"Would it be so bad to be a duchess?" Belinda's expression turned dreamy. "Just fink o' the fancy balls and 'ouses in the country, rubbin' shoulders wiv all 'em grand folk."

Tessa could sum all of that up in one word: *torture.*

During the Southbridge years, she'd hated every minute of pretending to be Miss Theresa Smith. Hated being forced to hide her name, family, and heritage—and for what? To be ridiculed by milk-fed chits who didn't know their arse from their elbows?

Crikey, she had more important things to do than being a wallflower. Grandpapa's empire was under attack. She had to protect her people, her world.

She lifted her chin. "No title is worth giving up my name and who I am."

"From what I've 'eard, Ransom 'as merits other than 'is title," Daisy said with a smirk. "One *big* merit in particular."

"'Old your tongue," Francie admonished. "Tessie's 'ere."

"It's all right—" Tessa began.

Francie shook her head. "It's *not* right. You're an unwed miss."

"Sorry, forgot meself," Daisy said contritely.

Seeing Francie's stony expression, Tessa sighed: there was no point in arguing. Her friends had always been overly protective about her "innocence." Never mind that she'd grown up in a brothel, they persisted in treating her as a lady, especially when it came to sexual matters. The resulting irony was that the three wenches were as prudish as spinster aunts around her. And they weren't persuaded by her logic that she'd seen and heard things that would cause a typical virgin to fall into a dead swoon.

Tessa considered herself a virgin only in the physical sense. Her *mind* was far from chaste, and, indeed, she was proud that she was no silly naïf (her knowledge of French was *nothing* compared to her vocabulary of vulgarities). Nonetheless, Francie, Belinda, and Daisy persisted in shielding her; since they did it out of love, she couldn't fault them for it.

"The point is, I'm not going to give up who I am for anyone," she said unequivocally. "Weren't you the ones who told me that no man is worth losing one's freedom for?"

What her friends *had* shared with her were their histories, using them as cautionary tales. All three women had endured abuses at the hands of men. All had chosen their profession because, as they put it, at least they got paid for their services... and kept their money and freedom.

"You're a clever one," Francie said with pride. "Let's 'ope your grandfather recognizes that before it's too late."

Seeing Belinda's stifled yawn and the drooping of Daisy's eyelids, Tessa realized she'd overstayed her visit. Her friends worked long hours and needed their rest.

"I've kept you up too long." She rose, and Swift Nick bounded off the bed. "I'll be on my—"

The door swung open.

Sam Bennett filled the doorway, his broad shoulders nearly brushing the frame. To enter, he had to duck his head which, she noted, looked damp. A dark lock curled upon his brow; it looked incongruously boyish against his scowling countenance.

"How did you find me?" she blurted.

"It's my damned job."

At his dark, growly voice, one she'd never heard from him before, the hairs on her skin rose to tingling attention. His brown eyes were no longer calm. 'Twas as if the earth's crust had split open, molten emotion glowing behind his spectacles. The scar through his eyebrow stretched taut. Every inch of his lean and muscled frame radiated barely leashed anger.

She swallowed. Wetted her lips.

"Sweet Jesus," Daisy breathed into the taut silence. "Never say *he's* your Bennett?"

8

Keep a rein on it, he warned himself. *Do not lose your temper.*

It was a refrain he'd repeated during his journey over. Tracking the maddening minx hadn't been difficult. A quick survey of her chamber had revealed her escape route via the balcony window. After questioning the staff, he'd learned that Miss Todd had a habit of visiting her "friends"...at her father's club.

She'd gone to a damned *bawdy house*.

He could scarcely credit it. Yet here she was, looking utterly at home with three wenches.

Even though the others were brightly and scantily clad, Miss Todd commanded his full attention. She was once again dressed like a lad, only this time her outfit wasn't bulky or concealing. She wore no jacket, her shirt draping over her delicate curves. Her trousers fit her legs like a second skin, her cravat highlighting the swanlike grace of her neck. The simple, glossy plait of her hair set off her large eyes and vivid features.

Instead of hiding her femininity, the masculine attire emphasized it. Her fresh, artless loveliness would tempt any man. A primal beat pounded in his blood.

Doesn't the bloody chit know the danger she invites?

Near his left eye, a muscle twitched. Never a good sign.

"We are leaving now," he told her.

"I'm not going anywhere with you." Her chin jutted out. In fact, her entire posture smacked of belligerence: her fists were planted on her slim hips, her slender booted legs braced apart.

Stop looking at her legs, you idiot.

Beside her, her damned ferret bared its fangs at him.

"If you don't want to go wiv the cove, Tessa, I'll take your place."

Harry's gaze veered to the brown-haired wench who'd spoken. Winking at him, the tart leaned forward on the bed, adjusting the neckline of her yellow satin dressing gown, exposing more of her generous assets. Hastily, he looked away.

"Ooo, the big fellow's blushing. Ain't 'e adorable?" she cooed.

"Cork it, Daisy." Irritation edged Miss Todd's voice. "And you, *Professor*,"—she turned to him, her chin lifted at a mutinous angle—"can toddle off. I'll go home when I'm ready."

All bloody week she'd been needling him with the sobriquet of "Professor." With her uncanny talent for annoying him, she'd unknowingly picked up a shard of his broken dreams, wielding it the way a cutthroat does a blade in a dark alley. Relentlessly and without mercy.

His simmering temper edged toward the boiling point.

"You'll come with me now, you bloody brat. And if I were a professor," he bit out, "I would be sorely tempted to give you a lesson in propriety. No, make that *common sense*. What in blazes are you thinking, dressed in that indecent attire and in a *brothel*, no less. You could have been accosted or worse!"

The last words left him in a roar, shocking him. He was known for calm, measured discourse. He didn't shout, especially not at a female.

Miss Todd had the temerity to *roll her eyes* at him. "I can take care of myself."

"How?" he shot back. "How, precisely, would you fight off a man's advances?"

"With these." She bent, and he blinked as she removed a *dagger* from each boot. With blithe expertise, she juggled the small cloisonné-handled knives in the air.

"Where in blazes did you get those?" Harry asked in disbelief.

"Ming. He trained me, too. My aim is excellent."

Her underlying (and rather immodest) threat was clear. Jaw clenching, Harry was contemplating hauling her out over his shoulder when the redheaded wench came to her side. She was older than the others, a handsome woman with a hardened mien.

At her nudge, Miss Todd sighed...but she caught her blades, tucking them back into her boots.

The redhead addressed him. "I'm Pretty Francie, the madam of the club. Tessa's safe 'ere. We keep an eye out for 'er, and she uses the 'idden corridors so none o' the patrons see 'er."

"I am obliged to you, Miss Francie, for looking out for my charge," he said curtly. "Nonetheless, this is no place for a young lady. The fact that she has been allowed to run amok for so long is a disgrace."

To his surprise, the madam gave a slight nod, her expression rueful.

"Ignore Bennett," Miss Todd burst out. "He's an overbearing *prig*—"

"It is not only my opinion that your behavior needs reforming, but also that of your grandfather."

Harry's deliberate evoking of Bartholomew Black did the trick.

The madam put a hand on Miss Todd's shoulder.

"You'd best go wiv 'im, luvie," she said quietly.

Miss Todd's shoulders slumped a little, and she gave her friend an oddly hurt look.

Spotting a long black cape hanging on the wall, Harry said, "May Miss Todd borrow that?"

"O' course." The blonde wench went to fetch it.

She returned, and, up close, he saw the fading bruises on her face. When he reached to take the garment from her, she flinched instinctively, confirming his suspicions. His chest tightened. There was nothing more despicable, more cowardly, than a man who'd hit a woman.

Slowly, he turned his hand over, palm up, waiting for her to give him the cloak.

"Thank you, miss," he said gently when she did.

"Oh…you're welcome. You can call me Belinda." She twirled a blonde curl around her finger and gave him a hesitant smile.

He inclined his head, then turned to Miss Todd. "Put this on."

She scowled at him. "I'm not taking Belinda's best cloak."

"I'll see that it's returned. You cannot prance about in those indecent trousers," he snapped. "Put on the bloody cape, or I'll put it on for you."

She hesitated, and he had a fiendish desire for her to disobey him. *Just try me.*

She snatched the garment. Knotted the strings and glared at him. "Satisfied?"

"Not until you're safely home." He pointed to the door. "To the hidden corridor. Now."

She bent to scoop up her ferret. Exchanging swift goodbyes with her friends, she marched out into the hallway. Approaching the paneled wall, she pressed down on a section of the plaster molding. The panel swung open, revealing a corridor behind the walls.

She entered, swiveling to say smartly, "Don't forget to close the panel behind you."

He bit back a retort. Once inside, he shut the panel, cloaking them in dimness. He followed her through the cramped passageway. As he bent his head to avoid hitting the ceiling, a visceral memory struck him: of rock crashing down all around. Of being trapped in suffocating darkness. The old panic sparked, his heart racing, palms going clammy...

"Blood and thunder, this isn't a stroll through Hyde Park." Miss Todd's tart voice jerked him out of the memory. "Stop dawdling and hurry up."

He didn't know whether to be relieved or exasperated by the distraction. Either way, the panic receded. He sped up, her scent reaching him through the gloom, the fresh sweetness banishing the lingering, acrid traces of gunpowder and cindered earth. In truth, her feminine fragrance had been teasing him for days, a mysterious alchemy of perfume, soap, and...her.

They headed down steps and continued their way on the lower floor. She halted, and he did the same, his nose inches from the top of her head. Her essence filled his nostrils, clean and vibrant and heady. He couldn't stop himself from inhaling deeply.

"Why are we stopping?" he murmured.

"*Shh.* I think I hear someone coming."

He strained, listening. The sounds were faint at first...footsteps? *Thump, thump, thump.* Accompanying voices grew louder, taking the shape of words.

"Ooo, you're so big and 'ard," a female voice moaned.

"Like my cock, do you? Then take it deep in your cunny!"

Sweat misted on Harry's forehead as groans escalated along with the thumping, clearly not from boots against the floor...but bodies on a mattress.

Someone *was* coming. Just not the way Miss Todd had imagined.

Unbidden urges heated Harry's blood. He was acutely aware of Miss Todd: her delicious scent and nearness, the escalating cadence of her breath. His body's reaction was instantaneous. Warmth flooded his loins, and he hardened with shocking swiftness.

Devil take it. Get a grip on it, man.

"This time of day I wasn't expecting..." She sounded flustered. "We can, um, continue on."

She rushed ahead, and he followed at her heels.

What, precisely, is the extent of the minx's sexual experience? Since their first meeting, the question had intrigued him. Here was a woman who played with dirty cards, called a brothel home, and took the sight of an orgy in stride. Unlike Celeste, who'd hidden her true nature beneath the mask of an angel, Tessa Todd flaunted her wickedness.

If you willingly drink her poison, you'd be the biggest fool alive, he thought darkly.

"Dash it, I think it's my *father*." Miss Todd's panicked whisper jerked him back to the present. "He'll murder me if he finds me here."

Harry heard it too: male voices, footsteps emerging from the dimness just up ahead.

"Where's the closest exit?" he said tersely. "Ahead or behind?"

"Behind—"

He wasted no time, trading places with her. "Get us there. *Now*."

They dashed back the way they'd come. His pulse thudded as the voices behind them seemed to grow nearer and nearer. Looking over his shoulder, he saw the lick of lamplight against the tunnel wall.

Miss Todd came to a halt. She triggered a mechanism in the wall: a soft click, and the panel opened. They jumped out, Harry sealing the exit shut behind them. He waited, muscles bunched, as the steps paused...directly on the other side of the wall.

A man's brusque tones filtered through the thin barrier. "Have the Roman orgy atrium cleaned up. They left a mess there last night."

"Yes, Mr. Todd. Do you want to check the rooms on this floor?"

Harry looked at Miss Todd. Her green eyes were stormy with dread, the pupils dilated.

"Ain't got time." Todd's voice bristled with impatience. "That's your job, ain't it?"

"Yes, sir. Beg pardon, sir."

"Let's get on with it."

When the steps moved on, Harry released a breath. He did a quick survey of the hallway. Doors lined one side, a stairwell at the far end.

He said in a low voice, "Can you get us out of here?"

Miss Todd nodded shakily. "We'll have to take the back stairs."

One of the doors suddenly opened, voices floating out.

"Come again soon, gents," a woman's voice purred from within the room.

A chorus of male laughter. "With you, Sally, we always do."

Two men emerged into the hallway.

Bloody hell. They would be in the men's line of sight in an instant—nowhere, no time to hide. The best Harry could do was shield Miss Todd's body with his own, try to keep her out of the newcomers' view.

Before he could make the move, fingers slid into his hair. His head jerked, his startled gaze colliding with Miss Todd's. He saw her determined expression the instant before she raised herself on tiptoe, crushing her mouth to his.

∽

Kissing Bennett was a risky move.

Yet Tessa didn't want to have to deal with her grandfather's wrath if she was discovered here, and this stratagem was the best one to keep her identity concealed. The approaching men would pay no mind to an embracing couple. Bennett obviously agreed with her plan because he crowded her up against the wall, his big body shielding her from view, his mouth covering hers.

She'd seen people kissing, but she'd never done it for herself. She wasn't certain exactly *what* she was supposed to do beyond smooshing her lips against Bennett's. The truth was, having him so close was affecting her ability to think. She was acutely aware of his rigid form pressing into her, his strength and heat, and it was...distracting.

She tried to say something, but his mouth suddenly slanted, and the kiss deepened. Her thoughts blurred to awakening sensations. Bennett kissed the way he seemed to do everything: with focus, intensity, and skill. His lips dragged against hers, firm and velvety, stoking a feverish heat beneath her skin.

He tastes of peppermint, came the nonsensical thought.

Her mind fogged with sultry heat. Of their own accord, her lips parted to take in more of him. He shuddered around her, and, an instant later, she felt a hot, thick invasion between her lips.

Zounds...his tongue was in her *mouth*.

She'd glimpsed others kissing this way, and she'd thought it absurd (and, frankly, unhygienic), but experiencing it for herself changed her perception altogether. Bennett's kiss was delicious, thrilling, *addictive*. He licked inside her, and a spark danced along her spine, igniting a flare between her legs. Her hands clenching in his hair, she tipped her head back, a desperate, silent plea for more.

In the next instant, she was crushed against the wall. Sandwiched against wood and Bennett's harder length. Her unfettered breasts surged against his granite-hard chest as the kiss caught *fire*. His mouth consumed her, possessed her, laying claim with each bold thrust of his tongue. He'd taken control over the kiss, yet she felt strangely safe. Protected.

And *hot*. Dear God, she was burning up inside. His big hands splayed over her bottom, yanking her closer. His thigh wedged between her legs, the intimate invasion lodging her breath.

He nudged deeper against her sex, hitting an exquisite peak, and her breath popped free, turning into a moan as it left her lips.

Her woman's place was throbbing, aching, shockingly wet. Delirious with need, she rocked against the hard trunk of Bennett's thigh, gasping at the blissful friction.

"God, yes," he rasped against her lips. "Ride me."

She couldn't stop if she tried. As she rode his sinewy appendage, she felt another one pressing into her thigh. His male member, she realized dizzily. It was as hard and heavy as a steel pike, and when she squirmed against it, he groaned, the rumble hitting the back of her throat. His tongue pushed even deeper into her mouth, and, on instinct, she sucked—

"Couldn't make it to a bedchamber, eh?"

"Must be a tasty wench. Care to share?"

She jerked at the leering male voices, but Bennett kept her pressed against the wall, his body shielding her from view.

Without turning, he snapped, "Mind your own bloody business, or I'll make you."

His lethal tone was enough to make the men scurry off.

When the coast was clear, Bennett stepped back.

Panting, her lips and breasts still tingling, Tessa watched as he removed his spectacles, studiously polishing them on his shirt. Watching the care with which his large, rough hands handled the delicate frame sent a quiver through her belly.

Dazed wonder seeped through her. *So this is desire.*

This was what she'd understood in theory but now *actually* understood. She'd attributed the magnetic, pulsating energy between her and Bennett to animosity...but it wasn't that. Or not just that. Antagonism and attraction, she realized in a flash, were two sides of the same coin.

Bennett shoved on his spectacles, met her gaze.

"What the *devil* was that?" he ground out.

His fury came out of nowhere. Stunned, unprepared, she scrambled for words.

"I th-thought it was a good stratagem," she stammered. "I didn't want to be recognized."

Before she could gather her wits, try to articulate herself better, he cut her off.

"The next time you wish to use me as the means to an end," he said icily, "give me some goddamned warning. Unless you wish to be taken up against the wall like a bloody trollop."

She stared at his harsh countenance, his smoldering eyes, and humiliation churned sickly. *What was I thinking?* Even if her aim had been to protect her identity, it didn't excuse the way she'd acted. The way she'd lost herself, *thrown* herself at Bennett... Stupidly, she'd thought that he'd enjoyed the kiss, that he felt the same vibrant, life-altering attraction that she did.

But he didn't. He thought she was a trollop.

God, she was worse than a trollop: she was a *fool.*

Words forced themselves through the tight ring of her throat. "I—I'm sorry."

"We're leaving." His eyes dared her to defy him as he pointed to the stairwell. "*Now.*"

For once, pride abandoned her. It was all she could do to hold onto her composure. Silently, fighting back the heat behind her eyes, she fled toward the exit.

9

The next evening, Harry broodingly observed the proceedings of Baroness Lucia von Friesing's supper party. He did not want to be here. In fact, if he'd been given the choice between shopping for a new wardrobe and being where he was now, he'd have taken off like a shot to Bond Street.

The reasons behind his desire for escape were multifold.

First, the dining room was small and stuffy. The dark paneled chamber barely accommodated the intimate gathering, and Harry was as out of place as the hastily-added and mismatched china setting in front of him. Yet, for some reason, Black had insisted that he have a seat at the table rather than wait in the carriage.

The second reason was that Harry found himself taking an instant dislike of the guest of honor. His reaction confounded him; it wasn't his nature to rush to judgement—nor to experience so strong and irrational an antipathy.

Nonetheless, the Duke of Ranelagh and Somerville set his teeth on edge.

His Grace, who went by the sobriquet of "Ransom"—what kind of bloody name was that?—occupied the place of honor next to the hostess. A thin, silver-haired woman, Baroness von Friesing was fawning over him, the jet beads on her turban quivering as she nodded at something he'd said. Her expression was as rapt as if he were explaining to her how he'd discovered the Holy Grail.

Tall and fit, the duke had dark hair and arresting features. His tawny hazel eyes, slashing brows, and sculpted cheekbones hinted at an exotic influence in his lineage. He sported a mustache and, on his chin, a small patch of hair as carefully trimmed as a garden hedge. In Harry's opinion, the latter was an affectation that no decent Englishman should adopt unless all razors were to vanish off the face of the earth.

But facial hair wasn't the reason for Harry's rancor toward the duke: it was the other's languid arrogance. Ransom never spoke but in a mocking drawl, and his gaze flicked from guest to guest, as if he couldn't bear the sight of any of them too long. And his treatment of Tessa, his supper partner, was downright shoddy.

Placed next to the duke, Tessa had looked ill-at-ease all evening, and no wonder. Whenever Ransom deigned to look at her, his mouth curled sardonically beneath his mustache...as if she were a cruel joke that had been played upon him. The few words he'd spoken to her were outwardly polite yet infused with condescension.

Arrogant prat. Harry's hands balled under the table. *She deserves better than the likes of him. She deserves better period.*

Which led him to his third and most pressing reason for not wanting to be here.

He felt...guilty.

A steel band tightened around his chest. His treatment of Tessa yesterday had been unforgiveable. Her kiss had caught him by surprise: it had set fire to his blood, hardened his cock, made him lose control. When the bastards had interrupted them, his haze of lust had bled into a memory he'd kept buried deep.

Celeste. Her surprise midnight visit to his bachelor's lodgings. How she'd looked like an angel descended from the heavens to his shabby apartments...and how she'd kissed like one too. She'd tasted of honey, the sweetness hiding poison. With her soft, cool lips, she'd coaxed him into taking more and more...until he'd met his own demise.

The memory of her manipulation, of his *stupidity*, had roared over him. He'd vowed never to let a woman use her wiles upon him again, yet yesterday he'd found himself ensnared in another feminine web. Used *again* as a means to an end. Risking his mission and his honor in the process.

He'd taken his anger out on Tessa. When his fury had subsided—at least enough for him to think clearly—he'd seen his behavior for what it was: uncouth and uncalled for. He owed her an apology.

All day, he'd wrestled with what to say to her. How to explain his atrocious treatment of her without revealing his past. Not that she'd given him a chance.

Bold, willful, sprightly Tessa had cloistered herself in her bedchamber all day. She'd had her guard dog Lizzie in there with her, so he couldn't exactly break down the door to offer her an apology. An apology that he hadn't yet figured out. An apology that was overdue and growing more overdue with each passing moment.

As he watched her now, he couldn't deny another fact. A discovery that made self-disgust rise like bile in his throat. One that made him want to kick himself and offer to let her do so, too.

Beneath that wicked, wild exterior, Tessa Black-Todd was...soft.

Vulnerable.

And unmistakably innocent.

Watching her avoid eye contact with him and leave her food untouched (she hadn't eaten anything Mrs. Crabtree had sent on trays throughout the day either) and feeling the tension between them, he knew he'd hurt her. He recalled her stricken expression, her stammered apology when he'd called her a trollop, and the self-disgust turned to shame. Because as sweet and passionate and wanton as her kiss had been, it had also been inexperienced. Unambiguously virginal.

He had been the one to take their passion into dangerous territory. *He* had been the one to lose control. And yet he'd blamed *her* for it.

His throat clenched. Aye, he needed to beg forgiveness…and he would do so at the first opportunity. For now, however, he needed to get through the night. To keep his mind clear and on his assignment.

He would make up for yesterday's lapse in judgement by gathering information tonight. This was the first time since being hired that he'd been in the same room as Black, and he planned to make the most of the opportunity. To be the eyes and ears that he was here to be.

Decked out in his usual antiquated glory, a bewigged Black occupied the end chair next to Harry. On Harry's other side was Black's daughter, Mrs. Todd, a mousy, frail woman dressed in heavy velvet despite the summer heat. She wore a great deal of jewelry, rubies and diamonds glittering on her neck and hands. Next to her was her husband, Malcolm Todd, a short, balding man with hard eyes and a brusque air. He'd checked his pocket watch three times in the last quarter hour.

Awkward silence reigned. Stilted from the start, conversation had now come to a full halt. Luckily, liveried footmen provided a diversion in the form of the soup course; Baroness von Friesing cleared her throat at the other end of the table.

"What do you think of the mulligatawny, Mr. Black?" she said.

"I've 'ad worse." Black waved his spoon at the center of the table, which was crowded with silver candelabra and epergnes filled with hothouse flowers. "'Ope soup and oysters ain't all we're being served. When I 'ave guests, the table's full and not with bleeding flowers neither."

The baroness did her best to mask a cringe. "Supper is being served *à la russe* this eve, sir." At Black's squinty look, she clarified,

"The courses will be presented in sequence, sir, rather than all at once. Such a style is all the rage."

"Rage, eh? Don't doubt that." Black harrumphed. "'Ungry guests ain't 'appy ones."

Seeing the glint in Black's eyes, Harry suspected that the cutthroat might be amusing himself at the baroness' expense. As she sputtered, Ransom cut in.

"If food will liven things up, then by all means," he drawled, "summon the next course."

"Present company ain't lively enough for you, Yer Grace?"

At Black's ominous tone, Ransom did a smooth turnabout.

"*Au contraire*, the company is charming." Turning to Tessa, the duke flashed an insincere smile. "May I compliment you on your looks this eve, Miss Todd? I find your gown quite delectable."

Tessa stirred her spoon around her soup. "Probably because you're starving."

At her smart reply, the duke blinked.

Harry did not like the sudden speculative interest that flickered in the man's hooded gaze.

"My stepdaughter's gown was made by Madame Rousseau," Mavis Todd roused herself enough to say. "She's a famed modiste, you know. Caters only to the *crème de la crème*."

"You don't say." The duke sounded bored again.

"The French do know their fashion," Mrs. Todd prattled on. "Indeed, I have been admiring your coat, Your Grace. It is cut in the latest French style, I believe?"

"I maintain a residence in Paris," Ransom said indifferently.

That explains the bearded chin, Harry thought. *Smarmy bastard.*

"Not only is Tessa fashionable," Mrs. Todd said, her voice beginning to strain with effort, "she's accomplished. Why, Mrs. Southbridge of Southbridge's Finishing School called Tessa her most 'outstanding' pupil amongst her many aristocratic peers. Did you know Tessa went to school with the daughter of the Marquess of Chetley?"

Harry suspected Mrs. Todd was trying to help, but her praise and name-dropping bore an unfortunate whiff of desperation. Like a fishmonger's wife trying to sell yesterday's catch.

"Is that a fact?" His Grace's eyes were mocking as they regarded Miss Todd. "I didn't know you had such high connections, Miss..., ahem, Smith."

Tessa's flushed cheeks roused Harry's protective instincts. Earlier in the carriage, she'd had a row with her grandfather, refusing to go through with the sham of being the baroness' distant niece.

Black had put his foot down. *The duke says you can't be a Todd and move in 'is circles. 'E and I both agreed: from 'ere on in, you're Miss Smith.*

Although Harry did not always agree with Tessa's unconventional ways, he had to admit that he admired her pride: her desire to be true to herself. He saw her struggle now to keep her composure. It was clear she wanted to dish Ransom some sauce. The only thing keeping her in check, he suspected, was her grandfather's glare of warning.

"How long is this 'roost' business going to take?" Malcolm Todd interjected.

"It's *russe*, not...never mind." The baroness sighed. "There are several courses yet to come, Mr. Todd. No more than three hours, I expect."

"You must be joking." Todd's round face turned red. "I'm an important man. I can't sit around twiddling my thumbs for three bloody hours!"

"Please, not so loud," Mavis murmured. "Noise triggers my megrims, as you know."

"You didn't tell me this was going to take *three hours*," her husband hissed at her, albeit at a lower volume. He gestured to the duke. "I thought this was a done deal. Bought and paid for."

"Nothing has been agreed upon." Ransom's tone was glacial.

"You can say that again." Expression mutinous, Tessa tossed

her proverbial hat into the ring. "I won't have my future decided without my consent!"

The duke slid her another look, and this one didn't stop at her face. Harry's muscles bunched, his temperature rising as that tawny gaze roved over her figure. Despite what His Grace might think of Tessa's origins, there was no doubt that he appreciated the view. That any man would.

She was beautiful, and tonight was no exception. Her leaf green gown trimmed with seed pearls enhanced her slender femininity. Her hair was parted down the middle, her dark ringlets twisted into two clusters and twined with oak leaves made of golden silk. Anger brought a flush to her milky skin and a rebellious sparkle to her eyes; to Harry, she looked like a sulky, sensual wood nymph.

As plentiful as Tessa's physical charms were, her spitfire spirit was equally captivating. From the start, she'd had the ability to arouse strong emotions in him, be it annoyance or fascination or, aye, lust. Knowing this, he would have to be on guard. He couldn't let his attraction to her interfere with his judgment or his work.

"You'll do as you're told, girl," Malcolm Todd snapped. "I didn't get dragged 'ere just to 'ave my time wasted—"

"*Enough.*" Black's fist pounded the table, rattling the dishes (and the hostess, whose hand flew to her bosom).

"You, missy,"—he jabbed a finger at Tessa, whose eyes flashed defiantly—"will mind your manners and behave like a lady. And you, Yer Grace,"—like the needle of a compass, his finger moved to Ransom, whose face had turned blank—"will remember the terms o' our agreement. As for you,"—Black addressed his son-in-law—"God's blood, cease your goddamned whining. It ain't the time or the place. Now all o' you, do I make myself clear?"

Tessa said nothing, her delicate jaw clenching.

His Grace drained his wineglass.

Malcolm Todd muttered, "I wouldn't need to whine if you'd make up your bloody mind."

"What did you say?" Beneath his wig, Black's countenance darkened like a gathering storm.

"The vultures 'ave been circling Covent Garden," Todd burst out. "The territory needs a new leader, and it should be me. I *deserve* it."

Black has a territorial war on his hands? And who are the 'vultures' Todd is referring to? And is it a coincidence that they're circling Covent Garden, where The Gilded Pearl was located?

Keenly, Harry watched on.

"If I've told you once, I've told you a 'undred times: you *deserve* nothing." Black threw his napkin onto the table. "Respect is earned, you bloody imbecile, which is why you'll ne'er amount to anything."

"If you're in danger, Grandpapa," Tessa blurted, "you must let me help—"

"Shut your yap," her father said.

"Stay out o' this," her grandfather barked.

She looked between the two men, and, for an instant, her mask slipped. Harry's chest constricted as he glimpsed what lay beneath: the hurt, bewildered look of a child who's being punished and doesn't know why. An instant later, her mask was back in place, her pain concealed behind a lifted chin and defiant eyes.

"As for you, Todd," Black thundered, "you'd better watch—"

Beside Harry, Mavis suddenly mumbled, "I feel...rather faint..."

Harry reacted on instinct, catching her before she toppled from her chair. "I have you, Mrs. Todd." She slumped against him, her weight no more substantial than that of a feather.

"Heavens," the baroness said in alarm. "Shall I send for smelling salts?"

"Won't do no good." Black hobbled over, his brow lined. "Are you all right, poppet?"

Mavis shook her head with effort. "I have to go. I'm sorry, Father."

"Ain't nothing to be sorry about," Black said gruffly.

"I'll go with you, Mama." Tessa dashed over to Mavis. "I'll make your special tonic."

"No, dear, you stay here. Get better acquainted with His Grace." Mavis gave her stepdaughter's hand a weak squeeze. "Your father will take me home."

"Let's go." Malcolm Todd was the only one who didn't seem worried. In fact, he looked like a prisoner given a reprieve.

"After you get 'er 'ome," Black said in low tones to his son-in-law, "you stay there. Take care o' my girl. I'll be by after supper's done."

Todd gave a curt nod. He and Mavis made their way out.

The remaining guests returned to their seats, and Harry wondered what catastrophe would strike next. He didn't have long to wait.

As the fish course was being served, Black declared, "Let's cut to the chase. The point o' this evening was for the parties to get acquainted. Can't do that, can they, with all these prying eyes."

"*Grandpapa*," Miss Todd hissed.

"Don't Grandpapa me, missy. You're the one who wanted a say in 'er future. Can't do that without getting to know 'Is Grace better."

Miss Todd opened her mouth to argue—*and rightly so*, Harry thought hotly—but Ransom said, "Perhaps Miss Todd would honor me with a turn in the garden?"

Harry did not trust the man. There was no telling what a rake like Ransom might attempt alone in the dark with a beautiful young woman. The duke's gaze roved over Tessa again, and this time he bloody *undressed* her with his eyes.

Harry gnashed his teeth.

The baroness cast a longing look at her poached turbot. "I suppose I can chaperone."

"You stay," Black commanded. "Bennett will escort them."

Harry thought quickly. "I ought to secure the environs first. Make sure it's safe."

"Secure the environs?" Brows arching, Ransom said to Black, "Are all your servants this thorough? Or is it just this earnest fellow?"

"A man can't be too careful," Black said through a mouthful of fish.

Harry resisted the impulse to plow his fist into the duke's smirking face. Instead, at Black's nod, he headed to the garden. To ensure that nothing, and no one, would harm his charge.

10

The Duke of Ranelagh and Somerville escorted Tessa out to the garden, Bennett trailing behind them. The fog-filtered moonlight revealed a small rectangular courtyard surrounded by hedges. Lanterns lit the two graveled paths that crisscrossed the space, a gurgling stone fountain standing at the center of the "X." Tessa couldn't see why it had taken Bennett ten minutes to "secure" the place, unless he'd turned over every leaf of the skimpy flower bed.

She was acutely aware of his presence behind her. The truth was, she'd been acutely aware of him since their kiss, and it was taking all her wherewithal to avoid looking at him. Yet she couldn't escape the sensations: her lips still felt seared by his, the hard ridges of his muscles imprinted upon her skin. The barest whiff of his soap made her heart race with longing...and humiliation.

She finally understood what Pretty Francie and the others had warned her about. Before, she'd scoffed at the idea of being seduced by a man, but Bennett's kiss had changed that. And his reaction afterward had shown her just how painful losing oneself to passion could be.

At least he'd gotten one thing right: she *was* a trollop.

Having had a day to contemplate the matter, she wasn't overly surprised or embarrassed by the fact. Blacks prided themselves on being a hot-blooded lot. While she was adopted into the family, the Black spirit ran in her veins as true as blood, and she reckoned it was the family legacy of passion showing itself in her.

Her grandfather oft described his first meeting with his wife-to-be as akin to being struck by lightning. He'd chanced upon Althea Bourdelain at a fair: one look at her and he'd known there would be no other woman for him. She'd felt the same way. Her upper class family had opposed the match and disowned her when she chose to elope with her love.

Althea and Bartholomew Black remained devoted to one another until the day she died. Grandpapa had never remarried.

A Black mates for life, Tessie, he'd said.

Tessa had always found her grandparents' story romantic. She'd secretly yearned to someday feel that intensity of emotion: to know love that would endure suffering and celebrate joy and never fail. Thus, she didn't mind being a trollop if it meant finding and being true to her heart's desire.

What she did mind was being a *rejected* trollop.

Blast it, why do I have to want a man who doesn't want me back?

Even as she recognized her feelings for Bennett, she also knew it was too late to eradicate them. In truth, they'd taken root from their very first encounter, and, despite his harsh repudiation, continued to bloom. Frustration tangled her insides. While she grappled with yearning, *he* was entirely unaffected by their encounter.

He continued to do his job as if it was exactly that: a job. Tonight, he'd watched on while her family tried to auction her off like a prime article at Tattersall's, his handsome face devoid of emotion. Obviously, he couldn't care less if she were to be married off to another man. In fact, he was aiding and abetting her grandfather in the godforsaken scheme.

Damn his eyes, she thought on a surge of shivering anger.

"Cold, my dear?" a silky male voice asked.

She'd almost forgotten about the duke. Which was odd, since he was a large man, nearly as tall as Bennett, and he was standing right next to her. In the moonlight, his tawny eyes appeared silver, and his long, manicured fingers were undoing the carved buttons of his coat.

Before she could reply, wool slid over her shoulders from behind. She was engulfed in warmth...and Bennett's masculine scent. Just like that, her nipples budded, tingling beneath her bodice.

Bennett's gruff voice emerged from behind her. "Take mine."

She swiveled to look at him. She didn't know what she hoped to see, but it wasn't his composed expression. Her frustration swelled.

And be tormented by your smell all night? I don't think so.

She shrugged off the jacket, tossing it back to him. "It's not necessary."

"I think you'll find this more to your liking." To her surprise, Ransom placed *his* jacket over her shoulders. "The superfine is woven for me specially."

The material was softer and plusher than that of Bennett's jacket. And, rather than soap, it smelled of an exotic cologne, one that she found cloying. She was about to refuse the garment when she caught a glimpse of Bennett.

Lines bracketed his scowling mouth. His jacket was bunched in his fist, and that unruly lock had once again escaped to curl upon his brow. He looked...irritated?

Hope burst into bloom. She decided to wear Ransom's jacket after all.

Presenting her back to Bennett, she gave the duke her most dazzling smile. "I am much obliged, Your Grace."

The duke's eyelashes flickered. They were long for a man, she noticed, and suited his debonair style. With his striking feline eyes and bearded chin, he made her think of a pirate. He was handsome, sensual, and faintly exotic, the sort of man debutantes would swoon over.

Unfortunately, *she* seemed to prefer men who were stoic, brooding, and extremely annoying.

His Grace offered her his arm. "Shall we?"

They started down one of the paths towards the fountain. As Bennett's steps plodded close behind, Tessa's mind worked furiously. Could it be that Bennett *did* feel something for her? She thought back to their embrace: he might think her a trollop, but she hadn't been the only one doing the kissing. It hadn't been *her* tongue taking the plunge into his mouth. And, thinking on it more, there'd been unmistakable proof of his arousal: she hadn't imagined the poker-like object prodding her thigh.

As her mood lifted, she was able to analyze the situation more clearly. There *was* evidence to support that Bennett wasn't indifferent to her. So why had he been so angry?

The next time you wish to use me as the means to an end, give me some goddamned warning, he'd growled at her.

Was it because he'd felt used by her...manipulated? Didn't he realize that she was attracted to him? That what had begun as subterfuge had quickly given way to true desire?

Would he care?

"Penny for your thoughts, Miss Smith?" the duke drawled.

She was determined to discover the answers to her questions. To do so, she would have to get through Bennett's armor of indifference. And she had an inkling how to go about it.

Seizing the opportunity, she said sweetly, "We both know that's not my name. Why don't you call me Tessa instead?"

"If you'll return the favor and call me Ransom." He paused. "You surprise me."

She tipped her head to one side. "How so?"

"You seem different. From the rest of your family."

"You insult me, sir," she said hotly.

"I don't mean to." He studied her with those curious eyes of his, which had a slight upward tilt to them, like a cat's. "You really don't want to marry me, do you?"

I'd rather take a hot poker in the eye. Aware of their audience, however, she traded her retort for a more diplomatic reply. "I don't know you. How could I know if we'd suit?"

"The prospect of being a duchess suits most women."

"I'm not like most women."

"I'm beginning to see that," he murmured.

Her cheeks warmed at his blatant male appreciation. In the past, she'd never had reason to flirt. No man had been worth the effort, and she had little patience for the subtleties of fan twirling, eyelash fluttering, and meaningless flummery.

She snuck a glance backward. The muscle ticking in Bennett's square jaw buoyed her hope. Perhaps flirtation had its uses after all. If the simpering simpletons at Mrs. Southbridge's could master flirting, then, by God, so could she.

Deliberately, she turned back to the duke. Put on her most charming smile. "And I'm beginning to see that you're not as bad a fellow as I assumed."

Ransom stared at her a moment. Then he laughed; it was a surprisingly hearty sound.

I wonder what Bennett's laugh sounds like, she thought wistfully. He'd never laughed in her presence. He was too busy brooding or giving her a lecture.

"What are my presumed faults, pray tell?" Ransom led her past the fountain.

"You're a rake," she said baldly.

"I find that bachelorhood is a state that requires the occasional relief from tedium."

"More than occasional from what I've heard."

Instead of denying it, Ransom smiled. "I don't like tedium. I have a feeling we have that in common…Tessa."

Although she'd given leave for him to call her by her first

name, the way his voice caressed those syllables made her cheeks heat. The intimacy felt indecent, as if she'd been caught without her unmentionables.

"You'll address her as Miss Todd." Suddenly, Bennett was by her side. He no longer looked calm. In the moonlight, his face was hard, menacing, his body taut with leashed power. "She is a lady, and you'll pay her the proper respect."

A thrill coursed through her.

"Call off your guard dog." Ransom sounded annoyed. "He's foaming at the mouth."

She recalled herself enough to say, "Step back, Bennett."

He didn't move. His gaze was locked on Ransom, his big hands curled into fists.

Zounds, she couldn't allow bloodshed to happen. She placed a hand on his chest, the powerful thud of his heart making her own throb in unison. "I said *step back*."

His gaze swung to her. Her breath caught at the banked fire behind the wire frames.

Then he stepped back.

Adjusting his lapels, Ransom said, "Let's continue, shall we?"

Tessa was keenly aware of the crunch of Bennett's boots behind them as they walked along the perimeter of the garden. She knew she ought to flirt with Ransom some more, but she was already bored with it. Bennett absorbed her attention. She wondered what he was thinking. If he'd intervened because of his personal feelings for her...or if he was only doing his duty.

"Other than my intolerance for boredom," Ransom said smoothly, "do you have any other aversion to marrying me?"

"Other than my dowry, do you have any other reason for marrying me?"

"No."

She slanted him a look, surprised by his frankness. They'd circled back to the fountain again, a tall, vertical structure topped by a large stone pineapple. Water sprayed upward from its leaves before tinkling into the tiered basins below.

Instead of walking past, Ransom stopped. Turned her to face him.

"Marriage is a necessity for me, I don't deny it. But I would not have you be an unwilling bride." He tipped her chin up with one finger. "While my title might hold little appeal, there are other enticements I could offer you."

Silver crescents reflected in his eyes. It was oddly mesmerizing.

Bennett's deep voice cut in. "Miss Todd, you should go back inside."

She twisted her head, saw the familiar shuttered look on his face. Resentment surged.

"Why?" she challenged.

Bennett's nostrils flared. "For once, just do as you're told."

Just because she desired him didn't mean that she'd let him lecture her as if she were a *child*. Moreover, she was tired of his contradictions. Of being led on by crumbs of hope that led nowhere.

Her temper sparked. "Why don't *you* do as you're told and stay out of my way, Professor?"

"Your master's orders were to escort not interfere." The lethal edge in Ransom's tone gave Tessa pause. Made her wonder what lay beneath the duke's disaffected veneer. "Make yourself scarce."

Bennett's frame vibrated with tension, his shoulders up and jaw clenched. For an instant, she feared that he might retaliate. While she was confident he could pound Ransom to a fare-thee-well, there would be consequences for trouncing a duke.

Before she could intervene, Bennett turned heel and stalked to the other side of the fountain. His desertion was oddly deflating. It obviously didn't take much for him to give up on her.

Because he doesn't give a damn about you.

Hands cupped her shoulders, and she was turned to face the duke.

"Now, where were we?" he murmured.

I don't know about you, but I'm stuck on that idiot on the other side of the fountain.

The truth was not just annoying, it was mortifying. Why was she setting her cap for a man who didn't want her? Why was she setting herself up for more rejection? Hadn't she suffered enough from her father, her grandfather, and even those blasted twits at Southbridge's?

Ransom reached out, tucking a stray curl behind her ear. "Ah, yes, I believe I was about to demonstrate some of the advantages of being my duchess."

She saw his intent, and a desperate notion struck her. Maybe the reason she was hooked on Bennett was because he was the first man to kiss her. Maybe if she kissed another man, she'd find it just as earth-shattering.

Maybe if I kiss the one in front of me, I'll realize there's nothing special about Bennett…

She held still as Ransom's face came closer. He was a rake, so if anyone knew how to kiss, it ought to be him. Seeing the practiced smolder in his half-lidded eyes, she had to quell a sudden, inappropriate urge to laugh. His lips touched hers: the kiss was refined, smooth, skilled. It was pleasant…and as exciting as tepid tea.

Drat and double drat.

A sudden blast jerked her head back. The next instant, icy water rushed over her.

She gasped, and Ransom sprang away from her, shouting, "What the devil?"

Tessa stared at the fountain: the top had…blown off? Pieces of the stone pineapple littered the fountain's basin. Instead of a sedate trickle, water was spraying everywhere, soaking both her and Ransom. With a squeak, she jumped back just in time to avoid another dousing.

"Put this on." Bennett appeared by her side. Yanking off Ransom's sodden coat and tossing it aside, he replaced it with his own. The sturdy wool was dry and warm.

Cocooned in his heat and scent, she sputtered, "Wh-what happened?"

"It appears that the fountain malfunctioned," he said.

His tone was bland. Too bland. Before she could question him, she sneezed.

In the background, Ransom cursed as he emptied water from his shoes.

"His Grace will be awhile." Taking her arm, Bennett steered her toward the house. "Let's get you inside before you encounter any other mishaps."

11

"You've been a naughty miss," he told her.

Tessa sat in front of him, perched on his desk, her plump mouth sulky and eyes inviting. With her legs crossed, one hand leaning insolently on the blotter, she said, "Then why don't you teach me a lesson...*Professor?*"

The sparkling challenge in her eyes moved him into action. Rising from his chair, he stripped her layers until she was bared to him. All the while, she watched him, lips parted, eyes heavy-lidded. He laid her against the desk, his cock swelling as he took in the erotic contrast between her snowy skin and the dark wood.

"Be a good girl, and don't move," he told her.

For once, she obeyed him. He rewarded her acquiescence by tasting her...everywhere. Her plush mouth, the plump lobe of her ear, her impudent little nipples. He left no inch of her silken loveliness unexplored. She sighed as he trailed his tongue down the shallow valley between her tits, over her white, quivering belly. His hands clamped on her sleek thighs, spreading them wide.

The sight of her pussy made his rod jerk, pre-seed wetting the head. Parting her silky nest, he ran a finger along her exposed pink slit, and satisfaction rolled through him.

"Christ, you're wet," he murmured. "Do you like me petting your pussy?"

"Yes." Her eyes were smoky green with desire. "Do it some more."

"Ask me nicely."

"Please," she said, pouting.

"Please what?"

Her bottom lip caught beneath her teeth. "Please pet my pussy?"

A request he wasn't about to deny. He caressed her slick folds, his breath coming harshly as her honey dripped over his fingers. When her hips arched into his touch, her head moving restlessly on the desk, he knew she was close. Knew how to take her over. Lifting her thighs over his shoulders, he bent to taste her sweetness.

A shocked moan broke from her as he ate her pussy. Her slender thighs tensed around his head, and he kept at it, licking her until her wanton pleas filled the room. *Oh yes, Professor, please...*

He found her pearl, sucking it at the same time that he eased his middle finger into her untried passage. God, she was small and *tight*. Heat roiled in his balls as her virginal cunny squeezed him. She cried out, and he groaned as his own climax came roaring over him...

Harry awoke with a start. He was in bed, naked, his chest heaving. The sheet was tangled at his waist, tented by his enormous erection. He was rock-hard, pulsing, his cockhead weeping in anticipation.

He itched to finish himself off.

Instead, he raked both hands through his hair and stared up into the darkness.

What the hell am I doing?

Things were getting out of hand. First, he'd lost control kissing Tessa, then he'd rigged the fountain to prevent the duke from kissing her, and now he was having an erotic dream about her. A dream that had felt so real the scent and taste of her still lingered, making his gut clench with hunger.

Even Celeste hadn't managed to rouse such an intensity of feeling, not that she hadn't tried. She'd pitted him and her other suitors against one another, using jealousy to control them. As besotted as Harry had been, he'd seen through that particular ploy and refused to play her game.

Seeing the Duke of Ranelagh and Somerville with Tessa, however, he'd experienced a strong primal urge to tear the bastard from limb to limb. To lay claim to Tessa, even though she wasn't his and could never be. She was the granddaughter of the suspect he was investigating; his very presence in her life was a lie.

There was only one logical solution to this present mess: he had to complete this assignment and get the hell out of here. No more waiting, passive observing. After leaving Baroness von Friesing's party tonight, Black had gone to stay with his daughter: this was the perfect time to search his study. Either Harry would find evidence of the cutthroat's guilt or he would inform Inspector Davies that his objectivity was compromised. That he could no longer carry out the mission.

Dressing quickly, Harry left the mews for the main house. Passing the front drawing room, he noticed a slant of light up ahead. The door to the billiards room, next to Black's study, was ajar. He thought about turning around, but soft murmurs came from the room, drew him forward. He peered through the crack in the door.

Christ. It was Tessa.

Turn around. Don't go in.

But he couldn't tear his eyes from her. Couldn't stop the need that shot through him like a potent drug. She was clad in a frilly white wrapper, her glossy curls tumbling free, and she appeared to be playing billiards by herself. The enormous baize-covered table dwarfed her, creating a whimsical tableau in which she might have been a little girl playing at being a grown-up.

As he watched, she made a shot. His brows raised as the ball dropped neatly into a pocket.

"Your turn," she said.

Who the devil is she playing with?

Curiosity got the better of him. Unable to see through the narrow opening, he cracked the door open wider...and saw Swift Nick perched on a corner of the table. The ferret rose on its hind legs, waving its front paws, and Tessa laughed.

The merry sound slid through Harry like warmed brandy.

"All paws tonight, are you?" She scratched behind the animal's ears, and Swift Nick's long body arched in contentment. "Never fear, dearest, I shall play for you."

In spite of himself, Harry felt his lips twitch. Her playfulness was charming. If that trait didn't lead her to play devious tricks on him, he might find her...adorable.

"Let's up the ante, shall we?" she went on in a conspiratorial whisper. "If I make this shot, then it means he *does* like me."

Harry stilled. *Who is she talking about? That bastard Ransom...?*

She circled the billiards table, flitting in and out of his view like an elusive hummingbird. Finally, she leaned over the green baize, her back to the door, presenting him with a view of her pertly rounded bottom. He swallowed as she wriggled about, trying to reach the ball with her stick. When she couldn't manage it, she hiked up her nightgown, hoisting herself onto the table's edge.

Christ Almighty.

Lust and fascination riveted him to the spot. She was perched on the side of the table, her skirts pinned beneath her, her *bared* legs swinging idly as she contemplated her shot. Those limbs were white, slender, even shapelier than he'd imagined; he swallowed as the image flashed from his dream: her legs draped over his shoulders, her heels digging into his back as he feasted on her...

"Drat and double drat."

Her curse pierced his erotic thrall. She'd missed the shot, the ball hitting the rail and rolling lazily toward the opposite end of the table. She hopped to the ground, her hands planting on her hips. In a blink, she transformed from siren to sprite. She looked so annoyed, so damned delightful, that he had to choke back a laugh.

She whirled around. "Who's there?"

Ah, hell. He expelled a breath. Feeling like a damned Peeping Tom, he entered the room.

"*Bennett.*" She stared at him. "You gave me a fright."

He stopped a safe distance from her. "If a pack of cutthroats didn't scare you, I doubt I could accomplish the feat."

Her wide gaze didn't waver. "What are you doing here this time of night?"

Since he couldn't very well tell her he'd been about to break into her grandfather's study, he fished for an excuse. "I couldn't sleep and thought I'd look for something to read." He spotted the half-empty glass on a nearby table, and his brows inched upward. "Brandy?"

"I couldn't sleep either. I thought brandy and billiards might help." She wrinkled her nose. "If I go to bed now, however, I'll just have nightmares about that missed shot."

He stifled a smile. Her competitiveness was damned cute.

"You can't make an accurate shot when you're off-balance," he told her.

"I wasn't off-balance. My height makes it necessary to lean on the table." Her gaze narrowed. "Don't tell me you're an expert at billiards?"

Billiards had nearly funded his education at Cambridge.

He shrugged. "I've played."

Her brows lifted. "Care to go a round?"

Her invitation surprised him. Accepting it, he knew, would be extremely ill-advised. The smart, rational thing to do was to turn around and leave.

On the other hand, he'd never in his life backed down from a sporting challenge.

He inclined his head. "All right. One game."

～

Tessa managed to keep her expression calm while excitement tumbled through her.

Being no fool, she was certain that Bennett had been behind the exploding fountain. She had to admire his ingenuity: rigging a fountain was no small feat. One that required more expertise than even her bucket-over-the-door gambit. The fact that he'd taken the pains to set up the elaborate prank filled her with hope.

Could he be interested in me? Even a little?

Lying in her bed, she'd come to a realization: she wanted Bennett. He was the man she was supposed to spend her life with. He was her lightning, and she'd been struck. Of course, this led to some problems. Her grandfather wanted to marry her off to Ransom, and there was the matter of securing Bennett's affections. She'd deal with the former when necessary, and as for the latter...

Blacks never gave up without a fight. They didn't *mope* because of one rejection; they dusted themselves off and went another round. And another and another, as many as necessary to achieve their goal.

Since her goal was Bennett, she would have to fight to win his heart (and other body parts).

The truth had been dazzlingly simple. And contemplating matters further, she'd recognized that she hadn't exactly done a stellar job of endearing herself to Bennett. What man would want a woman who served him salty tea, embarrassed him in a tea shop, had him nearly arrested for theft, and destroyed his favorite boots? Then, to top it all off, she'd thrown herself at him without any warning.

Crikey, she needed to work on her flirtation skills. She'd decided to turn a new leaf. Her new strategy was this: instead of plaguing Bennett, she would try to act in a more pleasing manner. To be more accommodating and biddable, more in the usual mold of females.

Now she had the unexpected opportunity to try out her plan.

Anticipation squeezed her lungs; it felt like the whole room was holding its breath.

Bennett crossed over to the collection of billiard accessories hanging on the wall. She watched, captivated by the care he took choosing his instrument. His long fingers glided over the sticks, testing each for balance and weight, and she shivered, imagining that masterful touch on her skin.

His final selection was a cue of polished ash. She, herself, preferred playing with a mace, a shorter, carved stick with a small shovel-shaped block at the end.

"What shall we wager?" she said.

"I don't take money from ladies," he said dismissively.

As if you'd beat me. She managed to bite back the rejoinder. Men, she knew, didn't like being bested; if she meant to flirt with Bennett, she should probably let him win.

Drat. Flirting was *difficult*.

Then an inspiration hit her. Flirting was about getting to know one another, wasn't it? If she wanted to ascertain Bennett's feelings, there was one sure way to do it.

"Let's play for something more interesting than money," she suggested.

His brooding look was a bit too penetrating. "Such as?"

"Whoever loses the given shot answers a question of the other's choice," she said innocently. "If it's a tie, we both have to answer."

His scarred eyebrow lifted. "You name the first shot."

Careful to contain her excitement, she said, "Hitting from the baulk line, the ball that lands closest to the back cushion wins."

The shot was her specialty. She'd practiced it hundreds of times.

"Ladies first," he said.

Placing her mace on the table, she lined up her shot. As she bent over, her medallion slipped from the neckline of her wrapper, the heavy gold getting in her way. She pulled it off, put it on the table's edge. Taking aim with her mace, she gave a precise shove.

Her white cue ball hit the far end of the table and rolled back, stopping a mere two inches from the back cushion. A winning shot, if she'd ever seen one.

She turned triumphantly to Bennett, whose gaze appeared riveted on her medallion.

"Your turn," she said.

His eyes snapped to her ball. "Not bad."

"Let's see you do better," she retorted.

Oops. Habits were hard to break.

He didn't seem put off by her challenge. Instead, a wolfish gleam appeared behind the polished lenses of his spectacles. Removing his jacket, he casually slung it over a chair and took his position at the table.

Her heart pitter-pattered at his splendid form. He radiated virility in his unadorned blue waistcoat, his rolled-up sleeves revealing sinewy forearms sprinkled with hair. His wide shoulders lowered as he set up his cue ball. She wetted her lips as his long trouser-clad legs formed a powerful stance, the muscles of his thighs subtly flexing as he leaned over his cue.

He thrust, the movement fluid and powerfully controlled. The ball glided across the table, rebounding from the far end. Her eyes widened as it rolled toward hers, then past it, coming to a stop...a hairsbreadth from the mark.

She blinked. "You win."

"Lucky shot."

She didn't believe it for a moment. Admiration rolled through her. And, being no sore loser, she said, "What's the forfeit?"

He studied her, his gaze inscrutable. "I can ask you anything?"

She nodded.

"Where did you get that medallion?"

"This?" She retrieved her necklace from the table's edge. "Grandpapa gave it to me. Why?"

"I was intrigued by the markings. It's unusual jewelry for a lady."

"Oh...I suppose it is." After a moment's hesitation, she held it up, showing it to him. "This is the crest for the House of Black. Grandfather modeled it after a medieval device. See the crossed swords? One represents protection, the other vengeance." She tapped her fingernail against the small ruby embedded at the tip of one of the blades. "The blood is what binds our kin and warns our enemies not to cross us."

"The medallion is a calling card to your enemies?" There was a harshness to his voice that she didn't understand. "If they receive it, they know vengeance has come calling?"

"No." Frowning, she tried to explain it better. "Grandfather doesn't give the medallion to foes, only family members, loyal retainers, and those to whom he wishes to grant a boon. The medallions are meant to *protect* the wearers from anyone who might do us harm."

Something passed through Bennett's eyes. She didn't know what he was thinking, but she felt the shift in his emotion. It invaded the room, as heavy and ripe as the air before a storm.

Uncertainty pelted her. "Um, ready for the next shot?"

The long case clock counted the moments as he studied her. Just like that, the storm seemed to pass. His expression cleared, and he nodded.

Relieved, she said, "Let's play a winning hazard. You go first this time."

He set up the balls. After executing a flawless shot, he stepped aside for her to go.

I can still tie. Gripping her mace, she visually lined her cue ball up with the red object ball. As she prepared to make her shot, however, awareness prickled through her. She could *feel* Bennett's intent focus upon her. He didn't look at her the way the duke had; Ransom's flirtation had been casual, meaningless, his interest in her no deeper than the challenge of the moment. She was a diversion for his tedium, a way to refill his coffers so he could resume his rakehell ways.

Bennett, however, gave her his full attention. As if she were a creature he'd never encountered before and he wanted to understand her inner workings. No man had ever looked at her that way.

She forced herself to concentrate. But her arms were trembling, and when she shoved her mace, her ball veered off-course.

Annoyed at herself, she watched as her cue ball missed the red one completely. "You win again. What's your question?"

Her plan wasn't going well. At this rate, she'd never get to ask him if he did, indeed, rig that fountain and why. With an inward sigh, she wondered what mundane thing he would ask her now.

"Will you forgive me, Tessa?"

Her heart punched against her ribs. Bennett's expression was stark, yet the tautness of his large frame conveyed that her answer mattered to him.

"For what?" she whispered.

"My treatment of you yesterday was unforgiveable. I was at fault. I lost control, and I blamed you for it." A muscled ticked along his jaw. He gripped the upright cue in one hand, the ropey muscles of his forearm shifting. "I was no gentleman, and I ask for your forgiveness."

"It was my fault," she blurted. "I shouldn't have thrown myself at you."

"It was a good stratagem," he said quietly. "But you caught me off-guard, and I don't like being surprised."

She took a few steps closer. "I'm sorry."

"Don't be. I'm the one who took my anger out on you." He set his cue down on the table, shoved his hands in his pockets. "If I could take back those words," he said gruffly, "I would."

His apology flooded her with warmth. And wonder. No one had ever taken such care with her feelings—had taken such care with *her*.

"It's all right," she said softly...because now it was.

"No, it isn't." His gaze was steady, earnest. "What I called you—it's not true."

"I did assault you in a brothel," she said with sudden humor. "Many might agree with your assessment."

"You're *not* a trollop." His fierce rebuttal made her strangely giddy. "What I said reflects on me, not you. I spoke out of anger... because of something that happened in my past. But that has nothing to do with you. And I won't have you calling yourself a trollop or making a joke of it. Or even thinking it."

"What happened in your past?" she said.

"I don't talk about it." The steel shield slid over his expression. "I mention it only to prove a point: what happened was not your fault but mine. Now will you accept my apology or not?"

His brusque tone told her not to push...for now. Besides, she'd never shared such aching honesty with anyone before. She wasn't ready for the intimacy to end.

You wanted to win Bennett's affections. 'Tis now or never. Be brave.

In that moment, she realized that honesty—exposing one's true desire—required more courage than any contrived stratagem.

Drawing a breath, she closed the remaining space between them. He stilled, tension tightening his broad shoulders. Tipping her head back, she looked into his guarded gaze.

"I'll accept your apology," she said, "if you'll accept mine."

His brows drew together. "You've naught to apologize for."

"I don't mean for the kiss. I mean for everything else," she said tremulously. "For all the tricks I've played on you. They were childish and...not nice."

"Apology accepted." His expression eased, his eyes crinkling with humor. "Although I must confess that your bucket over the door was quite inventive."

"No more inventive than rigging a fountain." She said it without thinking and could have kicked herself for his guard went up immediately. "I didn't mean—"

"It's all right. I did rig the fountain." His lips twisted. "I owe you an apology for that too."

"You don't. I'm glad you did it," she said in a rush.

He stared at her. "You are?"

Be brave. Be bold. Be a Black.

"I didn't want Ransom to kiss me. That is, I did..."—she fumbled, and seeing his scowl, she forged on hurriedly—"but only because I wanted to forget you. To forget our kiss."

Emotion flared in his scorched earth eyes. "Tessa—"

"But I couldn't. I can't." Even though her heart was racing, she held his gaze. She placed a hand on his chest, felt his hard, pounding vitality beneath her palm. "Because, Bennett...you're the only one I want to kiss."

12

Ah, hell.

Staring at Tessa's beautiful face, her shy confession in his ears, Harry knew he was lost.

He was attracted to her for so many reasons. Her artless beauty, her playful irreverence, the way she made him want to either throttle her or laugh aloud or kiss her senseless and it didn't matter which because in the end it came down to this: she made him *feel*.

To top it off, she was gazing at him as if he was the only thing she wanted in the world. There was a vulnerable glimmer in her eyes, her sensual bottom lip caught beneath her teeth. She looked worried...as if she wasn't sure the attraction she felt was mutual.

All of it, all of *her*, was like setting a match to the powder keg of his suppressed desires.

The lust he'd been keeping in check exploded, blowing reason to smithereens.

Before he knew it, he'd lifted her onto the billiards table, crowding into the vee of her legs. She gasped, but her arms lifted to his neck, her head tilting back. Whipping off his glasses and tossing them onto the green baize, he took what she offered.

What he'd been craving since the last time he'd kissed her. Their mouths fused, his tongue delving into her sweetness. He feasted, and, *Christ Almighty*, she let him, encouraged him.

When she shyly licked his tongue, he felt that stroke all the way in his balls.

Hungrily, he found her earlobe, sucking it between his lips. Her wanton whimper made him shudder, his erection straining against his trousers. God, *God*, he had to have more.

Untying her wrapper, he pushed it off her shoulders, and it fluttered like a shed cocoon onto the table. He cupped her breast through her night rail. The fruit was delicate, not quite filling his palm, its firm, rounded shape infinitely pleasing. Her nipple was stiff beneath the fine muslin, the size of a small raspberry. When he drew a thumb across the taut peak, her eyes grew dazed, her mouth slackening.

"Like that, sprite?" he murmured.

"Oh, yes," she sighed. "Do it again."

Despite his arousal, he felt a tug of amusement. Hell, who knew that her boldness could have its benefits? He found himself torn between the desire to laugh and to wring more of those lusty sighs from her lips. The choice wasn't difficult.

He bent his head, sucking her clothed nipple into his mouth.

"Zounds." Her fingers speared into his hair, holding him close. "*Bennett.*"

He had the irrational desire to hear her say his real name. Instead, he tongued her, plastering the wet fabric against the prominent berry, flicking it until she moaned. He did it to her other tit, and she wriggled against him, so hot and needy that he reached for the hem of her nightgown. Pushed it up and up. The sight of his large, roughened hand on her milky thigh was unbearably erotic...and brought reality crashing back.

What the devil am I doing? I can't—

"Please, don't stop," she panted. "Don't."

He couldn't resist her sweet pleas, the verdant need in her

eyes. His hand moved up her sleek thigh, toward the apex, and lust slammed into him at what he found.

"Your pussy is so soft and wet," he said thickly.

Her thighs tensed as he parted her dark, silky nest. He slid a finger along her slit, ripe and juicy as a summer peach. When his thumb skated over her hidden bud, she jolted.

"That feels...odd," she gasped. "I don't know if I like it."

He hid a smile. "Let me know what you decide."

Entranced by her expressive face, he adjusted his strokes to maximize her pleasure. Soon she was moaning, her dew coating his fingers. *Damn*, but she was responsive. So sweetly lusty. Her hips rocked demandingly into his touch, and he rubbed her nubbin harder at the same time that he cupped her breast, pinching the needy tip.

Her lips formed an "O" of surprise. She came suddenly, beautifully. Her moisture gushed into his palm, and his turgid cock jerked in response, seed leaking and dampening his smalls.

Groaning, he was bending to claim her mouth again when he heard a shattering noise.

His head swung up. "What was that?"

"Wh-what?"

She blinked at him, cheeks flushed and eyes languid, tempting him to forget whatever he thought he'd heard. But his gut told him something wasn't right. Swift Nick apparently sensed it too, for the ferret was bounding toward the door that separated the billiards and drawing rooms.

"It sounded like glass breaking." Shoving on his spectacles, Harry retrieved his pistol from his jacket before striding to join the animal, who was now doing an agitated dance by the door. He swung to look at Tessa. "Stay here."

She nodded, eyes wide.

He readied his weapon, yanked the door open, and saw the cause of the noise: a gaping hole in the front window. As he headed toward it, he glimpsed figures moving in the darkness beyond.

"Who's there?" he shouted. "Answer me, or I'll shoot."

"Toss 'em in. No time to light the rest," a man's voice hissed. "Let's get out o' 'ere!"

Before Harry could take aim, two objects came hurtling through the broken window...iron canisters with lit fuses, rolling in opposite directions. Harry ran to the closest one, stamping out the flame. The other was out of reach, fuse almost burned, no time to get there. Moving on instinct, he scooped up the device he'd deactivated and sprinted toward the billiards room.

He made it through the doorway, grabbing a frozen Tessa, dragging her to the billiards table. Shoving her beneath the heavy wood frame, he dove under, covering her body with his. A blast tore through the night, the ground shaking. Plaster rained onto the table overhead.

He lifted his head. "Are you all right?"

"Yes." She looked stunned but unharmed. "What happened?"

"Explosive device. I have to check the drawing room."

He rolled off of her, pulled them both to their feet. As he did, the unexploded tube bumped in his pocket. He removed it carefully, set it on the billiards table.

"Is that...?" Tessa stared at the canister, the cotton stuffing coming out of one end.

Cotton that looked innocent but could kill.

"It's highly volatile," he warned. "Don't touch it."

He would examine it later, but he already knew what it was.

Because he'd created it.

How did the explosive cotton end up in a blasting device? Is this the work of Aloysius De Witt?

"There's smoke coming from the drawing room," Tessa gasped.

Bloody hell. Pushing aside his turmoil, Harry scanned the room for something to fight the fire. He went to the window, yanked down a velvet drape. "Wake the house, go!"

She took off running.

Gripping the fabric, he sprinted to the drawing room to face the rising flames.

13

THE GREY, GHOSTLY LIGHT BEFORE DAWN MATCHED THE SOMBER mood in her grandfather's study.

Although Tessa hadn't slept, she'd done a quick ablution and changed into a frock. Now she and her father occupied chairs across the desk from Grandpapa. Bennett stood next to her, Ming by her grandfather's side. In the wingchair behind the massive oak desk, Grandpapa looked haggard. He'd left off his wig, his shorn grey head aging him, making him look his three-and-sixty years.

Rage smoldered in his eyes as he looked at the black iron tube on the blotter. Earlier, Bennett, who was familiar with blasting materials from his time as a navvy, had disassembled the device. He'd removed the guts, placed them carefully in a box. To Tessa, the shredded cotton had looked innocuous, but having seen the damage done to the drawing room, her insides had chilled.

"I'll carve out the guts o' who'ever did this," Grandpapa growled. "Use 'em to string 'im up!"

He'd been uttering such threats ever since he'd been summoned home to find that his fortress had been attacked. Two of his guards had been killed protecting the front gate. Thoughts of Ned and Josiah swelled Tessa's throat. Both men had families, young children now left without a father. She and Grandpapa would go to give their condolences to the grieving widows, to assure them that their families would be looked after, yet no amount of money could replace a loved one.

An evening that had held such promise had ended in tragedy. In her marrow, Tessa felt the shifting tides, the dark and menacing undertow; when she glanced up at Bennett, the trepidation in her heightened. He seemed so distant that the few feet separating them might have been thousands. His expression was once again clad in steel, his gaze as opaque as wood. There was no trace of the passionate lover who'd held her and shown her such exquisite pleasure.

She told herself his reserve was due to the fact that he didn't want to rouse her family's suspicions, yet her instincts told her that wasn't the reason. Bennett could be stoic, yes, but this was more than that. Since the fire, he'd withdrawn into himself, barely uttering a word to her, even while she'd bandaged the superficial burns he'd sustained from fighting the blaze.

Over the past several days when they'd been at odds, he'd shown little of his feelings, but she'd still sensed his focus on her. His attention. Now that was gone: snuffed out like a flame.

What she felt from him was...nothing.

She tried to calm herself. Perhaps it was the aftermath of the life-or-death situation he'd just faced. Or perhaps he was just exhausted from battling the fire.

Or perhaps he regrets making love to you.

Her anxiety burgeoned. She didn't have the wherewithal to contend with that possibility on top of everything else. An enemy had attacked her family, and she needed to focus on how to protect them. It would be too much to deal with a broken heart as well.

She'd fallen in love with Bennett. That was the way it happened for Blacks: as sudden and powerful as a lightning clap. She'd been struck at last, and she knew, for her as for her grandfather and all the Blacks before him, that there would be no second time.

Inhaling, she twisted her head to look at Bennett again...and her midsection churned.

Steely composure. Eyes that didn't even see her.

"Leave us, girl."

Her gaze turned to her father, who waved a hand at her the way one might swat at a fly. He was still dressed in the clothes he'd worn at the baroness' supper, which seemed like it'd taken place a lifetime ago.

"Got a crisis on our 'ands," Father snapped, "and you're in the way."

She fought the surge of despair. Was this to be her destiny? To spend her life being unwanted?

"I have a right to be here." *I will not be shut out...by any of you.* "I am a part of this family, and we face our foes together."

Her father's face turned florid. "None o' your lip, girl, or by God, I'll—"

"Stop your bloody yammering, Todd!" Grandpapa's fist hit the desk, the iron tube rocking. "Ain't got time for this shite. Got a pox-ridden bastard to find and all you can do is flap your gums."

Tessa bit her lip; her father fell silent, scowling.

"Well, Ming?" Grandpapa addressed his right-hand man. "Who's the blackguard behind this?"

Ming's long braid swung slowly side to side. "Not know yet, Mr. Black. Still looking."

"Well, look 'arder!" Grandpapa roared. "What am I paying you for? My 'ome has been attacked by infidels, and you're of no more use than a bump on a bleeding log!"

Ming didn't flinch at his employer's show of temper. Tessa knew he understood that, beneath Bartholomew Black's rage, lay the grief of a man who'd failed to protect his own. But seeing the furrows that deepened on the loyal manservant's forehead, knowing that he, too, had lost comrades this night, Tessa spoke up.

"It's not Ming's fault, Grandpapa. Whoever is behind this planned the assault well. The villain struck right before the change of guards, when our security is at its weakest. If Bennett,"—her voice trembled as she said his name, but hopefully no one noticed—"hadn't caught those villains in the act, they might have set off all their devices and blown up the entire house."

As it was, only the drawing room had sustained damage. Bennett, assisted by the staff, had managed to put out the flames before they spread farther. He'd even saved the family portraits: they now leaned against the walls of the study, the faces looking out with reproachful stares.

"As to that, missy,"—her grandfather's eyes burned into her like hot coals—"what in *bleeding 'ell* were you and Bennett doing together at that time o' night?"

Her breath wedged in her throat. Beside her, Bennett went still. With all the chaos, the two of them hadn't had time to work out a story. One thing she knew for certain: there was *no way* she could tell her grandparent the truth. She would never endanger Bennett.

"It was a coincidence," she said in a rush. "I was playing billiards because I couldn't sleep. Bennett heard something and came to investigate. That was when we heard the attack."

None of this was a lie. She'd just skipped over a few parts. Like Bennett's scorching kiss, the way he'd touched her, shown her incandescent pleasure...

"If it weren't for Miss Todd's swiftness in alerting the others and ringing the fire bell, the damage would have been far worse," Bennett's deep voice said.

At the unexpected praise, she sent him a startled look. Bennett's expression hadn't changed all that much. Yet the approval in his eyes made her pulse throb with hope. She shot him a tremulous smile; was it her imagination, or did his stern features thaw a little?

"My Tessie shouldn't 'ave been put in that dangerous position," Grandpapa barked.

Grabbing his cane, he got up from his chair. He went to the portraits, his proud gait betrayed by its visible unevenness. He stopped in front of Grandmama's proud visage, reaching out to touch the burnt edge of the frame. Some of the paint had melted, red dripping down the velvet curtains behind Althea Bourdelain Black. Thankfully, Grandmama herself remained preserved: beneath her pearl-studded coronet, she gazed out with serene green eyes, untouched by time and fire.

"No one in my family should e'er feel anything but safe and free," Grandpapa said.

Although his back faced Tessa, she heard the emotion roughening his voice. She went to him, placed a hand on his sleeve. "Grandpapa, it's all right."

"Soon it shall be." He straightened, turned. "Leave us, Tessie."

"I will *not*. I can help. I'll disguise myself, go to the taverns frequented by our enemies and spy on them—"

"Shut up, you stupid girl!" Her father sprang from his chair like a predator who'd been biding his time. "Or, so 'elp me God, you'll get a whipping you shan't soon forget."

Anger got the better of her. "Seeing as God is more likely to take notice of me than you are, I suppose the whipping *ought* to come from him."

"You insolent little *bitch*—"

She stood her ground when her father came at her, but both Bennett and Ming moved like lightning. Bennett shoved her behind him while Ming restrained her swearing father.

"Todd, control yourself," Grandpapa said sharply. "Bennett, take Tessa upstairs."

Frustration beat against Tessa's breastbone. Her grandfather's expression was as unyielding as a mountain. He wasn't going to allow her to help her family in its most dire hour of need.

Resolve filled her. *Good thing I don't need his permission.*

~

As Tessa stormed past her still-restrained father, Harry slowed, his hands fisting. He was sorely tempted to give Malcolm Todd a thrashing. The bastard's treatment of Tessa was despicable: all she'd wanted to do was help. Only Ming's shake of the head and the fact that the other had Todd subdued made Harry move on. He wouldn't hit a man who couldn't hit back.

Moreover, as satisfying as pummeling Todd would be, Harry couldn't afford to be dismissed from his job. He had to stay by Tessa, to protect her...from the demons rising from his past.

He followed her as she stomped down the hallway in a fit of pique. In spite of the darkness that threatened to swamp him, he felt a spark of amusement. This was Tessa: part brave, passionate woman, part adorable brat. He could no longer deny his illogical and ill-fated attraction to her. He didn't know where it would lead, where it *could* lead given the tangled mess of the situation, but he did know one thing.

He would do anything to keep her safe.

"*Oof.*"

Tessa had come to an abrupt halt, and he'd run into her, pitching her forward. His hand shot out, yanked her back by the waist. Her softness hit his hard edges, and, despite his inner turmoil, desire flared. An awareness of how perfectly they fit together.

Releasing her, he muttered, "Pardon. I didn't see—"

"Keep your voice down." She kept her gaze averted. "And walk as quietly as you can."

Puzzled, he watched as she tip-toed back the way they'd come, all signs of temper gone. Had her tantrum been for show?

What is the minx up to now?

She turned into the billiards room, crooking her finger at him. Brows lifting, he followed her inside, and she closed the door with obvious stealth. She padded over to the bookcase on the wall that separated this room from Black's study; kneeling, she began to pluck volumes off the middle shelf.

"What are you doing?" he asked.

"If you want to stay, be quiet." Her voice hushed, she kept at her task.

Curiosity got its hooks in him. He knelt, stacking the books she passed to him on the floor. She reached to the back of the emptied shelf and extracted a small, cut-out piece of wood.

"Hell," he murmured. "You made yourself a squint?"

In answer, she placed a finger to her lips. The peephole into Black's study wasn't big, and its view was limited. Nonetheless, the voices of the room's occupants came through clearly.

"...one o' the dukes is behind the attack," Malcolm Todd's voice was insisting. "Only they would 'ave the power."

"I know it's one o' 'em. Didn't get to where I am by being an imbecile," Black's voice shot back. "Question is, which bloody one? Ming's been working on this since that bastard tried to off me at Nightingale's last month."

Someone tried to assassinate Black before this?

Frowning, Harry wondered if Inspector Davies was aware of this fact. His certainty in his mission had already suffered a blow when Tessa had explained about the medallion last night—that it was used as a symbol of protection rather than vendetta—and now to learn that someone had tried to kill Black *twice?*

Harry's gut told him something wasn't right. Yet as he took in Tessa kneeling beside him, her full pink skirts spread like petals around her as she spied like a naughty schoolgirl, he also knew his objectivity had been compromised. He wanted Black to be innocent because he wanted *her.*

"The assassin named John Loach." That was Ming, succinct as

always. "So far find connection between him and three of the dukes. Don't know which one ordered shooting at Nightingale's."

"Who are the three suspects?" Todd demanded.

There was a pause; Harry guessed the loyal manservant was looking to Black for permission to answer. And he knew he guessed correctly when Black muttered, "Tell 'im."

"Loach frequent visitor to tavern in the docklands. Owned by Francis O'Toole."

Tessa's hands balled in her lap.

"Loach has brother," Ming continued. "Brother is one of Severin Knight's men."

Harry was not familiar with Knight. Seeing Tessa's sharp intake of breath, he leaned closer, whispering, "Who's Knight?"

"The Duke of Spitalfields," she whispered back. "He oversees and gets a cut of most of the trade that happens there."

"Finally, Loach owe money," Ming said. "Five hundred quid to Adam Garrity."

Garrity was a name Harry knew. The infamous moneylender was married to his sisters' friend, Gabriella nee Billings. Harry had met Gabriella once, years ago before her marriage, and had the memory of a plump, redheaded chatterbox.

He'd never met Garrity, but he knew his sisters did not approve of their friend's match. According to them, Garrity was a shady character, and they bemoaned the fact that they'd seen little of Gabriella since her marriage.

"Garrity is the Duke of the City," Tessa murmured. "He's a moneylender, and men from all strata of society are indebted to him."

"Make me a duke," Todd said suddenly. "With John Randolph dead, you need someone to take over Covent Garden. Give me that territory, and I'll stand with you against all your enemies. I'll mount an attack on O'Toole, Knight, and Garrity."

"These ain't men to cross, you stupid bastard," Black growled. "Which is why I 'aven't made my move yet. Got to 'ave evidence before I strike back. As to your allegiance, I gave you my Mavis. Made you part o' my family. Ain't your fealty already sworn to me?"

"Yes, o' course. I just meant—"

"I know what you meant." Steely warning threaded Black's voice. "I ain't making no decisions about Covent Garden until my enemies are vanquished. If you want a dukedom, then you'd best show yourself useful."

"What do you want me to do?" Todd said sulkily.

"Give Ming your best men. 'E's got a watch on the three bastards and could use extra sets o' eyes and ears." Black paused. "Whoe'er is behind this will feel the fire of my vengeance: 'e'll pay for what 'e did to my guards this night. And to those under my protection at The Gilded Pearl."

The truth plowed into Harry. *Black had been protecting the bawdy house.* The medallion found on the victim had been a symbol of his protection...just as Tessa had claimed.

"This enemy not fight with fire, Mr. Black," Ming said somberly. "He use *hellfire*."

"'Ellfire?" Todd let out a derisive laugh. "Your Chinaman's got a screw loose."

"Between you and Ming, one man knows what e's talking about, and it ain't you." Disgust dripped from Black's voice. "'Ellfire is what we're calling this shite on my desk. Ming found the same bloody stuff at The Pearl."

"Found one device not blow," Ming clarified. "Same material inside."

"Don't know 'ow this shite is made, but it's twice as powerful as gunpowder. Ming and I tested it." Black's voice was stark. "Stuff burns cleanly and through everything in its path. If Bennett 'adn't stopped those buggers from lighting more tonight, they would've razed this place. Just like they did The Pearl."

Harry's gut coiled. All the properties Black described were those of the explosive material he'd accidentally created in his laboratory. The one that had been stolen from him by fellow scientist Aloysius De Witt, Celeste's father.

"I can keep track o' gunpowder by tracking its components. No sales o' saltpeter 'appen in the underworld without my knowing. But this 'ellfire is different," Black said grimly. "We don't know its ingredients. Some bastard might be making it right beneath our noses."

Harry swallowed, thinking of the volatile compound he'd produced out of nitric acid, oil of vitriol, and cotton. When Aloysius De Witt had learned about Harry's discovery, he'd wanted to produce and sell it for industrial purposes. Harry had argued that the substance, which he'd named "explosive cotton," was too volatile and dangerous to market.

De Witt had proposed a partnership. He'd funded Harry's attempts to produce a safer product, but then he'd grown impatient. Even though the explosive cotton wasn't ready, he'd insisted that it was time to bring it to investors.

Harry had refused, and his decision had cost him his future. Yet his shattered ambitions paled in comparison to the present threat. Had De Witt managed to stabilize the compound? Had he turned it into a useable weapon of destruction?

"On top o' all this, the Peelers are bloody thorns in my side," Black raged on. "Their spies are everywhere, so watch your backs."

"I ain't afraid o' the police," Todd scoffed. "I'll slit the throat o' any spy that dares set foot in my 'ouse."

"No, you'll bring 'im to me." Black's decree was cold, as final as death.

Harry's pulse thudded. Obviously, revealing his identity was not an option.

Beside him, Tessa gave a start. She scrambled to cover up the peephole.

"Grandfather was walking toward the squint," she said urgently. "He might have seen it."

Wordlessly, Harry shoved the books back in place. Tessa ducked her head out in the hallway, looking this way and that before gesturing to him. Numbly, he followed her down the empty corridor and up the stairs, his mind consumed by all he'd learned.

By *hellfire*...which he might have inadvertently unleashed on the world.

14

Filled with agitated energy, Tessa entered her sitting room. She dismissed Lizzie, who'd been tidying up her watercolors. The lady's maid pointedly left the door wide open, and Tessa didn't gainsay her. If Grandpapa stopped by, the closed door would rouse his suspicions. Despite the less than private situation, Tessa was determined to gain clarity on two points.

First, would Bennett help her family in their time of need?

Second, what were his feelings toward her?

Her heart palpitated. Since their spying session, Bennett had withdrawn even more, and she didn't know the cause of it. Whether it was the looming threat of the hellfire that absorbed him…or his regret over their passionate encounter.

What she did know was that she couldn't stand on pins and needles any longer.

She turned to face him, blurting, "Are you in or out?"

Despite her anxious state, she felt a quiver of longing just looking at him. He was wearing a tobacco brown frock coat and buff trousers, his masculinity starkly pronounced in her feminine chamber. Framed by the primrose silk walls and delicate furnishings, he was as out of place as a stallion in a tea shop. At present, he stood by the table she used for painting. Thanks to Lizzie, the pots of colors were neatly lined up, the ivory-handled brushes organized in their filigreed holders.

"Beg pardon?" His dark brows drew together. "In or out...of what?"

She decided to start with the easier issue. "Are you going to help me protect my grandfather? Or are you going to get in my way?"

She refused to stand by idly while Grandpapa's life was in danger, while her beloved streets were being threatened. She knew she was taking a risk in disclosing her intentions to Bennett. He might take the stance of every other man in her life and forbid her from doing what she needed to do.

Yet she'd taken the risk of trusting Bennett because...he was *Bennett*.

Time and again, he'd shown that he was a man who could be relied upon. He was one of the steadiest, most intelligent and competent men she'd ever met. Tonight, he'd risked his life saving her family home and all its occupants.

If she were going into battle, he was the knight she'd want by her side. Which was why she was asking for his help. Having Bennett as an ally would be a double boon: not only would she have his indisputable talents at her disposal, she could also save the precious energy that would be required to evade him.

Bennett's deep brown eyes studied her. She was relieved beyond measure to see that he seemed more like his normal self. His demeanor was less detached, his focus once again upon her.

"Those are my only two choices?" he asked.

"My family is *under siege*. Grandpapa may be too proud to admit it, but he needs all the help he can get. I'll not just wring my hands whilst our enemies come knocking."

"I don't imagine hand wringing is one of your talents." His tone was grave, but the glint of humor in his gaze gave her hope. "Perhaps you would consider letting the men handle this?"

"Isn't it obvious that they *cannot* handle this?" She listed off the facts on her fingers. "An assassination attempt was made on my grandfather. A bawdy house under his protection was blown to smithereens by hellfire. And, tonight, his home was attacked by the same vile means. We are at *war*, Bennett."

"Which is precisely why you should stay out of harm's way."

Why had she thought that he might be different from the rest? That he might see her as more than a nuisance, more than a girl who had nothing to offer?

Are you such a fool that you thought a few kisses would change anything?

"You're not going to take my side." She hated the quiver in her voice.

"I didn't say that."

Hope soared again, almost painful in its intensity. "Then... you'll work with me?"

At his slow nod, she dashed over to him. Impulsively took one of his large, calloused hands in both of hers. "*Thank you.* You don't know how much that means to me. I'll do anything—"

"That you will not. If you want my help, you'll follow the rules."

She dropped his hand. Frowned. "Rules?"

His gaze was brooding behind his spectacles. "Rule number one: you won't go running around pell-mell. In fact, you won't do *anything* without my permission."

"Your *permission*? Now see here—"

"Number two: when I tell you to do something, you do it. No questions asked."

Her resolve to be pleasing dissolved in a flash of indignation. "Who in blazes do you think you are? I'll not be dictated to!"

"I'm the man you need to protect your family. The family you'd do anything for."

At Bennett's blunt words, her arguments fizzled. Looking at

him, seeing his physical strength, the intelligence gleaming in those eyes, she knew he was right.

She couldn't go at this alone; she needed his help.

"Dash it all," she muttered. "I can't decide."

His brows lifted.

"I don't know whether I'm annoyed at your high-handedness,"—she huffed out a breath—"or relieved that you'll help."

His lips twitched, softening the lines on his face. "And for the last rule."

She narrowed her eyes at him. "Don't push your luck."

"If we are to be partners in this venture, then no one else is to know of our plans." He paused. "Not your family, not your friends at The Underworld, no one."

The word "partner" made her heart pitter-patter like that of a debutante asked to dance. He was willing to take her side, even against the wishes of her powerful family.

He believed in her quest, in *her*.

"On everything I hold dear, I vow not to tell a soul." Wanting him to know how much his trust meant, she said earnestly, "Would you like me to take a blood oath? I could get a penknife."

He stared. Then he burst out laughing, and that sound—rich, a bit rusty from disuse, and utterly masculine—was worth waiting for.

Smiling, he shook his head. "Keep your blood, silly chit."

"Shall we shake on it, then?" She extended her hand.

Instead of taking it, he curled a finger under her chin. The rasp of his toughened skin made her breath hitch. Beneath her bodice, the tips of her breasts budded, and, farther south, another place grew wet and wanting. Anticipation bloomed in her as he tilted her head up. Would he kiss her again? Her lips parted...

He didn't bend his head, merely turning her head left and then right. Examining her?

"I believe you," he said.

"You...do?"

"Your eyes give you away. When you're lying, the irises get cloudy," he said intently, "like flecks of verdigris in an insoluble solution. Right now, however, your eyes are clear."

He'd noticed her *eyes*? Even if she didn't quite understand his analogy, she'd take it as a compliment. Her chest melted like wax beneath a flame. His praise even made up for the fact that she apparently had a telltale sign that she needed to work on eliminating.

"Are we settled then?" she said breathlessly.

He stilled. Dropping his hand, he muttered, "Not quite."

"You can't go back on your word—"

"I'm not referring to that. I'm referring to what happened in the billiards room." He clasped his hands behind his back, said gruffly, "I owe you an apology. I took advantage of you—"

"You *didn't*." She couldn't let him believe that. "I was a full and willing participant."

"I'm responsible," he said stubbornly. "I'm the gentleman, and you're an innocent lady."

"I'm not innocent! For God's sake, I grew up in a bawdy house."

His face was as stony as a statue's. "Be that as it may, it was wrong of me to—"

"I wanted it." Despite her flaming cheeks, she said, "I wanted you to kiss me. Asked you to do it."

"Tessa..." His shield lifted, and she saw the flare of longing in his eyes before they shuttered again. "I cannot do the honorable thing by you."

Her heart twisted. "Because you don't want to?"

"Because I...can't." He rounded the corner of the table, putting distance between them. He touched the tip of one of her paintbrushes, his gaze on the silken bristles fanning between his finger and thumb. "Believe me, you could do better. You're beautiful, clever, rich. You could have any man."

"Even a duke?" The words left her before she could stop them.

"If you wanted the Duke of Ranelagh and Somerville, then he would be yours."

His tone was flat. Yet the telltale muscle ticking in his jaw told her everything she needed to know. The tightness in her chest eased.

"I don't want him," she said. "I want you."

There it was again. That flicker in his eyes: *naked longing*.

"Tessa, I'm not in a position to offer for you—"

"Then don't. Working together to protect Grandpapa will give us the chance to spend more time together," she said on impulse. "To see if we suit, without the pressure of expectations."

As she thought on it, it was the perfect plan. She didn't expect Bennett to be as sure of his feelings as she was, not after her regrettably juvenile behavior. Her plan would give her time to make up for all the tricks she'd played on him, to woo him...show him that she would be a worthy mate.

She also needed time to figure out how to manage her grandfather. How to convince the stubborn old goat that Bennett would make a far better husband for her than Ransom.

Bennett scowled at her. "Damnit, Tessa, you deserve expectations."

"I'd rather have you," she said truthfully.

He heaved a breath. Raked a hand through his hair. "Christ, what am I to do with you?"

Elation flooded her. His conflicted yet hungry look told her that she'd *won*. She would have the chance to convince Bennett that she was the woman of his dreams.

"Get to know me?" She edged closer to him. "Work with me to save my family?"

Slowly, as if he couldn't help himself, he reached out, tracing his thumb along her cheekbone.

"A loyal sprite, aren't you?" he murmured.

"We Blacks are always loyal." She shivered with pleasure when he brushed her lower lip before letting his hand fall. "Why do you call me that?"

"Sprite, you mean?"

She nodded.

"Because you're wee and mischievous..."

She wrinkled her nose. Zounds, that didn't sound attractive.

"...and also adorable."

He thinks I'm adorable?

"Adorable? Me?" she breathed.

His mouth quirked again. "When you're not getting me arrested or embarrassing me with farting contraptions or ruining my boots? Aye."

"I'll never play a trick on you again," she said ardently.

"Don't make promises you can't keep."

Entranced by his crooked smile, she lifted her hand, traced her fingertip over the scar in his eyebrow. The one she'd always wondered about. "How did you get this?"

His smile faded. "A blasting accident. I got trapped under rock."

"Blood and thunder, that must have been *terrifying*."

"I'd had better days."

"Is that why you stopped working as a navvy?"

"I suppose." He hesitated. "To this day, I don't like being trapped in tight spaces."

"I don't blame you—"

A rustling sounded outside the chamber. Heart thumping, Tessa whirled around, saw the departing swish of skirts. Just one of the housemaids passing by in the hallway. Nonetheless, it broke the spell, reminded her of where they were, what they still needed to do.

"We don't have much time," she said in a rush, "but I have a plan for finding the villain behind the hellfire attacks. First, we'll locate the taverns where O'Toole, Knight, and Garrity gather." She chewed on her lip, working out the details as she went along.

"Nighttime would be preferable for reconnaissance, and I'll disguise myself, of course—"

"The hell you will. You'll be staying here."

At Bennett's implacable tones, she stiffened. "We're *partners*. I'm not going to stay here whilst you risk your neck spying on those scoundrels."

"I'm not going to spy on them. That plan is risky, and you heard your grandfather. Ming's been tracking them for weeks now to no avail."

Bennett had a point. "Pray tell, Professor, do you have a better plan?"

She thought the sobriquet might lighten the mood; instead, his jaw clenched.

"There's another clue we can follow. The hellfire."

She considered the idea. "That cottonish stuff? But we know little about it."

"In my past line of work, I encountered a blasting compound similar to that material. It was created by a man I knew."

The revelation came as a surprise. But it made sense. Bennett had been a navvy; it wasn't surprising that he was familiar with explosives.

"Who is this man?" she said with dawning excitement. "Did he work with you on the railway?"

"He's dead. And he's not responsible for the hellfire: he knew his compound wasn't stable enough to use for any practical purpose and kept the formula a secret because of the dangers. He knew it was likely to harm whoever came in contact with it." Lines slashed around Bennett's mouth. "He was right: he died because of his discovery."

"How *dreadful*," she whispered. "It's like the story of Dr. Frankenstein."

Bennett gave a curt nod. "The inventor is gone, but it's possible that one of his associates gained the recipe for the compound. That they managed to stabilize it and turn it into this hellfire."

"Do you know who these associates are?"

He gave a grim nod.

She worried her lip. "Why didn't you mention this to Grandpapa? Shouldn't we tell him?"

"I don't want to implicate anyone, to cause anyone to suffer Black's wrath, until I have solid evidence of guilt."

Bennett had a point. In Grandpapa's present mood, there was no telling how he might react.

"Let me help you. There's so much danger afoot. You heard Grandpapa: Peel's Bloody Gang might be involved, and no one plays a dirtier, more despicable game than them," she said in disgust. "I'd trust anyone before a policeman."

"My rules, Tessa." His tone was unduly sharp. "I cannot be carrying on an investigation and simultaneously be worried about your safety."

She bit her lip, wanting to argue. As much as she wanted to be part of the adventure, however, too much was at stake. Her family's well-being and Bennett's. She'd never forgive herself if either came to harm because of her.

"I'll keep my end of the bargain. As long as you keep me apprised," she added hastily, "of *everything*. I'm your partner, don't forget."

"Rather difficult to." His voice was dry. "Now I'd best let you get some rest."

The unmistakable thump of a cane came from the hallway. Nonetheless, she risked getting on tiptoe and brushing her lips against his jaw, which was hard and bristly with his night beard.

"Thank you for helping Grandpapa. And for taking a chance on me," she whispered.

His eyes heated. He curled a finger under her chin. "You can count on me, sprite."

15

Two nights later, as Harry made his way to his destination on Cheapside, he replayed his interaction with Davies. In the wee hours of the morning, he'd met again with the inspector on the Thames. He'd reported on Black's enemies and the territorial war in the underworld, including the assassination attempt by Loach. He'd shared about the hellfire and his conclusion that Black was innocent in the matter of The Gilded Pearl.

"Goddamnit, we still cannot pin that bastard Black to a crime?" Swearing, Davies had raked a hand through his wiry hair. To his credit, however, he'd seized upon the bigger issue. "The situation is worse than I thought. We must contain this hellfire for such a weapon isn't safe in anyone's hands. If a war erupts, we won't have the manpower to control it."

Exhaling, Harry had told Davies about his suspicions concerning Sir Aloysius De Witt. That, of course, had necessitated giving an abridged version of his disgrace at Cambridge. He'd waited, uncertain how his superior would react.

"We all make mistakes, Kent. Yours was merely trusting the wrong people."

Relieved, Harry gave a curt nod.

"The question is, how do we structure our investigation? Our resources are already stretched to the limit." Davies' face lined with frustration. "Now we have three additional cutthroats to monitor as well as this bastard De Witt."

"Let me take on De Witt," Harry said. "If I find his laboratory, I can identify any substance he may be making and verify that it is, indeed, the hellfire."

Davies scrutinized him. "You'd be willing to take this on, Kent? Much will rest upon your shoulders. I cannot afford to provide reinforcements, nor would it be wise. Black hates the police, knows we're watching him. If he suspects any connection between you and the force, you'll be in grave danger."

It wasn't the peril that made Harry hesitate but the thought of Tessa. He *hated* that he would have to continue lying to her. Yet how else could he prevent the hellfire from threatening her world and his? How else could he stay by her side and protect her?

"I created this hellfire," he said. "I will extinguish it."

"You're a good man, Kent. An honorable one." Davies shook his hand. "When we win this battle, I'll see to it that you receive the recognition you deserve."

Before parting, the police inspector had suggested a way for Harry to get some assistance with the mission. This led Harry to his present destination: a small confectionery between St. Mary le Bow and Old Change. It was half-past eight in the evening, and the curtain was pulled over the shop window, an outline of light shining through. Harry found the door unlocked and entered the small shop, the scents of caramelized sugar, toasted nuts, and fruit surrounding him like a cozy blanket.

Mrs. Parbury, a rosy-cheeked matron, was bustling behind the large wooden counter. She looked up from organizing the jars and pans of boiled sweets, jellied fruits, and other sugary delicacies.

Harry doffed his hat. "Good evening, ma'am."

"And to ye, sir." Beneath her cap, her eyes twinkled, and she lowered her voice to a hush, even though no one else was in the room. "Go on back, lad. He's waiting for ye."

Harry went on, passing through the door that led to the kitchen. He exchanged greetings with Mr. Parbury, a stout man whose belly was barely contained by his splattered apron.

"Harry Kent, as I live an' breathe." The confectioner possessed the same good cheer as his wife, making Harry wonder if the line of work sweetened a person's disposition.

"It's been a while, sir," Harry said. "Good evening."

"It is at that." The confectioner stirred a pot. "Now can ye guess what I'm cooking up?"

Harry sniffed the air. "Something with citrus?"

"Lemon drops, sir. A favorite o' the ladies. I add a splash o' rosewater to sweeten the breath. 'Tis a good gift for sisters or, better yet,"—the confectioner winked broadly—"for a sweetheart."

The mention of a sweetheart reignited Harry's turmoil.

I don't want him. I want you. Tessa's bright honesty tautened his insides with desire...and guilt. He was lying to her about who he was. He'd infiltrated her family on a pretense and was spying on them for the police, an institution that all Blacks clearly despised.

Even without those looming problems, he wasn't sure that he was capable of giving her what she wanted. What most women, in his experience, wanted. He had no skill for sentiment or flattery; after the pain of Celeste, he'd vowed not to expose his heart again.

And, to be honest, he didn't know if he and Tessa were suited. She was...unusual. Did he really want a future that included ferrets and cutthroats and untold mayhem?

Ambivalence gripped him. Because the folly of it was he *did* want her.

God, he did.

"I'll take a tin," he heard himself say.

"I'll 'ave the missus wrap it up specially." Mr. Parbury beamed. "It'll be ready after your visit."

Thanking the confectioner, Harry exited the cooking area, going down a short hallway to an unpainted door. He knocked before entering the cramped but cozy sitting room.

"Harry." Ambrose unfolded his long frame from the chair where he'd been sitting, his lean face creasing in a smile. "It's good to see you, lad."

Shutting the door, Harry returned his older brother's firm handshake. "You as well."

"Come, sit." Ambrose waved to the table, which was laden with an assortment of pastries and sweets. "I told the Parburys it wasn't necessary, but they insisted on the hospitality."

He took the chair opposite his brother. "They've never forgotten what you did for them."

"It was a trifle." Ambrose poured tea into two chipped cups.

It was typical of Ambrose to call hunting down a burglar with no more than a set of muddy footprints a trifle. The eldest Kent was as modest as he was capable.

"You look well." Harry helped himself to a slice of iced gingerbread. "How are Marianne and the children?"

"Marianne is well and sends her love." Ambrose's amber eyes were warm as he spoke of his beloved. "Little Sophie continues to be a sweet, mild-mannered child, and Edward is…Edward."

Harry's lips twitched. Ambrose's heir Edward had gone from being a precocious boy to a certifiable genius whose curiosity oft landed him in hot water (a fate Harry could identify with). Edward was undoubtedly responsible for some of the silver swathing through his papa's dark hair.

"Enough about me. What is going on with you, lad?" Ambrose said quietly. "First Davies contacts me, telling me to keep the family at bay. Then I receive that cryptic message via mudlark that you wanted to meet in secret today."

Seeing the lines on his brother's brow, Harry felt another tug of guilt. Being the eldest by some dozen years (Ambrose's mama had been their papa's first wife), Ambrose took the responsibilities of being the family patriarch seriously.

He proceeded to fill his brother in on the last fortnight. He shared most details but left out the intimate ones concerning Tessa. Despite what she might believe, she *was* a lady and deserved his protection. Moreover, he wasn't comfortable discussing feelings that he, himself, did not fully understand.

At the conclusion, Ambrose swore. "Bloody hell, you're spying on *Bartholomew Black*? Are you out of your mind? The man's the most dangerous cutthroat in all of London!"

While his brother had a point, he was also beginning to see the underworld king through a different lens. He'd witnessed Black's devotion to his family and people. He thought about what Mrs. Crabtree had said: about all that Black had done for her and for the common folk, the ones to whom the government turned a blind eye.

"Black's not all bad," he said slowly.

"His enemies have been found in the Thames. In *pieces*."

With care, Harry said, "I recall that you and Marianne had some personal dealings with Black?"

"Marianne owed him a debt. It was paid, and I shall say no more," Ambrose said firmly. "Black may not be entirely evil, but he's not to be crossed. Davies was right to send you to me. I'll find a way to extricate you from Black's employ. After that, I'll be at your disposal: I'll personally help you investigate that bastard De Witt."

Hell. He wasn't going to be able to evade the truth. "I cannot leave Black's employ."

"Is this about proving your worth? Because of what happened two years ago?"

Bitterness and humiliation welled. Harry couldn't deny that that was part of it. He'd lost everything: the job at Cambridge, the membership with the Royal Society, his standing with his peers. Was it wrong to try to redeem his good name?

"Brother, it wasn't your fault. You were duped by a pair of conniving thieves...and worse than thieves, if they are indeed behind this dastardly hellfire."

"That doesn't excuse me for being a fool." Self-disgust throbbed like a festering wound. "For being blinded by my emotions."

"You were young." Ambrose's golden gaze was steady. "You've always held your cards close to your chest, lad, yet I wish you would have told me what was happening at the time—"

"There was nothing you or anyone could have done. In the scientific community, Aloysius De Witt is nothing short of royalty, and he decreed that I was a thief. And Celeste helped him to frame me."

The betrayal still burned.

"Let the past go," Ambrose urged. "For two years, you risked your neck playing with explosives in that navvy camp. Now you're back, and you've jumped straight into a pit of vipers. You've done your penance, Harry, you've nothing to prove. You must move on."

The words struck an uneasy chord. He hadn't thought of his actions as penance, only a desire to do something right. To reclaim the honor he'd lost.

Now, however, there was more at stake. There was Tessa.

No more hedging.

Taking a breath, he said, "Black and his family are in danger, and I cannot abandon them."

"You're worried about Black and his family? Why the devil would you care...oh, hell." Ambrose's keen gaze narrowed. "The *granddaughter?*"

"Tessa's not like her grandfather," he said defensively.

"*Tessa?*"

And this is why I like to hold my damned cards close.

Neck heating, he muttered, "She's...a nice young lady."

That might not be the most apt description, yet it was difficult to convey the precise nature of Tessa's appeal. She was a creature of contradictions. She was undoubtedly brazen, a mischief-maker and an occasional hellion. At the same time, she could be sweet, a vibrant sprite and a young woman with hidden vulnerability. She was unique, damned endearing.

Just thinking of her offer to give a blood oath made him want to laugh.

In truth, Harry didn't fully understand the intensity of his attraction to her. He only knew that, in her presence, he felt *more*. More alive, more...himself.

"Didn't you say that when you met the chit, she was disguised as a lad and fleecing a band of cutthroats?"

"Well, yes, but there's more to her than that." Seeing his brother's look of incredulity, he explained, "She is high-spirited, yes, but mostly in a fun-loving sort of way. She cares a great deal about her family. Her loyalty to those she cares about is unquestionable."

He thought of their visit this morning to the families of the fallen guards. Of Tessa's unexpected maturity and grace as she consoled the grieving widows. Afterward, she'd spent time with the children, passing out the treats she'd brought and having Swift Nick perform tricks to entertain them. For a short while, she'd succeeded in easing some of the pain from those small faces.

That her bright spirit could touch others shouldn't have come as a surprise. After all, her light touched him too. Just thinking of her impish smile spread warmth through his gut.

"As much as I hate to point this out, I fear I must. You are one of the most intelligent men I know, Harry. When it comes to females, however..."

Clearing his throat, Ambrose didn't finish. Didn't have to.

The past had proved that Harry's judgement when it came to the opposite sex was far from sound. Forced to question himself now, he couldn't deny that Tessa did have traits in common with Celeste. The main ones being her ability to trick and, aye, manipulate—he thought of their first blistering kiss—to achieve her end.

Yet he told himself that she was *not* Celeste. She was loyal and fierce and feisty: Celeste had been none of those things. Moreover, he wasn't the green lad he'd once been. While he desired Tessa, he wouldn't offer her, or any woman, his heart on a silver platter. He wouldn't lose control of his heart or head again.

"I learned my lesson the last time," he said shortly.

"Well, I'm glad we are discussing the matter instead of you brooding in isolation like you did before." Ambrose leaned forward. "Lad, I want what's best for you. And I'm telling you this Tessa Todd is nothing but trouble."

Harry couldn't help but raise a sardonic brow. "Are you saying you've never been attracted to a woman who promised trouble?"

Ambrose's cheekbones turned ruddy. "That was a different situation entirely."

"As I recall, Marianne was a suspect you were investigating."

"Touché." Sighing, Ambrose held up a hand. "If you won't be swayed, how can I help?"

"I need you to look into De Witt's financials. To see if money could be a motive for him."

"Done." His brother paused. "What about his laboratory? How are you planning to find it?"

"I've watched De Witt for the last two nights. His schedule was the same: he goes to some *ton* event, then spends the rest of the night gambling at Crockford's. Tonight, while he's out, I'm going to search his house."

∽

Harry parted from his brother with a revised plan. Ambrose had convinced him to hold off the search of De Witt's home until tomorrow, so that Ambrose could gather reinforcements. Thus, Harry now found himself with some unexpected time. Recalling an errand, he stopped briefly at his room before heading to another destination.

Upon arriving at The Underworld, he saw a long line of patrons snaking out the front door. He took the back entrance and asked for Pretty Francie. A few minutes later, the bawd emerged, dressed for work in a low-cut purple gown, a matching feather in her auburn hair.

"Mr. Bennett." Curiosity sharpened her painted features. "Weren't expectin' you."

"Pardon the intrusion." Bowing, Harry proffered the reason for his visit. "I'm making good on my promise to return Miss Belinda's cloak."

"That's thoughtful o' you." She took the garment. "Not many coves would remember such a trifle."

He thought wistfully of his favorite pair of boots, the ones Tessa had ruined with honey, and he muttered, "It's not a trifle if it's one's favorite."

"True enough." Francie's expression turned grave. "Ow's Tessa faring since the attack?"

This time around, Black hadn't managed to suppress the gossip about the attack on his home. Tongues wagged in the underworld as much as in any *ton* ballroom. The only thing Black had managed to quash were the details concerning the weapon used in the assault. Hellfire remained a secret.

"She's fine, but she won't be returning here in the foreseeable future." Harry didn't wish to be unkind, but he needed Tessa's friends to understand what was at stake. "I cannot allow her to compromise her safety."

Rather than offended, the madam seemed relieved. "'Bout time someone looked after that girl."

"That's why Mr. Black hired me. I'll do my best to keep a rein on her."

"Our Tessa don't need no reins." Francie snorted. "What she needs is *understanding*. Much as 'er grandfather dotes upon 'er, 'e don't understand 'er."

Unable to help himself, Harry said, "What doesn't he understand?"

The bawd turned assessing eyes upon him. "You care about 'er?"

"She is my charge," he said stiffly. "Her wellbeing is my responsibility."

"That's all she is to you, then? A responsibility?"

Faced with those unblinking eyes, Harry found he couldn't lie. He said nothing, and Francie must have read the truth in his silence for she gave a satisfied nod.

"The thing you got to know 'bout Tessa is that she does things for a reason. Now that reason ain't always clear—bit o' a trickster, that one—but she ain't a spoilt brat like you think."

Recalling his and Tessa's very public argument here, he flushed. "I don't think she's a brat."

Not most of the time, anyway. He'd gotten to know her better. He'd even formed a hypothesis as to the cause of her willfulness. Having witnessed her interactions with her father and grandfather, he suspected that her defiant behavior resulted from a history of having her wishes ignored or denied.

In the face of that adversity, many ladies would become subservient or compliant or just give up. But not Tessa: she was a fighter. Harry had to admit he admired her bold spirit, even if he sometimes felt the brunt of her strong will.

"Tessa's got a sense o' honor stronger than most men. Gets it from her grandfather, though 'e don't see it. When you found 'er dressed like a lad, cheating that bastard Dewey O'Toole at cards, she weren't doing it for fun. Not *just* for fun anyway," Francie amended.

Harry frowned. "Then why did she do it?"

"On account o' what O'Toole did to Belinda."

The truth slammed into him. "O'Toole was the one who put the bruises on her?"

"Blighter did more than beat Belinda: 'e stole 'er blunt, too. Not because 'e needed the money, but just because 'e could," Francie said starkly. "Belinda weren't 'erself after that, and *that's* why Tessa stepped in."

"Why didn't Todd do something about it?" If possible, Harry's esteem for Tessa's father dropped even lower.

Francie darted a glance around, hushing her voice. "'E ain't got the bollocks to stand up to the O'Tooles. And 'e don't give a damn about us wenches, not like Tessa does. Girl's got a 'eart o' gold and looks after 'er own."

It was the second time someone had said that about Tessa. A feeling spread through Harry, like the prickly pleasure-pain of an awakening limb. And along with it another feeling...

Remorse.

He'd underestimated her. His mind had failed to recognize the truth he'd *felt*: the goodness at her core, the virtue rooted in her like a sturdy flower abloom in the rookery's dirty streets.

Shaking his head, he said, "Why didn't she tell me or her grandfather? She let us believe she was just out on a lark."

"Belinda made 'er swear not to tell anyone. And Tessa's a woman o' 'er word."

Remorse bled into self-recrimination. To think, he'd compared her to Celeste, questioned her suitability to be his bride.

"She is a remarkable woman," he said in a low voice.

"She's no wilting violet, that's for certain. But she's more fragile than she lets on, thanks to that bleedin' finishing school."

He frowned. "What happened there?"

"High-kick twats treated 'er like rubbish is what. Bullied 'er without mercy." Francie's lips pulled tight. "Four years and weren't a day she didn't arrive with 'er eyes puffed up from crying."

Harry's chest clenched. That Tessa had been subjected to such cruelty made him want to punch something. It explained her prejudice against the upper class, why she wanted no part in the charade of being Miss Theresa Smith.

"Our Tessa's blood might not run blue, but she's a real lady." Francie's tone was as stern as that of any schoolmistress. "See that you treat 'er like she deserves."

He'd earned the admonishment. For not recognizing what had been plainly in front of his face. For being a blind fool.

Harry thanked the madam and took his leave. He stepped into the night air, his head spinning like a man who'd just received a blow to the head. Or one who was finally waking up.

16

Tessa stealthily crossed the courtyard toward the mews, her arms wrapped around a large box. She'd forgone a lamp and timed her journey to minimize the chance of being detected. The night air brushed against her cheeks, cool and invigorating after the hour she'd spent tossing in her bed. She hadn't been able to sleep. The moment her eyes closed, she'd seen the faces of Ned and Josiah and those of their weeping families whom she'd visited today, and helpless anguish had filled her.

She could do nothing for those two brave soldiers, and the menace was still at large. Her hope lay in Bennett: before supper, he'd told her he would be out this evening pursuing a lead. As glad as she was that he was making progress, she was also worried about his safety.

To distract herself, she'd decided to plant his surprise while he was out.

Hence the box in her arms and her climb up the steps to Bennett's room above the stables. At his door, she saw the darkened window and knew he was still out. Her timing was perfect. When he returned, he would be surprised and, hopefully, pleased by her gift.

It was part of her campaign to win him over. She was reasonably certain that he desired her physically. She might be a virgin, but she couldn't miss his obvious arousal the two times they'd kissed. Thus, she reasoned his ambivalence toward her must have to do with her other shortcomings.

Glumly, she recalled how Bennett had called her a spoiled brat. A man like him had probably had his share of bedpartners, women who were more fetching, sophisticated, and feminine than she was. Ladies who didn't run around in trousers, who knew how to properly flirt, and who didn't, well, *annoy* the man they wanted to marry.

Drat. If only she hadn't played so many tricks on him. She winced as she reviewed her trespasses. To be fair, he *had* got his revenge with the exploding fountain (neat trick, that), yet she had a lot to make up for.

Her chest squeezed. *If only I could get Bennett to* like *me*.

Gaining approval had never been her forte. For years, she'd tried with her father and her classmates, to no avail. Even Grandpapa, for all that he loved her, refused to see her for who she was. The thought of another rejection, especially from Bennett, caused fear to trickle through her, yet she had to try to win his heart...because he had hers.

Even if it meant exposing herself to ridicule and pain, she had to try. She was going to use a high-risk and potentially high-reward strategy: honesty. Since Bennett had seemed to like her disclosures that night in the billiards room, she reasoned she ought to stick with that tactic. To try to win his admiration by being herself.

It's worth a try, she thought. *I can't bungle this up any more than I already have, can I?*

She reached for the knob. When it didn't turn, she put down the gift, pulled two hairpins out of her cloak pocket, and made short work of the lock. She pushed the door open, picked up the box, and entered the shadows. Thin ribbons of moonlight slipped through the shutters, limning the outlines of furniture.

Before she could locate a lamp, a rustle sounded behind her. In the next heartbeat, she was yanked backward. Her back slammed into a wall of muscle, an arm circling her throat. Panic swelled.

"Bennett, it's me," she choked out.

"*Tessa?*"

The pressure around her throat instantly eased. She was set on her feet. As she gulped in air, a lamp flared on a nearby table. The glow illuminated the room and Bennett's austere expression.

"Bloody hell," he grated out. "Did I hurt you?"

"No, I'm fine. Just need to catch my breath," she wheezed.

"I could have—" He bit off an oath, shoving a hand through his tousled hair. "What the devil were you thinking, sneaking into my room at this hour?"

Before she could answer, he steered her into the single chair at the table before stalking off. He returned a minute later and shoved a glass into her hands. She took a tentative sip; the brandy's warmth soothed her throat.

"Well?" Bennett said.

He stood, scowling at her, his arms crossed, and it hit her: he was wearing a dressing gown...and nothing else. The well-worn navy fabric molded to his broad shoulders and revealed the strong column of his neck. Her gaze darted downward to the vee between his lapels, her pulse tripping. His chest looked like carved granite, the slabs of defined muscle dusted with dark hair.

The robe clung to his sinewy arms and narrow hips, ending below his knees. Below the hem, his naked calves bulged. His feet were large and bare.

Heat that had nothing to do with the brandy pooled in her belly. Beneath her cloak, her nipples tingled against her night rail. Zounds, he was beautiful.

"I'm waiting," Bennett ground out.

And, unfortunately, not in a lovey-dovey mood.

"I thought you would be out tonight." Popping up, she went to retrieve the gift she'd dropped in the scuffle. "And I came to leave you, um, something."

A wave of self-consciousness struck her. Suddenly, she felt like an awkward schoolgirl bringing an apple for the tutor for whom she's developed a tendre.

Bennett's stare transferred from her to the box she was clutching. "What is it?"

"It's nothing," she hedged.

Too late, she realized her impulsive gift was unusual. Far too intimate. Not something a lady would give to a gentleman unless she was brazen and utterly ignorant of social niceties.

God, what was I thinking? Heat scorched her cheeks.

He held out his hand. His long fingers crooked in a gesture that conveyed, *Hand it over.*

Her grip on the box tightened. "I've actually, um, changed my mind."

"You can't take back my gift."

"Since I haven't given it to you, I'm not taking back anything."

"Despite your tendency to argue over everything,"—while his expression was grave, his voice held a trace of humor—"do you think, in this one instance, you might make an exception and give me the damned gift without prolonged debate?"

"I don't argue over everything..." She bit her lip, feeling supremely foolish.

He quirked a sardonic brow.

"Oh, all right." She shoved the box at him. "But don't blame me if you think it's stupid."

"I won't think it's stupid."

On pins and needles, she watched him set the box on the table, untie the string, and lift the lid.

His brows drew together. "You brought me...boots?"

Mortification tautened her insides. "I told you it was stupid.

It's just that I ruined your best pair because I was being silly and thoughtless and—"

"How did you know my size?" Lifting one of the boots from the box, he ran a hand over the supple black calfskin.

Despite her embarrassment, Tessa thought those boots would look smashing on Bennett. She'd asked the bootmaker to model them after those made by the famed but now defunct Hoby's of St. James, the shop that had made footwear for the Duke of Wellington. The so-called Wellington boots were taller, closer-fitting, and less fussy than Hessians, and she thought their utilitarian elegance suited Bennett to a tee.

"I retrieved your old boots from the rubbish heap and gave them to the bootmaker. He was able to construct this pair from those measurements." Seeing the way he caressed the leather shaft, almost reverently, she ventured, "Do you...like them?"

"They are very fine. Finer than any I've owned," he said softly.

Relief and pleasure hummed through her. "Oh. I'm glad."

Clearing his throat, he said, "As it happens, I have something for you as well."

She faltered into stillness, her heart jerking oddly. "You do?"

He replaced the boot in the box and went to his jacket, which hung on a hook on the wall. Rummaging in one of the pockets, he returned with a small package.

"It's just a trifle," he muttered.

Bennett brought me a gift! Whatever it was, she would treasure it forever.

With trembling hands, she took the parcel, removing the cheerful yellow ribbon and brown paper. Her eyes widened at the sight of the tin, which was affixed with images of hearts, flowers, and cherubs.

"How *pretty*." Opening the lid, she breathed, "You brought me lemon drops?"

"I told you it wasn't much."

"Lemon drops were my *favorite* as a girl. I haven't had one in ages." Eagerly, she selected one of the jewel-like confections and popped it into her mouth. The tart sweetness spread over her tongue like sunshine. "These are delicious. Would you like one?"

Belatedly, she remembered to offer him the tin.

His lips twitched. "Thank you, no. But I'm pleased you enjoy them."

The fact that he'd thought to bring her a present, that he'd thought of her at all, made her buffle-headed with happiness. "When did you have time to go to a confectionary?"

"It was, er, on my way." He shoved his spectacles up his nose. "I returned your friend's cloak."

Her chest melted as sweetly as the candy on her tongue. He was *such* a good chap, one who was always good to his word. "Thank you for remembering Belinda. And for the sweets."

"You're welcome."

Their gazes held in the intimate, flickering light. A charge of awareness electrified her senses. Yearning ripened every cell of her being until she felt she might burst with anticipation.

He reached out, his knuckles grazing her cheekbone, and her breath hitched. He was looking at her intently, almost as if he were seeing her for the first time. And, for once, his rich brown gaze was unguarded...and smoldering with longing.

"Christ, Tessa," he said hoarsely. "I want you."

His admission weakened her knees.

"Then take me, Bennett," she whispered. "I'm yours."

∽

How the devil could he resist her?

From the moment she'd awkwardly given him the new pair of boots, he'd known there was no more fighting his attraction to her. To this woman whose willful exterior hid a pure, generous, and fiercely loyal heart. A woman who wouldn't betray the whores who were her friends, even if keeping her word was to her own detriment. Who treated a tin of lemon drops as if they were diamonds. Who looked at him as if he made the sun rise for her... just by being who he was.

By God, he was *tired* of reining in his desire for her. He wasn't going to any longer.

Whatever the consequences, he would deal with them—because Tessa was *his*.

He cupped her face in his hands, drinking in the beauty of her eyes, her petal-soft skin, her lush mouth. Then he lowered his head, and the taste of her, part tart, part honey, and all Tessa, was more thrilling than a scientific discovery. More potent than any blasting powder.

Her hands slid into his hair, and he shuddered at their insistent grip, the eager press of her dewy lips against his. In an easy motion, he swept her into his arms, carried her to his bed, tossing his glasses on the bedside table. He lay her down, and her luxuriant sable curls spilled over the threadbare quilt, her eyes a glowing beacon in the darkness.

Lying beside her, he ran his thumb over her bottom lip. "Are you certain you want this, sweetheart?"

"As certain as death." She reached up, tugged at the lapels of his robe. "Do hurry, *please*."

At her unabashed eagerness, he fought a smile. "What's the rush?"

"I don't want you to change your mind," she whispered.

His chest clenched at the insecurity in her beautiful eyes. It amazed him that she could be so strong yet fragile at the same time. And he hated himself for ever causing her to doubt herself.

Cupping her jaw, he said firmly, "I'm not going to change my mind, sweetheart. And I'm not going to rush either. I'm going to take my time with you."

"So you will...make love to me?"

"I'm going to pleasure you, sweeting, but I won't take your virginity."

As a gentleman, he wouldn't do that to her. He wouldn't do anything irrevocable until he knew for certain that he could do right by her. That she would want him to...after she learned that he'd been lying to her this entire time.

Guilt knotted his chest. For a wild instant, he contemplated letting the truth spill out: his position with the police, his mission to stop the hellfire, his real name. But Tessa was a daughter of the underworld, her hatred of the police ingrained.

No one plays a dirtier, more despicable game...I'd trust anyone before a policeman.

And he knew he couldn't risk it. Couldn't risk her ejecting him from her life when he needed to stay by her side. To protect her from the imminent peril.

"Is...is something wrong, Bennett?"

Her tremulous words punctured his dark thoughts. *When the threat is over, I'll tell her the truth,* he vowed to himself. *And I'll do whatever it takes to win her forgiveness.*

"Nothing's wrong," he said huskily.

"Then why are you brooding?" Her eyes searched his. "If I've done something wrong—"

"Tessa, you're perfect. This,"—he claimed her mouth once more, lifting his head only when she was breathless and wearing that delightfully dazed look on her face—"is perfect. The only thing I'm thinking about is how I want to pleasure you tonight."

"Oh." Her mouth took on a sudden, impish curve. "Do you need suggestions? Because I still have that deck of cards Alfred lent me..."

He didn't know whether to groan or laugh. "I'd forgotten about those damned cards, or I would have confiscated them."

"Confiscated?" she said saucily. "And what would you have done with them, *Professor?*"

Hearing her use that sobriquet brought echoes of his erotic dream of her. He was as stiff as an iron pike, but he was determined to slow things down. To pleasure her and explore her sensual bounty. As if she read his thoughts, her laughter faded, her eyes growing heavy-lidded, an invitation he could not resist.

He kissed her neck, inhaling her sweet, unique scent. When he nipped her earlobe, she made a sound halfway between a moan and a whimper, as adorable as it was arousing. Impatient with the layers that separated them, he untied her cloak, tossing it to the ground. A few moments later, her night rail followed.

Staring down at her, he was rendered speechless. With her delicate curves and flawless skin, she was like a nubile water nymph rising from a spring. Seeing the dark, shy thatch between her slender thighs, the glint of clinging dew, he swallowed heavily.

"Do you find me...pleasing?"

At her hesitant words, he dragged his gaze back to her face. Incredulously, he saw that she was serious. And worried?

"Christ, sprite," he said with feeling, "you could not be more so."

He cupped her breast, the silken weight fitting perfectly in his palm. She bit her lip, and just watching her pearly teeth sink into that luscious pink ledge, the same color as her budded nipples, made his mouth pool.

"You don't think they're...too small?"

It took him a moment to understand what she was asking.

Startled, he said, "Your breasts, you mean?"

She averted her gaze. "The girls at school used to make fun of them. Said I ought to water them so they'd grow." Her laugh sounded forced. "They said gentlemen preferred ladies who were more, um, endowed."

Anger spiked in him at the cruelty she'd experienced. At the same time, he felt a fierce surge of tenderness for the girl Tessa must have been. For the girl who lived inside the woman...the woman who he was finally beginning to understand.

"The silly chits don't know what they're talking about." He curled a finger beneath her chin, made her look at him. "You are perfection."

"Truly?"

The wonder in her eyes made his chest ache. And his erection throb. In answer, he grazed her right nipple with his thumb and heard the sharp hitch of her breath.

"See how responsive you are, sweeting? How your nipples bud and blossom at my touch? There's nothing prettier than that," he said thickly. "Nothing more arousing to a man than knowing a lady likes what he's doing."

Her lashes swept up against her brows, myriad emotions darting through her eyes.

Then she dazzled him with a smile. "In that case, you ought to know that I like what you're doing *very* much."

"Brazen minx."

Lips curved, he kissed her, marveling at how everything felt different with her, different and new. Being with her in the moonlight beat back the shadows of his past. She was unlike the ladies he'd known and the women he'd bedded in the navvy camps. He'd never been with a female who blended passion with humor, innocence with the instincts of a siren, playfulness with devastating honesty.

She moaned when he rolled the needy tip of her breast between finger and thumb. Tearing his mouth from hers, he kissed a path down the slope of her collarbones, fragile as a bird's wings. Lust pounded in his veins as he continued on to her breasts, the petite, firm curves shivering beneath his tongue. When he closed his lips around one perfect, pink peak, her spine arched off the bed.

"Blood and thunder," she gasped.

He suckled her harder, going from breast to breast. He flicked the taut tips, then laved them with his tongue, loving her breathy moans. He reached between her legs, and the extent of her arousal whipped through him like a storm.

"You're drenched." Reverently, he slid his finger up her dew-soaked slit.

"I can't help it." Her bottom lip caught beneath her teeth again even as she wriggled deliciously against his stroking finger. "It just happens whenever I'm with you."

God, her honesty. It made him feel taller than a mountain.

And randier than a green lad with his first wench.

"You're as juicy as a peach, and I'd wager you taste even sweeter," he rasped.

He spread her thighs wide and prepared to feast.

17

Tessa considered herself well-versed when it came to sexual matters, at least in a theoretical sense. In fact, the Queen of Hearts in her deck of cards depicted a man performing this particular act on a lady sitting atop a throne, her hands holding up her skirts. When Tessa had first seen the image, she'd thought it outlandish: what man or woman would wish to engage in such a perversion? Yet, as always, her first-hand experience with Bennett made her realize how little she understood.

Because the act might be outrageous, but it was also...*sublime*.

Her embarrassment at having Bennett's mouth at her intimate juncture was no match for the incendiary pleasure of his kiss. Her inhibitions melted in the searing bliss. As he licked into her secret cove, flames flared in her lower belly.

"Just as I thought," he muttered. "Sweeter than a peach."

His words, the feel of them against her damp folds made her shiver helplessly. Then he was licking her sex again, the bold swipes streaking fire down her legs. His tongue edged higher, finding the hidden peak of sensation, and the fire raged out of control.

"Come for me," he urged thickly. "Give me your juice."

His tongue flickered like a flame. Hot, teasing. She squirmed as it stoked her desire higher and higher. Suddenly, he drew on her with fierce suction, and she cried out his name as ecstasy blazed through her.

Before the tremors faded, his mouth was on hers. Tasting herself in his kiss sent a shiver of shock through her. He licked her mouth as thoroughly, as masterfully, as he had her pussy, and, despite her recent climax, arousal rekindled in her.

He raised his head. His hot gaze studied her face, and, touching his thumb to her lower lip, he murmured, "Not done yet, sprite?"

"No, I am. That is, I just, um, *did*."

Her cheeks flushed as she contemplated how to answer his question. All Pretty Francie and the girls had said about a woman's pleasure was that it was a rare occurrence. Tessa knew what she'd just experienced with Bennett was wondrous and extraordinary; what confused her, however, was that, even with her recent release, she wouldn't mind...more?

"I know you came, sweeting." A smile entered Bennett's dark eyes. "I'm asking if you want to do it again."

She blinked. "Is that possible?"

The smile migrated to his lips. "For some women, yes. For you, absolutely."

"Does that mean I'm a wanton?" she said doubtfully.

Although, if being a wanton meant that she could enjoy that extraordinary pleasure over and over again...maybe she didn't mind being one.

"It means you're a sensual, passionate woman." Tenderly, he tucked a tress behind her ear. "And I'm a damned lucky fellow."

His words made her heart swell. They also reminded her of another pressing reality. A reality that was, in fact, pressing against her thigh like a bar of iron.

Summoning her courage, she said, "Bennett?"

"Yes, love?"

"Is there anything I ought to, um, do…for you?"

Her courage was rewarded by a look of pure male longing.

"Do you want to?" he asked intently.

"What's sauce for the goose." Humor struck her, and she couldn't resist adding, "Or, more apropos to the situation, what's sauce for the hen is sauce for the, um…cock?"

He stared at her. Then his shoulders rocked with laughter.

Rather pleased with herself, she said, "Will you show me what to do? How to please you?"

"You do please me, just by being you. But if you want to explore…"

"I do," she said, nodding eagerly.

"…then do to me what you liked me doing to you."

She thought about it. "But I liked everything."

His grin was slow, wolfish. "Then I'm even luckier than I realized."

A host of ideas crowded her brain, all of them bold, brazen.

Exciting.

"I want to see you," she blurted. "Without the dressing gown."

Rising to his knees, he shed the garment. At the sight of his brawny virility, her breath jammed in her throat. He was like a living, breathing Titan: powerfully honed, no excess flesh anywhere, just slabs of muscle rippling on his big frame.

Moonlight silvered the sinew twisting over his broad shoulders and bulging at his biceps. Whorls of dark hair covered his broad chest. The hair narrowed into a trail that drew her gaze downward toward his corrugated abdomen, the prominent vee of muscle that girdled his pelvis, the taut hollows of his hips. And there, hanging between his muscular thighs…

Zounds. He was huge…*everywhere*. His long, thick cock jutted out like a heavy branch.

She lifted dazed eyes to his. "You're beautiful."

His lips tipped up. "Men aren't beautiful, sweeting."

"You are," she said with feeling.

His eyes flared again, and the next instant he was atop her. His hard, warm, naked body pressed against hers for the first time, and she sighed at the heady pleasure. At the arousing contrast between them. She could lie there for hours, just feeling him, being close, skin to skin.

"You're soft as a kitten," he said huskily.

"You're *not*." Wonderingly, she ran her hands over his shoulders, the ropes of muscle shifting beneath the sleek skin. Feeling the pulsing heft of his erection against her belly, she wetted her lips and noticed how his gaze followed the movement. "You're hard...all over."

He bent his head, spreading her lips with his tongue, thrusting into her mouth. She drew eagerly on his offering, sucking it like a sweet, and his growl filled her throat. As they kissed, his body moved over hers, his hair-covered chest titillating the tips of her breasts, tingles shooting to her sex. She moaned as his rock-hard thigh wedged into her cove. He nudged deeper, and she could feel her dew slickening the friction.

"Devil and damn," he said in a guttural voice. "You're ready again."

Was she *ever*. But there was something else she wanted to do.

"Wait," she said breathlessly. "It's my turn to pleasure you."

"If you give me any more pleasure, I'll explode."

"That's the general idea, isn't it?"

She tasted his laughter when he kissed her again. Kissed her so hard and deep and long that she nearly forgot what she'd intended to do. Until he took her hand, dragging it down the granite-hard planes of his body to his manhood. Her breath caught as he wrapped her hand around his rampant arousal, her fingers barely circling the thick, heavy stalk.

"It's so big," she blurted. "How do you walk around with this?"

"It's not usually this way." Humor glinted in his eyes. "Unless I'm around you."

She liked that. Liked that she could arouse him. It made her feel feminine and powerful. Intrigued, she ran her fingertips up the rearing shaft, feeling the raised veins, the virile pulse. She swept her thumb over the wide tip, and satiny moisture seeped from the tiny hole at its center.

He folded her fingers firmly around his turgid shaft.

"Like this," he muttered.

They lay on their sides facing one another, and he taught her how to touch him. The pace and pressure he liked. How to squeeze the tip of his member and bring her fist all the way down to the root. The act of pleasuring him, of pumping his hard cock, feeling that supple slide of skin over the rigid core, made her dizzy with desire. He reached between her thighs, and she moaned as she felt herself drenching his fingers.

"Keep frigging me," he rasped. "I'll pet your pussy, and we'll see who comes first."

His wicked challenge set her aflame. She grasped his cock tighter, and it pulsed, a spurt of slickness easing the drag of her fist. Their mouths collided in a hot, hungry tangle of tongues. Her thighs tightened as she felt his long finger slide down her swollen cleft, circling the place where she ached to be filled.

"Please," she whimpered.

She felt him nudge deeper, deeper yet, and then his finger was inside her, and her muscles clenched on the unfamiliar yet exquisite sensation.

"Goddamn, you're small. Tight," he said hoarsely. "Does it hurt, love?"

"No," she moaned. "Do it *more*."

With a sound that was part-groan, part-laugh, he obliged. His finger thrust deeper and deeper, and she panted as the tension in her coiled tighter and tighter. Then his thumb circled her pearl as he simultaneously caressed some high, transcendent place inside, and she catapulted over pleasure's edge.

"So bloody *sweet*," he growled. "Ah, God, you're going to take me with you..."

His hand trapped hers against his cock. His hips surged upward, and, even floating and boneless, she realized how much he'd held back. Now he unleashed his passion, driving his huge erection into their combined grasp. With each powerful shove, her pussy clenched.

Then his mighty body tensed. His shaft burgeoned, straining the limits of her hold. With a groan that sounded like mountains moving, he climaxed. Her breath held as he shuddered, load after load of creamy heat shooting from his cock, splattering his lean belly and drenching her palm.

He collapsed onto his back, dragging her on top of him.

With her cheek pressed against his thundering heart, a thought occurred to her. She giggled.

"What's so amusing, sprite?" his voice rumbled.

She raised herself up to look into his sated eyes. "Since I came first, I *finally* beat you at something!"

His roar of laughter was her reward.

18

BENNETT WAS WAITING FOR HER OUTSIDE THE BREAKFAST ROOM at eight o' clock the next morning. Despite the fact that he'd gotten little sleep, he was the picture of male vitality. His dark hair gleamed, his strong jaw was freshly shaven. Dressed in his usual stark attire, he was wearing the boots she'd given him. He was beyond handsome, every inch a gentleman. And having felt every inch of that big, hard body against hers just a few hours ago, she felt a quiver in her belly.

"Good morning, Miss Todd. I trust you slept well?"

At the primal gleam behind his spectacles, which matched not at all with his polite enquiry, Tessa tried unsuccessfully to fight down a blush. "Quite well, thank you. And you?"

"Like the dead," he murmured. "'Twould seem that recent activities wore me out."

"I don't recall you lacking in stamina," she returned under her breath.

For her daring, she got a twitch of his lips. After teaching her how to pleasure him, he'd given her a third climax before sending her back to her room. In fact, he'd absorbed her senses so completely that she'd forgotten all about the hellfire until she was alone again. Which was why she'd sent a note this morning, letting him know she'd be down earlier than usual.

"We have to talk." Casting a glance down the empty hallway, she said in a hush, "About you-know-what."

Some of the humor faded from his eyes. She was learning to read his emotions better, and the deepening grooves around his mouth told her that he *had* discovered something.

"Bennett, you promised you would keep me apprised—"

The rattle of an approaching cart cut her off.

"Not here," Bennett muttered, opening the door. "We'll talk inside."

Entering, they were greeted by Jeffries, the butler, and Will, the first footman. Light streamed through the tall arched windows, gleaming off the silver domes on the sideboard. The place setting at the head of the table was untouched, an ironed newspaper next to it. Grandpapa had not yet come down to breakfast. She and Bennett could have a few moments of privacy... once she got rid of the servants.

She went to the sideboard. Lifting the domes, she released the delicious aromas of coddled eggs, bacon, deviled kidneys, kedgeree, and kippers. There was a selection of crusty rolls, pastries, and toasted bread as well, accompanied by an assortment of preserves.

Turning to the grey-haired butler, she gave her brightest smile. "Jeffries, I don't suppose Cook has any of her delicious lemon curd left? I have a craving for it this morning."

"I'll send William to fetch some." The butler nodded to the footman.

Once William was out of the room, she said, "I was noticing that *The Times* is on the table."

"Yes, miss. That has always been the master's preference."

"True, but just the other day, Grandpapa told me that he enjoys *Bell's Life* even more than *The Times*," she said innocently. "Wouldn't it be lovely to surprise him with this week's edition?"

"I'll procure a copy," the loyal retainer said at once. "That is, if you wouldn't mind…"

"I can manage on my own." She gave him a cheery wave.

After the butler departed, she turned to Bennett. His firm mouth was quivering.

She arched a brow. "What is so amusing?"

"You. The way your mind works." He shook his head. "And you wonder why I call you 'sprite'?"

In truth, she loved his pet name for her. Loved *him*, moreover. But she couldn't get distracted.

"We haven't much time. You were home earlier than expected last night. I take it you've made progress?"

He hesitated. "Yes."

"What have you discovered?" When still he paused, she prodded, "I've kept my end of the bargain, stayed at home and out of trouble. If you don't want me investigating on my own—"

"All right, all right. You win." His eyes gleamed. "Again."

She'd found a brooding Bennett attractive. A flirtatious one was downright devastating to her senses. Although his reference to her "victory" last night quickened her pulse, she kept her gaze determined and steady on his.

He sighed. "I've located a suspect. A man who I believe was connected to the inventor of the explosive. Tonight, I'm searching his house to look for any connection to the hellfire."

"Let me go with you," she said immediately.

"No." His jaw set. "It's too dangerous."

"Which is why you *need* me." Her concern for him made her rush on. "No one knows the stews better than I do. Why, think how I helped you escape that first night—"

"First of all, I won't be in the stews. Second, as I recall it, I was helping *you* to escape."

"Not the stews? Where does the blighter live—Mayfair?" Her facetiousness faded at Bennett's slight flinch. Blinking, she said, "The suspect lives in Mayfair? He's a *blue-blood*?"

"Devil take it." Bennett shoved a hand through his hair.

"Who is he? You promised—"

"I ought to have nicknamed you 'bulldog' instead of 'sprite'."

"'Sprite' is more flexible; 'bulldog' works less well for intimate moments." Instead of arguing, she switched tactics. "After everything we've shared, don't you trust me?"

"That's hardly playing fair."

"Please, Bennett." Because he seemed to be responding, she worked up the courage to say, "I care about you. I couldn't stand it if you came to harm because you were helping me."

He stilled. A panicked feeling came over her. She'd exposed too much, too soon. She was just beginning to win him over and now she'd scared him away with her talk of feelings...

"I'll tell you his name *if* you'll remember your vow to do as I say."

With trembling relief, she dipped her chin in answer.

"Sir Aloysius De Witt," Bennett clipped out. "He's a scientist, a member of the Royal Society."

She frowned. "Why would a man like that be involved with hellfire?"

"A title is no guarantee of character," he said stiffly.

"I know *that*. What I meant was why would a respected scientist make weapons for the underworld...oh." The reason hit her. "For money?"

"De Witt keeps up appearances, but I'd wager that's a good guess. I plan to dig deeper into his financial situation, but, first things first, tonight I'll search his house to look for evidence." Bennett pinned her with a stern look. "You will give me your word to stay home and not interfere."

In her heart, she knew what was right. What she had to do. Surreptitiously, her fingers crossed in the folds of her skirts.

"You have my word," she said.

Grandpapa's voice boomed from the hallway. "We're all set for the morrow?"

"Yes, sir." It was Ming's voice. "All dukes confirm."

Grandpapa came through the doorway, leaning on his cane, periwig in place. "Good. Now I want extra guards...Tessie." He caught sight of her by the sideboard. "You're up early, ain't you?"

"What's going on tomorrow?" Tessa said.

He tromped to his seat at the head of the table. "Can't a man 'ave 'is tea before being bombarded with questions?"

"I'll get your tea, Grandpapa."

Hurrying over, she sat next to him and reached for the pot. She made his tea the way he liked, with ample cream and two spoonfuls of sugar, a task she'd enjoyed doing since she was a girl. She bided her time while he blew on the hot beverage before tasting it.

"Good?" she said.

He grunted in answer. Slurped more tea. When he reached for the newspaper, however, she couldn't refrain any longer. "What's happening on the morrow?"

"God almighty." He scowled at her. "Can't a man enjoy 'is breakfast in peace?"

"You said you needed your tea, and you have it. Now what is going on? If you won't tell me, I'll ask Ming."

She looked to her grandfather's right-hand man, who stood a little way from the table, Bennett beside him. Ming's expression remained impassive, but his eyes rolled slightly upward, as if to say, *Do not drag me into this.*

"Ming's silent as the grave 'less I say so." Looking smug, Grandpapa shook out his newspaper.

"Fine. Then I shall simply keep asking you until you tell me," she said determinedly. "What's happening on the morrow?"

He drew his newspaper up higher.

She pulled down the top edge. "What are the dukes confirmed for?"

"Bloody 'ell, you're wrinkling the damned paper—"

She rose, palms flat on the table, her gaze locking with her grandfather's. "I'm a Black. What happens to this family happens to me. I'll ask again, and I'll keep on asking until you tell me: *What is going on?*"

"God's blood, all right! Quit your yappin'," her grandfather growled. "I'll tell you."

She tilted her head, waiting.

"I've called a meeting tomorrow at Nightingale's. Ming 'as identified three suspects—three o' the dukes—and I've invited them for a parley. Nothing to worry about."

Was he daft? How could she *not* worry? "You're going to be in a room with a bastard who tried to *kill* you."

"Gor, that wouldn't be the first time." Grandpapa gulped more tea, wiping his mouth with the back of his hand. "Wouldn't even be the first time this week."

"That is not amusing. What if something happens to you? In the past month alone, you've been shot at, your home attacked. You're not a c-cat, Grandpapa, you haven't got nine lives." To her horror, her voice quivered, heat rising behind her eyes. "I don't have a good feeling about this—"

"Ming'll arrange plenty o' protection." He set a strong, age-mottled hand over hers on the table. His signet ring, the seal of the House of Black and a symbol of its power, shone richly in the morning light. "Now 'ow many times 'ave I told you, missy? A true Black'll shed 'is blood afore 'e sheds a tear."

"If you'd let me, I would shed blood for you," she whispered. "I would stand by your side."

"I know that. Always said, you might not be o' my body, but you're o' my heart. And your job is to not strain the ol' ticker, eh?" He chucked her under the chin with the old, familiar affection. "Now you know I can't take you tomorrow. But know that you're with me, 'ere,"—he thumped a fist over his heart—"where'er I go."

She did know it. Knew the depth of his love for her, the love she returned with every fiber of her being. She might not be able to protect him, but she knew who could.

"Take Bennett with you tomorrow," she said. "For added protection."

She shifted her gaze to Bennett, who said, "I'd be glad to be of service, sir."

"For my peace of mind, Grandpapa," she pleaded, "please take Bennett."

"Fine, if you'll cork that gob o' yours," Grandpapa muttered.

Relief washed through her. "Consider me corked."

"But there's one condition."

Isn't there always? She suppressed a sigh and waited.

"Received an invitation from Ransom. 'E's throwing a masquerade in three days, and 'e wants you there. You'll go and without a fuss. And while you're there, you'll make a proper go o' it with 'Is Grace. Understand?"

She bit her lip, sliding a look at Bennett. His face betrayed little emotion, but she was reassured by the tensing of his wide shoulders.

He *did* care about her, he had to. He wouldn't make love to her the way he had if he didn't feel some affection toward her. He wouldn't say she was adorable and call her "sprite."

Their relationship was far from settled, but she knew they were making progress. One day, he would fall in love with her, the way she'd fallen in love with him. She trusted Bennett with all her heart: he wouldn't stand by and watch her be married off to the duke. No, he would sweep her off into the sunset, the same way Grandpapa had done with Grandmama. She and Bennett would have a love that would endure suffering and celebrate joy and never fail.

"We got a bargain, missy?" her grandfather demanded.

Beneath the table, her fingers crossed yet again.

"Yes, Grandpapa," she said.

19

Harry entered the De Witt townhouse.

He'd waited until the last light had winked off in the servants' quarters before picking the lock of the back entrance. His senses on high alert, he now traversed the dark cavern of the kitchen. At a rustling sound, he tensed...relaxing as vermin scurried past.

Taking the steps up to the ground floor, he followed the arterial corridor. As he passed the shadowy entertaining rooms, he took note of the furnishings, which looked expensive and new. A pianoforte dominated the music room, a chandelier dripping crystals above it.

His jaw clenched. It would be the perfect stage for Celeste: she would appear like an angel with her pale blonde hair aglow, her long, tapered fingers gliding across the keys. For an instant, he recalled watching her play, how besotted he'd been, how he'd have given anything for the favor of her smile, and humiliation twisted his gut.

Yet a more recent memory came to him. Tessa...wreaking havoc on the violin during her lesson this afternoon. How in God's name she'd managed to make the instrument sound like a cat in its death throes was beyond him. And, apparently, her hapless violin master.

As far as Harry was concerned, however, she had far more important skills. She was, for instance, a prodigy when it came to the love arts. The memory of her sweet passion stirred his blood. A lusty sprite, his Tessa was.

In truth, no other woman had ever aroused such desire in him, nor made him feel so desired in return. No other had made him laugh the way she did. No other had given him such light and warmth and asked for so little in return.

It made him want to offer her more. If not his heart, then at least his name. To do that, he first needed to get to the bottom of the hellfire.

He found De Witt's study at the end of the hall. Closing the door behind him, he lit a lamp, shadows flickering over the bookcases as he headed to the large desk. He scanned the leather blotter: a tray of writing implements, green glass paperweight, and stack of correspondence. Sifting through the mail, he paused at the cream and gilt card.

An invitation to the Duke of Ranelagh and Somerville's masquerade three days hence.

The De Witts were fixtures in Society, and it wouldn't be unusual for them to be rubbing shoulders with the *crème de la crème*. Yet finding a connection between Ransom and the suspect was an odd coincidence, one that didn't sit well in Harry's gut. For now, he tucked the fact away.

With the help of his picks, he bypassed the locks on the drawers and sorted through papers and ledgers. Nothing there. Frustrated, Harry shut the last notebook. He'd found naught of use, nothing to tie De Witt to the hellfire.

There has to be more. I know that cunning bastard is behind this. If I were him, where would I keep the evidence of my nefarious activities?

He surveyed the room for possible hiding places. Moving along the bookcase-lined wall, he removed volumes at random, rapping his knuckles against the wood. On his third try, a hollow resonance made his ears perk, his pulse accelerating. There was an empty space behind that bookcase—an antechamber, perhaps? But how to get in?

He pushed the bookshelf; it didn't budge. Some mechanism must be locking it in place. He examined it, inch by inch, and didn't find any hidden levers. From another room, a clock chimed midnight; he couldn't afford to dally. As he weighed the pros and cons of removing the barrier with a mild explosive (not subtle but effective), the door opened.

He pivoted, his hand plunging into his greatcoat pocket. He whipped out his pistol, aimed it at the figure emerging through the door.

"Don't shoot, Bennett," came the familiar, feminine voice. "It's me."

"*Tessa?*" He stared at her trouser-clad figure in disbelief. "What the devil are you doing here?"

"*Shh*, or you'll wake the house." Beneath her cap, her eyes were huge. "I'm here to help you."

"Goddamnit." His shock turned into pure rage. "You gave me your *word* that you'd stay put."

"I know I did, but I got so worried that I couldn't just sit there and wait. And I only intended to keep watch for you," she rushed on. "Then I saw suspicious characters lurking outside. Three of them, I counted, and they have the shifty look of Peel's Bloody Gang." Her mouth curled in disgust. "They're not in uniform, but you know how those spying bastards work. De Witt probably greased their palms to watch his lair."

If Harry wasn't so infuriated, he might have been impressed with her surveillance skills. She'd only missed on one point: it wasn't De Witt who was responsible for the watch, but Harry. Ambrose and his partners, Lugo and McLeod, were keeping a lookout for him. The three men had whistles that made a distinctive sound like a gull's call, and they were to sound a warning if the De Witts returned unexpectedly.

Harry hadn't heard any whistles going off, which meant that Tessa had somehow got by the seasoned investigators. And he couldn't tell her about Ambrose without revealing his own identity.

Leashing his anger, he bit out, "How did you get past them?"

"Child's play." She made no effort to appear modest. "I gave a crossing sweep a guinea to create a distraction. You know, the pretend-to-get-hit-by-a-carriage trick? Works every time. The Peelers were so busy helping the lad that I snuck right by them and into the house."

Bloody hell. Looking at her beaming face, he didn't know whether to shout at her for risking her neck or congratulate her for duping three experienced investigators. Since they were in the middle of breaking into a house, he could do neither, and his fury mounted to a dangerous degree.

There was a wriggling in her jacket. Swift Nick poked his head out to hiss at Harry.

She quickly pushed the ferret back into her pocket. "Hush, Swift Nick. We're in the middle of a break-in."

Harry breathed through his nose, his hands bracing his hips as he strove to control his temper.

She peered up at him through her lashes. "Are you, um, angry?"

With Herculean effort, he wrestled his emotions into place. Forced himself to focus on what he needed to do. He would deal with the lying chit in due course.

"We'll discuss that later," he said coldly. "Time is of essence. There's an antechamber behind that bookcase, and I'm trying to find the mechanism to open it."

Even in the dimness, he could see her eyes light up. "Let me have a look."

She dashed to the bookcase, repeating his earlier actions. "Hmm, there's no obvious switch."

"I know that." Impatiently, he surveyed the room. "It's likely hidden in the study somewhere."

"If it was me, I'd want it in a convenient place. The desk, perhaps?" She trotted over, started rifling through the stack of papers. Brows lifted, she held up the invitation he'd seen earlier. "The De Witts move in Ransom's circles?"

"Apparently," he said. "Leave everything as you found it. We don't want to raise suspicions."

"That's a pretty paperweight. Is that a real flower in it?" Blithely ignoring his instructions, she reached for the green glass.

"I said don't..." He paused, seeing the line between her brows. "What's the matter?"

"The paperweight. It won't move." She frowned, tugging at the object. "Maybe if I..."

She twisted, and an audible click came from the direction of the bookcase.

"Crikey," she breathed.

Harry was already striding to the bookcase. Placing his hands on its side, he pushed, and this time it moved easily. It slid along the wall, revealing an entryway into gaping darkness.

Tessa was by his side in a heartbeat, lamp in hand.

He took it from her. "Stay behind me."

She gave an avid nod.

He led the way, and, as the circle of light fell, the hairs on his nape rose. The small chamber was a replica of his laboratory at Cambridge. The lamp's flame gleamed off glass vessels, burners, and metal implements, each step he took bringing him closer to the past. As a numbing chill spread through him, his mind turned as clear as ice.

"Is this where the rotter is making the hellfire?" Tessa whispered.

"I doubt it. Even De Witt wouldn't be so foolish as to risk

blowing up his own house. At most, he's conducting preliminary experiments here." Harry stopped at a table lined with stoppered flasks. As a precaution, he handed Tessa the lamp. "Keep the flame at a distance."

Eyes huge, she took a step back. He lifted the first flask. It was filled with a clear, colorless liquid. He uncorked it and wafted the scent toward his nose. He knew the acrid, suffocating scent: the smell of destruction and failure.

"What is it?" she asked.

"Nitric acid."

She peered at it warily. "Is it explosive?"

"Not on its own." When she looked relieved, he said, "It is highly corrosive, however, and, more to the point, an agent that can cause other flammable substances to combust. It plays a similar role to that of saltpeter in gunpowder."

She chewed on her lip. "So if the nitric acid were combined with a flammable substance, it could make the hellfire?"

He nodded, setting down the flask and picking up another. This one was also filled with a clear liquid, one with an oily viscosity. He knew what it was; he confirmed it anyway.

Tessa wrinkled her nose at the released odor, like that of rotted eggs. "Is that oil of vitriol?"

He gave a tight nod. "Also known as sulphuric acid. It acts as a catalyst, enhances the effect of the nitric acid. All you need is a source of fuel..." He pulled open a drawer. "And here it is."

She stared at the folded linens. "*Towels* are the principle ingredient of hellfire?"

"Soaked in a solution of nitric and sulphuric acids, the cotton becomes highly combustible. All you would need is a spark and —boom."

And he would know, he thought grimly. One fateful night back at Cambridge, he'd been heating a mixture of the two acids when the flask shattered. He'd grabbed the nearest cloth, a cotton apron, using it to wipe up the mess. He'd hung the apron up to dry by the fire, and a minute later, *whoosh*. Before his startled eyes, it had gone up in flames.

His accidental discovery had opened a new door of experimentation. That door had been shut when De Witt stole his invention and discredited him. Disgraced him so that he was no longer welcome in the scientific community.

"Didn't you say the compound was unstable? If so, how is De Witt producing and storing it?"

A good question. One that Harry still didn't have the answer to.

"He's making the hellfire somewhere," he said darkly, "and I have to find that factory, see it with my own eyes. As of now, we have no proof of anything. De Witt could claim he's just running a few experiments—"

He cut short as a shrill, bird-like call sounded in the distance. Ambrose's warning signal.

"Damn it, they're back."

She frowned. "I don't hear anyone."

"We have to go. *Now*." Closing the drawer, he pulled her out of the laboratory and back into the study. He pushed the bookcase back as the whistle sounded again. Tessa hurriedly twisted the paperweight back into its original position, locking the door in place.

Together, they dashed out of the study. In the hallway, Harry heard someone coming up the front steps. At the same time, the wood-soled tread of a servant's shoes sounded inside the house, heading towards the entrance hall. Hinges squeaked as the front door opened. Harry pressed against the wall, concealing himself in the shadows, motioning for Tessa to do the same behind him.

"How was your evening, Miss De Witt?" a man's voice said.

"A bore. Have some warmed milk sent up to my chamber." Celeste De Witt's voice hadn't changed, was still as musical as silver bells, but now the sound stirred not delight in Harry but seething anger. "I need it after all that palavering."

The servant murmured a reply. Footsteps sounded again, Celeste's light ones up the staircase, the other's down toward the kitchen.

"We'll have to make a run for it out the front door."

Tessa's urgent whisper snapped Harry back to reality. He took her hand, and they crept stealthily to the entrance hall. Seeing no one, they exited the main door and were halfway down the street when a sleek carriage rolled up.

The door opened, revealing Ambrose's urgent expression. Without a word, he grabbed Tessa by the arm, Harry boosting her into the carriage from behind. Harry had an instant to glimpse her shocked expression before he jumped in after her.

20

Tessa landed with a thump, plush seat cushions breaking the impact. In the next instant, she reached into her boot, her fingers closing around the cloisonné handle of her dagger. She whipped it out, taking aim at the grim-faced policeman on the opposite bench.

She let it fly, nailing his hat to the carriage wall.

"Next one is through the heart, Peeler," she spat. "Let us go."

In reply, the Peeler's dark brows inched up. "A 'nice young lady,' you said?"

The odd words were made even odder by the fact that they were directed at Bennett.

"She has her moments," Bennett said shortly.

Another look was exchanged between the men.

"You two know one another?" she burst out.

"Put away the damned daggers," Bennett said. "This is my brother."

"Your *brother?*"

She'd had no idea that he had siblings. She realized she knew little about him other than the fact that he had worked as a navvy, was good at just about everything, and could make her feel swoony just by smiling (or even scowling, which was what he presently was doing).

With a yank, Bennett's brother freed her dagger and his hat. He passed the former back to her, and, a bit abashed, she took it and stowed it back into her boot. When Bennett made no move to introduce her, she did it herself.

"Pardon the misunderstanding, sir. I'm Tessa Todd," she said politely. "Bennett never mentioned you to me before."

"I don't imagine he has." Strangely, Bennett's brother didn't elaborate.

"This is my brother Ambrose," Bennett said in curt tones. "He was keeping a lookout for me."

Drat. She'd unknowingly pulled the wool...over *Bennett's brother's* eyes.

Determined to make a good first impression, or at least improve the bad one she'd made, she said penitently, "I'm very sorry about the mix up, Mr. Bennett. I hope you'll forgive the, um, decoy involving the crossing sweep. I thought you were a Peeler, you see, and I was worried about Bennett. I used the ruse to get past you so that I could warn him."

"Did you now?" The carriage lamp revealed that Ambrose Bennett's eyes were a golden color and that they were regarding her acutely. "How singular."

She was relieved to hear curiosity, rather than disdain, in the man's deep voice. Now that she had a chance to examine him, she could see a likeness between the brothers.

Both were tall, lean, and starkly handsome (her Bennett was, of course, the handsomer of the two). Both also had an aura of trustworthiness: big men who made one feel protected rather than intimidated. She guessed that Ambrose had some two decades on his brother, the veins of silver in his dark hair adding to his distinguished aspect.

"Singular, that's me." Belatedly, she realized that her cap had fallen to the carriage seat, and her hair was tumbling pell-mell down her shoulders, "On top of tricking you and ruining your hat, I hope you'll also pardon my appearance."

"There's naught to pardon." A hint of a smile was in Ambrose Bennett's eyes, making him almost as handsome as his brother. "But may I ask...what is that moving in your pocket?"

"Oh. That's Swift Nick Nevison." She unbuttoned the flap, and the ferret bounded out onto the carriage seat, nose twitching and eyes blinking in his furry mask.

"Say hello to Bennett's brother," she told him.

Swift Nick raised his head, lowering it in a distinct nod.

A muffled sound came from Ambrose. "You brought a ferret... to a break-in..."

"If we're done with the circus tricks," Bennett said cuttingly, "I need to speak with Miss Todd."

The chill in his tone snaked down her spine. His gaze was unreadable, his old armor in place. Her fingernails bit into her palms.

"I'll leave you two to it," Ambrose said soberly. "My partners are following behind and will convey me to my residence." So saying, he opened the window, instructing the driver to stop.

He got out, and Bennett said to him, "I'll be in touch."

"Will do. Miss Todd?"

She tore her anxious gaze from Bennett to look at the other man. "Yes?"

"It was a pleasure to meet you," Ambrose Bennett said gently.

To her surprise, he took her cold hand in his gloved one and kissed it. He gave her a slight squeeze before letting go, communicating something that she didn't quite understand. Something that was, nonetheless, oddly comforting.

The conveyance started off again. Swift Nick, clearly bored with the domestic drama, scooted to an unoccupied corner, curled up, and fell asleep.

"You lied to me," Bennett said.

Though calm, his words struck her with the concentrated force of bullets. He'd moved to the bench vacated by his brother, and his blank expression made her reel.

And blurt the first stupid thing that entered her head.

"I crossed my fingers when I made that promise."

"Pardon, I didn't realize," he said with scathing sarcasm. "That makes lying all right then."

"No, it doesn't." Swallowing, she tried to explain. "I'm sorry I went back on my word, but you left me no choice—"

"This is my fault, is it? Of course it is." Bitterness infused his voice. "Why should you take the responsibility for your wrongdoing, your bloody *lies*, when I'm here as the convenient dupe?"

Despite her anxiety, something in his words struck her as strange...and unfair.

"I'm not blaming you," she said quietly. "The responsibility is mine. I decided to break my promise and come tonight."

"Yes, you did." A muscle ticked along his jaw. "I gave you my trust, and you showed me, without a doubt, that you are not deserving of it."

Although she flinched at his harsh words, she did not back down. She couldn't. She had resolved to win Bennett's favor, yes, but not by altering the essence of who she was.

Moreover, she'd believed that he was the one man who wouldn't ask it of her. Who'd seen something special, of value, in her. Had she been wrong?

"Perhaps it is you who is not deserving of my trust," she said.

His brows slammed together. "The devil you say."

"While I did break my word, I did so because you gave me no other choice." She lifted her chin. "You wouldn't listen to me. Wouldn't even consider that I might be of use to the mission, that I might contribute something which, by the by, I *did* seeing as I got us into the laboratory."

"At what risk?" he ground out. "Christ, Tessa, you were

traipsing alone at night, breaking into a house. Anything could have happened to you!"

"So you're angry," she interrupted, "because you were worried for my safety?"

"I'm angry because you *betrayed* my trust," he snarled.

At least his controlled calmness was gone. She was no good at battling sarcasm and subtle attacks (which was why she'd been thoroughly trounced by the debs at Southbridge's). But she *excelled* at direct combat because she never backed down.

"You betrayed my trust too," she shot back.

"That's shite."

"It's not shite! It's the truth."

"How?" he clipped out. "How did I betray you?"

She was working herself into a fine rage, and she didn't care. "By not believing in me. By treating me like all the men in my life do: like I am nothing more than a nuisance!"

"If you stopped acting like one, you wouldn't be treated like one," he said acidly.

That was *it*. She could take no more. All the hurts of a lifetime came rushing to the fore, blasting her composure to smithereens.

"Do you think I *want* to have to break my word? I state my reasoning, but *no one* listens to me. Not my father, grandfather, and not you. No one gives a damn what I think and feel. No one sees me for who I am. *Me*, Tessa." She jabbed a finger at herself. "A woman, yes, but one who has a mind and heart of her own. Who cannot just stand by and twiddle her thumbs while the man she loves heads into danger alone. Do you *know* what it's like fretting over your safety? When I have no idea where you are or what you're doing or what peril you might be facing—*oof*."

Her words were lost as Bennett hooked her around the waist with one arm, yanking her forward. Stunned, she found herself on his lap. His arms tightened like steel bands around her.

"What on earth?" she sputtered.

"Be quiet," he said.

Oh no, he didn't. "Do *not* tell me to be quiet—"

"Fine. But if you keep talking, you'll miss my apology."

She quieted. Stared at him.

His expression was still taut, tense, but his eyes...they were no longer shuttered. Emotion glittered in them like raw diamonds trapped in rock. Her breath held.

"You're not a nuisance," he said roughly. "The reason I'm keeping you out of this is because I don't want you to get hurt. I want to protect you."

"And I want to protect you." Since she'd shown her cards, she might as well double down. The truth flowed molten in her veins; there was no holding it back. "I've fallen in love with you, Bennett," she said with calm conviction. "I don't expect you to return those feelings, and it's all right that you don't. Truly. My love is a gift. But I'm telling you how I feel because that is why I broke my promise tonight. Because I cannot watch the man I love go into battle alone. I am not that woman. And I'll never be."

"Tessa—"

She had to finish this before she lost courage. "It was my mistake to try to be other than who I am. You see, I thought if I could be more pleasing, more biddable, more in the usual mold, you might...like me." Although embarrassment scorched her cheeks, she held his gaze. "But the truth is I'll always be me. I'm sorry I betrayed your trust, but I can't betray myself either. If that means that you no longer wish to continue our...affair,"—she forced herself to go on—"then so be it."

She was trembling from head to toe. Heat pressed behind her eyeballs; somehow, she found the strength to hold them back. To hold onto the pieces of herself that might fly apart if she didn't.

"You will never be in the usual mold, Tessa."

His blunt words hit her like a mallet. Pain spread through her like a crack in porcelain, and she could feel the tears welling. She struggled to free herself from his hold, yet his arms trapped her.

"Let me go," she said in a muffled voice.

"I can't," he murmured in her ear, "though God knows I've tried. I *do* like you, sprite, precisely because you're different and rare. I've never met anyone like you, and I know that if I wandered this earth for fifty years more, I still never would."

The words sunk in.

She tipped her head back to look at him, breathing, "You like me? Truly?"

"Christ." Tenderly, he thumbed away a tear that slipped free. "How could you not know that?"

"I know you like me in a ph-physical sense," she stammered, "but I wasn't sure about the rest. After all, I played those tricks on you. And flirted with the duke. And tonight you said I wasn't deserving of your trust, made you a dupe—"

"Sweeting, I don't like you putting yourself in danger. I was angry, and, out of that anger, I spoke unfairly." He hesitated. "I've been lied to before, and I don't react well to it."

His words rang a bell. That night in the billiards room, he'd also mentioned his anger being triggered by something that had happened in his past.

Tentatively, she said, "Who lied to you?"

When he remained silent, she said in a rush, "I don't mean to pry. Well, I do, I suppose, but only because I want to understand you. So I can do better," she said earnestly. "*Be* better."

"You don't need to be anything but you, Tessa. I'm the one who needs to do better."

His words were a balm to her hurts.

"You don't need to be anything but you either," she said softly. "Although if you wish to talk about it…I'm listening."

Just when she thought he wouldn't take her up on the offer, he spoke.

"I courted a woman once. I was in love with her, and she led me to believe she returned those feelings. I trusted her, wanted to marry her, but she betrayed my trust," he said flatly. "She'd never had any intention of marrying me, and by the time I realized she was using me as a means to an end, she'd destroyed my good name and the future I'd planned."

Tessa's head whirled. Bennett had never been a disclosing sort, and his revelations only raised more questions.

"You loved her?" she burst out.

"Yes."

Beneath her bottom, Tessa felt his muscled thighs quiver like that of a stallion readying to bolt, and she asked in a rush, "Do you still love her?"

Bennett stared at her. "Bloody hell, no."

Relief percolated through her. At least he wasn't carrying a torch for this mystery woman.

"I'm glad. Because she doesn't deserve your love," she said frankly. "Any woman who'd relinquish your heart is a feather-wit."

He tipped her chin up, looked into her eyes.

"You really believe that," he murmured.

She nodded. "If you were to give me such a gift, I would never let it go."

"Tessa...I don't want to lie to you." His voice was raw. "I don't think I can open my heart that way again. That I could love that way again."

"Oh," she said faintly. What else could she say?

"I want you, I like you, and, God willing, when this mess is over, I'll do the honorable thing by you, if you'll have me." His gaze was steady. "I would be faithful, committed to your happiness. And I'd lay down my life to protect yours. That is what I can promise you."

Her heart thumped at Bennett's proposal. While she might not have his love, she'd have his passion and devotion. How many women had that from their husbands?

Optimism burgeoned alongside joy. Bennett wanted to marry her. He liked her *as she was*.

I'll earn his trust. Determination filled her. *One day, he'll put his heart in my safekeeping.*

"I'll have you," she whispered.

His eyes darkened with hunger and other emotions she couldn't name.

He growled, "Then you're mine."

21

SHOVING HIS SPECTACLES INTO HIS POCKET, HARRY CLAIMED Tessa's mouth. Tessa, being Tessa, kissed him back with a generous ardor that lay waste to his brain.

The fact that he was concealing his identity, that he had no idea how he would convince Tessa to marry him once he told her the truth (and never mind how her grandfather was going to react), that he wished he could offer her more than what he had... all worries were incinerated by the passion of their kiss.

There was only now. How sweet she tasted. How soft she was.

How perfectly her pert bottom nestled against his bulging cock.

For once, he was glad that she was dressed like a lad for it gave him easier access to what he wanted. What he craved. He tore off her jacket and cravat, burying his face in her neck, nuzzling the downy curve while his hand roved beneath the hem of her shirt. His palm covered one soft breast, his fingers playing with the budded tip, and she whimpered.

"You're so sensitive," he murmured. "I'd wager I could bring you to climax just by petting your breasts."

"I'd put money on it," she gasped.

His lips twitched at her candor. At the same time, guilt stabbed him at his mistreatment of her. His knee-jerk reaction had been wholly unfair; of the two of them, who was doing the true deceiving? Worse yet, he'd compared her with Celeste. Tessa had broken her word, true, but not to manipulate or hurt him. Her motivations had been pure, born out of loyalty and...love.

I've fallen in love with you, Bennett.

God, he didn't deserve it. Didn't deserve her.

And he bloody *longed* for the day when he could hear her call him by his real name. Still, he had her in his arms, and he wasn't about to let opportunity go to waste. He pushed her shirt up; in the dim light, her skin gleamed like the finest alabaster. Her nipples were tight, beckoning rosebuds, and he leaned to suckle them.

Her hands clenched in his hair as he laved her eager tips. A minute later, she was panting, squirming in his lap. A minute and a half later, he unfastened her trousers, shoved his hand inside—and groaned at how ready she was. He slid a finger through her wet petals, finding and diddling her slick bud, and, a minute after that, she came.

He swallowed her cries, her shivers tightening his stones.

Staring at her pretty, flushed face, he reckoned Ambrose's driver could circle a while longer. It was worth the risk to make Tessa come again for him, and, besides, it wouldn't take long. For his sprite was as generous in her passion as she was in everything else. She gave him everything and held nothing back.

The thought made him randier than hell. He kissed the corner of her plump, decadent mouth. "Ready for another go, sweeting?"

Even though he knew the answer, when she whispered, "Oh, yes," in the sultry voice of a woman who's been thoroughly pleasured, he thought he might explode on the spot.

But he'd rather do that with his mouth between her legs, her sweet juice on his tongue.

"Lie back, love," he instructed.

He lifted her from his lap, intending to lie her across the bench, but she wriggled out of his reach.

"I don't want to," she said firmly.

Not that he was surprised...but he was surprised. "Well. All right, I'll tell the driver to—"

He broke off as she tossed her jacket onto the carriage floor by his boots. In a graceful movement, she went to kneel on top of the garment, making room for herself between his thighs. When her fingers started working on the placket of his trousers, he found his voice.

"Er, what are you doing?" He had his suspicions, and the very notion made his erection swell so fiercely that it threatened to pop off the buttons she was busily undoing.

"I don't want to lie back. Last time, you said I could do to you what I liked you doing to me. And that's what I want to do."

Ah, Christ. Paralyzed by lust, he watched as she took hold of his cock. He was so burgeoned that her fingers scarcely fit around the girth, so sensitive that he could feel the pulsing of the raised veins beneath her fingers. Gently prying the erect beast from his belly, she looked up at him, the naughty gleam in her eyes straight out of his fantasies.

"I like touching you," she said and proved it by running her fist from root to tip.

"I like your touch." *Understatement of the century.*

"Am I doing this right?" Her mouth had a teasing curve. "I'm trying to recall the lesson you gave me last time, Professor."

Hell, did she know that she'd just tapped into his erotic fantasy of her? Of taming his wicked minx, channeling her energy toward more pleasurable ends? With past lovers, he'd experienced varying degrees of intimacy, but never anything like this. Never this combination of lust, humor, and tenderness. Never this desire to prolong the lovemaking so that he could...play.

"You're doing very well," he allowed. "But you could tighten your fist, stroke me harder."

"Like this?" Her saucy pout nearly undid him, as did her firmer grip. "But you're so big I can hardly get my fingers around you."

"Then use both hands, sprite."

She obeyed, and watching her dainty fingers pump his rod was like being tortured on a rack of pleasure. Then she leaned closer, her lips just inches from his prick, and his breath held. Devil and damn, she wouldn't consider...?

"You used more than your hands on me." Her breath puffed against his turgid flesh, and he gripped the cushions as he strove to stay in control. "Shall I do the same?"

Hell, yes.

"Only if you want to, sweeting," he managed.

Her answer was to place the sweetest, gentlest kiss on the tip of his cock.

His reply was to leak a bead of seed.

She paused...then *licked* it off.

The feel of her lapping him, the sight of her between his legs, her pink tongue circling his engorged crown, tore a groan from his chest. Her delicate licks tautened his muscles, pushing harsh breaths from his lungs. With her inexperience, she kept him on the razor's edge, providing enough sensation to drive him wild, not enough to make him spend. With a flash of humor, he recognized that, even in this, she had a special affinity for testing the limits of his control.

Mid-lick, she peered up at him. "Am I doing this right?"

"You've a native talent, love." He hid a grin at the way she beamed, looking supremely proud of herself. "But perhaps a few pointers would not be amiss?"

"Fire away, Professor."

God, he *loved* her cheeky ways.

He spent a moment contemplating how to convey the essential information. It was a unique situation. With a wench or worldly lover, he'd never had to broach the topic of how to give fellatio. With a lady, he wouldn't try. But Tessa was both eager and innocent, and he wanted to do this properly. Wanted her to have a positive introduction to this carnal delight. Wanted to be the one and only man to give it to her.

"Remember those lemon drops I brought you?" He tucked a wayward tress behind her ear. "How you enjoyed them, savored them?"

Her head tipped to one side. "Yes."

"Pretend I'm a lemon drop."

Her curly lashes swept up. Even in the dimness, he saw understanding and excitement light her eyes. "You mean I should do it...like this?"

He groaned as her mouth engulfed his glistening dome.

"Yes, sprite, suck me. As much of me as you...*goddamn*." His neck arched in bliss.

When she had a mind to obey, she *excelled* at it. With her fingers wrapped around the root, she took the rest of his cock into her wet, hot hole. She drew on him tentatively at first, then with increasing confidence, the eager pulls making fire race up his spine.

He reveled in the decadence of having her thus: between his legs, her hair spilling over his thighs, her lovely mouth working his prick with determined ardor. Reaching out, he cupped her cheek, and feeling his hard shaft moving inside that downy curve was nearly his undoing. In the next instant, he dragged her up so that she straddled his lap.

"I wasn't finished," she said.

Her pout was so endearing that he couldn't help but kiss her. The taste of his own salt on her lips was another blow to his already shaky self-discipline.

"I'm too close, love," he told her. "A gentleman doesn't finish in a lady's mouth."

"Oh." A line worked between her fine brows. "But didn't I, um, finish...in yours?"

Bloody hell. It was too much. She overwhelmed him.

He shoved his hand down her opened trousers to find her pussy swollen, dripping for him. He thrust his middle finger into her snug sheath.

Her spine arched, her hands clutching his shoulders. "*Bennett.*"

"Ride my finger," he ordered. "Up and down. Take me deep into that sweet cunny of yours."

Her hips bucked at his words. He hissed out a breath as she sank deeper, taking him to the knuckle, surrounding him with her tight, humid heat. When she rose, her sheath clutched at him as if it wanted more, so he gave it to her. Eased two fingers into her on the next pass and searched out her nubbin with his thumb.

"Zounds," she moaned, "it's too much..."

"You can take it," he growled.

And he was right because not two seconds later, she was riding him. Bouncing on his fingers with a wanton exuberance that made his blood sing. His palm slapped against her wet petals, his thumb diddling her pearl, and with his free hand he fisted his cock. Feeling the lush squeeze of her pussy, imagining his prick was buried where his fingers were, he could hold back no more.

"Kiss me, Tessa," he grated out.

She crushed her lips to his, her hips slamming down at the same time that he thrust his fingers deep, hard, curling them to reach that special spot. She stiffened as if electrified. He drank in her sounds of fulfillment, the milking spasms of her pussy decimating his self-control. The pressure in his bollocks surged as he jerked his cock fiercely, steam boiling up his shaft. He groaned into her mouth as he exploded, his seed a hot geyser against his palm.

She sagged against him like a rag doll. With no little regret, he pulled out of her clinging sweetness. He neatened them both up as best he could. With the musk of their intimacy lingering in the air, he wrapped his arms around her and held her as the carriage rolled on.

"Bennett?" Her voice was drowsy.

"Hmm, sweeting?"

"In case I forgot to mention it, I like being yours."

His chest tightened. As usual, he struggled to put into words what he felt.

He settled for, "Good, because you are."

It wasn't much, but she snuggled deeper into him. A minute later, she was asleep.

He directed the driver to take them toward home. As the carriage swayed in the darkness, he still couldn't put it into words, but he knew. Knew in his bones that everything had changed.

22

THE NEXT MORNING, HARRY PASSED BENEATH COOING PIGEONS perched on a sign that read "Will Nightingale's Coffee House." He, Ming, and a coterie of armed guards made up Black's entourage for the meeting with the dukes today. As he entered Black's stronghold, he had a sense of traveling back in time. Coffeehouses had had their heyday several decades back, and the interior of this one, while well-kept, belonged in the prior century.

Shaved wood floors softened the thump of booted feet, the walls paneled in dark wood. Trophies of the hunt were mounted here and there, staring out with glassy eyes. Next to those worn heads, watercolors provided a discordant note, and the sight of them made Harry's lips quirk. He had no doubt who was responsible for the cheerful slaughtering of paint and paper.

Egad, but his sprite lacked the usual graces.

Yet if he had to choose between a wife who could paint a pretty scene and one who made love the way Tessa did, with such sweet, generous abandon...so much for art. Memories of their steamy carriage interlude fogged his brain before he pushed them aside. He couldn't be fantasizing about Tessa while he dealt with a bunch of cutthroats, one of them being her grandfather.

The proprietor bowed low before Black, assuring him that his usual table was ready. Harry followed the cutthroat past long tables crammed with customers who fell into a deferential hush as they passed. One fellow rose, sweeping off his cap, stammering thanks to Black for finding him employ, and the king gave a regal nod as he continued on his way.

Black's table turned out to be a massive oak trestle set in a secluded alcove. Red velvet drapes were tied back and could be drawn to afford additional privacy. There were eight seats in all, and Black took the carved, throne-like chair at the head.

As usual, Ming stationed himself behind his master. Harry went to stand beside him but was stopped by Black's curt command.

"Bennett, sit there." The cutthroat jabbed a finger at the seat to his right. "Want to talk to you before the others arrive."

Harry looked to Ming, whose slightly raised eyebrows were the equivalent of a surprised exclamation from another man. Warily, Harry folded his long frame into the appointed chair. For long moments, Black aimed a brooding stare at him, his beringed fingers drumming on the table. A serving boy dashed forward with a silver pot, filling their cups with steaming, pitch-dark brew.

Black took his time doctoring his coffee with cream and sugar. As the silence stretched, so did Harry's nerves. Black's manner made him uneasy.

His intuition came to bear when Black declared, "What's your secret, Bennett?"

Bloody hell, does Black know about me and Tessa? Cold sweat prickled his palms. *Or did he discover my connection to the police force?*

"Er, what secret, sir?" he managed.

"Your secret," the cutthroat said impatiently, "for managing my Tessie. I've 'ired more bodyguards than the chit's got years, and not one o' 'em could 'andle 'er. Yet since you've been around, she's been as docile as a lamb."

Relief tumbled through Harry. At the same time, his brows lifted. If Black would describe Tessa's behavior in the past fortnight as docile, what had she been like *before?*

"Told you she 'ad spirit, didn't I?" Black countered, clearly reading his mind. "Yet there she was at breakfast, all smiles and biddable as you please. Told me the dressmaker's coming around today, and she's gettin' measured up for 'er costume for Ransom's masquerade. She didn't give me no lip about that or pester me about coming 'ere either." The cutthroat harrumphed. "Worked a bloody miracle, you 'ave."

Harry thought it prudent not to share how he'd brought about Tessa's dreamy-eyed, glowing acquiescence. As for the dressmaker, he knew she was going along with it because of the bargain she'd struck with her grandfather. She wanted Black to have Harry's protection, and her loyalty and love overrode everything else.

He suspected there was one additional motivation for her attending the masquerade: the invitation she'd found at De Witt's. Harry had lectured her not to approach the De Witts if they showed up, and her ready agreement hadn't been at all convincing. One more thing he'd have to keep an eye on. Luckily, the event would be a masquerade, allowing him to attend incognito.

"I've worked no miracles," he said carefully. "She's an exceptional young lady."

"Exceptional is one way o' putting it." Black slurped his coffee. "Must say I don't mind 'aving someone else deal with 'er antics."

"Miss Todd means well. She's loyal and wants to do her family proud." The words left him before he could think twice.

Black's eyes narrowed. "Know my granddaughter well, do you?"

Including in a biblical sense. "I know she has many fine qualities."

"That she does. Now, Bennett, a gel like that, she's worth protecting, ain't she?"

"Yes, sir."

"And, when the time comes, if I can't be there, I can count on you to take care o' 'er?"

He frowned. "Why wouldn't you be there?"

"Ain't saying I won't, but got to plan for hypotheticals." Black leaned forward, his voice low, strangely pressured. "After 'ow you 'andled the 'ellfire attack, I know I can trust you. If the need arises, I want you to keep Tessie safe. You got a place to stow 'er?"

"Pardon?" Chilly premonition gripped his nape.

"If anything were to 'appen to me, you got a safe place you can take 'er? Beyond London. Somewhere my enemies wouldn't know to go."

Harry immediately thought of Chudleigh Crest, the sleepy village in Berkshire where he and his siblings had grown up. "Yes, I know a place."

"Keep it to yourself. Tell no one, not even me. And if the day comes when you need to take Tessie there,"—urgency blazed in Black's gaze—"you go and await instruction. Understand?"

"Yes." He didn't know what else to say. He would protect Tessa with his life.

"Good." Black leaned back, his expression wiping clean. "Company's arrived."

Harry rose as the newcomers approached. Their respective guards stopped several yards from the table, forming a wall between the alcove and the rest of the coffee shop. Harry recognized Malcolm Todd's scowling face, but the other three men were strangers.

The ginger-haired one stepped forward and bowed. He was a large man with a greying auburn beard. He'd gone soft in the middle with age, and Harry had seen his sly, currant-like eyes before...in the face of Dewey O'Toole.

"Top o' the morning to you, Black," the man said with false cheer.

"And to you, O'Toole." Black looked over the man's shoulder. "Where's your boy? I thought he was learning the ropes."

"Dewey ain't one for mornings. You know the younger generation," O'Toole said easily.

"I know that if the younger generation were to spend less time rabble rousing and more time earning their keep, they'd save us all a world o' trouble."

O'Toole's smile wavered, but he managed to keep it in place.

Black waved him into the seat to his left and greeted the next in line.

"Severin Knight," he said. "Been a dog's age."

"Mr. Black." Knight's polished accent was at odds with his rough-hewn features and burly frame. His rather exquisite silk cravat was offset by his swarthy skin. "Pardon if I haven't paid my respects of late. Business has been occupying my attention."

"You ain't the only one. 'Ave a seat so we can get down to it."

Knight inclined his dark head, seating himself beside O'Toole.

The last stranger came forward. Even if the process of elimination hadn't verified his identity, Harry could guess who the man was from his sisters' description of their friend's husband. They'd said that Adam Garrity was a fastidious man whose good looks were diminished by his ruthless, cold-blooded aura; as usual, they were spot on.

Garrity was not the tallest, burliest, or loudest of the group, yet intangible power emanated from his lean and subtly honed frame. His eyes were hard onyx, his brows black slashes, his cheekbones blade-sharp beneath his pale skin. When he inclined his head, not a single strand of ebony hair fell out of place.

"Thank you for coming, Garrity," Black said.

"My pleasure." Garrity's gaze flicked to Harry, and Harry felt his muscles constrict beneath that piercing stare. "New man?"

"Can't 'ave too much protection these days," Black said.

"Indeed." Garrity proceeded to the chair at the opposite end of the table.

As everyone took a seat, Malcolm Todd's beady eyes roved over the remaining chairs. Apparently finding none of them satisfactory, he went over to Harry, who was to Black's right.

"Take your place by the Chinaman," Todd snapped.

"Bennett ain't going nowhere," Black said. "Sit your arse down in another chair."

Todd's angry gaze burned into Harry, yet he obeyed his father-in-law's command. Remaining in the contested seat, Harry felt the assessing stares of the other men. Something significant was happening, although he didn't know what.

Serving boys arrived to fill cups with coffee and lay out a collation of meat, cheese, and pastries. When they left, Black nodded to his guards, who drew the red velvet curtains, shrouding them in privacy.

"Ain't going to beat around the bush. This ain't a social call," Black said.

"Reckoned your summons made that clear." O'Toole dunked a biscuit into his beverage. "What's this about then, eh?"

"There's a rat in our midst," Black said. "It needs to be exterminated."

If Harry had wondered what tactic Black would take, he now knew. The straight talk caused glances to shift around the table, expressions instantly wary.

"Surely you don't mean at this table," O'Toole began.

"That's precisely what I mean. All o' you know I was attacked outside this very coffee house last month, and if you say you don't, you're lying. One o' you is twitching a tail 'neath this table, and I'm giving you a chance to show yourself."

"I resent your implication, Black. I ain't no rat." In a show of outrage, O'Toole waved a meaty hand at the others. "Neither are any o' these fine fellows."

If he thought to stir up a rebellion, he was bound for disappointment. Knight looked pensive, Garrity faintly amused.

"It is not the nature of the rat to expose itself." Garrity arched a dark brow. "Surely you did not expect one of us to scurry forward and accept responsibility?"

"I didn't, but rats are motivated by one thing: self-interest."

Black's gaze circled the table, and Harry noted that not one of the men looked away. A show of defiance, fear, or strength, he couldn't tell.

The king had more to say. "I've ruled this roost since two o' you were in leading strings. You may not remember the time before, when chaos and bloodshed were tearin' the stews apart. That was why I drew up the territorial lines and established the Accord. Society's rules were made to keep men like us down, but that don't mean we don't need rules o' our own. We may be cutthroats, thieves, and moneylenders, but we 'ave our own code, our own sense o' 'onor that demands we defend what's ours and be loyal to our own. That's what I'm reminding you o' today. An attack on me ain't just on me: it's an attack on our way o' life. It's pitting brother against brother and weakening us all."

Harry's estimation for the cutthroat grew. Black might be responsible for multiple crimes in the eyes of society, but he was a man who lived by his own code of conduct. In the underworld, he stood for law and order, and, without him, chaos would reign.

"We ain't always seen eye to eye, you and I, but I'm grateful for all you've done, Black." Once again, O'Toole was the first to speak. "But I resent being accused of a crime that I didn't commit. What proof do you 'ave that one o' us,"—again, he gestured to the table at large—"is involved in this treasonous act?"

"All o' you 'ave a connection to John Loach, the bastard who tried to assassinate me."

At Black's reply, Harry observed little reaction on the dukes' faces. Yet something shifted in the air, like the gathering of energy before a storm. His gut told him that that name was a stranger to none of the present company.

"That's not much to go by. Loach had many connections in the stews." Knight's blunt features were devoid of emotion even as he admitted knowledge of the culprit.

"Not just in the stews," Garrity said with equal equanimity. "According to my sources, he worked as an occasional informant for that policeman Davies."

Harry's nape went cold. *Bloody hell...Loach worked for Davies? Why didn't Davies mention it when I told him about Loach's assassination attempt on Black?*

"Know a lot about the bugger, don't you?" O'Toole narrowed his eyes at the moneylender.

Garrity shrugged, the dark superfine on his shoulders remaining smooth. "I know a lot about many things and especially about those who owe me money. Loach had been a client for some time. When the situation called for it, he paid off his debts by selling information to Peelers."

"Called for it, eh?" Malcolm Todd sneered. "When one o' your brutes threatened to shatter 'is kneecaps, you mean?"

Garrity's smile was razor sharp. "My methods are proprietary."

"You'd take blunt earned by squealing?" O'Toole said in disgust.

"I take money that is owed to me," Garrity said coldly. "Pity Loach is dead: he still owed me five hundred pounds."

"Enough." Black's command cut short the repartee. "Loach may be dead, but the threat lives on. Someone attacked The Gilded Pearl and my own 'ome using the same weapon. An explosive capable o' burning down the streets. O' destroying territory lines, which means no one at this table is safe."

The air crackled with an invisible force, as if someone had attached an electrifying machine to the alcove and was madly cranking. Harry had to appreciate Black's move. The appeal to self-interest was a brilliant stratagem to enlist the dukes' help and to flush out the traitor.

"What do you want us to do?" Knight said.

"Bring me the rat," Black said flatly. "I'm giving you a week. Produce the traitor, or I'll be forced to do a purge, bloody casualties be damned."

Black was offering them a chance to find the culprit before he was forced to do so...by any means necessary. Speculative glances were traded around the table, the question in everyone's mind clear: *Which among us is the rat?*

"That's all," Black said.

Dismissed, the three dukes took their leave. Todd remained.

Black nodded, and the guards shut the curtains once more.

"Well?" Black said without preamble.

Ming's braid swung side to side. "Not know. All could be guilty."

"I don't like that bastard Garrity." Todd's lips curled. "Don't trust any man who takes money from a squealer. And, for all we know, the Peelers are behind this: maybe they paid Loach to take a shot. God knows they've tried every other way to take you down."

Goddamnit, we still cannot pin that bastard Black to a crime? Inspector Davies' words rang in Harry's head. Davies had made it his life's mission to capture Black, yes, but surely a man of the law wouldn't stoop to murder?

"Wouldn't be the first time one o' Peel's Bloody Gang tried to frame me." Black grunted. "Protecting the public, my arse. They only protect one kind o' people, and it ain't our kind."

Harry's insides knotted. Who could he trust? Was he helping the right side?

Black was no saint, yet he brought a semblance of order to his rowdy domain. He did charitable works, helped those in need. And he was under siege by an evil that, if uncontained, could threaten all of London.

"Well, Bennett, what do you think?"

Black's question broke Harry's brooding.

"I think that surveillance needs to be kept on O'Toole, Knight, Garrity...and anyone with a link to Loach," he said starkly. *Including Davies.*

"We 'ave the men for that, Ming?" Black said.

"Stretched thin. Could use help."

"I could—" Harry began.

"No." Black's tone was unequivocal. "You got your assignment, the most important o' all."

Harry didn't argue because the other was right.

Todd said, "I'll send o'er reinforcements."

Black nodded grimly. "The seeds are sown. Now we'll wait and see which way betrayal grows."

23

"You have no idea who is the guilty one?" Tessa pressed as the carriage swayed on.

"It could be any of them." Bennett's face was set in austere lines, and no wonder, given how he'd described the meeting he'd just returned from.

Despite the grim topic, the fact that they could talk about it gave Tessa a warm tingle. The intimacy between them was deepening. Bennett was treating her like a *real* partner: he'd shared what happened with the dukes and with little prompting on her part.

Not only that, but he was *listening* to her.

During her fitting for the masquerade, while Madame Rousseau had fussed with fabrics and accoutrements, Tessa had meditated upon how to investigate De Witt. Upon Bennett's return, she'd excitedly shared her idea: they could ask her friend Alfred Doolittle to help. When Bennett had asked if Alfred could be trusted, she'd replied with the truth, that she would trust her chum with her life. As a result of the ensuing discussion, they were at present en route to pay Alfred a visit.

To observe proprieties, she'd had to bring Lizzie along. At

least she'd been able to coax the maid into riding up top with the groom so that she and Bennett could have a few moments of privacy.

"And the Peelers? You think they're involved as well?" she said.

"I...don't know." His brows drew together.

"Well, it wouldn't surprise me one bit. It's as I've always said: one can't trust a policeman farther than one can toss him." She sniffed. "Spies, mercenaries, and brutes, the lot of them."

"Right." Bennett cleared his throat. "At any rate, your father is lending men to the cause, so a close watch is being kept on anyone attached to Loach."

"Papa *ought* to help."

Although her father and Grandpapa had never got on, she was glad that the former was finally showing backbone. She hoped it would improve the state of affairs between them because she hated having dissension in the family. The thought of family reminded her of other questions she had for Bennett.

The unexpected meeting with his brother had made her realize how little she knew about his background. About his kin, where he'd come from. Their whirlwind courtship had consisted mostly of butting heads, escaping danger, and making passionate love. Now that they'd reached a temporary calm, she wanted to know more about him.

"I enjoyed meeting your brother last night," she ventured.

After a few seconds, he muttered, "The feeling was mutual."

"You think so?" she said eagerly.

She *wished* it were true. Wished with all her heart that Bennett's family would like her and welcome her into the fold. Yet she couldn't shake the fear of a different kind of reception, the kind she'd more often received in her life.

Ambrose Bennett had seemed nice, but his carriage, clothing, and manner had all pointed to the fact that he was a gentleman and a well-to-do one at that. He might not approve of his brother's involvement with a daughter of the underworld. In order to understand what she was up against, she needed to find out more about Bennett's family.

"Ambrose was charmed by you. Then again,"—Bennett's eyes softened—"who wouldn't be?"

She didn't have enough fingers to list all her detractors, but his faith in her charms made her heart go pitter-patter. "Do you, um, have other siblings?"

"I have sisters."

"How many?"

"Four."

When he said no more, she said wistfully, "I've always wanted siblings."

"When our parents passed, Ambrose and my eldest sister took care of the rest of us, so, in a way, they were like parents, too."

"How old were you when your parents passed?"

He hesitated. "I was a grown man when my papa passed. My mama died when I was twelve."

"Did you miss her?" Tessa said softly.

"Yes. We all did. She was a wonderful mother, loving and patient, and she was our rock." His voice had a hoarse edge. "Sometimes I think…"

"What do you think?" she prompted.

He studied his hands. "That those years before she died were the happiest of my life."

A spasm hit Tessa's heart. How difficult it must have been for him to lose his mother, whom he'd clearly loved, and at such a tender age. She wondered if his reluctance to open his heart had something to do with this early loss as well as the betrayal he'd suffered.

Resolve filled her. *Your happiest years are yet to come, Bennett. I'll see to that.* Seeing the rawness in his eyes, however, she decided not to push.

Instead, she smiled. "I'd love to meet the rest of your family."

"I'd like that too," he said quietly. "One day."

"Do they all live in London?"

"Not all."

"But your brother does?" When he gave a curt nod, she said earnestly, "I should like to send him a note of thanks."

"It's not necessary."

"But he was inordinately helpful. Come to think of it," she said, canting her head, "he conducted himself with remarkable poise. Does he have prior experience with such situations?"

Bennett's brows lifted. "Are you asking if my brother has participated in break-ins before?"

Her cheeks heated. "I didn't mean to imply—"

"Ambrose has a steady temperament. He's a gentleman through and through."

"Yes, of course," she said hastily. "I meant no insult."

Why, oh why, do I constantly put my foot in my mouth? In the taut silence, her heartbeat clip-clopped along with the horses. She cast about desperately for another topic.

"I got fitted for the masquerade," she blurted.

A pause. "How did it go?"

"Fine, I think. The theme is 'Wonders of the Animal World.' Madame Rousseau said she could make me any costume I wanted."

"What animal did you choose?"

"It's a surprise," she said on impulse.

His lips twitched. "I'm certain you'll be charming, no matter what costume you wear."

"I wouldn't be so certain."

When he tilted his head in question, she admitted, "The truth is that I dread the masquerade. I, or Miss Theresa Smith rather, was never a smashing success at these blasted affairs."

"Why not?"

"Um, because I lack social graces? Because I flirt as well as I play the violin?" She pursed her lips. "Or perhaps it's because I'd rather encounter armed cutthroats in an alleyway than fan-wielding chits in a ballroom?"

"I, for one, have no complaints about your flirtation skills." His heated glance made her pulse flutter. "As long as you use them only with me."

"I wouldn't want to flirt with anyone else."

"Which proves my point," he murmured. "Your lack of artifice, sprite, don't you know how irresistible it is? How irresistible *you* are?"

Her lips parted as she stared at him, loving him so much that her chest ached with it.

"Christ, stop being adorable. A man can only take so much," he said in a low growl. "As it is, it's requiring all my willpower not to drag you onto my lap and have my way with you."

"I wouldn't mind," she whispered.

His smile was her favorite one: slow, a bit wicked. "Don't tempt me, sweeting. Else I'll forget that we're in a carriage, in the middle of the day, with the maid and groom within earshot."

Details that mattered, she supposed. She sighed.

"I thought I told you to stop being adorable."

"I'm not doing anything," she protested.

"You're being you. That's enough. Now tell me why you dread the masquerade."

It felt good to confide. And Bennett's gentle teasing made it easy to share her insecurities.

"For one, it's likely that some of my former classmates from the Dungeon of Horrors will be there." Just thinking of those smirking faces churned her insides.

His lips quirked. "By Dungeon of Horrors, I take it you're referring to Mrs. Southbridge's?"

"I hated every minute of that school," she said with emphasis. "It wasn't just the tedious lessons, either. The other girls made fun of me. How I looked..." She looked at her lap, fiddling with a primrose ribbon on her skirts. "How I *am*."

"Can this be true?" Before she could argue that yes, it definitely *was*, he clarified, "You're intimidated by a bunch of chits?"

"You don't know how they are. They're *mean*."

"They're mean because they're jealous," he said flatly. "Of your beauty, spirit, and uniqueness. They'll never hold a candle to you, and they know it."

His compliment rendered her speechless. And he wasn't done.

"You're not the same girl you were back then. You know your worth. If someone is malicious, you hold your head up high and smile. Take no notice of their pettiness and envy."

"Easy for you to say," she grumbled. "What do you know about being an outcast?"

"More than you'd know." Shadows darkened Bennett's gaze. Before she could ask him what he meant, he stated, "Trust me, you won't be a wallflower at the ball."

"I suppose since Ransom invited me, he's obligated to ask me to dance," she said reluctantly.

"I wasn't referring to the bloody duke."

"Then how do you know I won't be a wallflower?"

"I just know. Trust me on this," he said resolutely.

The carriage was slowing. The ruckus of tradespeople doing business signaled their arrival at Alfred's place in Whitechapel.

She took in all that was Bennett, his strapping good looks and noble nature, and longing throbbed in her voice. "I wish you could dance with me at the masquerade."

"One day, sprite." His eyes held a molten promise. "Until then, I'll be there watching over you."

24

After a thorough scan of the narrow, bustling street, Harry handed Tessa down from the carriage. She wore a white muslin, the tightly fitted bodice emphasizing her slender torso, the full skirts swishing elegantly around her silk shoes. With her pretty face framed by a flower-trimmed bonnet, she reminded him of a porcelain shepherdess he'd once seen in a shop.

Thinking about her confession about the bullying she'd endured made him want to punch something. How dare anyone try to trample her spirit? Even though he couldn't be by her side at the masquerade, he'd see to it that she was protected from those insipid chits.

His Tessa was no wallflower. And no one would put her in the corner.

His hand closed fiercely around hers before letting go.

She smiled up at him, warming him with her special light. "Here we are."

Their destination was a shop crammed jowl to jowl with other businesses. It was distinguished by an enormous sign hanging over the window, which announced in gold gilt that this was "Doolittle's Emporium of Wonders."

Emporium of wonders, his arse. The plethora of random goods visible through the glass revealed what this place was: a pawn shop. Harry's only question was whether Tessa's friend Alfred received his inventory in an honest manner...or if he was an out-and-out fence.

Harry instructed the groom to keep watch outside with a weapon at the ready.

"There's no need to worry," Tessa said. "Today is Wednesday."

He didn't follow. "What is special about Wednesdays?"

"Alfie's wife on Wednesdays is an excellent shot."

Opening the door for her, he said, "His wife...on Wednesdays? I don't understand."

"Alfred has a different lady for each day of the week," she explained.

He frowned. "Your friend is a bigamist?"

"Alfred's no bigamist," she reassured him. "He's not legally married to any of them."

Inside, the shop was a maze of shelves, all of them crammed with merchandise, everything from teapots to garments to exotic oddities. The effect was bizarre. Next to a chipped crystal vase sat a stuffed monkey with a lace cap on its head. A curious potpourri of tobacco, lemons, and wet dog pervaded Harry's nostrils.

They arrived at the shop's counter. A buxom blonde in her forties stood behind it. She was haggling with a short, havey-cavey sort of fellow wearing a battered hat and threadbare coat. Silk handkerchiefs were piled on the counter between them; immersed in their negotiations, the pair took no notice of Tessa and Harry.

"A crown, and that's my best offer," the blonde said.

"That wouldn't pay for one o' these billys, let alone all six." The man snatched one of the handkerchiefs, held it up. "The silk's first-rate. See 'ow this billy gleams in the sun?"

"It's 'otter than the sun, too." Despite her disheveled locks and rather skimpy dress, the woman's shrewd expression suggested that she didn't suffer fools readily.

"I didn't pinch these," the would-be supplier protested. "They be family 'eirlooms, passed down to me by my dear ma, God rest 'er soul."

The blonde's gaze slitted. "Thought your name was Jenkins."

"Right-o, dove." He winked at her, leaned an elbow on the counter. "Call me Big Bobby Jenkins, they do, and it ain't on account o' my height."

"If your last name is Jenkins, then why would your ma 'ave the initials,"—she stabbed a finger down on the embroidered crest of the handkerchief—"*L. M.?*"

"Gor, is that what it says? Ne'er learned my letters." Big Bobby's smile held not one whit of repentance. "All right, dove, ten shillings for the lot. Billys like these sell for six shillings a piece in those posh shops on Pall Mall."

"*Those* ain't stolen goods." She rolled her eyes. "Christening these'll take time and talent with a needle, so a crown's all you'll get from me."

"Eight shillings."

"A crown, you cly-faking bastard, and not a shilling more."

Sighing, the man said, "You've a 'ard 'eart, dove."

"Next time, bring me goods that ain't marked, and I'll be softer than a lord's arse." The proprietress tossed a coin over the counter, and Big Bobby good-naturedly caught it.

"Good afternoon, Sal," Tessa called.

The blonde turned. "Tessa! 'An't seen you in a dog's age."

"I've been a bit busy," Tessa said apologetically.

Sal's penciled brows shot up, and she jerked her chin at Harry. "Who's the swell?"

"This is Sam Bennett. He's my, um, bodyguard." A hint of pink crested Tessa's cheeks. "Bennett, this is Sally Doolittle."

"Strapping fellow, ain't you?" Sal eyed him, licking her lips in the manner of a mongrel presented with a meaty bone.

Egad. He cleared his throat. "Pleased to meet you ma'am."

"Call me Sal, 'andsome. Everyone does." She wriggled her shoulders, a motion that tested the limits of her low neckline.

"Pardon, sir." Big Bobby, who was making his way out, brushed against Harry. He flashed a smile of not very white teeth.

"No harm done," Harry said.

With a doff of his hat, Big Bobby continued on his way.

"Hold it right there," Tessa demanded.

Big Bobby froze.

"Whatever it is you pinched, give it back, you sticky-fingered blighter," she said.

Harry blinked. Patted his waistcoat. "My pocket watch. The bastard stole it."

Big Bobby made a run for it.

Before Harry could give chase, a shot blasted through the room.

Big Bobby cried, "Goddamnit, Sal, that was my favorite 'at!"

He bent to pick his headwear up from the ground. Harry's brows inched up at the sight of the precise hole punched through it.

Sal tucked a small, pearl-handled pistol back into the folds of her skirts. "Ought to know be'er than to shit where you sup. If I see that bony 'ide o' yours again, I'll blow a 'ole through it too. Now give the ticker back to the toff, and be quick 'bout it."

Jamming on his holey hat, Big Bobby did as he was told before skulking out.

"Perfect aim, as usual," Tessa said.

Sal preened. "No be'er than yours with those pretty daggers."

The mutual admiration society was interrupted by the emergence of a young man through the velvet curtain behind the counter.

"Bloody 'ell," he said, yawning widely, "can't a chap get some shut-eye around 'ere?"

"*Alfredkins!*" All of the hardness melted from Sal's features. She rushed over to the newcomer, cooing, "Sorry we disturbed you, love, but Tessa's 'ere."

"Can see that, my peepers ain't faulty. But who's the four-eyes?" Alfred Doolittle ambled up to Harry and gave him a once-over.

Harry returned the favor. Up close, Doolittle was older than he'd first appeared; he was probably near Harry's age, those years softened by an angelic boyishness. Slight and bran-faced, Doolittle had a mop of brown hair and large, wide-spaced eyes.

"Name's Sam Bennett," Harry said evenly. "I was hired on by Mr. Black to protect Miss Todd."

"Ain't shook this one loose yet, eh?" Doolittle addressed Tessa.

"Hello to you, too," she said smartly. "And I have no intention of shaking Bennett loose. In fact, we came because we need your help."

"'Ain't 'eard that before," Doolittle muttered. "All right, to the office, the pair o' you." Turning to his lover, he said, "Keep watch, Sal, and don't 'esitate to put that talent o' yours to use."

"Which talent, Alfredkins?" Sal purred, running her fingers through his hair.

"With the pistol, you tart." Doolittle gave her bottom an indiscreet squeeze, and Sal giggled. "Your other talents'll keep 'til bedtime."

A moment later, all business, Doolittle crooked his finger at Harry and Tessa, and they followed him through the curtain.

His office turned out to be a surprisingly well-appointed room at the back of the shop. The furnishings were of high quality, though mismatched. There was an oak desk, a half-moon rosewood table, and a zebrawood curio cabinet crammed to the gills. Peering inside the last, Harry saw a familiar-looking pig bladder device; he narrowed his eyes at Tessa, who just gave him a cheeky grin and tugged him over to a chintz settee.

Doolittle took the leather wingchair by the fire.

"State your business," he said as grandly as any lord of the manor.

"First of all, I want to return these." Tessa opened the large knitting bag she'd brought with her, and Swift Nick's head popped up. In his mouth was yet another familiar item: the pack of naughty cards Tessa had used to fleece Dewey O'Toole.

"If it ain't the furry bandit," Doolittle drawled.

The ferret relinquished the deck to Tessa and, grinning, vanished back into the bag.

Tessa set the cards on the coffee table, next to a chess set missing several pieces. "Thank you for lending them to me."

"Come in 'andy, did they?" Doolittle said easily. "'Eard about the bull and cow at Stunning Joe Banks' establishment."

During his tenure in the Black household, Harry's vocabulary of rhyming slang had grown considerably. Thus, he knew that "bull and cow" meant a row.

"Let's just say the cards provided the necessary distraction," Tessa said.

Seeing the conspiratorial smile that passed between her and their host, Harry frowned. "How, precisely, do you know one another?"

"Known Tessie since she was a poppet with eyes bigger than 'er 'ead," Doolittle said.

"Alfred and I met at The Underworld when I caught him stealing," Tessa added fondly.

"Worked for the previous owner o' the club, see, cove by the name o' Hunt."

Harry jolted. The prior owner of The Underworld was Gavin Hunt, and Hunt's wife Persephone happened to be as thick as thieves with Harry's sister-in-law, Marianne. The Hunts and Kents were friends, and, before he'd left for Cambridge, Harry had spent no little time in the company of the Hunt family. The fact that this Alfred Doolittle had a connection to them as well made him wary.

Yet he didn't think he'd met Doolittle before. Nor did the other evince any sign of recognition as he palavered on.

"Now Hunt didn't mind my borrowing a pair o' candlesticks now and again, so 'ow was I to know that the rules were changed under new management?" Doolittle's tone was utterly reasonable, his expression as innocent as a babe's. "Turns out, Tessie's pa don't take lightly to a bit o' skimming. 'Is 'ounds caught my scent, so I took cover in one o' the wenching rooms. Imagine my surprise to find it already occupied by this wee chick. And my further surprise when she didn't make a peep when the guards arrived and asked if she saw anyone come in. Not a single peep, even though she saw me dive under the bed not a minute earlier—"

"And we've been friends ever since," Tessa finished.

"Ah," Harry said as if it were perfectly normal for a girl to befriend a thief. But that was his sprite: her loyalty was unfaltering. It was a trait apparently shared by Doolittle, for he looked at her with undisguised—and, fortunately for him, *brotherly* —affection.

"Right, then. What do you need your ol' chum Alfred for this time?" Doolittle said.

Tessa glanced at Harry, who nodded. He trusted her judgement.

Moreover, they needed all the help they could get.

The connection between Inspector Davies and Black's would-be assassin Loach had been too glaring for Harry to ignore. Not knowing who to trust, he'd asked Ambrose to make discreet enquiries into the activities of Inspector Davies. Yet this added another burden to his brother, who was already looking into De Witt's financials and had his own cases to investigate.

Furthermore, Harry's gut told him that the meeting at Nightingale's had been a portent of bad things to come. Black had thrown down the gauntlet; anything could happen in the next sennight. It was imperative that they hunt down the villain before the bastard struck again.

Enter Tessa's plan involving Doolittle.

After she finished summarizing the details of the hellfire, she said imploringly, "No one knows the streets like you do, Alfred. Since Bennett and I cannot keep watch on De Witt on our own, we need your help. You're to tail him only, mind, and keep a safe distance while you're doing it."

Doolittle, who'd remained quiet throughout, scratched his ear. "Why don't you tell your grandfather 'bout this?"

"You know how Grandpapa is: he never wants me involved, nor does he take me seriously," she said darkly. "And, in this case, we have no proof of De Witt's wrong doing. Any scientist could have a laboratory in his house. But if we trail him to the factory where the explosive is being produced, *then*,"—she snapped her fingers—"we've got him. Then Grandpapa will have to believe me. And only then will we be able to put an end to this menace on our streets."

Doolittle's sigh was that of a man who knew Tessa well. "Made up your mind, 'ave you?"

Her vigorous nod caused her bonnet to shed a violet onto the carpet.

"Give us the cove's address," Doolittle muttered.

"*Thank you*, Alfred." Tessa beamed at him.

"The two nights I followed De Witt," Harry said, "he left his townhouse at nine in the evening. After making an appearance at a society affair, he headed to a club. Crockford's in St. James."

"Crockford's, eh?" Doolittle whistled. "Play there gets steep."

Which was precisely why Harry wanted to know more about De Witt's financial situation. Was he in debt? Was money motivating him to produce and sell hellfire to the underworld?

"Both times, he didn't leave the club until dawn." Harry paused. "From what I know of De Witt, he is a man of habit, so tailing him will likely involve late nights."

"Late nights ain't the problem." Doolittle stretched his arms, yawning. "It's the days stuck in this 'ere shop. A chap gets rusty from too much respectability."

If running a fence was respectable, Harry wondered what Doolittle considered disreputable...and decided he didn't want to know.

At that instant, a blast came from the front of the shop.

"Zounds." Tessa's eyes widened. "Should we go help?"

"Nah. If it were Monday,"—Doolittle exchanged a significant glance with Tessa, making Harry wonder about the "wife" on that day of the week—"my arse would be catapulting from this 'ere chair, but it being Wednesday means all I got to do is nuffin'." He yawned again. "Come to fink o' it, I might catch a few winks."

"We won't keep you." Tessa rose, and Harry followed suit. "We'll hear from you soon?"

"Long as I 'aven't lost my touch." Doolittle wriggled his fingers and waved them off.

25

Two nights later, Tessa sat before the vanity as Lizzie put the final touches on her hair. Madame Rousseau, the modiste, had suggested trying a new, softer coiffure to go with the costume, one that she claimed was all the rage. Mavis had arrived to supervise Tessa's toilette, and she reclined on the adjacent chaise longue, a blanket tucked over her slight form.

Mama hadn't recovered completely from her last episode. In the mirror, Tessa saw the other's pale lips, the skin on her cheeks so translucent that a tracery of blue veins showed through.

Tessa bit her lip. "You really didn't need to come, Mama."

"Of course I did. My condition prevents me from accompanying you to the masquerade," Mama said, "but I refuse to miss this part as well. A girl needs her mama to be present for her grand entrée."

"This isn't my first foray into the *ton*."

Tessa felt obliged to point it out. During the years at Southbridge's, she'd blundered through her share of such events, and she didn't want her mama's hopes to be raised...only to be crushed if she once again failed to be a success.

She, herself, had larger game to hunt. The De Witts might be in attendance tonight. Although she'd given Bennett her promise not to approach them, she could *monitor* them surreptitiously if the occasion permitted.

"Things are different now," Mama said. "With the Duke of Ranelagh and Somerville at your beck and call, doors will be opened for you."

"His Grace is hardly at my beck and call."

"Ransom is *dazzled* by you."

Tessa let out a huff of amusement. Because of Mavis' physical frailty, people often overlooked the fact that she had steel at her core. She was a Black, after all. Her strength of will showed itself frequently when it came to her stepdaughter: it seemed nothing could put a dent in her optimism about Tessa's future.

Tessa turned in her chair to face her stepmama, earning her a grunt from Lizzie.

"Hold still, Miss Tessa. I ain't done."

"Sorry, Lizzie." To her mother, she said, "It isn't me he's dazzled by: it's the dowry Grandpapa has promised him. He admitted as much during our turn in Baroness von Friesing's garden."

"He did?" Distaste thinned Mama's mouth. "That's not very gentlemanly of him, is it?"

"I prefer honesty to flattery."

"Nonetheless, a fellow ought to show proper respect for the lady he is courting. I shall speak to Father about it."

"*Please* don't, Mama." The last thing she needed was her grandfather pressuring Ransom into a pretense of romance. "Such niceties are unnecessary, I assure you."

"Every lady deserves niceties," Mama said primly. "Especially during the courtship."

Before Tessa could argue, Lizzie said, "That's that, I think. Have a look."

Tessa turned back toward the looking glass. She swung her head this way and that, admiring Lizzie's handiwork. The maid had plaited several sections of her hair, arranging the dark braids to lie softly against her ears before twisting into an elegant coil at the back of her head. Her only hair ornament was a headband from which sprouted a pair of small, furry, triangular ears. The ears were made of cream-colored ermine and matched the trim on Tessa's gown.

"Come here, dear," Mama said, "so I can have a better look."

Lizzie left, and Tessa went to sit on the chaise longue.

After a thorough inspection, her mama declared, "You are a diamond of the first water. Mark my words: Ransom will propose before the night is out."

Crikey, that was the *last* thing Tessa wanted. With prickling unease, she realized that she would have to find some way to discourage Ransom whilst appearing to her family that she was going along with the courtship. Not an easy balance to strike.

If only I could tell Mama and Grandpapa the truth: Bennett is the only man for me.

She slid a glance at Mama, who was happily exclaiming over the costume's merits, and wondered how the other would react. Could her parent understand marrying for love rather than practical reasons?

On impulse, she said, "How did you know you wanted to marry my father?"

Mama blinked. "Well, he asked me. Or, rather, he asked Father for my hand. I had been recently widowed, and your father seemed like a nice man."

"Were you...in love with him?"

"I don't suppose I was." Mama gave a slight shrug. "Love is not a requirement for marriage."

Although Tessa was aware of the state of affairs between her parents, she couldn't help but press, "Didn't you want to love your husband?"

"I loved my first husband. Loving once was enough." Mama's lips pressed tightly.

The other did not discuss her first marriage...out of grief, Tessa assumed. From the rumors she'd heard, Warren Kingsley had been an inordinately robust and handsome man, one who'd died far too young in a boating accident. Poor fellow had been found floating in the Thames, hardly recognizable after dining with the fishes.

"Why this talk of love, Tessa? Are you in love with Ransom?"

"No." Faced with Mama's shrewd eyes, Tessa was glad she didn't have to lie. "And that's the problem. I *want* to love my husband."

An amused sound rustled from Mama's throat. "Heavens, what a romantic you are turning out to be. You're almost as bad as Father. But take it from me," she said with crisp pragmatism, "it is better not to burden a marriage with love. Tolerance and affection are more peaceful goals."

Before she could reply, a fist pounded on the door.

"Tessie, you ready yet?" her grandfather's voice bellowed. "At this rate, I ain't going to live long enough to see this 'secret' costume o' yours."

"Let him in," Mama advised, "before he breaks down the door."

Tessa hurried to comply, and her heart flip-flopped as Bennett entered behind Grandpapa. Since she couldn't very well have a bodyguard by her side at the ball, Bennett was to pose as Baron von Friesing's footman. The plan was for him to keep a low profile and a watch on things.

To that end, he was dressed in formal livery, the stark black and white garb fitting his tall, muscular frame to perfection. He was the epitome of virile grace, the snowy folds of his cravat emphasizing his clean-cut handsomeness. The gleam behind his wire frames caused her insides to flush with heat.

"Let's 'ave a look at you." Dressed in an emerald silk banyan, a matching tasseled cap on his head, Grandfather made a twirling motion with his finger.

Tessa did an obedient spin. Made of champagne-colored velvet, the gown was cut *à la mode*: the neckline was low and off the shoulders, the bodice fitted, the skirts full. Ermine trimmed the décolletage and elaborate sleeves, and fur had also been sewn to the back of the dress to resemble a short tail.

She thought the costume was beautifully made. There was only one potential problem.

"Ain't you a pretty kitty?" Grandpapa said with approval.

Drat. When Mama had first seen the costume, she'd also assumed Tessa was dressed up as a cat. Which meant that Tessa's clever idea was missing the mark entirely.

Why, she thought sulkily, *would anyone think I'd go as something as mundane as a cat? And then take such lengths to keep my costume secret?*

"I don't think Miss Todd is a cat, sir." Bennett's deep voice held a hint of humor.

"With those ears, fur, and a tail, what else would she be?" Grandpapa demanded.

Bennett's eyes smiled at her. "I believe she is a ferret. Her favorite animal."

And that *is why I love him*. No one had ever understood her like Bennett did.

She beamed at him, and his lips twitched.

Her grandfather glowered at her. "God's teeth, Tessie, you could 'ave chosen any animal you wanted, and you're going to a duke's ball dressed as a bloody *rodent*?"

She glowered right back. "First of all, ferrets aren't rodents—"

"That's enough," Mavis called from the chaise. "Tessa, we don't require a lecture on ferrets. Father, everyone will mistake her for a cat, so don't worry about it."

Grandfather snorted; Tessa rolled her eyes.

After a moment, he said with a grunt, "Your costume's missing something."

"Obviously. Since only Bennett recognized that I'm a ferret."

Grandpapa raised his gaze heavenward before reaching into

the pocket of his banyan and pulling out a small velvet box. "Been waiting for the right time to give you this. Belonged to your grandmama, one o' 'er most prized possessions. She would 'ave wanted you to 'ave it."

Tessa dropped any pretense of being miffed as she reverently took the box from Grandpapa. Even though she'd never met her grandmother, she'd heard countless tales of the other's beauty, courage, and virtue. Althea Bourdelain Black was the stuff of *legend*.

"What is it?" Tessa breathed.

"Open it, and you'll see."

With hands that trembled, she lifted the lid. Her throat cinched at the sight of the familiar, heart-shaped ruby framed in gold. Small but distinctive, it was the pendant Althea wore in her portrait. In real life, the ruby had even more fire. When Tessa turned it over, she saw words engraved in the gold.

To A. B. The Pride of a Family.

"Oh, Grandpapa," she said tremulously, "how Grandmama must have cherished this gift from you. I'll strive to be worthy of it."

"I didn't give Althea that necklace or the matching ring. Both were from 'er family."

Tessa looked at Mama, who'd worn the ruby ring for as long as she could recall; the other, too, looked surprised.

"I always thought you gave Mama these jewels, Father," Mavis said.

A misty, faraway look entered Grandpapa's eyes. "When Althea made 'er choice to be my wife, it weren't without sacrifices. The Bourdelains came from noble stock and refused to forgive Althea for marrying beneath 'er. Not only did they disown 'er, they wouldn't let 'er see 'er younger brother. She adored the lad. A few years later, she discovered 'e'd died, and she ne'er got to say goodbye. For years, the sight o' those rubies brought tears to 'er eyes."

Tessa's chest ached at the tragic tale. "Poor Grandmama."

"Althea ne'er stopped wearing that necklace and ring because she ne'er stopped loving the Bourdelains, no matter 'ow they treated 'er. She was strong enough to bear the pain with the love. 'Ad the 'eart o' a lioness, my Althea did, and now it lives on in our daughter,"—he looked at Mavis, who gave a watery smile—"and our granddaughter. 'Tis only right that each o' you carry a part o' 'er."

"I am honored," Tessa said softly.

"And let it be a reminder: like my Althea, you are a true lady. You bow to no one," Grandpapa said sternly. "No matter where you go, you 'old your 'ead up 'igh, you 'ear me?"

"Yes, Grandpapa."

His words seemed to soak into her skin, her veins, becoming the throbbing truth of her heart. She looked at Bennett; in that instant, his gaze was unguarded. She saw herself in those rich dark depths…and the reflection was beautiful.

"Blasted clasp," Grandpapa grumbled. He'd lifted the necklace from the box and was attempting to undo the tiny fastener. "My 'ands ain't what they used to be." He shoved the necklace at Bennett. "You do it."

Taking the necklace, Bennett went to stand behind her. The knowledge that mere inches separated them caused her respiration to be erratic. Energy crackled in that sliver of space, his virile scent spinning her senses. And the more she tried to hide her desire, the more heightened it became.

Holding the ends of the necklace, he lowered the pendant onto her bosom. Her breath hitched when the ruby heart made contact with her skin, the gentle friction like a caress. The pendant dragged up, up, and when his fingers brushed against her nape, her nipples were already budded against her bodice. The rasp of his calloused fingertips melted her insides like wax. Warmth flooded her heart, between her thighs, all of her turned molten with wanting.

"There you go." Bennett's words had a husky edge. Had he, too, been affected by their exchange? One that, by all rights, ought to have been ordinary and mundane?

Gathering herself, she turned to face him, and her knees grew wobbly at the banked fire in his eyes. Longing that he was doing his utmost to hide, but that she could see: because she knew him. Because she loved him. Because her lioness' heart had led her to this man and no other.

"It suits you, Miss Todd," he murmured before stepping aside.

Not half as well as you do, she thought.

She vowed to herself that they would be together soon enough. Once they stopped the villain behind the hellfire and her family was safe, she would let *nothing* keep them apart.

The butler arrived with a tray of champagne, and Mama came to join them.

Raising a sparkling flute, she said, "To Tessa's second debut. May she make us proud."

"She always does," Grandpapa said gruffly.

Tessa blinked back sudden heat and held her own glass up high. "To the House of Black. May we never succumb to enemies and always fight for family and for love."

"For family and love," her mama and grandpapa echoed.

Tessa looked at Bennett—and saw the flash of naked longing on his face. She felt the urge to abandon pretense, to invite him to join the circle, be by her side where he belonged; the slight shake of his head warned her not to.

It took all her willpower, but she quelled her impulse. For the good of everyone, she would keep their affair secret. For now.

26

THE BALL WAS A CRUSH.

Mirrored walls amplified the seemingly endless throng of people, all dressed in extravagant finery. The gilded columns and towering potted palms added to a closed-in feeling despite the large size of the ballroom. Cloying perfumes mingled with the heavy scent of burning beeswax from the three blazing chandeliers.

"May I compliment you on your costume?" the Duke of Ranelagh and Somerville said as he guided her into a waltz. "You make a most charming kitty."

Tessa didn't bother correcting him. Since she'd arrived at the opulent ball, the handful of people who had deigned to speak to her had all mistaken her for a cat. Even the demi-mask she was wearing didn't help. In the carriage, Bennett had helped her to don the brown velvet mask decorated with swirls of gold embroidery and seed pearls.

Now you and Swift Nick could be twins, he'd said with his crooked smile.

How she *wished* she could be dancing with him instead of the duke. But knowing that he was somewhere in the crowd, keeping watch over her, made her feel better. It was past midnight, and she hadn't heard the De Witts being announced; she was losing hope that she'd have the opportunity to do some clandestine sleuthing.

Unfortunately, she *had* seen some other people she knew, including her nemesis Lady Hyacinth Tipping, now the Countess of Fyffe. Hyacinth had looked past her as if she were invisible. Surprisingly, Baroness von Friesing had been the one to observe that Ransom's attentions to Tessa were likely the cause of the snub.

Lady Fyffe's husband is a mere earl, and a Scottish one at that, the baroness had said tartly. *A fact you would know if you used your Debrett's as more than a doorstop.*

How well her chaperone knew her.

As Tessa whirled by the orchestra, she caught a glimpse of Hyacinth standing next to one of the gilded columns, staring at her with a sour expression. Tessa decided that dancing with Ransom wasn't so bad after all. In all honesty, he *was* being nice to her, which was more than she could say of the rest of the snobbish lot.

She smiled up at him. "And you are the king of that particular family, I see."

Ransom was a stylish lion, his bronze velvet tailcoat immaculately fitted to his lean frame, his demi-mask trimmed in golden fur. Embroidered lions pranced across his black silk waistcoat.

"I like to be the head of the pack," he drawled.

"Pride, Your Grace."

"Pardon?"

"A group of lions is called a pride, not a pack."

"Right." His smile flashed white against his mustache and trimmed beard. "You have an unusual fount of knowledge, Miss Smith."

He didn't know the half of it.

"I like animals." On impulse, she added, "And I'm supposed to be a ferret."

"A ferret, hmm? Well, you're the first of that I've seen. Most ladies prefer something more..."

"Elegant?" she guessed. "Exotic?"

Looking around her, most of the ladies were garbed in eye-catching extravagance. She'd seen peacocks, parrots, and goldfish by the dozen.

"I was going to say conventional. But you're not, are you?"

"One of many virtues I cannot claim," she said ruefully.

He swung her into a turn, and his speed and sudden closeness made her head spin a little. As did the words he murmured into her ear. "Virtue is overrated, my little ferret."

The dance ended, and she found herself looking up into his golden hazel gaze. He was a handsome rake. And so adept at flirting that he could make one feel as if his interest was genuine.

"How do you do that?" she marveled.

"Do what?"

"Be so sincerely *insincere*."

He gave a shout of laughter. The sound drew looks; clearly, everyone was wondering what she'd said to amuse him.

"Are you always this forthright?" Ransom murmured as he led her off the dance floor.

"Oh no. I'm an excellent liar when the occasion demands."

In fact, she was living a lie at this moment. She wished she didn't have to keep up pretenses, that she and Bennett could be open about their feelings—that Grandpapa could accept that she wanted to wed her bodyguard and not the duke (however nice the latter was being).

Maybe if Bennett and I solve the mystery of the hellfire, Grandpapa will see how worthy he truly is. She felt the gentle yet powerful weight of her grandmama's necklace, the legacy of love and strength. *Maybe the De Witts will yet make an appearance...*

"A trait we share," Ransom said.

"You're a good liar, Your Grace?" She was surprised that he admitted it.

"This entire ball is a lie, is it not?"

Intrigued, she tilted her head. "Because everyone is pretending to be something they're not?"

"That too. But I was referring to the fact that the ball is the picture of luxury." He smiled without humor. "One that I cannot afford."

"Then why host a ball at all?"

"Appearances, little ferret, are everything."

Ransom returned her to Baroness von Friesing, who'd planted herself close to the buffet table. She'd been chatting with another duenna and looked rather put out to have her *tête-à-tête* interrupted.

Nonetheless, she fixed a smile upon her face. "Done with my charge so soon, Your Grace?"

"Alas, rules do not permit for more than a second dance," Ransom said easily. "But perhaps I might claim you for a stroll around the ballroom later on, Miss Smith?"

"Why not?" Tessa held up the empty dance card dangling from her wrist. "'Tis not as if I have anything better to do."

"*Miss Smith*," her chaperone hissed.

Ransom's lips curved, and he kissed her hand before departing.

"Flaunting one's deficiencies is no way to reel in His Grace." The baroness gave her a dark look. "Why can't you at least *try* to flirt?"

Because I don't want to marry him.

Tessa shrugged. "Why bother when my dowry is the true bait?"

"Your flippancy is unbecoming, Miss Smith. Your grandpapa will be made aware of this," von Friesing warned. "I shan't be held accountable for your lack of cooperation."

"Crikey, I've danced with His Grace *twice*," she protested. "To cooperate any more, I'd have to offer to do the buttock jig with him on the dance floor."

"Mind the *vulgarity*."

"Who's going to hear me?" Tessa crossed her gloved arms over her chest. "Everyone's avoiding me like the plague."

It was Mrs. Southbridge's all over again. She was alone (except for the bristling company of the baroness which, frankly, was worse than being alone). And seeing Lady Hyacinth huddled with her cronies, their smirks as they whispered behind fans, Tessa knew who, once again, was the ringleader behind her social ostracism.

She told herself she didn't care. Held onto the advice that Bennett had given her.

You're not the same girl you were... You know your worth... Take no notice of them...

She craned her neck for any sign of Bennett. She was scanning the alcoves along the perimeter when a female voice said, "What a delightful costume."

Tessa swung around to see that she'd been approached by a lovely brunette and an equally lovely blonde. The former's orange-and-black striped gown suggested she was a tigress while the latter wore the soft, white plumage of a dove. The ladies were escorted by tall, dazzlingly attractive gentlemen who'd eschewed costumes, their black demi-masks their only nod to the masquerade.

Tessa blinked. "Are you, um, talking to me?"

Beside her, the baroness froze at the sight of the newcomers, her jaw going oddly slack.

"Why, yes. I wanted to complement you on your ferret costume." The brunette's smile and tea-colored eyes radiated genuine warmth. "I have great respect for originality."

"Oh...thank you." Tessa didn't know what shocked her more, the lady's perceptiveness or her compliment. "You're the first person here to guess that I'm a ferret."

"My wife is shockingly astute." This came from the black-haired gentleman. His wicked good looks could appear quite cold, Tessa imagined, but his jade eyes were warmly amused as he regarded his lady. "And original also. For instance, she eschews introductions and launches into conversation."

"Oh, dear. How amiss of me." The brunette flushed prettily. "I am Emma, and the gentleman teasing me mercilessly is my husband, the Duke of Strathaven. This is my younger sister Polly,"—she waved to the voluptuous golden-haired lady—"and her husband Sinjin. They are the Duchess and Duke of Acton."

"How do you do?" Hastily, Tessa sank into a curtsy. "I'm Miss Theresa Smith. And this is my, um, aunt, Baroness von Friesing."

"A pleasure, Your Graces." The baroness bowed low.

"How are you enjoying the ball?" The Duchess of Acton possessed a shy smile and stunning aquamarine eyes.

"I'm not really—*ouch.*" Tessa glared at the baroness, who'd elbowed her in the side. "What did you do that for?"

"My charge has enjoyed herself immensely," von Friesing gushed. "In fact, the Duke of Ranelagh and Somerville has paid particular attention to her and asked her to dance *twice.*"

"Which is the sum total of the times I've been on the dance floor," Tessa muttered.

"A fact that must be remedied." The Duchess of Strathaven tilted her head at her husband. "Strathaven, weren't you just saying you fancied a dance?"

The duke bowed. "Would you do me the honor, Miss Smith?"

To her bemusement, Tessa found herself doing a Scottish Reel with Strathaven. And then a Quadrille with the Duke of Acton. After that, the duchesses took her under their collective wing, insisting that she call them "Emma" and "Polly" and introducing her to a plethora of people. To Tessa's surprise, she was welcomed into the fold.

Her dance card began to fill up. And even though her partners were aristocrats, they were actually *nice* to her. Her current partner was the Earl of Ruthven, a fit man with thick, greying hair and an avuncular manner. He led her into a waltz, navigating the constellation of bright, spinning gowns.

"What a charming cat you make, Miss Smith," he said.

"I'm a ferret, actually." When she saw his green eyes flicker behind his black feathered mask, she said quickly, "If it makes you feel any better, I'm not sure what you are either. A crow or raven perhaps?"

"I'm open to your interpretation." He smiled. "In truth, I was a late addition to the guest list, and my valet scavenged this mask from God knows where."

"Are you well acquainted with the host?" she asked as they whirled to the music.

"I do not know anyone in this room well. I am newly come into the title, you see, and from a distant branch of the family that no one expected to inherit." He looked rueful. "Yet here I am."

Feeling a sense of kinship, she confided, "I don't know these people well either."

"And yet you are swarmed by admirers."

"Only because the Strathavens and Actons were kind enough to take me under their wing."

"You are being modest," Ruthven said. "You are as lovely and unique as that necklace you are wearing."

"It belonged to my grandmama," she said with pride.

She could feel Althea watching over her tonight. Guiding her past pitfalls and toward success.

After the dance, Ruthven returned her to her friends. Tessa noted a newcomer to the group; it was difficult not to. Petite and curvaceous, the lady had bright red hair and was dressed as some sort of yellow bird, an extraordinary quantity of feathers and ruffles on her gown. The duchesses were hugging her with unbridled delight.

"There you are, Miss Smith," Emma said, beaming. "We just

ran into our dear friend, whom we haven't seen in ages. Miss Theresa Smith, meet Gabriella, Mrs. Garrity."

Tessa's nape stirred. *Zounds, it couldn't be* that *Garrity...could it?*

"How do you do, Mrs. Garrity?" she said cautiously.

"I'm very well. And do call me Gabby, everyone does. I must confess, I'm ever so relieved to be out of the nursery. That is where I spend most of my days, you know. Not that I'm complaining. Well, perhaps I am a little, aren't I?"

Confronted with the flurry of words and big blue eyes, Tessa could only manage, "Um..."

"Oh dear, I'm talking too much, aren't I? It's a terrible habit of mine to chatter when I'm nervous," Gabby said guilelessly. "It was bad before, just ask dear Emma and Polly, but I fear it's gotten worse now that I'm with the children all day. I'm simply starved for adult conversation—"

"If that's the case, Gabby, dear," Emma (thankfully) cut in, "why haven't you come to call? You've turned down my last several invitations."

"I've been a dreadful friend—that is, if you still consider me a friend. I wouldn't blame you if you didn't." Remorse was written all over the redhead's pretty face, which was rounded and sprinkled with golden freckles, so that even her look of despair was somehow charming. "I've *wanted* to see you, but it's been one thing after another. Between the children and the new country estate, Mr. Garrity is *very* particular about how it is to be renovated, not to mention Papa's health not being what it was—"

"Take a breath, dear." Polly patted Gabby on the shoulder. "Or *several* breaths."

The lady gulped in air.

"Neither time nor distance will change our friendship," Emma said gently. "I meant only that we've missed you."

"I've missed you. Ever so much." Gabby bit her lip. "I don't know how the two of you do it."

"Do what?" Emma asked.

"*Everything.*" Gabby waved a hand. "Be a wife and mama and still have time left over for anything else. And Emma, you even do detection work."

Detection work? Tessa's ears perked. *Blood and thunder, that's something you don't hear duchesses doing every day.*

"I only take on the occasional case," Emma said. "And no one can do *everything.*"

"Even with oodles of servants and Mr. Garrity's clearly detailed schedules, I can't seem to manage very well," Gabby said glumly.

Polly's forehead pleated. "Mr. Garrity gives you schedules?"

"To help me organize my day. That way, I don't forget anything. He's ever so thoughtful," Gabby said, her eyes dreamy.

Tessa saw the duchesses exchange a look that suggested they might use a different adjective to describe Mr. Garrity and his schedules.

"Is your husband here tonight?" Emma said.

Gabby's red curls bounced against her cheek as she nodded. "He prefers we stay at home, but we're here tonight because he had business to discuss with some clients."

Emma's brows rose. "Here at the masquerade?"

"Everyone is in need of money, and the *ton* is no exception. Mr. Garrity's influence is quite far-reaching these days. Why else would Cits like us be invited to so elevated an affair?"

Gabby's shrug revealed a streak of pragmatism beneath all that effervescence. And left no doubt that her husband was indeed *that* Garrity: the one who might be plotting against Grandpapa. Was it a coincidence that Garrity was here at an event that De Witt was invited to? Tessa stiffened as another possibility struck her. Could there be a connection between Garrity, De Witt…and Ransom?

Apparently misreading Tessa's reaction, Gabby said in a rush, "Beg pardon, that was vulgar of me to mention money, wasn't it? Being the daughter of a banker and the wife of a moneylend—a man of business, I mean, I forget we aren't supposed to talk about such things. I meant no offense."

"I'm not offended," Tessa said truthfully.

Gabby's relieved smile gave her a twinge of misgiving. She couldn't help but like the redhead; it would be a pity if her husband turned out to be an enemy of the Blacks.

A footman dressed in smart livery approached and bowed. "Mr. Garrity wishes to depart. He is waiting for you at the carriage, Mrs. Garrity."

"Tell him I'll be right there." Turning back to the group, Gabby said hurriedly, "I must go, but Emma and Polly, will you please come to call tomorrow afternoon? I should like to visit with you ever so much. And with you, too, Miss Smith, if you are free."

Tessa blinked. Couldn't believe the opportunity that had just presented itself.

When the other ladies murmured their assent, she added quickly, "I'm free."

"Splendid." Rummaging in her reticule, Gabby produced a rather crumpled card and gave it to Tessa. "Here is my address. Look forward to seeing you all!"

She rushed off, a trail of yellow feathers drifting in her wake.

"Is she quite all right, do you think?" Emma murmured.

"We'll find out tomorrow," Polly murmured back.

Tomorrow, Tessa would have the opportunity to investigate Garrity in his own lair...as long as Bennett was willing to cooperate with her plan. She looked for Bennett in the crowd, bursting at the seams to share the new developments. The evening could not have gone any better.

Then a sonorous voice announced a new arrival.

"Sir Aloysius De Witt and the Honorable Miss Celeste De Witt!"

27

"Harry...is that you?" a voice like trembling silver bells asked.

Bloody hell. For an instant, Harry was tempted to deny it and continue down the carpeted hallway outside the ballroom. When he'd seen the De Witts arrive, he'd felt a surge of fury. Just as quickly, he'd locked away the emotion. Made certain to stay out of sight as he monitored them.

Aloysius had quickly made the rounds, Celeste by his side. He'd exchanged niceties with a number of guests, including Garrity and a man Harry did not recognize but who had waltzed with Tessa. Aloysius also spoke at length with Ransom, who'd danced a set with Celeste.

Aloysius had departed a quarter hour ago, leaving his daughter with her chaperone. Harry had thought his presence had gone undetected. Apparently, he'd underestimated Celeste...for a second time.

He forced himself to turn around.

Celeste had always suited her name, and tonight was no exception. Her swan costume accentuated her angelic grace, the white, feather-trimmed frock perfectly draped over her tall, slender frame. Her pale blonde ringlets quivered; she stared at him with eyes that he'd once compared to the color of heaven.

When he looked at her now, however, it was through the eyes of a man not a lad. She was still beautiful, but he saw how fragile that beauty was. How it didn't have the bones for endurance, the character that would enhance and deepen attractiveness over time.

When he removed his mask, shadows flitted through her eyes. Or maybe it was the candelabrum flickering on the side table.

"I thought it was you," she whispered. "Were you going to leave without speaking to me?"

She must be joking.

Anger flared. Knowing there was no way to avoid the interaction, he calculated his options. Going to the nearest door, he looked inside. The music room was empty.

Wordlessly, he gestured for her to enter. Once they were both inside, he left the door open. If anyone happened upon them, he would play the part of a footman assisting a guest.

"What do you want?" he demanded curtly.

"I want to talk to you." Her voice quivered. "To say...how sorry I am. For what I did."

Did she really think he wanted her apology?

His jaw clenched. "It's a bit late for that, don't you think?"

"I know what I did was unforgiveable. That you must hate me." Her eyes welled. "I didn't want to tell those horrid lies, but Papa made me."

Two discordant thoughts struck Harry simultaneously. One was that Tessa wouldn't blame someone else for the choices she'd made. She wasn't above untruths and trickery, but she usually had a good reason for it. Regardless, she took responsibility for her actions.

His other thought was that he had a chance now to try to uncover De Witt's plans. Looking at Celeste's pleading expression, he didn't know if she was party to her father's nefariousness; either way, he didn't trust her. Yet it would behoove him to try to get some answers.

"Was it your papa's idea for you to try to seduce me, to distract me while he went into the laboratory that night and stole my work?" he said evenly.

She licked her lips, her gaze darting then returning to his. "Yes...but I wanted to go to your room that night, Harry. You're the only one who's ever been truly good to me," she said in a shaky voice. "The only one who listened and cared. The only one I've ever—"

"Was it his idea also for you to lie the next day? To destroy the only alibi I had?"

"I didn't want to." A single tear spilled over. "I've regretted my actions ever since."

Not as much as I have.

He forced himself to play along. "If that is true—"

"It *is*. How I hated deceiving you." She took a step closer, one hand held out beseechingly. "Despite what I did, my feelings for you were true. As true as the feelings you once professed having for me. I kept those poems you wrote, Harry, hid them from Papa." Her gaze searched his. "I read them every night before I say my prayers."

If she had any sense, she wouldn't have reminded him of the damned verse. The words he'd so painstakingly and awkwardly penned. Yet his mortification no longer flowed like fresh blood, only itched like a healed-over scab. Ambrose had been right: he'd been a lad when he'd fallen in love with Celeste. He could forgive his younger self for trusting too readily. For being blinded by beauty.

What mattered was that he saw things clearly now.

And Tessa, he realized, had been the catalyst. With her spirit, humor, and honesty, she'd taught him to feel again. To trust again.

"What happened here?" Celeste extended a gloved fingertip toward his scarred eyebrow, not quite daring to touch him.

"What has your father done with my formula?"

Fear dilated her pupils. Her hand fell to her side, and she retreated a step. "I... I can't..."

He took hold of her upper arms. "Tell me, Celeste."

"I'm afraid," she whispered. "Papa will be angry."

He felt the quiver run through her and knew that, whatever else might be false, her distress was genuine. She'd always lived in fear of Aloysius De Witt. In the past, she'd denied physical abuses, but De Witt obviously controlled her with other methods. Harry could see that she'd been a pawn in her father's game. He remembered how he'd once wanted to rescue her, protect her, and the memory of that gentled his tone.

"Tell me," he repeated, "and perhaps I can help."

"I don't know the details. Only that he's involved in some bad business." She swallowed. "With bad men."

"Who are these men?"

"I don't know their names, but they're brutes." Suddenly, she launched herself at him, clinging to him like a vine. "Take me away from here. When you suggested it back then, I didn't have the courage, but now—"

Before Harry could extricate himself, he heard a gasp. His head whipped toward the door. He saw the shock on Tessa's face the instant before she ran.

∽

Tessa fled down the hallway, turning a corner—a dead end, save for a door. She ducked blindly into the room. The library...and thankfully it appeared abandoned. There was no movement or sound from the shadowed maze of bookcases beyond the fireplace and sitting area.

She closed the door. Sagged against the wooden partition as she tried to collect herself. To calm her raging emotions.

How could he? she thought with fury and despair.

Take me away from here. When you suggested it back then, I didn't have the courage.

Celeste De Witt's passionate words rang in Tessa's ears. Was Bennett having an affair with the woman? How long had he known her?

Even as Tessa's heart ached, a chill permeated her, numbing some of her pain. Was there more going on between Bennett and the De Witts than she realized? When he'd told her about De Witt being a suspect in the hellfire, she'd accepted it blindly because she'd trusted him. Because she'd believed that he would protect her family.

Now she realized her mistake. Bennett had been lying to her, and who knew what else he was mixed up in? What if his intentions toward not only her but her *family* were dishonorable?

Panic joined the fray just as bootsteps stopped outside the room.

"Open the door," Bennett's voice commanded.

Tessa's heart hammered against her ribs. "Go away, you lying bastard!"

"If you won't open it, step aside."

He wouldn't dare. Just in case, she backed away.

The door exploded with such force that it hit the wall. Bennett stalked in, shutting the door behind him. He advanced toward her, his expression grim. "We need to talk."

"I don't want to hear any more of your *lies*."

"I owe you an explanation."

"Indeed," she said acidly. "The time for that was before I caught you making love to the *suspect's daughter*. Or was that a lie too? Did you fabricate the story of De Witt's guilt?"

"What the devil?" For an instant, he looked nonplussed. Then he snagged her by the wrist. "We need privacy for this."

He dragged her toward the bookshelves.

"Let go of me, you troglodyte!"

"Do you want to compromise your family's safety? If so, shout louder so that everyone at this damned masquerade can hear you."

She glared at him but kept her peace...for now. She allowed him to lead her into the labyrinth of bookcases. The stacks of leather-bound volumes created a strange hush. When they reached the dim and musty heart of the towering shelves, she shook free and faced him.

"I saw you with Miss De Witt in your arms," she said in a furious whisper. "And I heard her say that you'd proposed running off with her before!"

"I did."

His admission pierced her like a bullet. She reeled, unprepared for the impact.

"But that was a long time ago." He dragged a hand through his hair. "Until tonight, I hadn't seen her in over two years. Not since I was at Cambridge."

"What were you doing in Cambridge?" She didn't know why, but those were the words that popped out of her mouth.

"I was studying science."

"You said you were a navvy!"

"I was. After De Witt destroyed my career."

That information made her pause. All of a sudden, she recalled what he'd told her about the inventor who'd created the explosive. The one whose work had killed him.

"You...you're the one who discovered the hellfire?" she said incredulously. "The one you said died?"

"A part of me did die, in a way," he said tightly. "When I was accused of being a thief and liar, my reputation was ruined. I became *persona non grata* in the scientific community. Eventually, I left and used my expertise in explosives to find work as a navvy."

His stark words chased a shiver over her skin. And fed the sudden hope in her heart.

"Tell me everything," she said. "Start from the beginning and leave nothing out."

"I discovered hellfire by accident: an experiment gone wrong," he said darkly. "I made the mistake of sharing my discovery with Miss De Witt. I had been courting her for some time—"

"How long?" Tessa interrupted.

"Four years, give or take. I'd asked her to marry me, but she put me off. Said her father would never agree to let her marry a man of my prospects. I believed her. De Witt is a baron and an ambitious man; he wanted a title for his daughter. When I told her about my accidental discovery, she convinced me to tell her father, to use it to win his favor. He, in turn, expressed great interest in the compound, in its potential for industrial application." Bennett shook his head. "I cautioned him. Told him how dangerous and unstable the explosive was. How I almost blew up the lab and my own bloody self."

Tessa tried to digest the information. The part about him wanting to marry Miss De Witt stuck in her craw.

Of course he would fall in love with a beauty like Celeste De Witt. She's feminine and elegant and... tall. *Everything I'm not.*

"What happened next?" she forced herself to ask.

"We came to an agreement. He wanted me to work on stabilizing the compound, with the caveat that I was to keep my endeavors a secret. He didn't want others finding out about what I'd come to call 'explosive cotton' and beating us to the patent. He also hinted that if my work succeeded, he would offer no objection to my wedding his daughter."

"He knew how to sweeten the pot," Tessa said under her breath.

Harry frowned. "Pardon?"

"Never mind. What happened?"

"Nothing happened. I couldn't stabilize it," he said, "at least not within so short a period of time. After a fortnight, De Witt was breathing down my neck. Said he had investors lined up, industrial works ready to buy our product. After a month, he became unreasonable, irrational. Blamed me for deliberately sabotaging his plans and life's work. One night, following a heated argument, I was ready to end our partnership, to continue studying explosive cotton on my own, when Celeste showed up at my room."

Jealousy burned at the base of Tessa's throat. "What did she want?"

"At first, to apologize for her father. She said he was under duress from financial obligations. But then one thing led to another." He cleared his throat.

"Did you...bed her?" The words scraped painfully from her throat.

"God, no. Celeste would never have allowed such liberties. But we, er, kissed. It was more than she'd allowed in the four years of our courtship."

Relief flooded Tessa that he hadn't bedded Celeste. At the same time, she was glad for the dimness because she could feel her cheeks flaming. Celeste had allowed kisses after four years; Tessa had allowed far more after *three weeks*.

"The next morning, I arrived at the laboratory to find De Witt waiting for me. The Chancellor and other faculty members were present when he accused me of being a thief." Bennett's hands clenched at his sides. "He claimed that I'd ransacked his laboratory the night before, stolen the notes he'd kept of his experimentation. And he had proof. Before my arrival, he and the others had searched my laboratory. They found a journal, written in his hand, containing notes on the explosive cotton."

"He stole your notebook, made a version in his hand,"—Tessa put two and two together—"and then put it in your lab to be found?"

Bennett's glance was startled. "How did you know?"

"Because that's what *I* would do if I were dastardly enough to frame someone."

His features softened, and his words came out with a hoarse edge. "Thank you."

"For what?"

"For believing me," he said quietly.

"I believe you about *this*, but you still lied to me," she shot back.

"I know. And I'm sorry for it."

Although she didn't *want* to soften, the sincerity in his deep voice and the remorse in his eyes made her traitorous heart thump faster. "Tell me the rest."

"I had an alibi for the night before. During the time De Witt had claimed I was in his lab, I was with Celeste. As a gentleman, however, I could not mention it."

"Zounds," she burst out, "it was your career, your *name*, at stake!"

"I know." His mouth formed a tight line. "But I still couldn't ruin a lady's reputation. And I suppose I hoped that she would do the right thing."

"And?"

His expression hardened. "She supported her father's claim. Said she was with him when they saw me leaving his office that night."

"*Bleeding hell.*" Tessa's jaw slackened. "She was in on it?"

"Ensuring that I played the part of the fool," he said bitterly.

The pieces fell into place. What he'd told her in the carriage after they'd searched De Witt's study...about why he couldn't love again. Because he'd been betrayed by the woman he'd believed himself in love with.

Then Tessa remembered something else he'd said.

"In the carriage, you claimed you weren't in love with her anymore," she accused.

His brows drew together. "I'm not."

"Then why were you making love to her?"

"I swear to you I wasn't." He rubbed the back of his neck, muttering, "I was trying to get answers from her about her father, and she just threw herself at me."

"Likely story," Tessa said with a huff.

"You can't honestly think I'd want her after how she betrayed me."

Hearing the revulsion in his tone, seeing the hard set of his jaw, she said grudgingly, "Maybe not. But you wouldn't be the first man to think with an organ other than his brain. You cannot deny that Celeste De Witt is a Diamond of the First Water. She's blonde and willowy and bloody perfection."

"Not my version of perfection. My taste runs toward petite, curly-haired brunettes who look adorable dressed up as ferrets." His bespectacled gaze was steady. "I don't want anyone but you, sprite."

She tried to hold onto her anger. "Then why did you lie to me? Why didn't you tell me about your involvement with the De Witts?"

"I'm not proud of my past." His words were gruff. "And the last thing a man wants to tell the lady he cares for is that he was a stupid bastard."

He cares for me. It was the closest he'd come to saying that he loved her.

"Oh, Bennett." Unconsciously, she reached out a hand.

He gripped it like a lifeline. "I haven't always told you the truth, and I'm sorry for it. But, upon my honor, I vow that I have never lied about my feelings for you."

"You're forgiven." The last of her anger melted away, and she smiled tremulously. "Just don't lie to me again."

A spasm of emotion crossed his face, his eyes briefly closing. When they opened, the raw yearning there washed away her doubts. Made her feel confident and beautiful and, most of all, *wanted*. Made her believe that while she wasn't perfect, she was the one for him. Just as he was the one for her.

"I don't know what I've done to deserve you." His voice was guttural with wonder.

"I don't know either." She tipped her head back, whispered saucily, "But I know how you could show your appreciation."

28

As usual, she had terrible timing.

And, as usual, he was powerless to resist her.

He cupped her face with both hands, feeling how soft and delicate she was. How sweetly trusting. And the ever-present guilt pounded along with desire.

Looking at her heavy-lidded eyes, her parted lips, he burned with wanting...and the urge to unburden himself. To confess his identity, the fact that he was a policeman on a quest to stop the hellfire. What were the chances that she could forgive him, trust him?

I'd trust anyone before a policeman.... Spies, mercenaries, and brutes, the lot of them....

Just don't lie to me again.

Harry's gut knotted. He didn't *want* to lie to her. Yet, if he told her the truth, she would likely cast him from her life. Now, when she was in danger and needed his protection. Losing her love would be devastating...but putting her life at risk?

He couldn't do it.

"Bennett?"

The uncertainty in her voice undid him. While he could not

express the truth in words, he could show her how he felt. His longing for her which was real and raw and beyond anything he'd felt before. Holding her precious face in his palms, he lowered his mouth to hers.

He wanted her to know that no one, least of all Celeste, could hold a candle to her. He intended the kiss to be a tender worship. An expression of yearning that had no specific destination, nowhere to rush, that was wanting and gratitude rolled into one.

Yet the instant she parted her lips for him, beckoning him inside, the flavor of the kiss changed. He sank deeper, lured by Tessa's essence so sweet, tart, and fresh. Suddenly, her arms were looped around his neck, and he was pressing her up against a bookshelf, the gentle spark fanned into a blazing hunger. A hunger fueled by all he wanted to say and could not, by the fact that he shouldn't be doing this. But mostly by pure *need*.

He nuzzled her earlobe, drawing that plump morsel between his lips. She urged him on with breathy pleas, her honest passion as arousing as any aphrodisiac. He trailed kisses down her neck, the soft slope of her collarbones, over the inviting expanse of her décolletage. She didn't usually favor low-cut gowns, and while he hadn't appreciated the way other gentlemen had eyed her bosom, he couldn't argue with the convenience.

He hooked his middle finger under the line of ermine, finding the skin beneath even softer, silkier than the fur. Her stays restricted access, however, and he couldn't reach very far.

"I never thought I'd say this," he murmured, "but I think I prefer you in shirt and trousers."

The dimness couldn't conceal the playful twinkle in her eyes. "I've received many complements on this costume, you know."

"I know. I wanted to strangle the bastards who were ogling you."

"You noticed?" she asked happily.

In the past, he might have mistrusted a woman who expressed delight over his jealousy, but Tessa was different. He knew that she wasn't playing games. She was honestly happy that he'd noticed her success, that she had someone to share it with.

A fact proved when she went on to say, "It didn't start off well, but I recalled what you said and held my head high. I ignored Hyacinth and the others like her, and then I met some perfectly charming ladies. They were so nice that you wouldn't even believe that they're duchesses."

Harry did believe it—because they were his sisters. He'd asked Emma and Polly to look out for Tessa, and the pair had been good to their word. "You don't say."

Tessa nodded eagerly. "They introduced me to others and my dance card filled and—*oh*."

He'd managed to find her nipple, strumming the straining, velvety bud. "You were saying?"

"I can't talk when you do that," she said in that breathy voice he adored.

"Shall I stop?"

"Don't you dare."

He hid a smile. "Now if you were wearing a shirt, I'd take it off, lick you right here." His finger circled her other nipple. "Would you like that, sprite? My tongue on your sweet breasts?"

Desire turned her eyes a hazy green. "You know I would."

Removing his finger, he placed it against her lips. "Suck it for me, love. Make it nice and wet."

His cock jerked as she laved his digit with her soft tongue, sucking sweetly, reminding him of her oral talents. Breathing raggedly, he withdrew his moistened finger and found her nipples again, going back and forth between them.

"Now pretend I'm licking you, kissing you." He tugged gently. "Sucking you here."

Before long, she was making little sounds in her throat.

"At least there's one good thing about this gown," he muttered.

"What is that?" She squirmed restlessly against him.

In answer, he ruched up her skirts with one hand. "Hold them up for me, love."

He went down on one knee. His hands splayed on the bare skin above her pretty, beribboned garters, holding her open to his hungry gaze. Even in the dimness, he could see the dew clinging to her dark nest. His mouth watering, he leaned in.

"*Crikey*," she moaned.

One would think a man eating the sweetest pussy he'd ever had wouldn't want to laugh, but his shoulders shook as he feasted upon her. *Crikey* was right. She was ambrosia to his senses. He ran his tongue through her drenched petals, searching out her loveknot, flicking that pouting bead, then sucking hard.

She arched against his mouth as she spent, and he groaned, pre-come spurting from his raging erection. Still, her wriggling told him she was not quite finished. He surged to his feet, covering her mouth with his own; simultaneously, he notched his middle finger to her hole. He pushed in slowly on both ends, heat burgeoning in his groin as he penetrated her with finger and tongue.

She took him readily, her spine arching against the shelves. He added another finger, easing into her tightness.

"Too much?" he rasped.

"More," she moaned. "Oh, Bennett, give it to me..."

She didn't have to ask twice. He thrust harder, faster, sweat glazing his brow as her little sheath gripped him, her pearl slick beneath his thumb. He kissed her, and she kissed him, and somewhere in that tangle of tongues he felt her quick expulsion of breath. Her pussy fluttered like desperate butterflies around his pistoning fingers, and he swallowed her cries as she reached the summit yet again.

He gentled his kisses and touches as she calmed. She regarded him with dreamy, bliss-filled eyes. God, she was never more beautiful to him than after he pleasured her. He forced himself to rein in his unabated arousal. They'd been gone far too long as it was.

"We need to get you back." He stroked an escaped tendril from her damp cheek. "But first we must restore your coiffure and frock to rights."

Her long lashes lifted. A moment later, she dropped to her knees. His heart hammered as she found the fasteners on his waistband, working on them with alarming dexterity.

"After," she said.

∼

"Er, after?"

Bennett's voice came out strangled, likely because she'd shoved his trousers down his hips. But, surely, he didn't think she would leave him in his present state? She wrapped a gloved hand around his enormous cockstand. He was so aroused that she had to pry the meaty column away from the flexing ridges of his belly. Enough so that she could fit her lips around the bulging head, anyway.

He bit out her name, and she savored the sound, just as she did his delicious musk. She licked up and down the veined pillar of flesh, enjoying the satin-and-steel texture, the way he pulsed beneath her tongue. Remembering his instructions from the last time, she curled her fingers around the root and tried to fit the rest of the shaft in her mouth.

It was no easy task. He was huge, for one thing, and this was only her second attempt. If Bennett's reaction was any indication, however, her efforts were not unappreciated.

"*Christ*, your mouth." He sounded drunk, his voice slurred with passion. "Bloody heaven."

Hmm. Perhaps she was better at this than she realized.

She found a rhythm, bobbing her head in concert with the pumping of her fist. She liked taking him this way, liked that she could return what he gave her and watch *him* lose control. One of his hands was curled in the coiffure that he'd just moments ago fretted over righting. His other arm was extended, his palm flat against the bookcase behind her, as if he needed to steady himself against the onslaught of pleasure. His face was carved with raw, primal need.

All this made her double her efforts. She moved her fist faster, harder, trying to cram in more and more of his cock. His hips bucked, and she choked a little when he hit the end of her throat. When he tried to withdraw, she refused to let him, tightening her hold and taking him deeper.

"Sprite, let go," he bit out. "I can't hold back—"

She came up for air. And to whisper, "I don't want you to."

At her words, his control seemed to snap. His fingers tightening in her hair, he surged powerfully into her mouth. She welcomed his plunging strokes, savoring his abandon, his surrender to her. As an experiment, she used her free hand to cup his stones, rolling the heavy, velvety sac in her palm.

"Bloody *fuck*," he groaned.

He jerked suddenly and then *exploded*. His essence flooded her senses, the hot, salty spurts overflowing her mouth. His shattered breaths, the knowledge of the pleasure she'd given him, filled her with joy.

Still hard, he eased away gently, and this time she let him.

He drew her to her feet and kissed her.

"Christ." His voice ragged, he ran a thumb over her bottom lip. "You taste of me."

"I like it," she whispered.

The wonder in his eyes made her tremble. "Tessa, it's never been like this. I...I've never felt anything like—"

"Ahem." They both jumped at the Duke of Ranelagh and Somerville's loud and not-so-subtle tones coming from the seating area. "Is anyone back there in the shelves?"

Bennett cursed under his breath, his hands fumbling with his trousers.

Gathering her wits, Tessa said in hushed tones, "Stay here."

Before he could stop her, she drew a breath and marched out.

Ransom was standing by the hearth. He didn't look overly surprised when she emerged.

She forced a smile. "You startled me, Your Grace. I was just touring your library. It's, um...very well endowed." *Blast it, why did I say that?* Hastily, she added, "I mean, you have an impressive number of books in your collection."

"Size matters, my dear, and never let a man tell you differently." His brows arched. "Would you like a personal tour of my...collection?"

"No! That is,"—she floundered for an excuse—"I'm rather parched. I was just about to go in search of refreshment. Would you escort me?"

With a hope and a prayer, she made for the door.

"A moment, Miss Smith."

She froze as the duke came up to her. Her breath caught as he reached out...and righted the furry ears that she hadn't realized had been dangling from her coiffure. For an instant, the veil of indolence lifted from Ransom's eyes; his cold, predatory stare lent his costume a chilling authenticity.

"If pussy goes out to play, we must ensure she returns in her proper state," he said.

Crikey, does he know?

Heart thudding, she fought not to blush. Not to cast an incriminating look toward the shelves.

"Th-thank you, Your Grace," she stammered.

The veil fell back in place. Ransom smiled as he held out an arm. "Shall we?"

29

"Promise you'll stay close to the others," Harry said.

"I have promised. A hundred times *at least*."

He could tell that Tessa was fighting not to roll her eyes. He didn't care. He was already regretting that he'd let her talk him into her harebrained scheme. She'd sprung her proposal on him on the way home from the ball last night when the aftermath of pleasure had put him in an indulgent mood. The intimacy they'd shared, beyond anything he'd ever experienced, had primed him to yield to her whatever she wished.

Now it was too late: they were en route to the Garritys' townhouse in Bloomsbury.

Shaking his head, he said, "I don't know what you hope to discover."

"Anything is better than nothing," she said prosaically. "With Alfred on De Witt's tail, we're free to investigate other possible hellfire suspects. I'll keep my eyes and ears open for any clues at Garrity's."

She said this as if she were a seasoned investigator.

"Garrity is a dangerous man," Harry stated. "If he catches you in his home—"

"He won't recognize me. I've only met him once, and it was years ago, when I was just a girl and Grandpapa had taken me to Nightingale's. At any rate, I doubt Garrity will be home at this time of day. If he is, I'll just be plain Miss Smith, there to take tea with his wife."

"And that's *all* you're to do." Thank God his sisters would be there to keep an eye on things. Since he'd asked Ambrose to inform them of his mission and the dangers Tessa faced, they would be sure to protect her.

"Lecture received, Professor."

Tessa's cheeky manner never failed to stir his amusement. She was the picture of the demure debutante in her fawn silk carriage dress and blonde straw bonnet, but at heart she was a saucy wench...*Praise Jesus.*

"One day, young miss," he said, his tone deliberately pedantic, "you're going to learn that there are consequences for misbehavior."

"What kind of consequences?"

He snorted. "You're not supposed to sound excited about getting punished, minx."

"Well, punishments can be pleasurable, can't they?" she said knowingly.

He stared at her. "What the devil do you know about that?"

"There was a popular themed room at my father's club called 'The Headmaster's Office.' I wondered why anyone would find that exciting. Naturally, I had to take a peek."

"Naturally," he said dryly.

"It was all very strange. Rods and paddles and whatnot." She wrinkled her nose. "I asked Pretty Francie about it, and all she would say was something along the lines of, *To each his own.*"

Once again, Tessa's fount of knowledge astonished him. It was a hodgepodge, not unlike her friend Doolittle's pawnshop. She was a veritable storehouse of mismatched facts, half-truths, with a few gems strewn here and there. Being with her was like being on a perpetual treasure hunt: you never knew what jewel you might stumble upon next.

Tessa narrowed her eyes at him. "You wouldn't want to punish me...would you?"

Case in point. What other woman could he have this insanely improper conversation with? The answer was only the one across from him. A female who had the freshness of an ingénue and the mind of a guttersnipe.

The fact made him want to smile.

"Not with rods and paddles and whatnot," he said gravely. "But I might enjoy torturing you in other ways."

"How would you torture me?"

Her breathy voice and rosy cheeks suggested that she wasn't entirely opposed to the idea. His loins throbbed with heat. Egad, their chat was rapidly turning into foreplay. Which wouldn't do: they needed to concentrate on the upcoming visit, not to mention that Lizzie and the groom were just out of earshot on the driver's perch.

Not for the first time, Harry wished that he could have Tessa to himself. That he could take her somewhere secluded, away from the danger and deception and the rest of the world. Where it would just be him and her and nothing between them...

Indulging in the fantasy, just for a moment, he said in a low voice, "I might, for instance, prolong your pleasure by making you wait for it."

"I don't like waiting," she protested.

"Exactly. And if you disobeyed me, I would make you wait longer. I'd kiss you everywhere, but I wouldn't let you come." His voice turned husky at the thought. "Not until you asked me nicely."

Her lips formed a silent "o." The same shape they'd taken when they'd circled his cock. When she'd given him the most intense climax of his life, turning him inside out with pleasure. He'd never known a more generous lover and not just in bed.

Tessa accepted him, never asked for more than he could give, and, by God, it made him want to give her everything.

Unfortunately, the carriage was slowing, and as much as he wanted to continue the conversation—or, indeed, turn talk into action—this was neither the time nor the place.

Soon, he told himself. *The day will come soon when she is safe, and then I'll tell her everything. I'll beg her forgiveness and make her mine. For good.*

"Tessa," he said.

"Hmm?"

His lips quirked at her sultry response, the glazed-over look in her verdant eyes that told him she was reliving their moments of passion too. She was a lusty sprite, and he liked that about her. Liked everything about her.

"We're here," he said. "Stay close to the duchesses, don't go anywhere alone. Promise me?"

"I promise," she breathed.

~

"I'm ever so glad you could visit," Gabriella Garrity said.

"Thank you for your hospitality," Tessa replied and meant it.

Gabby had clearly put forth an effort for the day's visit. Upon arriving at the enormous, newly built residence, the guests had been ushered through an entrance hall of gleaming marble to the present sumptuous drawing room. Everything in the house spoke of wealth and exquisite taste. The silk-covered walls and rosewood furnishings had an understated elegance, the dove grey upholstery a subtle, luxurious luster.

In contrast, there was nothing understated about the refreshments. Earlier, the butler had rolled in a cart with enough iced cakes and finger-sized sandwiches to feed an army. The platter of sliced fruits was a work of art, and Tessa wouldn't have dared to disturb it. Yet Gabby had cheerfully dug in, using silver tongs to serve the pineapple, oranges, and sugared berries to her guests.

Now they were all sitting by the coffee table, Gabby on a divan and the rest of them in surrounding curricle chairs. They were talking and nibbling, and Tessa noted with appreciation that their hostess wasn't the sort to have food on her plate just for show. Gabby appeared to be enjoying every morsel of the cakes she piled on her plate.

"You needn't have gone to such trouble, Gabby." This came from Emma, whose rose satin carriage dress was the perfect foil to her brunette beauty.

"It's no trouble at all. When Mr. Garrity is home, he prefers midday refreshments, so I always have everything at the ready." In the same breath, Gabby said, "Thank you, Burke. That'll be all," to the aged butler, who gave her a deferential bow before departing.

Polly's tawny curls canted to one side, her turquoise eyes widening. "You make preparations like this *every* day?"

"Mr. Garrity likes it." Gabby forked up a bite of lemon cream cake.

"Strathaven would too," Emma muttered, "but that doesn't mean he gets it."

"You have been known to bake His Grace his favorite Scotch pie," her sister teased.

"True." Emma sipped her tea. Above the gilt rim of the fine Sèvres cup, her brown eyes had a roguish glint. "But I usually do so as an apology. Or a bribe."

They all laughed.

"Oh, I have missed you all so!" Gabby set down her plate, the sudden movement causing the ruffles of her lavender gown to shiver like leaves in a breeze. "And you, too, Miss Smith, although I only met you yesterday."

The redhead's words were nonsensical, yet so heartfelt that Tessa couldn't help but smile. "Please do call me Tessa."

Emma set her cup down. "It's been too long, Gabby. How are you, my dear?"

"Everything is quite wonderful. The children are well, although I'll admit it's no imposition to have them out of the house with their governesses. And Mr. Garrity's star continues to rise; Papa says he's one of the most important men in all of London, although,"—a frown worked between Gabby's auburn brows—"I do wish the two of them would rub along better. Such is family, I suppose. My main worry for Mr. Garrity is the demands of his success. Why just over a month ago, he had to deal with the most tragic—"

Just as Tessa's ears perked to hear what Garrity had been involved in, Emma cut in.

"Gabby, dear, you haven't answered my question. How are *you* doing?"

"Haven't I just been going on about that?" Gabby's bright blue eyes were confused.

"Not really, dear." Polly's gentle manner probably put her in good stead with small children and skittish animals. "You've told us about your husband, children, and father, but not about *you*."

"Oh." Gabby's eyelashes fanned against her cheeks. "Well, I suppose...I suppose there's not much to say on that topic."

She reached for her plate, devouring iced cakes in rapid succession.

Tessa saw the duchesses exchange worried looks. Even she, who didn't know Gabby well, felt a twinge of concern about the other's inner state of affairs. She couldn't help but wonder: how could this sweet, guileless lady be married to a man as reputedly cold and ruthless as Adam Garrity?

"Gabby, what is it?" Emma said quietly. "You can trust us."

Gabby swallowed a final morsel. "It's nothing. Only that sometimes I wonder...I wonder if..."

Since they didn't have all day, Tessa nudged her on. "Yes?"

"I wonder if I'm a very good wife," Gabby blurted and burst into tears.

Crikey. Tessa froze, uncertain what to do.

Luckily, Emma and Polly hurried over in swishes of silk, flanking Gabby on the divan.

"There, there," Polly said, patting the sobbing lady's shoulder.

"Get it all out, dear." Emma passed over a handkerchief. "And I have more of these in my reticule if you need them."

"I d-don't know what's the m-matter with me," Gabby said, dabbing at her teary eyes. "I'm not usually a w-watering pot…"

"We all have our moments," Emma said. "And husbands, as we know, have a tendency to strain the nerves."

Gabby let out a wail.

"*Em*," Polly muttered, "you're not helping."

"I was only empathizing with Gabby—"

"But that's just it. *Your* h-husbands adore you. And why sh-shouldn't they?" Gabby said between hitched breaths. "Both of you are perfect."

"But nobody's perfect," Tessa said. Then, realizing that she had inadvertently insulted the duchesses, she added quickly, "No offense to present company."

"None taken. That was sensibly said," Emma said.

Emboldened by the lady's approval, Tessa ventured, "Did something, um, transpire to make you think you are not a good wife, Gabby?"

"You can talk to us without fear of judgement," Polly said.

"I know." Gabby's bottom lip wobbled. "You are the best of friends."

"And the souls of discretion," Emma said.

Twisting the handkerchief in her hands, Gabby said haltingly, "A few weeks ago, Mr. Garrity came home earlier than usual. He was…unlike himself. Agitated, as if he'd undergone some shock. I'd never seen him this way before, not in all our years of marriage. Yet when I asked him what had happened, he told me nothing was wrong."

"If I had a penny for every time Strathaven said that…" Emma rolled her eyes.

"He shut himself in his study. That night, I couldn't sleep, and I decided to check on him. He was still in the study and…well, a trifle disguised."

"A trifle," Polly murmured, "or more than that?"

"He'd finished an entire bottle of brandy." Gabby shook her head in clear bewilderment. "My husband is not one to overindulge in anything. He is always in command of himself. Always."

"And that night, he was not?" Brows drawn, Emma said, "Did he hurt you, Gabby?"

"Oh no, nothing like that!" Gabby sounded aghast, which Tessa took as a good sign. "Mr. Garrity would *never* harm me. Not intentionally anyway." Her eyes filled again.

"Tell us the rest," Tessa urged. Her nape tingled; her intuition told her that she was about to discover something important.

"I asked him again what was wrong. I think, because he was foxed, he told me. He said…someone important to him had died. In a workplace fire. When I tried to get more out of him, he… well, he didn't want to talk." Her color notably high, Gabby mumbled, "The next morning, I saw in the papers that a fiery explosion had burned down a place called The Gilded Pearl… a house of ill repute," she said in a broken whisper. "The coincidence was too great. I had to ask Mr. Garrity, and, when I did, I saw the truth written on his face. I may not be clever, but I know my husband. The person he was so upset over, whom he got drunk over, was some *prostitute* at that bawdy house!"

Gabby dissolved into tears again. While Emma and Polly comforted her, Tessa tried to make sense of the revelation. Someone important to Garrity had worked at The Gilded Pearl? If so, that would most likely rule him out as a suspect in the brothel's destruction. Why hadn't he disclosed this to Grandpapa during their meeting at Nightingale's?

"Did Mr. Garrity admit his infidelity?" Emma was saying quietly.

"He denied it. Told me to stop being silly." Cheeks flushed, Gabby said with a flash of spirit, "But if my husband wasn't being unfaithful, then why would he be so torn up over the loss of some woman who worked at a bawdy house?"

It was a good question. Tessa mulled it over.

"Perhaps she wasn't a lover, merely a friend?" Polly suggested.

Gabby didn't look convinced, and Tessa didn't blame her. From what Tessa knew about brothels (which was quite a lot), visits were rarely platonic. And if Garrity had indeed been enamored of a wench at The Pearl, surely he would share that fact with Grandpapa? It was, after all, an alibi. Then it struck her.

"What if it wasn't one of the prostitutes?" she said.

"I beg your pardon?" Gabby sniffled.

"A lot of people work in brothels..." *Don't give yourself away.* "Or so I've heard. And according to the papers, prostitutes weren't the only victims at The Pearl. There were kitchen staff, footmen, and maids."

And perhaps Garrity had some secret connection to one of The Pearl's employees. Some relationship he wanted to keep quiet...for whatever reason.

"Excellent deduction, Tessa," Emma said.

"You think that's possible?" Gabby whispered. "That Mr. Garrity didn't have a paramour?"

"*Someone important* could mean many things," Tessa reasoned.

"It could be someone to whom Mr. Garrity owes something. A friend...or even some distant relation," Polly chimed in. "Perhaps there is a branch of his family you haven't met?"

"I haven't met any of Mr. Garrity's family," Gabby said slowly. "His mama is deceased, and he will not speak about the rest of his kin—if, indeed, he has any."

"If anything is complicated, it is familial relations." Emma gave a knowing nod. "Which might explain why your description of Mr. Garrity's initial reaction wasn't that he was heartbroken. I believe the term you used was *agitated*."

"You're...right. All of you are."

Hope spread like sunrise over the redhead's face, so dazzling that it was almost painful to see. To witness how desperately Gabby loved her husband. Recalling how she, herself, had felt, catching Celeste De Witt in Bennett's arms, Tessa shivered because she understood.

In her case, however, she knew Bennett could be trusted.

Garrity was another story.

"When Mr. Garrity first came home, he seemed more angry than sad," Gabby said in excited tones. "Then when I found him drunk in the study, he wasn't grieving, exactly. He was more...um, agitated and rather..."

"Rather what, dear?" Polly said.

"Impassioned." Gabby's cheeks turned as red as her hair.

"And there's been no other trouble between the two of you?" Emma said dryly.

Gabby shook her head sheepishly. "I think I may have jumped to conclusions." She broke into a beatific smile. "Thanks to all of you, I feel ever so much better—"

The opening of the door cut her short. Tessa's pulse sped up as a lean, dark-haired man strode toward them.

"Mr. Garrity!" Gabby said breathlessly. "You're home early."

"I hope I am not interrupting." He made an elegant leg. "Your Graces."

Emma and Polly murmured their greetings.

"Miss Smith, I don't believe you've met my husband," Gabby said with unmistakable pride.

Garrity's onyx gaze trained on Tessa. He had the look of a fallen angel, with his slicked-back hair and pale ascetic features.

"A pleasure." His eyes narrowed a fraction. "Have we met before?"

"No." Beneath that stare, she felt like cornered prey. "I'm, um, sure I haven't had the pleasure."

"Will you join us, sir?" Gabby reclaimed her husband's attention. *Thank goodness.*

"Alas, I have work. Do enjoy yourselves, ladies." He bowed once more, pausing to say to Gabby, "I shall see you at supper?"

Gabby nodded, face glowing, looking for all the world like a besotted bride. Garrity, for his part, was not demonstrative, but his eyes were distinctly proprietary as he regarded his wife. On the surface, the pair appeared rather mismatched, yet deep, ineffable currents passed between them.

Tessa knew she wasn't the only one to sense that energy, for Emma and Polly both looked bemused and not entirely at ease. As if they, too, found it difficult to trust Garrity with their friend's happiness.

The only one who seemed untroubled was Gabby, who said brightly, "Who wants more cake?"

30

Due to a light rain, Lizzie rode with Tessa and Harry in the carriage on the return journey. Thus, Harry didn't get to hear about the revelation concerning Garrity until they arrived home, and Tessa sent the maid off on a specious errand while she and Harry took tea in the drawing room.

Since the explosion, carpenters, builders, and other craftsmen had been working around the clock to restore the room. New furnishings filled the space. The windows had been replaced (and girded with wrought-iron bars that served the dual purposes of protection and decoration), and the walls had been rebuilt and repapered in forest green silk.

Even the portraits had been rehung. Althea Bourdelain Black watched on with serene green eyes as her granddaughter paced in front of her.

"This rules Garrity out as a culprit, doesn't it?" Tessa concluded excitedly. "After all, why would he set fire to the place where *someone important* to him worked?"

Standing by the hearth, Harry had to agree. "At the least, this brings Garrity down several rungs on the list of most likely suspects. Well done."

She beamed.

"We should tell your Grandfather," he added.

Her smile faltered. "I know. He's not going to be happy that I went to Garrity's house, is he?"

"He's going to be angry as hell at you for going and at me for taking you there," Harry said bluntly. "Nonetheless, this is too critical a fact to keep secret."

"You're right." Tessa hesitated. "Do you think we ought to take the bull by the horns and tell him everything, including what we know about the De Witts?"

A question that Harry had begun to ask himself. Five days had passed since Black had issued his ultimatum, giving the dukes a week to bring him the guilty party. In the next two days, anything could happen.

On the other hand, Harry had no proof of De Witt's wrongdoing. And bringing up his past with Black would lead to dangerous questions...the kind that could get Harry ejected from Tessa's life.

"Doolittle's been on the watch for four days; let's give him one more," he said. "If he can't get us evidence that De Witt is producing the hellfire, then I'll take my suspicions to your grandfather."

"That's a plan—" Tessa was interrupted by a knock.

The butler entered with a note on a salver. "This just arrived for you, miss."

"Thank you. By the by," she said, "do you know when Grandpapa will be home?"

"I believe the master will be at Nightingale's this evening."

She waited until the butler departed before breaking the wax.

"It's from Alfred." She raised eyes sparkling with excitement. "He wants us to meet him."

"We're alike, you and I," Doolittle said in conversational tones.

"How do you reckon that?"

Harry was only half-listening to his companion. They were in a tavern in Bluegate Fields, the notorious dockland slum, and they'd managed to secure a coveted table by the window. The bulk of Harry's attention was aimed through the grimy glass, on the building across the street. In the descending darkness, the warehouse appeared dilapidated, paint peeling from its windowless walls, its roof sagging. A locked gate barred the narrow entrance.

"You're certain you saw De Witt go in there last night?" Harry said under his breath.

"Certain as death." Doolittle's slurp from his tankard left a foam mustache, making him look like a drunken cherub. "For days, the bastard was giving me the slip. But I turned the tables on 'im yesterday."

Earlier, Doolittle had given a summary of his rather extraordinary surveillance. On the first night, he'd tailed De Witt to Crockford's; De Witt hadn't emerged from the gambling club until nearly dawn. On the second night, Doolittle had decided to take matters into his own hands, slipping into the club and disguising himself as a member of the staff. He'd followed De Witt and made a startling discovery: there was an old tunnel in the basement of Crockford's that connected it to the building next door.

Forced to follow De Witt at a distance, Doolittle had emerged in time to see De Witt exit the other building and hail a hackney. On the third evening, Doolittle had taken no chances. He'd borrowed a friend's hackney and lain in wait by the building next to Crockford's. Sure enough, De Witt had emerged, and Doolittle had picked him up, driving him to the present location.

"The ol' cheeseparer didn't even tip me a bob for my trouble," Doolittle said in disgust.

"You were spying on him," Harry pointed out.

"*'E* didn't know that."

Harry refocused on the warehouse. "What is our plan for getting inside?"

"Patience, my four-eyed friend. We can't just barge in. Been watching the place since last night, and five brutes are working there, the leader being twice my size. But, ne'er fear, Ol' Alfred's got a plan." Doolittle tapped a finger to his temple. "We 'ave to wait until the moment is right."

"When will that be?"

"When I give the say so. And while we cool our 'eels, we might as well 'ave a chat."

"About what?" Harry tried the ale, surprised to find it wasn't half-bad.

"Like I was saying, we've things in common. Both o' us got a way wiv the ladies, for instance."

"I wouldn't dream of comparing my skills in that arena with yours."

"What can I say? Morts like me." Doolittle flashed a gap-toothed grin, wiping his ale mustache off with his sleeve. "But you're playing yourself short, my friend. Don't know a single cove who could've kept Tessa from coming 'ere tonight. 'Ow'd you manage that feat?"

"With a great deal of trouble," Harry muttered.

Specifically, he'd spent the afternoon reasoning, arguing, and negotiating with her. When none of that had worked, he'd kissed her into submission. Or, rather, he'd kissed her until neither of them could breathe and *then* he'd told her he couldn't focus if he was worried about her safety. Only then had she promised him in a sweet, love-drowsed voice that she would stay put until his return...as long as he filled her in on everything.

Compromise was proving a winning strategy with her.

"She ain't an easy one, our Tessa. Now me, I'm a lazy chap who likes 'is 'ens biddable, but you've the look o' a bastard who likes a challenge, eh?"

Beneath Doolittle's knowing look, Harry's jaw heated. Bloody hell, was it that obvious?

"I'm her bodyguard," he said.

"Don't mean you ain't something else, too." Opening the paper twist of roasted chestnuts he'd bought from a street vendor, Doolittle shelled a nut, popped it into his mouth. "Seen the way you look at 'er, and seen the way she looks at you. Known 'er most of 'er life, I 'ave, and I ain't e'er seen 'er look at a fellow that way."

"In what way?" Harry couldn't help but ask.

"Like 'e's a fellow, that's wot. Not a pigeon to pluck or an ape to defy or a target for one o' 'er pranks."

"I've been those, too," he muttered.

Still, he couldn't help but feel proud that he was the first man Tessa had seen as, well, a man. That he would be her one and only. And he was beginning to question his belief that he couldn't love again. What he felt for Tessa was different from what he'd felt for Celeste.

It was deeper, stronger...real.

"Aye, and you're still standing, which is probably why she's got 'er 'eart set on you. Question is, what are your intentions?"

This from a fellow who had a different "wife" for each day of the week.

Harry lifted his brows. "*You* are asking if my intentions are honorable?"

"I'm a man who looks after 'is own. Just ask any o' my women. Now Tessa ain't my mort, but she's the closest thing to a sister that I got. And while she's feisty, she 'as 'er blind spots, one o' 'em being blind loyalty." Something menacing chased over Doolittle's features, reminding Harry that this man had not only survived the stews, he'd thrived in them. "Any cove stupid enough to take advantage o' Tessa answers to me."

Although Harry didn't appreciate having his honor questioned, he was glad that Tessa had a steadfast friend in her corner. For that reason alone, he responded to Doolittle's question.

"My intentions are honorable," he said evenly.

"Black ain't going to like it," Doolittle warned. "'E wants 'er to marry a nob."

"Once the danger is over, I'll find a way to convince him otherwise. Or I won't. Either way, I'm marrying Tessa."

Shrewd eyes studied him. "You mean that?"

"If I didn't, I wouldn't say it," he said impatiently.

"Glad that's sorted. We didn't come 'ere to flap our gums all day. Got work to do."

Before Harry could point out that he wasn't the one who'd instigated the *tête-à-tête*, Doolittle rose from his chair, his eyes on the window. Through the dirty pane, Harry saw a Goliath of a man leaving the warehouse, four others with him. The pack of five crossed the street toward the tavern.

"Now," Doolittle said, "we go."

∼

Harry and Doolittle headed to the alley behind the warehouse. The narrow lane smelled of rubbish and human waste. In this part of town, danger prowled in the dark, and Doolittle kept an alert watch while Harry picked open the locked gate. They crossed a tiny courtyard, tied-up horses nickering as they passed.

Unlocking the back door, Harry entered first, Doolittle on his heels. Lamps on the walls revealed a single cavernous room filled with cargo. The scent of coffee, tobacco, and exotic spices permeated the air. Sacks and wooden crates stamped with the logos of various shipping companies were piled high, forming a maze.

"Someone's been skimming from the docks." Doolittle poked his hand into an open crate, lifting out a swath of gold-shot Indian silk. "This would look fine on my Sal, wouldn't it?"

"Put it back." Harry scanned the dimly lit room. "We're not here to steal."

"Is it stealing to take what's stolen?" Doolittle said in philosophical tones.

At Harry's warning look, the other sobered. "Last night, the coves took less than an 'our for supper, so we'd best 'urry."

"Let's split up to look for the hellfire."

Harry wound his way clock-wise through the labyrinth of cargo, his partner going in the opposite direction. He did cursory searches of crates and sacks and found nothing resembling explosive cotton. When he met up with Doolittle on the other side of the warehouse, the other's expression conveyed the same frustration.

"It has to be here." Thinking of De Witt's townhouse, Harry said, "Let's do another round. Look for a trapdoor or any entryway to a hidden room."

They started off again. This time, Harry kept his gaze on the floor. A thick layer of sawdust covered the rough boards, and he saw no telltale seams that would indicate a trapdoor. He stopped at a corner of the room where a crate stood some seven feet tall and half as wide. He noticed that sawdust was absent around the crate...as if it had been scattered by heavy foot traffic.

He knocked on the side of the container. His pulse thudded at the hollow echo that came back.

"Find something?" Doolittle jogged over.

"This crate is empty." Harry ran his hands over the raised edges, feeling for a hidden mechanism. "I think it's a—"

His finger sank into an indentation in the wood. *Click.* The hairs on his neck rose as the panel of the crate swung open like a door, revealing a set of steps descending into darkness. Reaching into his pocket, he pulled out a candle and lit it.

"Follow me." He headed down, the stairs creaking beneath his boots.

When he reached the ground floor, the astringent smell of chemicals churned his gut. He held up his light...and beheld a scene from his nightmares.

"Bleeding 'ell," Doolittle breathed.

In the dimness, the laboratory had a sinister, otherworldly feel. It was outfitted with the latest apparatus, curves of glass and polished metal. Dread and anticipation unfurled in Harry; he suppressed both, forcing himself to observe with scientific detachment. Going to the long table, which stood against a wall, he found the process for producing hellfire, neatly laid out in stages.

At one end stood large jars labelled *Nitric acid* and *Sulphuric acid*, a vessel for mixing the two next to them. Moving on, he opened a hamper: a clean stack of cotton toweling. Beside it was a glazed earthenware pan, likely used for soaking the cotton in the acid mixture.

He examined the covered container next to it: beneath the glass, the length of soaked linen appeared innocuous. Hastily, he drew his candle back, knowing precisely how volatile that cotton was. A little farther down, a freestanding washstand occupied the corner. A bucket of water and jars labelled *Carbonate of potash* and *Nitrate of potash* rested on the shelves above its basin.

And Harry understood.

"Clever bastard," he murmured. "He washes the cotton, gives it a dip in the potash solutions to further remove impurities. And then presses it dry with this." He tapped the wooden press with rollers beside the washstand. "That's how he achieves a stable product."

He came to a large cabinet like that of an apothecary. He pulled open one of the small drawers and found the familiar iron tube. For safety, he set his candle down at a distance before picking up the sealed metal canister. A long, slow-burning fuse trailed from one end. Carefully, he removed the cap from the other end: guts of shredded explosive cotton spilled out.

Hellfire.

At that instant, footsteps stampeded overhead. A voice boomed, "Who's down there?"

No place to run or hide. Doolittle cursed. Acting on instinct, Harry shoved the cap back in place, holding onto the device and reaching for his candle.

Doolittle whipped out his neddy, a weapon that resembled a stocking stuffed with lead shot. He swung it above his head, gaining deadly momentum as five brutes pounded down the stairs, the Goliath in the lead.

"Intruders?" the beefy man roared. "Get 'em, boys!"

"Make a move,"—Harry held up the explosive, bringing the flame close to the dangling fuse— "and I'll blow this place sky high."

"The mad bastard means to kill us all," one of the brutes gasped.

"Clear a path," Harry said.

All five obeyed. The leader snarled as Harry edged toward the stairs, jerking his head at Doolittle, who clambered up the steps first. Harry followed, going backward, the flame wavering too close to the fuse when he stumbled on one of the steps.

He made it to the top, and Doolittle slammed the crate panel shut behind him, shoving a heavy sack in place, grunting, "It's not going to hold 'em."

The ringleader's voice boomed, "E's bluffing. No cove's stupid eno' to play with this fire. After 'em!"

Harry blew out the candle, shoved the explosive into his jacket. "Run!"

He and Doolittle raced through the maze of cargo, the sound of splintering wood behind them. Footsteps thumped, and Harry knew they weren't going to make it out without combat. Ducking behind a hill of coffee sacks, he grabbed one, threw it across the path to trip his closest pursuer, who flew headfirst into a crate.

The next brute rounded the corner with fists flying. Harry dodged and returned with an upper cut, bone cracking against his fist. The man groaned, stumbling aside, but three more were on his heels. One man faced Harry, one tackling Doolittle, the third running past.

"Take care of 'em, lads," the leader shouted. "I'll make the delivery!"

Harry had an instant to glimpse the sack of explosives in the departing Goliath's grip before his opponent attacked. Staying light on his feet, he dodged the wild swings. He feigned right, moved left, landing a series of swift blows to his foe's gut, finishing with a left hook. The blighter groaned, toppling like a tree, but the first man Harry had fought came charging like a bull. He wrestled Harry's arms behind his back.

"Got a live one 'ere," he shouted.

The ruffian who'd crashed into the crate rose, a blade gleaming in his hand. "'Old the bugger still while I gut 'im like a fish."

Harry struggled, his captor yanking harder. Swiftly, he changed tactics. He pushed backward with all his might. Went with his captor's momentum rather than against it. Caught off-balance, the blackguard shouted as he lost purchase, falling backward. His skull cracked loudly against the ground, Harry landing on top of him.

In the next breath, Harry rolled onto his feet and dove at the blade-wielding ruffian.

They hit the ground, the steel clattering out of reach. Both scrambled for the knife. Harry got to it first, his fingers closing around the hilt, and he twisted around just as he was tackled. He saw his opponent's eyes widen, felt the sickening thrust of metal into flesh, the warm trickle over his knuckles.

He rolled the man off of him and staggered to his feet. Chest surging, he saw that his foe was beyond saving. He surveyed the wreckage: two other men lay insensate, and Doolittle had the last one beneath his boot, his bloodstained neddy held at the ready.

Harry sprinted over. "You all right?"

Scowling, his button nose bleeding, Doolittle looked like an angry Cupid. "I'm fine," he spat.

"Where is your leader taking the explosives?" Harry demanded to the subdued villain.

"Too late." The ruffian's battered face worked into a sneer. "You won't reach 'im in time."

"I'll repeat this once." Harry took out his pistol, jerked the man up by the scruff. "Where. Is. He. *Going*?"

"My friend's got a temper," Doolittle warned. "Look what 'appened to your associate."

Looking over at his dead comrade, the man visibly swallowed.

Doolittle flicked him on the shoulder. "I'd spill the beans, if I was you."

Sweat trickled down the brute's forehead. "If I say anything, he'll kill me."

"Who is *he*?" For effect, Harry pressed the barrel of the gun to the ruffian's temple.

"If I tell you, you didn't 'ear it from me."

Harry cocked the weapon.

"O'Toole," the brute blurted. "'E was the one wot 'ired us. 'E's working wiv a nob named De Witt. De Witt is the brains behind the 'ellfire, showed us 'ow to make the bloody stuff."

"Where did your leader go?" Harry bit out. "Where's he taking the hellfire?"

The ruffian swallowed. "To the Seven Dials. A place called Nightingale's."

31

HARRY ARRIVED IN HELL.

Smoke everywhere, fingers of flame reaching into the night sky. Shouts and screams as people dug through the rubble that had been Nightingale's.

"Holy Mother of God," Doolittle breathed beside him.

Could I have prevented this? If I had acted faster, caught De Witt sooner...

No time to think now, only to act. Harry ran toward the building, intending to help when he heard his name being shouted. He turned, and relief pounded through him to see Tessa's grandfather looking unharmed. Behind him, Malcolm Todd was barking out orders to men hauling buckets of water toward the fire.

Accompanied by Ming and a coterie of guards, Black approached Harry. The soldiers formed a protective rank around the two of them.

"Sir—" Harry began.

"Aven't got time." Black had lost his wig, his eyes glittering in his soot-streaked face. "You remember your promise to me?"

To take Tessa away if necessary. To keep her safe.

"Yes," Harry said tersely.

"Do it. Go now."

He couldn't. Not without telling Black the truth. "Sir, O'Toole is behind this. The hellfire. He has a scientist working for him—"

"De Witt. I know," Black spat out to Harry's surprise. "'Ave the bastard in my custody—or 'ad, rather. 'E's buried 'neath that rubble, God rot 'is soul. Nabbed 'im today: 'e was going to be my surprise for O'Toole tonight, but that blighter didn't show up, and now I know why. O'Toole set a goddamned trap for us."

"How did you know—"

"I know everything...Harry Kent."

Harry froze, his insides turning to ice.

"Known all along who you've been working for. But I also know your family. Know that honor, loyalty, and a need for justice run in the Kent blood."

Stunned, Harry couldn't form a response.

"That's 'ow I know you'll keep your promise to me," Black said in a low growl. "Now if Tessie gives you any trouble, you give 'er this." He removed his signet ring, shoved it at Harry. "She'll know what it means. Take it."

The ring weighed heavily in Harry's palm. And on his conscience. Despite his betrayal, Black was still trusting him to do what was right.

Swallowing, he glanced around at the pandemonium. "I should help—"

"Damn your eyes, Kent, *Tessie's in danger*." The urgency in Black's voice coiled Harry's insides. "I'm countin' on you to take care o' 'er. Trusting you with the greatest responsibility."

"Yes, sir. You can count on me." Harry turned to go.

Black stayed him with a hand. "One more thing: do not tell Tessa your true identity and that you're a Peeler. Not until you 'ear from me that the danger's o'er. I know my granddaughter: if you lose 'er trust, you won't be able to keep 'er safe."

Harry gave a curt nod, then headed off to complete the most important mission of his life.

32

TESSA OPENED HER EYES...AND BLINKED GROGGILY AT THE SIGHT of the carriage interior. Where was she? Then it returned to her like flashes of a nightmare: Bennett's arrival at the house last night, his terse explanation of what had happened, their abrupt midnight flit...

Her hand flew to her throat; next to her medallion hung Grandpapa's ring.

Not a nightmare. It really happened, she thought numbly.

Only a true crisis would lead Grandpapa to part with the symbol of his authority.

She tamped down tears, pulled back her shoulders. What mattered was that Grandpapa and her Father were unharmed. They would defeat their enemies, she knew they would. In the meantime, she would do her duty by obeying her grandfather's command. She would stay safe and protect the future of the House of Black.

Her hand closed fiercely around the ring. *You can count on me, Grandpapa.*

She realized that the carriage wasn't moving. She had no idea where they were, how long Bennett had been driving; she was amazed that she'd fallen asleep at all. Now she pushed aside the curtain, and, beside her, Swift Nick roused, grimacing at the infusion of light.

The sight startled her. There was nothing but...trees?

"Crikey," she muttered. "Where has Bennett taken us?"

Throwing open the door, she hopped down. Her half-boots didn't land on pavement or mud or any of the usual London surfaces. Instead, she was standing on grass—acres and acres of it, as far as the eye could see. There were trees and shrubs, too, more greenery than in Hyde Park, more than she'd seen in her *life*.

Swift Nick alighted, ears pricking. He promptly bounded off into the grass.

"Don't wander too far," she called.

"Tessa. You're awake."

She spun around as Bennett rounded the side of the carriage. He'd shed his jacket and cravat, and his shirtsleeves were rolled up his sinewy forearms. A night beard shadowed his jaw. Behind his spectacles, his eyes were warm with concern.

No one had ever looked so solid, strong, and steady. A wave of emotion crashed over her. Her breath hitching, she pitched herself at him.

His arms closed around her. "Shh, love, there's no need to cry. Everything will be all right."

"I'm not crying," she sniffled against his waistcoat. "That would be stupid. Grandpapa is fine. He's going to take down O'Toole and then we can go home."

"Just so." He rubbed her back in a soothing circle. "We'll just wait here until it's safe to return."

Lifting her head from his chest, she peered up at him. "Where is *here*, exactly?"

"Chudleigh Crest. In Berkshire." He took her arm, steering her around the carriage. "We're at my family's cottage."

"You grew up *here*?" she said in surprise.

His lips quirked. "It's the countryside, sprite, not the Outer Hebrides."

To her, the world here was so different from her city upbringing that it might as well have been those isolated islands. "The farthest I've been from London is Hampstead. Mama's constitution is too weak for travel, and Grandpapa has always been too busy to leave the city."

"Then we'll grow two plants with one seed. We'll keep you safe here and give you a sampling of country living." Smiling, Bennett unlatched the garden gate for her.

She passed through a trellised archway blooming with yellow roses, and her eyes widened with wonder. "This is your family home?"

To her, the place could have come from a storybook. The cottage was built of gingerbread-colored brick, with cheerful windows and ivy climbing the walls. Surrounded by overgrown hedgerows and rose bushes, the cottage had a cozy, tumbledown charm.

"We sold the one that my siblings and I grew up in. This is Ambrose's cottage."

"He won't mind that we're staying here?" she said tentatively.

Taking her hand, he led her through the open door. "Family is always welcome."

Her chest swelled at being included in his family. At the recognition of how much he was doing for her. For so long, she'd gone at things on her own, and it meant everything to know that she had a champion who would help her slay dragons. That she didn't have to face the world alone. That when she needed him most, Bennett was there.

Her fingers tightened around his.

Inside, the cottage had a charmingly rustic feel. The parlor boasted plump, chintz-covered furniture and shelves of books; it was a place that invited one to curl up and relax. Bennett gave her a quick tour of the kitchen, dining area, and snug bedchambers at the back of the house.

"I put your things in here." He led her into the master suite, which had a massive tester bed and chaise longue by the fire. "There's a bathing room through that door. Perhaps you'd care to wash up?"

"In a moment." She bit her lip. "Bennett, will Grandpapa and Father be all right?"

"The situation is precarious." His tone was somber, and she was glad he didn't try to lie to her. "But Bartholomew Black has ruled this long for a reason. He's a strong man, and he's surrounded himself with strong allies. Moreover, he's smart: he knew about O'Toole and De Witt and..." He hesitated, some emotion crossing his face that she couldn't read.

"And?" she prompted.

"And everything important to him is at stake." Bennett cupped her cheek, and she absorbed his warmth. "Your grandfather has a plan, I'm sure of it. You must stay strong and play your part."

"You're right." Sighing, she nestled closer. "I don't know what I'd do without you."

∼

Sometime past midnight, Harry lay in bed, hands tucked behind his head. Without the fog and smoke of London, clear moonlight streamed through a part in the curtains, and he stared up at the shadows frolicking on the ceiling. He couldn't sleep. Because of worry...and guilt.

Black knew who he was, that he'd been working for the police. The cutthroat had chosen to trust him nonetheless because of his family. Because Black knew that Harry would do the right thing. Now Tessa was the only one who didn't know the truth, and Harry burned to tell her everything. To unburden himself of the deception, beg her forgiveness, and start afresh, no lies between them.

But he couldn't. Because Black was right. To break the news to her now would compromise her safety. Her focus needed to be on evading her family's enemies and to distract her from that would be an act of selfishness on his part.

The right thing to do now was to fulfill his promise to her grandfather. To protect her. Only when the danger was over could he be free to confess everything.

To ask her to marry him.

It had taken seeing Celeste again to make him realize that the wound of his past had healed. That the heart he'd given as a young man was not the heart that beat in him now. And what Tessa had bestowed upon him—the sweet, generous bounty of her love—humbled him down to his soul.

He was the luckiest bastard alive that she'd chosen him.

Devil and damn, he couldn't wait for this business to be over. Hopefully, it soon would be, with the help of his family. Before his departure, he'd entrusted Doolittle with a note to deliver to Ambrose. In it, he'd asked Ambrose to offer Black any assistance that he could. While Harry didn't want to risk exposing his present location should the note fall into unintended hands, he knew his family would worry if they didn't know where he was.

Thus, he'd written simply that he'd gone "home." He'd told them he would return when it was safe, and they needn't worry or come after him.

All there was to do now was...wait.

The soft squeal of hinges made Harry jerk, bolt upright in bed.

His heart raced as he saw Tessa enter the bedchamber. She wore a billowing white night rail, her bare toes peeping beneath the hem. Her hair was a glossy mass tumbling over her shoulders.

Having bid goodnight to her over an hour ago, he hadn't been expecting company and was in his usual uniform for bedtime.

That is, in the buff. Hastily, he pulled the bedclothes closer around his bare torso, where'd they fallen when he sat up.

He cleared his throat. "Something amiss, sprite?"

"I couldn't sleep. It's too quiet here...and too loud." She came to the side of the bed, her eyes wide. "Are those blasted birds going to chirp all night?"

He cocked his head, listening. He smiled slowly. "Those are crickets, love."

"Oh." Her head bent, she fiddled with the edge of the sheet.

Her scent and nearness spiked his desire. Beneath the bedclothes, he could feel himself getting hard. Yet he'd vowed to himself that he would act like a gentleman during their stay. He didn't want to take advantage of her when she was at her most vulnerable. There was only so much temptation a man could take, however: being naked, in bed, and inches away from the woman he loved was definitely testing his willpower.

"Was there, er, something you wanted?" he said.

"Actually, yes."

"If you could wait outside, I'll get dressed and—"

"That isn't necessary. What I want is you." Despite her brazen words, her gaze was shy. "May I stay in here tonight?"

Christ. Need clawed at him. He fought it back.

"That's not a good idea," he forced himself to say. "You're tired, and it's late. Tell you what, I'll get dressed, and we'll go back to your bedchamber. I'll stay until you fall asleep—"

"I don't need a guard. I need you." Before he could react, she clambered onto the bed. Onto *him*. Straddling his lap, she whispered, "Don't you want me?"

"It's not a question of wanting—bloody hell, *Tessa*." His fingers dug into her hips as she delicately licked the edge of his ear. "Stop that."

"Shall I do this instead?"

She kissed his jaw, his neck, her hair sliding seductively against his chest. The scent of her, the feel of her...the everything of her. Everything he wanted.

Which gave him the strength to thread his fingers through her hair. To pull her gently away.

"I won't take advantage of you, sprite." He looked into her eyes, luminous pools of moonlight. "You've had a stress—"

"You're right. I have. People I love are in danger, and I can't change that." Her expression was at once innocent, wise, and fierce. "But right now, you're here with me. I love you, Sam Bennett, and, while I don't know what tomorrow will bring, I know what I have in this moment. I know there's nowhere safer for me to be right now than here in your arms."

God, *God,* how could he resist her?

He tipped up her chin. "I want you so damned much, Tessa. Do you know that?"

"Now I do," she said with a tremulous smile.

He could take no more. He tumbled her to the mattress, rolling on top of her, kissing and kissing and kissing her. She answered his fervor with her own, and soon he was dragging off her night rail, impatient to be rid of anything between them.

Skin met skin, and they both sighed. At the bliss, the closeness, the perfection of now with no thought beyond the moment. He wanted to give her everything. To worship his lover, to bring his wanton minx to new heights of pleasure.

He rolled her over onto her belly, hiding a smile at her start of surprise. Her natural affinity for lovemaking could make him forget that she was still a novice. There was much she hadn't yet explored, and he felt a fierce pride to know that he, and only he, would be her guide.

Kneeling to the side of her, he swept her hair off her back and, for an instant, just took in her pristine beauty. Her supple lines and delicate firmness, her skin as unblemished as a field after a fresh snowfall. He bent to kiss the back of her neck, taking his time, savoring the feel and scent of her as he made his way down the lissome ladder of her spine.

"You're shivering," he murmured.

"You're kissing my *backside*," was her breathy reply.

He chuckled against the dip of her back. "You don't like it?"

"I do, but it seems rather wicked."

"Only rather wicked? I'll have to work on that."

He nipped her gently on one pertly rounded buttock. Her squeak of surprise melted into a moan as he licked away the small hurt, his fingers drifting toward the shadowed crevice just beyond. She twitched as his touch skated over her secret rosebud, down to her swollen folds. Hunger flared as he found her plump with juice, ready for him.

He rolled her over and put his mouth on her ripe flesh.

Her fingers curled in his hair, her hips arching as he teased her erect little love-knot. He licked and suckled, and it didn't take long before he tasted her bliss. Like a man starved, he wanted more, would never get enough. He parted her with his thumbs, stabbing his tongue into her pink heat, yearning to get to the heart of his woman. To possess her utterly and forever.

∼

"Bennett?"

Tessa scarcely recognized her own voice. It was sultry, hoarse from her cries of pleasure. Bennett had brought her to climax so many times she'd lost count. She felt utterly spent, as wrung out as a rag.

He lifted his head. Golden embers smoldered in his dark eyes. "Had enough, love?"

"Come here and kiss me," she whispered.

He crawled over her, muscles flexing, big and lean and powerfully aroused. For while he'd seen to her satisfaction with virile persistence, he hadn't yet found his own. When he lowered his head to kiss her, his erection prodded her belly. She reached between them, wrapping her fingers around the enormous shaft, and he groaned against her lips.

"It's my turn." She pumped him firmly, from root to tip. "Will you let me do whatever I want?"

"Whatever you want."

His heated intensity told her it was true. He'd give her anything.

Which meant she could give him…everything.

She scooted upward to align her body with his. Deliberately, she rubbed her soft, wet sex against his turgid length, the feeling so exquisite that her nerve endings reawakened. Instinctively, she lifted her legs, fitting her calves into the hard grooves of his hips, canting her pelvis. The new position notched the blunt head of his cock against her opening, sending thrills of anticipation through her.

"I want you inside me," she whispered.

Corded muscle stood out along his neck, his chest heaving. "Tessa, I don't want to take advantage—"

"You said I could have whatever I want." She wriggled, painting his hardness with her damp desire, and he exhaled harshly. "This is what I want. You inside me, Bennett."

"Christ, Tessa." He framed her face with his hands, his features hard-carved with passion. "Are you certain you want this?"

"I love you," she whispered. "I want to belong to you completely."

"If we do this, there will be no going back," he warned. "You'll be mine, and I will never let you go."

"I'm already yours, my love."

Her words seemed to undo him. His eyes blazed and then he was giving her what she wanted. Fitting himself against her, pushing into her softness, a steady, stretching incursion that made her gasp.

"I'll go slowly," he said. "Tell me if you want me to stop."

"Don't stop," she panted. "Give me more. Give me everything."

He groaned, obliging her. New sensations whirled her senses. His thick cock slid deeper, deeper, and deeper still; while there was a pinch of discomfort, there was also an opening to new delights. He nudged a hidden place, and she jolted at the radiating bliss.

"Am I hurting you?" He tensed above her, every muscle controlled, waiting for her.

"It feels so *good*," she sighed.

"Good doesn't describe the half of it." He lunged slowly, oh so slowly. Brows drawn, he said, "You're so tight, so beautiful..."

He began to withdraw. When she made to protest, he thrust his hips, and then, *then* she began to discover what pleasure truly was. It was indescribable: the heat and intimacy, the soul-searing friction of her lover inside her. Discomfort became a distant memory as she instinctively followed his lead, her hips moving to meet his, her body absorbing the impact of delight.

"Yes, love," he rasped, "move with me, let me have you, all of you..."

He shifted his angle and hers, opening her further. She gasped as the steely root of his cock grazed her pearl. Every time he hilted himself, he ground against her mound, triggering familiar tremors in her pussy.

"Come for me again," he bit out. "Take me with you."

The knowledge that she could bring him over the edge catapulted her into another crisis. Her pussy seized around his thick invasion as she came, and the bliss was better, deeper than anything she'd previously experienced.

He pulled himself from her with a growl. On his knees, he fisted his huge, glistening erection.

His virility would forever be branded in her fantasies. The flexing of all that muscle, his arm bulging as he frigged his magnificent cock. All the while, his hot gaze held hers. He roared her name as he exploded, showering her belly, ribs, and breasts with his creamy heat.

The scent of his satisfaction made her giddy, and she looked at him with a dazed smile.

"That was...that was..." She struggled to find the exact word.

"Everything," he said huskily.

Yes, it was. Exactly.

And it was only the beginning.

"When can we do it again?" she said.

With a groaning laugh, he bent his head and claimed her mouth with a tender kiss.

33

Two days later, Tessa dreamily washed dishes in the kitchen basin. It was the least she could do given that Bennett had prepared their luncheon. Actually, he'd prepared all their meals seeing as she had no clue how to do so (and thus proving her hypothesis that he really could do anything). Presently, he was chopping wood out front.

She could see him through the small window. The sun burnished the thick waves of his hair. His shirt was open at the collar, his sleeves rolled up his powerful forearms. As she watched, he swung the axe in an efficient arc, splitting a log neatly in two.

"Isn't he *perfect*, Swift Nick?" she sighed.

The ferret, who was lounging nearby on a rug, snorted and rolled over to his other side.

Still watching Bennett, Tessa absent-mindedly scrubbed a bowl. Despite her gnawing worry for her kin, she couldn't deny that the last two days had been magical. She'd given Bennett her virginity, and, in return, he'd given her hope that he might be falling in love with her, after all.

Their lovemaking opened up a world of wonder. They'd spent most of yesterday in bed, with Bennett introducing her to variations on the theme. He was masterful and endlessly creative. Her cheeks warmed as she thought of how he'd kissed and worshipped every nook and cranny of her body. Of how he'd drawn her up onto her hands and knees and filled her up from behind, his hips smacking gently but firmly against her bottom, her cries of satisfaction muffled by the pillow...

Yet it was more than the physical joy of sharing their bodies. Bennett was opening up to her in ways he never had before. He showed more of his playful side, revealing a levity to his character that had been dimmed in the past by his brooding intensity. He teased her mercilessly about her city ways, and they'd actually had a *food fight* during last night's supper. She still wasn't certain who'd won. Although, given the steamy bath they'd shared in the copper tub afterward, perhaps they were both winners...

He also shared anecdotes of his boyhood here in the country, the pranks he and his favorite sister Violet played on one another. It had sounded so wonderful that she'd blurted her desire to meet Violet and the rest of his family. And sudden unease had prickled her nape when his expression had abruptly shuttered.

Is he embarrassed to introduce me to his sisters? Does he think they won't approve of me?

When she voiced her fears, his gaze had softened. "My sisters will love you, sprite. That I promise you."

She had to believe him. And, truthfully, his wasn't the only family she had to worry about. Once the peril was over and Grandpapa was restored to his throne—and she believed with every fiber of her being that he would be—she would have to convince him and her father to let her marry Bennett.

Grandpapa might be the easier of the two to win over. He'd entrusted her to Bennett's care, after all, which showed his regard for her guard. Moreover, all that Bennett had done to help the House of Black fight their enemies would surely land him in Grandpapa's good stead.

Her father, however, was a different story. She knew he didn't like Bennett, and Malcolm Todd wasn't a man whose mind was easily changed. Perhaps the only one who could sway him might be Mavis. As soon as Tessa returned to London, she would speak to her mama.

Suddenly, something caught her eye...a plume of dust in the window. A carriage. Coming down the tree-lined lane toward the house.

"*Grandpapa*," she breathed.

With thrumming excitement, she ran for the door, Swift Nick bounding at her heels. She rushed past Bennett, who called her name, but she was too filled with relief and joyful anticipation to stop. She reached the carriage just as it halted.

The door opened; the words of welcome died on her lips.

The Duke of Ranelagh and Somerville descended from the carriage, elegant as always in a maroon frock coat and buff trousers.

"Your Grace," she said in confusion. "What are you doing here?"

Ransom bent at the waist. "Why, I've come to fetch you, my dear."

"I do not require fetching." She frowned at him, feeling Bennett's presence behind her. "How did you know I was here?"

"I know a great many things, Miss Todd. Including the identity of your, ahem, bodyguard here." Ransom slanted a cold and strangely triumphant glance at Bennett. "Do you want to tell her or shall I?"

"I know who Bennett is," she scoffed.

She looked to her lover for confirmation—and his flinch, the wary tension of his large frame sent a sudden shaft of apprehension through her.

"Tessa," he said in a low, urgent tone, "there are things I need to tell you. I would have told you earlier, but—"

"But he didn't want you to know that he's been lying to you for the entirety of your acquaintance." Ransom smiled thinly. "He lied to get into your grandfather's employ; Bennett is not his real name. He is, in fact, Harry Kent, a disgraced scientist and a member of the Metropolitan Police Force. He was sent on a covert mission to spy on your family."

"What?" Shock numbed her. "You...you're making that up. Bennett,"—she turned desperately to her lover—"tell him that isn't true."

The expression on Bennett's face struck her heart like a dagger.

"My name is Harry Kent, and I do work for the police. I was sent to investigate your grandfather," he said hoarsely, "but the goal of the mission soon changed to stopping the hellfire. We're on the same side. Once I got to know you, your family, I realized—"

"He realized he could land himself a bigger fish," Ransom cut in. "How paltry a policeman's wages must have seemed compared to the dowry of Bartholomew Black's granddaughter."

"Devil take you, that had nothing to do with it," Bennett—no, *Harry Kent*—snarled.

"My mistake," the duke drawled. "Perhaps I have you confused with that other Kent family. You know, Ambrose Kent, ex-investigator who married the divine, and divinely rich, Marianne Draven. Or Emma Kent, who netted herself the Duke of Strathaven—"

"One more word about my family, and I'm calling you out," Kent growled.

"A gentleman's duel? How ironic coming from you," Ransom shot back.

"Stop."

The word came from her lips, but it seemed to come from some place far away. Some place that was housed in ice, numbing the pain that was spreading like a crack, threatening to splinter her into pieces. The man she loved, the only man she would ever love, had betrayed her.

He'd never wanted her. He'd been using her as a means to an end: as an instrument to destroy her family.

"Tessa, I swear I was going to tell you everything once the danger was over." Kent was talking, but all she could think was, *You're lying. All of it. Lies.* "Your grandfather, he knew all along who I was. And he agreed that telling you the truth now would risk—"

"Likely story," Ransom drawled, "and difficult to disprove since Black has gone missing."

Panic flared, momentarily blocking out the pain. "What's happened to Grandpapa?"

"I'm sorry to inform you, my dear, but he's been missing since the day before yesterday. He and your father," Ransom said gravely.

"Oh God." She closed her eyes, dread washing through her. "My mama—"

"She is fine. From what I understand, your grandfather's man Ming got her to safety. She's staying with the Garritys...friends of your grandfather, I believe."

"I must get back to London." She focused on that purpose, on that hope. Her world may have fallen apart, but one thing did not change: she was a Black. "I must see to Mama, help in the search for Grandpapa and my father."

"That is why I'm here, my dear. To aid you however I can," Ransom said.

"Swift Nick, get in the carriage," she said.

"Don't go, Tessa." Kent gripped her by the arm, his eyes blazing into hers. "It's not safe. I don't trust this bastard—"

"That's rich," she said bitterly. "You've been lying to me since the moment we met."

"I know. And God, *God*, I wish for once that I had the right words." His hold tightened on her. "That I knew how to tell you how sorry I am."

She couldn't take any more of this. Her emotions were already a seething morass.

"Just stay away from me," she whispered. "Don't come near me again. Now *let me go.*"

"You heard the lady. Let her go, or I'll make you." Ransom snapped his fingers, and three large footmen descended from his carriage.

"Listen to me, sprite." Kent didn't let her go, his features harsh with desperation. "I lied about my identity, but I never lied about my feelings. *I love you.*"

The words she'd longed to hear now shattered her heart. Because they meant nothing.

She meant nothing to him.

One of the footmen tore him away from her.

Kent backed away as the trio circled him. "Tessa, don't go!"

She forced herself to turn away and walk to Ransom, who was waiting by the carriage door.

"You won't hurt him?" she said quietly.

"I abhor violence." The duke shuddered. "My men will restrain him so he can't be a nuisance."

She gave a dull nod and made to enter the carriage, but Ransom's words stopped her.

"There is just one more matter, my dear. I believe your grandfather made known his desire for us to marry. As a man who understands the value of kinship," he said, "I would consider it an honor to assist the family of my future bride."

His intention was clear: in exchange for his help, he expected her to marry him.

At least he's telling me what he really wants. He's not lying to me with words of love.

Anger and despair tangled inside her. Really, what did it matter if she married him—or any other man? She was done with love, done with being lied to and made a fool of. At least with Ransom, she knew the bargain she was getting.

In the background, Harry Kent shouted something to her; she blocked him out.

"Whatever you wish," she said flatly.

"You have made me the happiest of men." Ransom's teeth flashed white against his mustache and beard, and he handed her up into the carriage. "By the by, I went to the liberty of procuring a special license. We may be married upon our return to London."

34

Harry awakened, disoriented by his blurry vision. Then he felt the hot pain lancing across his forehead, the throbbing of his left eye which, strangely, refused to open. He registered that he was gagged by a strip of fabric. He was on the ground, lying on his side. He couldn't move his arms or legs; they were tightly trussed.

The memories blasted through him. Buried him in a darkness worse than that of the tunnel in which he'd almost died. Remorse suffocated him.

"Tessa," he groaned against the cloth.

But she was gone. Gone because he'd lied to her, betrayed her...treated her no better than Celeste had treated him. The pain he'd seen in Tessa's eyes made his own shut in self-disgust.

Why didn't I trust her? Why did I lie to the woman I love?

In retrospect, he saw the strength of her love, knew that, if he'd only taken the risk and told her the truth earlier, she would have forgiven him. Instead, he'd been a coward. He realized, finally, that he hadn't been protecting her—he'd been protecting *himself.* All along, he'd been falling in love with her and terrified of his own feelings. He'd been afraid of opening his heart completely, of exposing himself to the pain of a loss greater than any he'd experienced before.

Now she had left him, wanted nothing to do with him, and he bloody deserved it.

Even as despair swamped him, agonizing fear reared its head. Tessa was with Ransom, who was, at best, a fortune hunter. At worst, he could have a more sinister involvement in all of this. After all, how had the duke discovered Harry's identity? How did he know that Harry was working for the police?

Harry's gut clenched. If Ransom dared to harm even a hair on Tessa's head...

I'll tear him from limb to limb.

He had to get to Tessa before Ransom tricked her into marriage. Or compromised her in some fiendish way. She might not want Harry's heart, but, by God, she would at least have his protection.

He struggled to free himself, to no avail. Ransom's footmen had expertly bound the ropes around his ankles, knees, and wrists.

Think, Kent. You have to get to Tessa.

He needed something sharp to slice through the thick cords.

A knife—in the kitchen.

He tried to rise to his feet, but his bound legs made him fall backward. He grunted as the impact jarred his pounding head and bruised ribs. He waited to catch his breath, then, using his feet and tied legs, propelled himself awkwardly toward the closest wall. The journey seemed to last forever.

Finally, he got there. Propping his back to the wall, he managed to push himself to his feet. Breathing heavily, he estimated the distance to his destination: a dozen yards. He would jump there, get to a knife.

He took the first hop. His entire body shouted in protest.

Gritting his teeth, he repeated the motion.

The door flew open, two figures silhouetted in the doorway.

Ambrose and Strathaven. Thank God they hadn't heeded his instructions to stay away.

"Harry?" Ambrose exclaimed. "Bloody hell, what's happened?"

Relief poured through Harry as his brother came over, yanked off the gag.

"The Duke of Ranelagh and Somerville has Tessa," Harry blurted.

His brother-in-law was working on the restraints. The instant the knots loosened, Harry tore free and shook off the ropes.

He headed to the door in a run. "I'll explain everything on the way back to London!"

∽

"Do you not find the meal to your liking, my dear?"

Tessa paused in the act of pushing her food around her plate. "It's fine."

Ransom dissected his quail with a precision that made her feel a bit queasy. In fact, so did everything in the opulent dining room of his townhouse. They were having a late supper, having driven all day to get back to London. During the ride, her shock and fury at Bennett's betrayal had slowly faded. Now she felt heartache and despair...and realized that she may have jumped out of the frying pan and into the fires of hell.

Ransom had been pleasant enough, but she didn't trust him. His elegance, sensual good looks, and sophisticated ennui: all of it seemed like a mask. She had no idea who this man truly was or what he wanted, other than her dowry.

She pushed her plate aside. "I want to go to my mama."

"We'll fetch her tomorrow. On the way to our marriage ceremony." His golden hazel eyes had a predacious gleam. "She can bear witness."

Why, oh why, had she agreed so rashly to marry him?

"I cannot possibly marry you until my grandpapa is safe," she said quickly. "I want all of my family present at our wedding."

"Finding your grandfather will take resources, my dear. Alas, my coffers are empty," he said ruefully, "which means I will need access to your dowry in order locate him."

"I'll sell my jewelry," she said.

"Quid pro quo, Tessa."

Ransom's words were cool but hard. Much like the man himself. Which proved her theory that aristocrats were as ruthless as cutthroats; the only difference was the weaponry they preferred. The duke wasn't above using her family's safety to force her into submission.

Which made her wonder: what else was this man capable of?

"How did you find out that Bennett is Harry Kent?" she said suddenly.

"A little bird told me."

"If you want me to trust you, then I'll have to know your source," she said coldly.

Ransom sipped his wine. "Not that it matters, but it was the Earl of Ruthven."

Tessa recalled the green-eyed aristocrat who'd been kind to her at Ransom's ball.

"He saw Kent, thought he looked familiar," the duke continued, "and when he saw you with Kent's sisters, he recalled the scandal concerning the younger brother. He put two and two together and recognized Harry Kent. Then he saw you and Kent sneak off to the library alone. As a concerned guest, he thought it best to inform the host of what he'd seen."

"But how did he know that Kent was working for the police?" she persisted.

"Ruthven didn't discover that fact; I did. After learning that Kent was lying about his identity, I hired an investigator to look into him," Ransom said matter-of-factly. "It took less than a day; the investigator had a source on the police force who identified

Kent as a new constable. He also provided a report on Kent's family, including their countrified origins. Indeed, he was watching you when you and Kent took off from London. He guessed where you were headed; that is how I knew where to find you."

Her head spun. "You had someone *spy* on me?"

"I had to keep up with the competition." Ransom drained his glass of blood-red wine. "Now finish your supper. You'll want to be rested for our big day tomorrow."

"I'm not hungry."

"I'll have something else made up for you." He nodded at a footman, who came forward to take her plate.

Stubbornly, she held onto it. "I'll take it up to Swift Nick. He hasn't eaten all day."

"Yes. About that weasel."

The distaste that flavored Ransom's voice set her teeth further on edge.

"Swift Nick is a *ferret*," she said.

"I don't care what he is so long as he stops baring those fangs at me. Perhaps you'd consider a more docile pet? Thanks to the Queen, spaniels are all the rage."

It was the last straw. As *if* she would ever give up Swift Nick!

"If you wish for a docile pet or wife," she said pointedly, "you are bound for disappointment."

"I have no wish for a docile wife." Ransom cocked a brow. "At least not in bed."

His insinuation turned her insides cold. This was all wrong. She couldn't marry this man.

Now that she was thinking more clearly, she could see her options. She would find another way to rescue her grandfather. She and Mama would put their heads together; the House of Black looked after its own. She didn't need the help of Ransom—or any man.

I need to be rid of this blighter. To get out of here. The easiest way to accomplish her goals was to have *him* call off the wedding.

"On the topic of marriage," she said boldly, "you may wish to know that I am not a virgin."

She blocked out the memories of how she'd lost her innocence. All that mattered was dissuading Ransom from marrying her. Everyone knew that men valued purity in their wives.

"Another trait we have in common." He forked a morsel of fowl.

"That's it?" she burst out. "Don't you even *care* that I've shared a bed with another man?"

"As long as you don't come to me encumbered." He sliced a spear of asparagus into equal lengths. "Even then, I could always pass the brat off as my own."

What kind of man *was* this?

She shot to her feet. "I've changed my mind. I'm not marrying you."

He rose, depositing his napkin on the table. "To avoid a tedious scene, let me make myself clear." Although his tone was mild, his features were hard. "This is not a trip to the modiste; you cannot change your mind about this gown or that. We are getting married on the morrow. The experience can be pleasant—or less so. Either way, it is happening."

"You cannot keep me here," she bit out. "That's *kidnapping*."

Ransom sighed. When he spoke, it wasn't to her but the footman. "Escort the lady upstairs. And stay by her chamber. We wouldn't want her to get lost before the wedding."

35

Harry vaulted over the back gate, landing in the dark garden behind Ransom's townhouse.

Ambrose and Strathaven landed beside him.

The three rows of windows at the back of the house were dark. Taking this as a good sign, Harry sprinted to the kitchen door, the other two following him. Finding it locked, he took out his picks and crouched, ready to get to work.

"Hold up, lad," Ambrose whispered. "That might not be necessary."

He frowned up at his brother. "Pardon?"

Ambrose moved aside, pointing upward.

With his brother no longer blocking his view, Harry saw that a window on the second floor had opened. A rope made up of knotted bedsheets dangled out of the opening. As Harry watched, a small figure clad in a voluminous nightgown climbed over the sill and began the precarious descent from some twenty-five feet off the ground.

Holy hell, I'm going to kill her for risking her neck that way...if she doesn't kill herself first.

His heart hammering, he ran over, ready to catch her. He

wanted to call out, tell her to hold on tight, but he was afraid to startle her. To break her critical concentration.

She heard him coming, nonetheless. Her head whipped in his direction, and her makeshift rope swung with a momentum that made him break out in a cold sweat. Fear seized his insides.

"What in blazes are you doing here?" she hissed. "Go away."

"Christ, Tessa, don't let go."

"Of course I'm not going to let go." She sounded supremely annoyed, but at least she continued her descent, fist over small fist, each movement getting her closer to safety.

It seemed to take forever, but at last she was close enough for him to catch her.

"Let go, love," he called, "I've got you."

She ignored him, climbed down the last few feet, and landed nimbly. When she made to walk past him, he moved into her path.

"I thought I told you to stay away," she said, her hands fisting on her hips.

Her eyes flashed at him. Her loose, wild curls frothed around her face.

God, she was beautiful. She was *everything*.

"I'm sorry," he said urgently. "Sorry I lied to you. It's true that the police sent me to investigate Black; they thought he was responsible for the destruction of The Gilded Pearl. But once I informed my superior that Black wasn't responsible, the goal of my mission became to stop the hellfire. I was afraid to tell you the truth because I wanted to stay by your side. To protect you."

"I don't need your, or any man's, protection," she shot back.

She was probably right. "You are terrifyingly resourceful, it's true. So maybe I was wrong: you don't need me. But *I* need *you*."

Was it a trick of the moonlight or did her face soften a little?

"You can go to blooming hell," she said succinctly.

Trick of the light, then.

"I have news about your grandfather," he said in a rush.

"Before we left for Chudleigh Crest, I told Doolittle my true identity and asked him to contact Ambrose, to ask my brother to help your grandfather. But before Doolittle left Nightingale's that night, he saw Black and Todd being taken by O'Toole. He followed them: O'Toole is holding your kin hostage at his flash house in Blue Gate Fields. Doolittle informed Ambrose, whose men have been monitoring the place for the past two days. We have a plan for rescuing your family."

Emotions chased across Tessa's face: hope and fear. Then she lifted her chin. "My thanks for the information, Kent. Now remove yourself from my path."

There was nothing for it. He had to show her how he felt.

He got down on one knee. Took hold of her hand.

She tried to pull free. "What in blazes are you doing? Get up."

"When it comes to feelings, I'm an idiot. I'm not good at expressing or even understanding them, but I know this: I love you, Tessa Todd," he declared. "From the start, you've captivated me, and I'm overcome by you. By *everything* about you. Your spirit, beauty, courage, and..."

Swift Nick poked his head out from her hair and hissed.

"...and even your damned ferret," Harry forged on. "I thought I was in love once, but that was a shadow of what I feel for you. You make me laugh, keep me on my toes, and drive me mad with desire—sometimes all at once. It's as if I've been trapped in a tunnel this whole time, and you...you're the light at the end of it. You give me direction, purpose, and I...I need you, Tessa."

He sounded like a fool, wasn't making any sense, but he didn't know how else to convey the vastness of what he felt for her. She still said nothing. Just looked at him, wide-eyed.

He drew a breath. "And I realized something else too. I thought by not telling you the truth, I was protecting you, but really I was protecting myself. I was afraid to love you, to open myself to that kind of pain. It...it hurt like hell losing my mama. And the business with Celeste reinforced that exposing myself could only lead to disaster. But *not* exposing my heart led to the true disaster: I lost you. The woman I love, the only one I'll ever love."

When she remained silent, he said desperately, "Say something, sprite. *Please.*"

"What happened to your face?"

The slight curve to her lips made his throat swell with relief.

"I had a disagreement with Ransom's men," he said hoarsely. "They wanted to separate me from the woman I love. I wouldn't go down without a fight."

"Well, win next time, will you? That shiner looks terrible." She huffed. "You can get up now."

He surged to his feet, hardly daring to believe. "Am I...am I forgiven?"

"Yes." She narrowed her eyes, jabbed a finger at him. "But you're still on my List of Retribution."

Joy, relief, and love—so much bloody love—poured through him.

"It would be my honor to be on your list. Just as long as I'm in your life," he said tenderly.

He pulled her into his arms and kissed her with everything he felt.

And, Praise God, she kissed him back.

He felt a tap on the shoulder.

He released Tessa's mouth but kept his arms around her when he turned.

"Much as I hate to interfere," Ambrose said, "I suggest you postpone the reunion until we get out of here." He paused, smiling faintly. "A pleasure to see you again, Miss Todd."

"You as well, Mr. Kent," she said with an adorable blush.

Harry shrugged off his jacket, placing it over her shoulders. "Let's get going—"

"You're not going anywhere," the Duke of Ranelagh and Somerville said.

Oh, for heaven's sake.

Seeing Harry face off with Ransom, the former backed up by his brother and brother-in-law, the latter by a team of footmen, Tessa lost her patience.

"You're not really going to fight, are you?" she said.

"Damn right, I am," Harry snarled. "I'm going to pummel this kidnapping bastard!"

"I didn't kidnap her. She made me a bloody promise," Ransom returned.

"I've changed my mind. Live with it." She crossed her arms, glowered at the duke. "If you don't, you're bringing a world of trouble onto your head."

"I'm no stranger to trouble," Ransom scoffed.

"Not *this* kind of trouble. When I tell my grandfather that you forced me into marriage, what do you think he'll do?"

Uncertainty flickered on the duke's face before it hardened again. "He wants a title in the family. He'll give me your dowry as agreed upon."

"Not if I tell him you *coerced* me," she said with deliberate emphasis.

Harry growled in the background.

"Devil take it, I didn't touch you." Ransom sounded less confident now.

"One time, a man *looked* at me with disrespect, and do you know what happened to him?"

The duke hesitated. "What?"

She widened her eyes. "No one knows. He was never seen again."

Ransom's eyes darted as he made the calculation…and came to the expected conclusion.

He shrugged. "I suppose it is the lady's prerogative to change her mind, after all."

"Thank you for understanding, Your Grace," she said crisply.

"You didn't leave me much choice."

"I'm annoying that way. You see the trouble I saved you from?"

He studied her. Strangely, his mouth tipped up at the corners.

"Some kinds of trouble would probably be worth it," he murmured. "If I were a different sort of man."

He turned to leave.

"Not so bloody fast." This came from Harry.

She placed a hand on her lover's bulging bicep. "Let him go." When he stared stonily after the retreating duke, she said, "Please, darling?"

Slowly, Harry's hands uncurled. In the next heartbeat, he swept her into his arms.

He said, "Anything you want, sprite."

36

Soon thereafter, Tessa found herself in the Duchess of Strathaven's sitting room. She was surrounded by Harry's four sisters: Emma, Thea, Violet, and Polly. Rosie, Ambrose Kent's beautiful blonde daughter, who was about the same age as Polly, was also present. Apparently, Emma had written her sisters about Harry's troubles, and they'd all dropped everything to come to Town.

The love between the siblings glowed as brightly as the fire in the hearth. What was more, they had welcomed Tessa into their warm circle, keeping her company while the men went to ascertain Mavis' safety with the Garritys. Tessa had wanted to go too, but, given the lateness of the hour, Emma had insisted that she stay. In truth, she was tired, and it was no hardship chatting and sharing a snack with the ladies.

"How very brave of you to stand up to Ransom," Emma was saying now.

"It was nothing." Tessa idly stroked Swift Nick, who was snoring on the cushion beside her.

"You're *far* too modest," Rosie declared.

"From the way Harry told it," Polly said, her aqua eyes shining, "you were a *true* heroine."

"And not only for the way you stood up to the duke."

This came from Violet, Viscountess Carlisle, the sister closest to Harry in age. She was a tall, pretty brunette with caramel-colored eyes and a tomboyish quality that Tessa instantly liked. She was also obviously *enceinte*.

Violet crammed an entire cake into her mouth. She swallowed before saying, "Harry told me you climbed down from the window using a rope of bedsheets. Crumpets, that's ingenious. How I would have liked to have seen that!"

"Vi once wanted to be an acrobat," Emma said dryly.

"Carlisle doesn't mind that I'm unconventional." Vi's grin was that of a woman who knows her husband loves her for exactly who she is.

In fact, all of the ladies had that special glow.

"Our brother can't stop singing your praises, Tessa," Thea, the Marchioness of Tremont, said with a gentle smile. She was a quiet beauty with golden brown hair. "It's not like him at all."

"What isn't?" Tessa said curiously.

"How open he's being about his feelings," Em replied. "Our dear Harry is a genius, except when it comes to matters of the heart."

"When it comes to feelings, he's a clam." Vi polished off a plate of sandwiches.

Emma raised her brows. "Shall I ring for more refreshments?"

"Might as well," Vi said. "I am eating for two, after all."

Privately, Tessa thought the other was eating enough for six or seven.

"When he got entangled with that De Witt chit," Vi went on, "he didn't say a word to us. Just brooded and looked miserable. Next thing we knew, he was embroiled in some scandal at Cambridge, got tossed out, and ran off to become a navvy. Then he returns to London, again not telling us anything, and enlists with the police force, of all things!"

Since learning of Harry's true identity, an ember had embedded itself beneath Tessa's breastbone, and now it smoldered to life. After hearing Harry's heartfelt confession, she was no longer angry at him. She understood why he'd lied to her, knew he'd been trying to do the right thing. She believed that he loved her; how could she not, after his passionate speech and all his efforts to protect her and her family? Harry being the man he was, she knew that he would also do the honorable thing by her.

What she didn't know was whether she had the strength to do the right thing by him.

"Why did he choose to join the police, do you think?" she forced herself to ask.

"Serving justice runs in our family," Emma said. "Before Ambrose opened his private enquiry business, he worked for the Thames River Police for many years."

Not only was Harry a policeman, he came from a *family* of them? She, on the other hand, was descended from a long line of underworld cutthroats. The smoldering turned into a flame.

We come from two different worlds. How will we build a life together?

"After the scandal at Cambridge," Thea said quietly, "I think Harry felt a need to redeem his name. To him, joining the police might have been a way to regain his honor, although, in truth, he never lost it."

Tessa agreed. Honor meant *everything* to a man like Harry. If he married her, how could he continue working as a Peeler? If she married him, would she have to give up her dream of serving her grandfather, of making the underworld a better place?

She thought of her grandparents' story and, for the first time, wondered whether it was fair to ask the person one loved to sacrifice everything. She and Harry loved each other, yes. But what if love wasn't enough?

"Now we have Harry back because of you, Tessa," Polly said. "We have you to thank."

As the sisters chimed in their agreement, Tessa forced a smile. She told herself not to worry about the future right now. Her priority was the rescuing of her menfolk. Once they were safe, then she would face other decisions.

In the meantime, she had Harry, had his love, and she would make the most of these precious moments for as long as they lasted.

The door opened, and her heart thumped at the sight of her beloved. Then she registered that he was alone. She surged to her feet. "Where's Mama?"

He came to her, squeezed her shoulder. "She's fine, sprite, and with Ming at the Garritys'. As it turns out, Garrity is a true ally to your grandfather. After the meeting at Nightingale's, he and Black apparently met in private and came to an understanding. Although Garrity would not disclose specifics, he indicated that he is just as vested in finding the culprit behind The Gilded Pearl as Black is. He pledged to help Black and to provide safe harbor if needed."

"But why isn't Mama with you?"

"She'd had a dose of laudanum before bedtime, and Gabby suggested that we let her sleep and bring her over here in the morning."

Overwhelmed with relief, Tessa nodded.

"Morning will be coming soon enough," Emma said. "We should all get some rest so that we can be fresh when we plan the rescue of Tessa's kin."

∽

"Harry?" Tessa's voice called softly.

God, he loved hearing her say his name. His real name.

Closing the door that separated the rooms (and sending silent thanks to his oldest sister for the convenient bedchamber arrangements), Harry went to the bed. Dressed in a robe borrowed from Strathaven, he'd debated whether or not to go to Tessa.

It was late, she needed her rest, and it wasn't proper.

On the other hand, he was madly in love with her.

He smiled. "Expecting someone else?"

Tessa was sitting up, a lamp lit by the bedside. "Silly man. I was hoping you would come."

Her candor made his chest clench, but it was a sweet kind of pain. The sweetness intensified when she pulled back the coverlet, patted the mattress next to her.

Hell, he didn't need to be asked twice.

Settling against the pillows, he pulled her into his arms. Just held her and absorbed the rightness of doing so. The rightness of Tessa.

"I adore you," he said against her hair.

She tensed, and he felt a pang of remorse. Given his trespasses, he wouldn't blame her for not believing him. She'd forgiven him, yes, but that didn't mean she would forget that he'd lied to her. He was wracking his brain for a way to tell her it was all right, that he would earn her trust again, when she lifted her head from his chest and looked at him.

"Your sisters told me you weren't the effusive type."

Relieved at the teasing, loving sparkle in her eyes, he said, "I'm not. Only with you."

"Does that mean I'm going to get poems on my pillow?"

"If you want them." He'd give her poems. He'd give her any damned thing she wanted.

"What on earth would I do with poems?" Her hand slid inside his robe, the ridges of his belly flexing beneath her caress. When her fingers circled his cock, his breath hitched. Her touch made him instantly hard. And he got harder when she whispered in his ear, "I'd rather have this."

He turned onto his side, facing her. "We don't have to make love tonight," he said seriously. "You must be exhausted. Let me hold you until you fall asleep."

"Or I could hold you." Her fist tightened, and he couldn't stifle a groan. "And we could pleasure each other until the morning comes. Which sounds better, do you think?"

A question that didn't require an answer. He leaned in to claim her mouth...and found himself pushed onto his back instead. He blinked as she straddled his torso. "Sprite?"

"I've decided how I'm going to exact my retribution. You're going to lie back and let me have my way with you."

Well. This was new.

And bloody arousing.

His erection strained against her bottom. "Whatever you wish, love."

She bent over and kissed him. Sweetly, so sweetly that his blood sang and he reached for her—and found his hands swatted away.

"Keep your hands to yourself, Professor," she said.

God, he was going to come just from her saucy banter.

He let his hands fall to his sides, and she proceeded to kiss him again. Her lips fluttered over his injured face, gentle and sweet and healing. His chest heaved as her tongue traced grooves of muscle, as she licked, nuzzled, and nibbled her way down his body. Tasting him with a desperation that made his fists twist the sheets. When her nightgown got in her way, she yanked it over her head, and her loveliness struck him like a physical blow.

"You're the most beautiful sight I've ever seen," he said.

"So are you. I especially like this." Her finger traced the trail of hair that bisected his abdomen, the ridges leaping beneath her touch. "It's like an arrow pointing to my favorite part."

"Your, er, favorite part?" He couldn't help but grin like a fool.

"Well, after your eyes. And your mouth." Her smile was impish. "I suppose it's *one* of my favorite parts."

"Tessa?"

"Hmm?"

"Your favorite part likes you too."

She took his not-so-subtle hint, making a space for herself between his thighs, wrapping her fingers around his eager cock. He was so hard she had to wrench him gently from his stomach. She frigged him with both hands, his pre-seed lubricating her touch, and he prayed to God that he would last through her exquisite brand of torture.

She put her lips on him, and his hips bucked as she lapped at his erection. Her pink tongue worked over the fat, glossy dome, then down the veined shaft, then, *Christ*, over his pulsing stones. He didn't know what was more erotic: the sensations of her hot little mouth or seeing the pleasure she took in pleasuring him. Her cheeks were flushed, her eyes heavy-lidded as she came up again.

His neck arched as she took him deep into her mouth. "Ah, that's fine."

Her reply was muffled by his rod, the most sensual sound he'd ever heard. She bobbed up and down, up and down, taking more and more of him. When he butted against the back of her throat, her chin brushing his taut balls, he knew it was over.

"I'm going to spend," he grated out.

Her answer was to draw harder upon him.

He detonated with a roar, surging into her giving mouth, giving her everything that he was.

She released him with a pop that made his still-hard shaft twitch. She was panting, her lush lips wet with his seed, and hunger rushed through him. He would never have enough of this woman, never.

Clamping his hands on her slim hips, he hauled her up, heard her gasp of surprise as he planted her sex on his face. Her nectar dripped into his ready mouth, and he growled with pleasure at her abundance. She moaned as he ate her, licking her slit, sucking on her pearl. He stiffened his tongue, pushing into her tight little hole, fucking her sweetness until she came.

Before she finished, he dragged her back down his body. Pleasuring her had brought him to full arousal again. He notched his stiff cock to her entrance and yanked her down.

He held her still, savoring the perfection of their fit. Of her tight and slick around him. Of him hard and throbbing inside her. Everything as it was meant to be.

"Harry," she gasped, "I need to move."

"Go ahead, love. Ride me," he said huskily.

This position was new to her, but his sprite was nothing if not game. She moved her hips, lifting up, her brows knitting...and then she sank down, her lips forming a lush "o."

"I like this," she breathed.

"I thought you might," he murmured.

Soon, she found a rhythm. He kept his hands on her hips, guiding her as she rode him, as she impaled herself on his raging prick. Her pretty breasts bounced as she took him harder and harder, her wet petals kissing his abdomen, her lips chanting his name.

He surged up, capturing her nipple in his mouth. At the same time, he reached to where they were joined, his thumb finding her pearl, rubbing it as he shafted her.

"I love you, Harry," she gasped. "Never forget it."

"I love you, Tessa. So bloody much," he growled.

She came with a wild cry, and he just managed to pull out, groaning as his cock wedged into the crevice of her arse. Two thrusts between those pert hills and his seed blasted from him, raining over her backside.

He closed his arms around her, their heartbeats slowing in unison.

"Tessa?" he said.

She was so quiet that, at first, he thought she might have

fallen asleep. Then she lifted her head, her eyes as soft as seafoam. "Yes?"

"Do you want to know which part of you is *my* favorite?"

"Which one?"

He smiled slowly. "Everything, my love. Every single part."

37

THE NEXT MORNING, FRESHLY BATHED AND DRESSED (LIZZIE had arrived with a change of clothes), Tessa found herself once again in the midst of the Kent family. This time the husbands were present, and they were a handsome, virile bunch. They were also openly affectionate with their ladies, a rarity in Tessa's experience. To her great relief, the Garritys had also come, Mama and Ming with them. Though pale, Mama had returned Tessa's fierce hug.

Ming had stood before Tessa, his head bowed. "That night, O'Toole's men too many. Surrounded us. Master tell Ming go, get Mrs. Todd, take to safety. So I did." His voice was gritty, his hands balling at his sides. "I left him."

"You did what Grandpapa wanted you to do." She'd taken one of Ming's strong, capable hands in both of hers. "You couldn't have saved him. Because of you, Mama is safe. We owe you much, dear friend, and we'll be relying upon you again when we rescue Grandpapa from that villainous O'Toole."

Emotion had burned in Ming's eyes. With a curt nod, he'd withdrawn to the edge of the room.

Tessa now sat next to her mother on the couch, Alfred on her other side. She'd already thanked her friend profusely for all he'd done. Alfred, being Alfred, had waved aside her words of gratitude; currently, he was plowing his way through a plate of refreshments.

The rest of the group was sitting or standing around the coffee table. Although Tessa had slept little last night, the reason standing behind her, she felt invigorated. With all the heads in the room, they would come up with a plan to rescue her kin.

"Thank you all for coming," she said, and the chitchat quieted in the drawing room. "On behalf of the House of Black, I want to express my gratitude for your assistance."

"Any friend of Harry's is a friend of the Kents," Ambrose Kent said.

"Your grandfather once did me a great service, Miss Todd." The sultry voice belonged to Marianne Kent, Ambrose's wife, a glamorous silver blonde. "And I am not one to forget a debt."

During the earlier introductions, Tessa had discovered that Mama and Marianne Kent were acquainted. Although the two had not kept in touch, Mrs. Kent had apparently planned Mama's wedding, a fact that Tessa had been too young to remember.

Destiny meant to twine the paths of the Kents and Blacks, it seemed.

Feeling Harry's hand on her shoulder, Tessa looked up at him, and the steadiness of his bespectacled gaze strengthened her.

She turned to the Garritys, who occupied a love seat. "We Blacks are in your debt for taking care of Mama. May I offer my sincere apologies for the, um, subterfuge at my last visit?"

"No apology necessary." Gabby's smile was as bright as her red curls, her blue gaze clear. "With your family in danger, of course you had to be careful. And we were ever so happy to host Mrs. Todd. There must be no talk of debt, isn't that right, Mr. Garrity?"

Garrity's black brows lifted infinitesimally. "As you say, Mrs. Garrity."

Tessa had a feeling that the moneylender was not quite on the same page as his wife when it came to the debt he was owed. No matter. Once her grandfather was free, he would reward all those who'd been loyal to him.

"The House of Black does not forget a kindness—or a wrong. That scoundrel O'Toole will pay for what he has done." Mama's quiet voice rang with veracity. "Mr. Garrity, will you tell the group about the letter you received?"

Garrity removed a missive from the pocket of his dark frock coat. "It arrived this morning from O'Toole. He has declared himself the new king. He's giving the dukes three days to swear fealty to him. If not, he will execute Black."

A chill swept through Tessa, and Harry's grip tightened on her shoulder.

"The blackguard wouldn't dare," she said in a choked voice.

"At this point, it is clear O'Toole would dare pretty much anything." Garrity flicked a speck of lint from his trousers. "As far as I know, two dukes have crossed over to his side already. He has the men and means to take power. And if those loyal to Black resist, O'Toole will have an excuse to take Black's life."

Tessa's heart kicked against her ribs. "What do we know about the flash house where O'Toole is keeping my kin?"

"Based on the information from my men's surveillance, I've drawn a map." This came from Ambrose Kent, who laid out a piece of parchment on the coffee table. Everyone crowded in for a closer look.

"It is situated in Blue Gate Fields, on the bank of the Thames. My men have scouted four entry points. There are the obvious ones at the front and back of the building." Ambrose tapped his finger on the red X's that marked each spot. "In addition, we believe there are two hidden entrances. My men spotted people entering the adjacent tavern and leaving through the flash house."

"There is a tunnel below ground," Harry said, "connecting the buildings?"

"Precisely."

"What about this last entrance?" Tessa pointed to the remaining red X at the rear of the flash house. "It looks like it is in the river."

"Good eye, Miss Todd. That last entry point does indeed lead into the Thames. My men have spotted lighters going into the banks beneath the flash house."

"An underground water passage," Violet breathed. "It reminds me of all those secret passageways we found when we solved that murder—remember, Carlisle?"

Viscount Carlisle, a rugged Scotsman, sighed. "Aye, lass. No matter how hard I try to forget."

"That is four entry points," Harry cut in. "Have we the men to cover them?"

Kent looked grim. "That brings us to the next question: our plan of attack. Garrity, what is your estimate of O'Toole's forces?"

"O'Toole is the most powerful of all the dukes. With two others, Moran and Lavery, joining him, he will outnumber our combined forces at least two to one. And there is more." Garrity's dark eyes were forbidding in his pale face. "When Black and I met, we both agreed that O'Toole cannot be doing all this alone. He is a ruthless brute, yes, but there is a sophistication behind the hellfire, a subtlety and deliberation in how he has strategically been undermining Black's power that is uncharacteristic of him."

"O'Toole has a partner." To Tessa, this made sense. "Do you think it was De Witt?"

"De Witt was a pawn," Garrity said flatly. "For years, he's been swimming in gaming debts. According to colleagues of mine, he'd been trying to sell a rock blasting device to the railways, but his venture failed when that substance proved too unstable. His gambling got worse. My guess is that he became so desperate that when someone approached him to make the hellfire for a deadlier purpose, he agreed."

"Then someone else is pulling the strings behind the scenes."

Harry's brows drew together. "Someone clever enough to cover his tracks at every turn."

"Or *her* tracks," Emma pointed out. "Never underestimate the power of a villainess. Trust me, I've made that mistake."

At her words, her husband, the wickedly handsome Duke of Strathaven, put a possessive arm around her waist, pulling her snugly against his side.

"We don't have time to worry about this hidden partner," Tessa burst out. "The clock is ticking. We have only two days before O'Toole executes my kin. We must plan an attack."

For a moment, silence shrouded the room.

"It will be a bloody battle," Ambrose Kent said somberly. "One that might incur heavy losses, and, moreover, one that we cannot guarantee we'll win."

"Two to one are not winning odds," Garrity said. "I am not a man to bet on a losing horse."

"But we must help Tessa," Gabby said, her blue eyes rounded.

Looking around the room, Tessa saw concern…and determination. These people, who hardly knew her, would be placing themselves and their men in jeopardy for the sake of her family. Entering a battle they knew they could not win. And she knew she could not ask that of them.

Suddenly, she knew what she had to do. "Mr. Garrity, the traitors Moran and Lavery aside, what positions have the remaining dukes taken?"

His brows lifted. "Severin Knight, Christian Croft, and the Prince of Larks have declared no position in this. I believe they are waiting to see where the chips fall."

"Then it is time they are reminded of the fealty they swore to my grandfather," Tessa said.

"No offense, Miss Todd, but I do not think they will listen to a female."

"I may be a female," she retorted, "but I am also a member of the House of Black."

Standing beside her, Harry said, "I'll go with you."

And she loved him for it. She linked her hand with his.

"Sinjin and I have an acquaintance with the Prince of Larks." This, surprisingly, came from Polly. "Perhaps we could be of help?"

Tessa stared at the beautiful lady and her extravagantly handsome spouse, the Duke of Acton. How on earth would these nobs be acquainted with the leader of the mudlarks?

"It is a long story." Acton's dark blue eyes were amused as he regarded his wife. "We'll explain on the way there."

"We have another ally." Harry spoke up. "The police."

"You think *Peelers* will help us?" Then she recalled that her lover was one of them. "Um, no offense."

"None taken." Harry's reply was rueful. "When your grandfather mentioned that Loach had been an informant for Inspector Davies, I asked my brother to look into the matter. To make sure the police were in no way involved in the plot against your family."

"Davies is clean," Ambrose said quietly. "I spoke with several of his informants. All of them stated that he instructed them never to engage, only to observe. I, myself, have known Davies for over two decades, and my gut tells me he is an honest man."

Still, she hesitated. Old beliefs died hard.

"Just as good and evil exist in the underworld, both are found in the police force," Harry said.

It was difficult to argue with reason.

"Will you ask this Davies to join us, then?" she said reluctantly to her lover.

"Let me talk to him," Ambrose said. "Harry ought to accompany you on your quest."

Surrounded by staunch supporters, Tessa felt a surge of confidence. She grasped the chain of her medallion, pulling it from beneath her bodice. The gleaming disk and her grandfather's signet ring glinted in the morning light.

"From the bottom of my heart, thank you, friends," she said. "The House of Black will not forget your kindness this day."

∼

To Harry's relief, the meeting with the Prince of Larks went off without a hitch. This was not surprising, given the history between the Prince, Polly, and Sinjin. During the adventures that had brought Sinjin and Polly together, Sinjin had saved the Prince's life, and Polly was a mentor to the Prince's young sister. Indeed, the Actons ran a school in the countryside giving interested mudlarks a chance to learn a vocation, should they choose.

Nonetheless, Harry knew a fierce admiration watching his sprite in action. It struck him, not for the first time, that she had much in common with her grandfather. Given the chance to prove her mettle, she did so without hesitation. Her willfulness, pranks, and clever stratagems were but a shadow of what she was truly capable of, if given the opportunity.

She was fearless, resolute, possessed of a royal strength of will. She was a true leader in spite of her sex, diminutive size, and the ferret perched on her shoulder.

When she spoke, people listened. They believed because *she* believed.

Harry could not be prouder to stand by her side.

After securing the Prince of Lark's pledge to help with the siege on O'Toole, Harry and Tessa traveled on without Polly and Sinjin. Earlier, Tessa had sent notes, stamped with her grandfather's seal, to the other two dukes, Christian Croft and Severin Knight. Apparently, Croft was travelling and would not be back for a fortnight. Knight, however, had sent a prompt reply inviting them to meet at his office.

Their carriage navigated through the crowded, narrow streets of Spitalfields to arrive at a street of terraced houses not far from the Petticoat Lane Market. In the falling dusk, all the buildings looked the same, with plain brick fronts, the most distinguishing thing about them being the massive windows that graced all three storeys.

At Knight's address, Harry and Tessa were escorted in by a guard, who led them past lower floors that appeared to be dwelling spaces to the uppermost level. There, a vast room was filled with wooden looms presently unattended. The light of sconces flickered over the spindles of silk and unfinished swathes, giving the place a ghostly feel.

Severin Knight approached them, his large shadow sweeping over the abandoned looms.

"Ah, you must be Miss Todd." He took her hand and kissed it, the gesture unexpectedly suave for a man of his size. When he raised his dark head, there was a gleam of interest in his eyes that Harry did not like. "'Tis a pity we were not brought together by better circumstances."

"Mr. Knight." Pulling free of his grasp, Tessa acknowledged his greeting with a regal nod. "I'm sorry to disturb you, but you must know the situation is urgent."

"Come." Knight's casual wave included Harry. "We shall have the discussion in my office."

As they headed to the back of the room, Tessa said curiously, "I noticed the living quarters are below the workshop. Isn't that a bit topsy-turvy?"

"Depends on one's perspective," Knight said. "A weaver's work depends on light, so he must follow it where it goes."

"Hence the upper floor. And the large windows," Tessa surmised.

"Precisely." Knight ushered them through a door into an opulent chamber. Huge, intricate tapestries covered three of the walls. The remaining wall was nearly all glass, the clear panes refracting the last fingers of sunset clinging to the sky.

"How beautiful," Tessa exclaimed.

Smiling faintly, Knight waved them to chairs by his desk, settling behind it. "Now to business."

"The House of Black is calling all its loyal men to arms," Tessa began.

"Its leader has been captured." Knight steepled his hands. "I'd say the battle has been decided."

"It is far from decided. That coward O'Toole launched a dastardly attack on my grandfather, using the most underhanded of means. He is not fit to be the king."

"Nonetheless, he holds the current king hostage. And two of the dukes have joined him." Knight fiddled with the ornate silver wax jack on his blotter. "I do not enjoy conflict, Miss Todd, but I enjoy being on the losing side less. To be frank, what do I care which king I pay my tribute to? O'Toole will take no more of a cut than your grandfather does. In the end, it is all the same to me."

Seeing Tessa's face redden with anger, Harry said quietly, "Have you seen the effects of hellfire, sir?"

Knight's hand dropped from the wax jack. "I have seen Nightingale's, yes."

"And do not forget The Gilded Pearl. It's not just the destruction of property at issue," Harry said with emphasis, "but the loss of life. Bartholomew Black might not have been a perfect ruler, but in the time that I have worked for him, I've seen him grieve for his subjects, care for them, work to make the underworld a safer place. Do you honestly believe a man like O'Toole will do the same? Do you trust O'Toole to rule, with the power of hellfire in his hands?"

A pause.

Knight leaned back in his chair. "Your bodyguard is a convincing fellow, Miss Todd."

"He's not just my bodyguard." The glowing love on her face made Harry's chest burgeon with pride.

"Ah. Pity." Knight sighed. "Still, I cannot lead my men into a war they will not win."

"We will win, Mr. Knight." Tessa's voice had the ring of conviction. "Mr. Garrity and the Prince of Larks are on our side."

The duke sat up straighter. "This is true?"

"Yes," Harry said, "and Miss Todd will also have the backing of my family."

Knight's dark brows lifted. "And who is your family?"

"My brother is Ambrose Kent."

"I've heard of him." A hint of respect was in the other's voice. "An investigator, no?"

Harry nodded. "And my sisters have married powerful men with connections and resources to help in this fight."

"As you see, Mr. Knight," Tessa said, "there is only one right side to be on. When the House of Black is victorious, we will reward our friends—and woe to all who have crossed us."

Harry thought she might have gone too far with the threat, but Knight gave a bark of laughter.

"I see why the two of you work well together," the cutthroat said. "One woos with logic, the other brandishes a big stick. Very well, you have convinced me. You may count the House of Knight amongst your supporters."

38

Holding Tessa's shoulders in a firm grip, Harry said, "Promise me you'll stay here on the boat with Mavis and Alfred."

Tessa's smile was tremulous, entirely untrustworthy. "I promise."

Frustration knotted Harry's insides. He wanted her anywhere but here, yet she'd insisted on being a part of the rescue. And *Mavis*, of all people, had supported her.

"This is House of Black business," Mavis had said, and that was that.

Now *both* women were on this boat moored just downstream from O'Toole's flash house. It was after dark, and they would be keeping watch here while the men launched the attack. Yesterday, all players had met to plan the siege, which was to be four-pronged.

Knight's group would storm the front entrance, Garrity's men the back. The Prince of Larks, Harry's family, and the police would take the tavern. Lastly, Harry, Ming, and guards from the House of Black would row lighters into the water passage beneath O'Toole's fortress.

Even so, O'Toole had the advantage in numbers. Determined

to help his side win, Harry had worked through yesterday and today preparing special weapons for their attack.

As if reading his mind, Tessa said, "Are your devices and masks packed in the lighters?"

"Everything is ready," he assured her. "We're just waiting for Knight and Garrity's signal."

Knight and Garrity were to go in first, creating a distraction, drawing O'Toole's men up into the fight...and leaving the water way less guarded. Harry had given them a firework to set off once their attack was underway.

As if on cue, Ming poked his head into the cabin. "Time to go."

Harry took a moment to kiss Tessa, and she whispered, "Be careful, my love."

"You, too. Stay put," he repeated.

He boarded one of the lighters. As the small barge glided through the dark water, he looked back at the boat. In spite of the perils ahead, he felt his lips twitch.

Tessa stood on the prow of the boat, her ferret on her shoulder, her trousered legs firmly planted. The wind whipped the stray curls that had escaped her thick plait. She was waving at him, blowing him kisses.

He sobered as Ming distributed the weapons. In addition to the satchel of devices he'd made, Harry would be carrying pistols and ammunition.

"Once in, go to prisoners' cell." Ming reviewed their plan. "Get Mr. Black and others."

Yesterday, the mudlarks had done some additional scouting amongst the watering holes of O'Toole's men. Their keen, plentiful ears had caught wind of two crucial pieces of information. First, the prisoners were being kept behind bars in the basement of the flash house. Second, there was a secret password for entry via the underground water passage.

Harry nodded, silence falling as they approached the cliffs of O'Toole's keep.

He held his pistol in readiness as they passed into the dank cave beneath the flash house. The low ceiling of rock seemed to press down upon him, the memory of being entombed cinching his lungs. Clammy fingers gripped his nape. He started at the sound of movement, of ruffling air—ducking as a black veil swooshed over his head.

Bats, he recognized, heart hammering.

They reached a small, rickety dock, and Harry gladly alighted first. He motioned for the men to stay behind as he approached the huge door that guarded the entrance into the flash house. Pulling down the brim of his hat, he knocked.

A slit opened at eye level, suspicious eyes peering through it. "'Oo are you?"

"Name's Jones, one o' Mr. Lavery's men." Harry figured that the guard wouldn't know the names and faces of all his new allies. "Wiv the bloody bastards attacking above, Mr. Lavery wanted to send in reinforcements below."

"Wot's the password?" the guard demanded.

"*O'Toole the Conqueror,*" Harry managed to say with a straight face.

The peep hole slammed shut. The sound of a metal bolt sliding sounded from the other side, the door opening. "Well, 'bout time I 'ad 'elp down 'ere—*buggering hell.*"

Harry had shoved the door the rest of the way, holding the wide-eyed guard at gunpoint.

"Tie and gag him," he said to one of Black's men.

He led the way through the corridor, which snaked through the bowels of the flash house. Shouts and gunfire could be heard from the floors above, and he prayed their side was winning. He saw a corner up ahead, a falling of light. Heard voices and the rattle of steel.

He motioned to his men to halt. Carefully, he peered around

the corner. A dozen guards in the antechamber, brutes armed to the teeth. They were clustered around a massive door.

"Guard the cell," the leader barked. "And take no prisoners. Master's orders."

The bloodthirsty cheer that went up had Harry leaning back, reaching into his satchel. He readied three devices, donned his mask and gestured to his team to do the same. As soon as the protective gear was donned, he lit the fuses and tossed them into the room.

"What the devil?" Bewildered cries sounded.

Harry had designed the contraptions to smolder rather than explode. As smoke billowed through the room, choking and blinding the unsuspecting enemy, he led the charge.

He headed through the thick grey fog, straight to the leader, attacking with a right hook. His enemy coughed out a curse, weapon clattering to the ground, and they traded blows. A wild punch caught Harry in the gut, but he dodged the next swing, going in low. He tackled the other, plowing his fists until his opponent lay unconscious on the ground.

A hand landed on Harry's shoulder, and he spun, ready to attack.

"Free Mr. Black." Ming's words were muffled by his mask. "Men and I finish here."

Harry nodded, grabbing the ring of keys from the fallen foe. He sprinted through the smoke to the door, Ming and the others forming ranks to get him through. Ripping off his mask, he unlocked the barrier, ran through a corridor into another antechamber and—

He threw himself to the ground, a bullet whizzing by his ear. He skidded on his back, had an instant to register Black and Todd, shouting, trapped behind bars, before O'Toole took aim again. Harry whipped out his pistol. Shots fired simultaneously.

O'Toole stared at him, then at the red stain on the front of his own shirt.

The cutthroat toppled with a thud.

Chest heaving, Harry surged to his feet, staggered over the fallen body to the cell. He took out the key ring, fumbling slightly as he slid in the first key. It didn't turn...

"I'll take that, if you please," a cultured voice said from behind him.

Harry spun around. Found himself at gunpoint.

The grey-haired man holding the pistol looked familiar. *Where have I seen him before?* Something about his noble face and piercing green eyes...

Those eyes regarded him with deadly calm. "Throw your weapons down, or I shall be forced to put a bullet through you."

When Harry didn't obey, the stranger said, "Do you notice the quiet?"

With a sudden chill, Harry did.

"Your men outside have been surrounded by mine. Rounded up and brought upstairs. If you don't want them to die, you'll do as I say."

Bloody hell. With no other choice, Harry complied.

The man took the keys, kicking away the weapons.

"Who are you?" Black growled from the cage. "Why have you done this?"

The stranger laughed, a sound like steel etching glass.

"Look me in the eyes, Bartholomew Black," he said softly. "Look at me and tell me you do not recognize me. Tell me you do not know what you have stolen from me."

Moments passed as Black stared at the stranger. The color slowly drained from his face.

"Your eyes," the cutthroat king said hoarsely. "You...you're Althea's kin."

39

Crouching outside the room, Tessa jerked in surprise.

On the other side of the doorway, Alfred shook his head: a warning not to expose their position. She managed a nod, even as her mind spun.

The Earl of Ruthven...is Grandmama's relation?

She'd gotten tired of waiting on the boat; something had told her that her men needed help. Alfred wouldn't let her go alone, so she and he had taken one of the remaining lighters into the fortress, leaving Mavis with a guard for protection. They'd arrived to see Ming and their men being marched upstairs by O'Toole's gang. Two of O'Toole's men had been left behind to flank the prison entryway; Alfred's flying neddy had taken care of them.

Now it was up to her and Alfred to save Harry and her family.

Flattened against the wall, she risked peering into the room to get a quick lay of the land. Grandpapa and Papa locked in a cell. Harry standing in front...a dead body lying on the ground.

Ruthven was holding everyone at gunpoint.

"Yes, I am Anthony Bourdelain," Ruthven said. "Althea's younger brother."

"Why did you do this?" Grandpapa's voice was hoarse.

"You know why. I'm exacting my vengeance for what you did to my sister." Ruthven's cold tones turned Tessa's spine to ice.

"I loved Althea. And she loved me," Grandpapa said. "I never hurt her."

"You *destroyed* her. She was a debutante, poised to become a great lady. She could have had any title she wanted, but you tricked her, seduced her. You ruined Althea—and our family." Ruthven's words were choppy with fury, edged with a passion that burned with madness. "Do you know how many years my parents scrimped and saved for her launch into Society? We were gentry but destitute, and Althea was our sole hope for improving our fortunes. Then you came along like a bloody thief and stole everything!"

"I told Althea I would look after 'er kin. But your parents, they refused to see 'er. Disowned 'er. Broke 'er 'eart, it did," Grandpapa said raggedly.

"Althea was dead to us the moment she disgraced herself. The pride of the Bourdelains is not for sale. Did you know my father killed himself a year later? I, a twelve-year-old-boy, found him at his desk, his brains blown out, his blood soaking into the piles of his debts. My mother died of shock soon thereafter, and I was sent to an orphanage." Savagery frayed Ruthven's voice. "Everything I suffered was because of you."

"Althea tried to find you. But the orphanage where you were last seen had burned down," Grandpapa said. "She was told that you were dead. For years, she wept at the thought of you."

"I escaped that hellhole, have made my own way in the world since I was fourteen, and I have done things that would make you, a murderous cutthroat, quake in your boots." Ruthven's laugh had Tessa reaching for one of her daggers. "All the while, the thing that drove me to survive was the thought that one day I would avenge my family. Then Fate finally smiled upon me. Handed me a title and fortune and the means to destroy everything you hold dear."

"You didn't do this alone." Harry's voice was calm, reasonable, and Tessa knew he was trying to keep Ruthven talking, to buy time. "How did you recruit De Witt and O'Toole?"

"In order to have my vengeance, I had to take everything from Black. Not just his life, a pittance compared to what he owes me, but his empire too. I chose O'Toole because he is Black's strongest enemy. Or was, rather." Ruthven's voice dripped with contempt as he glanced at his dead partner. "No matter. He served his purpose. As for De Witt, I encountered him at a gaming hell. He was drunk, desperate, told me his sad tale of how he had the most powerful substance known to mankind, and no one wanted a thing to do with it. And I knew I'd found the missing piece."

"Why did you use the hellfire on The Gilded Pearl?" Harry asked.

"The Pearl was a test. And a way to shake the foundations of Black's power. To show that those under his protection were not safe, that his strength and rule were coming to an end."

"I ain't done a thing to you. I demand to be set free," Father declared.

"In the name o' revenge, you've shed the blood o' innocents," came Grandpapa's gravelly voice. "This must stop. Kill me if you must, but let the others go."

"You will not get off so easily." Ruthven laughed again. "Why do you think I convinced O'Toole not to kill you at once and keep you alive? My men will soon have your precious daughter and granddaughter, and you will watch as they die by my hand. As I take away *everything* from you as you have done from me."

Has the bastard captured Mama? Trembling, Tessa knew she had to stay focused.

"But first, I will rid myself of your present companions. They are annoyances," Ruthven said.

Terror struck Tessa's heart. Ruthven was raising his gun at Harry.

She had to act—*now*.

As Alfred tensed in readiness beside her, she gripped her dagger. In the next heartbeat, she leapt into the room, took aim, and let her blade fly.

Ruthven cried out in pain as the steel sunk into the shoulder of his weapon arm. He dropped the gun, and Harry dove for it, grabbing it, then spinning around. The earl snarled, trying to reach the knife embedded in him, but Alfred grabbed the hilt, tearing it loose. He held the bloody blade while Ruthven howled with rage.

Swift Nick darted from her pocket to her shoulder, hissing at the villain.

Harry aimed the gun at Ruthven. "Doolittle, tie him up."

"You're dead," the earl shouted as Alfred tucked away the dagger and withdrew a rope. "All of you. My men have yours surrounded—"

"Be'er stuff that gob o' yours, too," Alfred muttered and gagged the villain.

Tessa ran to Harry. "Are you all right?"

"You're supposed to be on the boat." He looked at Swift Nick. "You, too."

The ferret grinned.

"Never mind that. Let's get everyone free," she said. "Where are the keys?"

"O'er 'ere." Alfred retrieved the keys from Ruthven, tossed them over.

Harry caught them. Tucking away his pistol, he went to open the cell.

Grandpapa came out first, and Tessa threw herself into his arms. "Oh, Grandpapa!"

"Later, my brave Tessie," he murmured. "We ain't got time now."

"Yes," she said tremulously, "they may have Mama—"

Harry's curse startled her.

As did her father's calm words. "Move away from him, Tessa."

She whirled around, shock slamming into her. Her father now held the pistol, she saw numbly...must have filched it from Harry as he left the cell. Now he aimed it at Grandpapa.

"Anyone moves and Black dies instantly," Father said.

"What the bloody 'ell are you doing, Todd?" Grandpapa growled.

"I'm sick and tired o' your blustering, you old fool. Almost died on account o' you. Well, now the tables are turned," Father gloated, "and I got the power now."

"Father," Tessa pleaded.

On her shoulder, Swift Nick bared his fangs.

"Shut your mouth," he snapped. "Now all o' you, drop your weapons and kick 'em o'er 'ere if you don't want Black to die."

With clear reluctance, Harry and Alfred did as her father demanded.

"You too, girl," Father said.

Her hand trembling, Tessa tossed over her remaining dagger.

Her father waved Harry toward the cell. "Now get in. You too, Doolittle."

When neither moved, he cocked the pistol. "Do it, or he dies."

Tessa saw the conflict on her lover's face, and her desperation mounted.

"Please, Harry, just do as he says," she said.

Slowly, Harry moved to the cell. Alfred followed.

Swift Nick hissed—and, in a lightning-fast move, Father yanked the ferret from her shoulder. She cried out as he slung Swift Nick into the cage with such force that the creature's long body slammed into the back bars. With a moan, Swift Nick slumped to the ground.

Harry rushed to tend to the animal as Father locked them in.

"I'm doing this for us, Tessa. Once I get rid o' this bastard, I'll be king." His face shone with terrifying greed, an expression that made him a stranger to her. "When I'm in power, you'll 'ave riches beyond your wildest dreams."

"I don't dream of riches." Her voice hitched. "Don't do this."

Her father slowly circled Grandpapa, the gun steady in his hands. "This is what we'll do. I'll put a bullet in 'im. Then we'll say O'Toole did it, and I killed O'Toole in revenge. Aye, that'll make me a 'ero," he said, chortling, "and Black's natural successor."

"No, Father. You know this is wrong," she pleaded.

"Once I'm king, I can grant you anything you want. Even that bastard Bennett." His eyes glittered. "I'll let you 'ave 'im, Tessa: all you 'ave to do is back up my story."

"She won't lie for you, you bastard," Harry growled, shaking the cell bars. "Neither will I."

Her love: so strong, noble, and good.

"I love you." The words flew from her lips.

The love in Harry's eyes would have warmed her for a lifetime. "I love you."

"You've made your decision, Bennett. Dead men tell no tales." Malcolm Todd's evil smile snuffed out her last flicker of hope.

While this man may have sired her, he was not her kin.

"What will it be, girl?" He addressed her brusquely. "If you're with me, you leave the room while I take care o' business."

"I will not leave. Nor will I lie." She stepped in front of her grandfather.

"Go, Tessie," Grandpapa said heavily. "Ain't e'er asked you for nothing, but I'm asking you now. *Go.*"

"I will not go." She remained facing her father, her head held high. "I am a Black. If you're going to murder Grandpapa, then you'll have to kill me first."

In the background, she heard Harry's shout of denial.

Malcolm Todd's brows drew together. Then his expression wiped clean. "As you wish."

He took aim. She forced herself not to look away as the blast shot through the room.

Death was not as bad as she thought it would be. Her ears buzzed, she felt numb, but there was no pain. Only a strange, floating sort of sensation.

She heard a gasp. Odd, it didn't come from her...but Todd? Then she saw the red blossom on the man's chest.

An instant later, he crumpled to the ground.

She remained paralyzed, even as her grandfather scrambled to pick up the fallen gun.

"Is he dead?" A quiet voice...Mama's?

Tessa's head swung to the doorway. Mama stood there, a pistol in her outstretched hands.

"Not yet," Grandpapa said. "Stand back, my jewel, I'll finish 'im."

"No." Mama walked over to the fallen figure of her husband. "I want him to see me."

"*You?*" Todd gasped up at her. "You...shot me..."

"No one harms my family," she said.

His eyes wide, Todd let out a gurgling sound, and his head fell to the side.

Tessa remained frozen, her eyes on the man whose blood ran in her veins, who'd been willing to shed the blood of his own kin. Who now lay dead because of his greed.

And she felt nothing.

She heard the clang of the cell door opening, and, an instant later, Harry's warmth and strength surrounded her, flowed into her, bringing her back to life. She drew in a shuddering breath as he murmured to her. She felt the familiar scrabble of claws up her arm, and heat pressed against her eyes as Swift Nick's furry head nuzzled her neck.

"It ain't o'er," Grandpapa said urgently. "We got to get—"

At that instant, thundering footsteps sounded outside.

Harry shoved her behind him as the first figure burst into the room.

"Bloody hell." Ambrose Kent's gaze surveyed the scene, taking in the fallen bodies and the bound and gagged Ruthven. "What happened in here?"

~

An hour later, Tessa stood on the prow of the boat. Dawn hadn't yet broken, water and sky forming a seamless dark canvas. She was watching Harry talk with his supervisor. A stern-faced Peeler, Inspector Davies hadn't been exactly friendly to her, yet she owed him nonetheless for the role he'd played in defeating the enemy. At this moment, his men, along with others of her team, were rounding up the villains to bring them into custody.

She couldn't hear what Davies was saying to Harry, but the inspector clapped a hand on Harry's shoulder before exiting on a lighter.

Harry approached her, and her heart ached at his strength and virile beauty. He was everything she'd ever wanted. And, because she loved him, she had to let him go.

"How did it go with Davies?" she managed to say.

"He offered me a promotion and a raise." Harry looked bemused. "He even forgave me for suspecting his involvement."

Do it now. It'll only get harder if you wait. Set him free.

"You don't have to marry me," she blurted.

He blinked. "Pardon?"

"I know you want to do the right thing. But we're too different, you and me." Her heart breaking, she forced herself to go on. "We come from different worlds. You need to lead an honorable life, and you will, when the truth of De Witt comes out and the world discovers all you've done to defeat evil. In society's eyes, you'll be a hero. But you can't be that if you're married to me." Taking a breath, she said, "So I release you from any obligation."

Holding his beautiful, bespectacled gaze was the hardest thing she'd ever done. She waited, praying she had the strength to see this through.

His brows drew together. "Do you love me?"

Blooming hell. Why is he making this so hard?

She couldn't lie. "I do, and I know you love me. But what if love isn't enough? Look what happened with my grandparents. Grandmama lost her family, and Grandpapa was nearly destroyed. I won't let you make such a sacrifice for me. And the truth is...my own happiness would be tainted if I had to leave my world and my family behind."

"I turned down the promotion. Gave Davies my resignation."

Dumbfounded, she stared at him. "Oh, Harry, you can't do that for me—"

"I didn't do it for you. I did it for me." He cupped her face, and she shivered with longing at the familiar rasp of those big, strong hands. "You're what I want, Tessa, the meaning I've been searching for even though I didn't know it. There will be other jobs, and, to be honest, I'm better suited to being a scientist than a policeman anyway. But there will be no other you. You're my light, my anchor, my love."

Tears slipped free, and she didn't try to stop them.

"I love you so much," she said brokenly. "I'll be the wife of your dreams, I swear. I'll do everything in my power to be worthy—"

He kissed her. A kiss of love, passion, and tender persuasion that vanquished her doubts. That convinced her, once again, that love could conquer all.

When their lips parted, her eyelashes lifted, and awe flooded her. Behind him, dawn had broken, dazzling colors filling the sky. The light glinted in his thick hair, in his smiling, loving eyes.

Her heart overflowing, she smiled back.

40

THREE DAYS LATER

"If you pace any more, you'll wear a trench into the Aubusson," Mama chided.

"What's taking so long?" Tessa muttered. "Harry and Grandpapa have been closeted in the study for nearly an hour."

"I expect there are terms to decide. Marriage isn't just between two people, you know."

Hearing the hitch in Mama's voice, Tessa stopped pacing and joined the other on the settee.

"Are you all right?" she said quietly.

"Since you asked me a quarter hour ago? I'm fine, dear." Mama gave her a tight-lipped smile.

"But you've, um,"—Tessa struggled to find the gentlest way to phrase it—"...lost a husband."

"And you a father." Mama smoothed out her black silk skirts, her gaze not quite meeting Tessa's. "A father that I took from you."

Tessa blinked. The other couldn't be serious?

"He may have sired me, but he was no father. I only have one parent, and that is the one who saved my life. You protected me when Malcolm Todd would have killed me and Grandpapa too. You are my true kin, Mama," she said, her voice throbbing with emotion.

"I love you, Tessa." A tear slid down Mama's pale cheek. "I was so worried that once the shock had passed, you'd be angry…"

"Never at you." She touched her forehead to her mother's. "Neither of us will easily forget what happened, but we have each other. And we will get through it."

Their hands met and held. Their fitful breaths were the only sound in the drawing room.

Until Grandpapa's voice boomed from the doorway. "What did I say 'bout a Black not shedding tears?"

Tessa hastily wiped her eyes. Her grandfather hobbled over, and she rose, giving him a quick peck on the cheek before relinquishing the place next to Mama. She crossed over to Harry, who tipped up her chin, his gaze concerned.

"Everything's fine here," she whispered. "How'd things go in there?"

He smiled, putting an arm around her waist.

Relieved, she snuggled against him.

Grandpapa gave Mama his handkerchief.

"I'm sorry to put you through this, my jewel," he said gruffly.

"You didn't put me through anything." Mama blew her nose and straightened her shoulders. "We Blacks stick together. I haven't done anything for you that you haven't for me."

Before Tessa could puzzle out her mother's words, Grandpapa cleared his throat. "Speaking o' family, you'll want to congratulate the newest member."

Felicitations and a toast with champagne followed.

"Now that the danger's o'er, got work to do. The underworld's in shambles," Grandpapa said matter-of-factly, "and I'll need all 'ands on board. I expect you to 'elp with the rebuilding."

Thrilled at Grandpapa's acceptance of her beloved, Tessa looked expectantly at Harry.

"It would be my honor, sir," her fiancé said gravely.

She beamed.

"Well, missy, ain't you going to offer a 'and as well? God knows you've been pestering me 'bout it long enough. Now that I need you, all you do is stand there, smiling like a fool."

She stared at her grandparent's stern countenance, the loving acceptance in his dark eyes, and she blurted, "The House of Black can count on me, Grandpapa."

"It always 'as, Tessie."

He kissed her on the forehead and then declared it was time to give the betrothed couple some privacy. On his way out, Mavis at his side, he paused briefly at Grandmama's portrait. He said nothing, only smiled—a heartbreaking smile of love that had known joy and suffering and had never failed.

Tessa felt tears press against her eyelids once more.

"Am I marrying a watering pot?"

At Harry's gentle teasing, she sniffled. "Of course not. We Blacks don't cry. What took you and Grandpapa so long in the study? Did he give you any trouble? Because if he did—"

"He accepted my proposal straightaway." Harry looked bemused. "Told me he'd always wanted an alliance with my family."

"Then why was he pushing me to marry Ransom?"

"Can't you guess?"

"Grandpapa was campaigning for the duke...so that I *wouldn't* choose him?" She planted her hands on her hips. "Why, the devious old codger!"

"Don't you like the way things turned out?"

She did, but she couldn't very well admit that she liked being *duped*. "If Grandpapa wanted you to be his grandson-in-law so much, what took you so long in the study?"

"We had other things to discuss."

"Such as?"

"Black wanted me to arrange a meeting with Inspector Davies." Harry gave her an amused look. "In order to express his gratitude."

"I can't believe we owe a debt to Peelers," she muttered.

"They fought on our side, sprite. And they're disposing of the hellfire," Harry reminded her.

"With *your* help. You're the one doing all the work."

Harry had been working tirelessly to develop safe ways to handle the hellfire. He'd set up a laboratory and conducted experiments. Tessa hid a grin; she rather enjoyed seeing her professor at work.

She fiddled with a button on his waistcoat. "Is that all you and Grandpapa talked about?"

"We also discussed what to do about Ransom."

Seeing his taut jaw, she said quietly, "Leave it be. There was no harm done, and, besides, the duke has had to flee Town because of his debts. Let the moneylenders take care of him."

"When I think of him abducting you, trying to force you to marry him—"

"It wasn't quite like that." At her fiancé's glower, she said hastily, "I mean, nothing happened. It was child's play to escape—"

"The memory of you swinging twenty-five feet above the ground is not one to remind me of if you're trying to plead that bastard's case."

She didn't want Harry to suffer any consequences for trouncing the duke. Besides, she didn't think Ransom was evil, merely expedient. A prank seemed a more fitting punishment for his crime.

"Why don't you let me take care of Ransom?" she suggested. "I'll add him to my List of Retribution."

Harry's arms crossed over his wide chest, his brows lifted.

"Having experienced your brand of punishment, I can assure you that *no* man is going on that list but me."

Her knees quivered at his possessive tone, the steamy memories he evoked.

And, apparently, he had another memory to give her.

He got down on one knee. Her heart drummed as he took her left hand.

"On that note, I'd best make this official." He cleared his throat. "Tessa Black-Todd, daughter of the House of Black, mother of ferrets, and love of my life—will you do me the honor of marrying me?"

She laughed. "Yes, yes."

He slid a ring onto her finger. Set in a simple frame of gold, the opal glowed with a rare fire.

"Oh, Harry, it's *beautiful*." She turned her hand this way and that.

"It was my mother's." Rising, he brushed his knuckles along her cheek. "She would have loved to welcome you into the family, and my siblings are eager to do so in her stead."

Tessa looked into his handsome, steadfast face, and knew that she'd found her place of belonging. With this man by her side, she could face anything. For they had the kind of love that would endure suffering and celebrate joy and never fail.

The kind that lasted forever.

"I love you," she whispered.

"And I love you."

Their kiss was deep and passionate and sweet. By the time they pulled apart, they were both breathless, desire leaping between them. She couldn't suppress a giggle.

"What's so amusing, sprite?" he murmured.

"I was just thinking that Severin Knight was wrong. About how our partnership works."

He swept his thumb over her bottom lip. "How so?"

"Clearly, I'm the logical one," she said merrily, "and you're the one—"

Harry groaned. "Don't say it."

"—brandishing the *big stick*."

They laughed together—for the joy of the present, the promise of the future.

Then they kissed again.

EPILOGUE

"Harry...we're going to be late..."

Since his wife was naked and moaning those words as he took her up against the wall of her sun-drenched dressing room, Harry didn't think she was too concerned about tardiness. His hands gripped her slim hips, and he lifted her nearly off his cock before slamming her down again. Her tight sheath rippled around him, the pleasure racing up his spine, tingling at his scalp.

"You'll have to hurry up and come then, won't you?" he growled.

She peered up at him with luminous eyes. Her lips tipped up. "I already did."

Devil and damn, she was a lusty sprite. And she was his. All his.

The thought expanded his chest...and his cock. He relished her dainty and limber frame, how easily he could wrench her up and down his erection, holding her aloft with the thrusts of his prick. Her hands speared into his hair, and she pressed her mouth to his, kissing and kissing him as she took him deep inside. He drove in deeper and deeper still, yearning to be as close in body as they were in mind and soul.

Soon passion overwhelmed him, and he knew he couldn't hold

back much longer.

"Help me, love," he panted. "Rub your pearl, make yourself spend again."

Her cheeks flushed, she did as he instructed, reaching between their heaving bodies. His nostrils flared as he watched her slender finger work in her dark thatch, rubbing her little bud as his thick shaft spread her tender petals. The sight of her diddling herself, of his cock plowing her, was too much to bear.

For her, too, apparently.

She gave a breathless cry, her pussy quickening, gushing around his turgid member. The lush milking of her passage summoned his own climax. He shouted out as he blew his seed inside his wife in bursts of hot, endless pleasure.

He buried his face in her fragrant curls, trying to catch his breath.

"So now that we've christened my dressing room," Tessa whispered in his ear, "is yours next?"

"You'll have to give me some time to recover, you wanton minx." With a laughing groan, he reluctantly eased from her, setting her toes on the floor. He chucked her under the chin. "And if we're to christen every chamber of this place, I'll have my work cut out for me."

"Grandpapa may have overdone it," she muttered.

As a wedding gift, Black had given them this palatial residence in Mayfair. What was remarkable about the place wasn't just its many rooms...but the size of its nursery.

"Let's just say his hint was unsubtle," Harry said dryly.

He helped Tessa into her dressing gown before donning his own. He reached into his pocket for his new watch, his lips curving as his fingers brushed the engraved back. Tessa had given the piece to him last week when he'd been readmitted to the Royal Society. With De Witt's perfidy revealed, Harry's reputation had been restored.

The Society had also recognized Harry for his work in the

development of safety standards for the handling of explosive materials. How strange it'd been to have his old ambitions fulfilled, to recognize that, as grateful as he was for the honor, he'd been given a far greater one.

Tessa's cheeky inscription on the watch said it all: *To my husband and Professor of Love.*

There weren't any titles or honors he wanted more.

"Harry, I'm late."

"Now she worries." He shook his head, smiling. "Don't fret, we have an hour yet. We'll get you to the ceremony on time."

"I'm not talking about the ceremony."

Her meaning hit him like a blast of gunpowder. Obliterated his ability to speak.

Her cheeks were pink, her eyes sparkling. "If it's a boy, may I choose the name?"

"Whatever you want," he managed.

He snatched up her hands, kissed them one by one. He was overwhelmed with feeling, but, with Tessa, he didn't mind. Because he knew she would always keep his heart safe.

~

Entering Nightingale's, Tessa experienced a strange case of nerves.

After the hellfire, Grandpapa had funded the coffee house's reconstruction. Although the new interior looked much like the old one, there were some significant changes. He no longer conducted business from an alcove but from a separate suite added to the back of the building.

"You'll be fine," Harry said in an undertone as they approached the new chamber.

Her heart brimmed at the understanding in his warm brown eyes. Day by day, their intimacy had grown, and sometimes it seemed as if they could even read each other's thoughts.

"I hope they'll accept me," she whispered back.

"How could they not? You've been the leading force in rebuilding the underworld."

She smiled at his confidence in her. "I couldn't have done any of it without you."

At that moment, Swift Nick popped his head out...from the pocket of Harry's jacket. Tessa had wanted to look as commanding as possible for today's event, and her fitted cerise promenade dress, while smart, had limited space to house a ferret. Luckily, Swift Nick had grown quite fond of his other human.

"Wish me luck, Swift Nick," she said.

The ferret made a *took-took* sound as she petted his head. With a wink, he burrowed back into Harry's pocket.

She and Harry arrived at the oak doors flanked by a pair of guards who bent low.

"Ready, sprite?" Harry said.

She slid her hand into his, and their fingers linked.

"Ready, Professor," she said.

She drew in a breath and nodded at the guards. They pushed open the doors, and she walked into the grand chamber. A chandelier hung over the massive round table, around which sat the most powerful men of the underworld. They all rose at her entrance, and some—including Garrity, Knight, and the Prince of Larks—bowed as she passed.

She stopped at the empty chair next to her grandfather.

Grandpapa exchanged nods with her husband before taking her hand. She had an instant to see the pride in his dark eyes before he turned back to the table. She faced the waiting men as well.

In a booming voice, Grandpapa declared, "Long live the Duchess o' Covent Garden!"

A heartbeat passed...then answering voices soared to the rafters.

"*Long live the duchess!*"

AUTHOR'S NOTE

Those interested in science history may recognize that I borrowed Harry Kent's "invention" from Christian Friedrich Schönbein (1799-1868), a Swiss-German chemist who accidentally discovered the material that would become known as guncotton and, later, as nitrocellulose. Schönbein's discovery didn't happen until 1845, a few years after Harry's story takes place, but since I was already taking artistic liberty, I decided to take a little more. But it wouldn't have been impossible for Harry to have discovered his "explosive cotton" in 1838: Braconnot, a French scientist, treated wood fibers with nitric acid to form an explosive material he called "xyloïdine" in 1832, and Pelouze, another French chemist, did the same with paper and cardboard in 1838.

BOOKS BY GRACE CALLAWAY

GAME OF DUKES

Welcome to the *Game of Dukes*, a series that draws from Regency London's finest drawing rooms and the shadows of its dark rookeries. Some dukes are peers of the realm, others lords of London's underworld, but all are relentless in their pursuit of justice, power, and passion. They'll meet their match—in the strong, feisty women who capture their hearts.

Book 1: **The Duke Identity**

Shattered by betrayal, ex-scholar Harry Kent finds new purpose as a policeman. Sent to infiltrate a family in London's criminal underworld, he lands a job guarding the family's clever and wicked daughter, Tessa Todd. Neither is prepared for their passionate attraction—or the rising peril that threatens their lives.

Book 2: **Enter the Duke**

In order to escape his cutthroat debtors, the Duke of Ranelagh and Somerville ("Ransom") must flee to a remote country village. There he finds a woman from his past—and a chance for redemption. Will the rake learn his lesson and rediscover his heart? Find out in the next sizzling installment of the *Game of Dukes* series!

Book 3: **Regarding the Duke** (May 2019)
She married him for love. He married her for money.
For years, sweet, innocent Gabriella has adored her powerful husband Adam Garrity, London's most ruthless moneylender. Yet an accident leads to devastating revelations: her illusions about their marriage are shattered...at the same time that he realizes the truth of his feelings for his wife. Can a marriage that started with lies turn into a ravishing love story for all time?

HEART OF ENQUIRY

This series features the adventures of the Kent family. Each of the unconventional siblings finds laughter, steamy passion, and true love while unraveling mysteries and secrets in late Regency England. Join them in their sizzling escapades...

Prequel Novella: **The Widow Vanishes**
Fate throws beautiful widow Annabel Foster into the arms of William McLeod, her enemy's most ruthless soldier. When an unexpected and explosive night of passion ensues, she must decide: should she run for her life—or stay for her heart?

Book 1: **The Duke Who Knew Too Much**
When Miss Emma Kent witnesses a depraved encounter involving the wicked Duke of Strathaven, her honor compels her to do the right thing. But steamy desire challenges her quest for justice, and she and Strathaven must work together to unravel a dangerous mystery... before it's too late.

Book 2: **M is for Marquess**

With her frail constitution improving, Miss Dorothea Kent yearns to live a full and passionate life. Desire blooms between her and Gabriel Ridgley, the Marquess of Tremont, an enigmatic widower with a disabled son. But the road to love proves treacherous as Gabriel's past as a spy emerges to threaten them both... and they must defeat a dangerous enemy lying in wait.

Book 3: **The Lady Who Came in from the Cold**

Former spy Pandora Hudson gave up espionage for love. Twelve years later, her dark secret rises to threaten her blissful marriage to Marcus, Marquess of Blackwood, and she must face her most challenging mission yet: winning back the heart of the only man she's ever loved.

Book 4: **The Viscount Always Knocks Twice**

Sparks fly when feisty hoyden Violet Kent and proper gentleman Richard Murray, Viscount Carlisle, meet at a house party. Yet their forbidden passion and blossoming romance are not the only adventures afoot. For a guest is soon discovered dead—and Violet and Richard must join forces to solve the mystery and protect their loved ones... before the murderer strikes again.

Book 5: **Never Say Never to an Earl**

Despite their outer differences, shy wallflower Polly Kent and wild rake Sinjin Pelham, the Earl of Revelstoke, have secrets to hide—and both desperately fear exposing their true selves. Yet the attraction between them is too strong to deny, and they become entangled in a passionate adventure. Both will have to face their greatest fear in order to win the love of a lifetime... and to survive the machinations of the enemy who lies in wait.

Book 6: **The Gentleman Who Loved Me**

What happens when fate throws a headstrong miss on a

mission to find a titled husband together with a powerful and notorious club owner who is anything but a gentleman? Find out in this final passionate installment in the Kent family series, which stars Primrose Kent and Andrew Corbett in his long-awaited return.

MAYHEM IN MAYFAIR

Welcome to Mayfair, where passion and intrigue go hand-in-hand. This steamy romance series brings to life a Regency London of refinement—and depravity. From bawdy houses to Vauxhall, rakish heroes and plucky heroines discover that the path to true love can take some exciting and decidedly naughty turns...

Book 1: **Her Husband's Harlot**

How far will a wallflower go to win her husband's love? When her disguise as a courtesan backfires, Lady Helena finds herself entangled in a game of deception and desire with her husband Nicholas, the Marquess of Harteford ... and discovers that he has dark secrets of his own.

Book 2: **Her Wanton Wager**

To what lengths will a feisty miss go to save her family from ruin? Miss Persephone Fines takes on a wager of seduction with notorious gaming hell owner Gavin Hunt and discovers that love is the most dangerous risk of all.

Book 3: **Her Protector's Pleasure**

Wealthy widow Lady Marianne Draven will stop at nothing to find her kidnapped daughter. Having suffered betrayal in the past, she trusts no man—and especially not Thames River Policeman Ambrose Kent, who has a few secrets of his own. Yet fiery passion ignites between the unlikely pair as they battle a shadowy foe.

Can they work together to save Marianne's daughter? And will nights of pleasure turn into a love for all time?

Book 4: **Her Prodigal Passion**

Sensible Miss Charity Sparkler has been in love with Paul Fines, her best friend's brother, for years. When he accidentally compromises her, they find themselves wed in haste. Can an ugly duckling recognize her own beauty and a reformed rake his own value? As secrets of the past lead to present dangers, will this marriage of convenience transform into one of love?

CHRONICLES OF ABIGAIL JONES

Book 1: **Abigail Jones**

When destiny brings shy Victorian maid Abigail Jones into the home of the brooding and enigmatic Earl of Huxton, she discovers forbidden passion... and a dangerous world of supernatural forces.

ABOUT THE AUTHOR

USA Today & International Bestselling Author Grace Callaway writes steamy and adventurous historical romances. Her debut book, *Her Husband's Harlot*, was a Romance Writers of America Golden Heart® Finalist and a #1 Regency Bestseller, and her subsequent novels have topped national and international bestselling lists. She's the winner of the Passionate Plume Award for Historical Novel, and her books have been honored as finalists for the National Reader's Choice Awards, the Maggie Award of Excellence, and the Daphne du Maurier Award for Excellence in Mystery/ Suspense.

Growing up on the Canadian prairies, Grace could often be found with her nose in a book—and not much has changed since. She set aside her favorite romance novels long enough to get her doctorate from the University of Michigan. A clinical psychologist, she lives with her family in Northern California, where their adventures include remodeling a ramshackle house, exploring the great outdoors, and sampling local artisanal goodies.

Keep up with my latest news!
   Newsletter: gracecallaway.com/newsletter

facebook.com/GraceCallawayBooks

bookbub.com/authors/grace-callaway

instagram.com/gracecallawaybooks

amazon.com/author/gracecallaway

ACKNOWLEDGMENTS

First of all, to my readers, thank you for your support of my work. Your lovely messages mean the world to me. Many of you expressed sadness at the Kent family saga ending, so I hope you enjoyed Harry's story and the visit with the other Kent siblings.

To my wonderful editors, Diane and Veronica, thank you for helping make my work shine. This story is better because of you. Gina, thank you for your copyediting expertise. As always, thank you Seductive Designs for making my books look beautiful and for capturing the spirit of my work in your gorgeous cover art.

To my dear friends, the ladies of Montauk 8 and the Indie Intensive group: you inspire me and make the business of writing fun!

Last but not least, to my family, thank you for your support, understanding, and patience during the writing of this book. Love always.

Printed in Dunstable, United Kingdom